W9-AWB-317

PRIZE STORIES
1990
THE O. HENRY
AWARDS

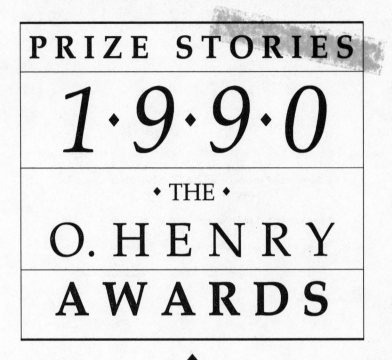

PRIZE STORIES

1·9·9·0

· THE ·

O. HENRY

AWARDS

◆

*Edited and with
an Introduction by*

William Abrahams

DOUBLEDAY

NEW YORK LONDON TORONTO SYDNEY AUCKLAND

PUBLISHED BY DOUBLEDAY
a division of Bantam Doubleday Dell Publishing Group, Inc.
666 Fifth Avenue, New York, New York 10103

DOUBLEDAY and the portrayal of an anchor with a dolphin
are trademarks of Doubleday,
A DIVISION OF BANTAM DOUBLEDAY DELL PUBLISHING GROUP, INC.

Library of Congress Cataloging-in-Publication Data

Prize stories. 1947–
    New York, etc. Doubleday.

        v. 22 cm.

    Annual.
    The O. Henry awards.
    None published 1952–53.
    Continues: O. Henry memorial award prize stories.
    ISSN 0079-5453 = Prize stories

    1. Short stories, American—Collected works.
PZ1.011   813'.01'08—dc19   21-9372
                                                               MARC-S
Library of Congress   [8804r83]rev4

ISBN 0-385-26498-4

Printed in the United States of America

April 1990

FIRST EDITION

RRC

CONTENTS

PUBLISHER'S NOTE

This volume is the seventieth in the O. Henry Memorial Award series.

In 1918, the Society of Arts and Sciences met to vote upon a monument to the master of the short story: O. Henry. They decided that this memorial should be in the form of two prizes for the best short stories published by American authors in American magazines during the year 1919. From this beginning, the memorial developed into an annual anthology of outstanding short stories by American authors, published, with the exception of the years 1952 and 1953, by Doubleday.

Blanche Colton Williams, one of the founders of the awards, was editor from 1919 to 1932; Harry Hansen from 1933 to 1940; Herschel Brickell from 1941 to 1951. The annual collection did not appear in 1952 and 1953, when the continuity of the series was interrupted by the death of Herschel Brickell. Paul Engle was editor from 1954 to 1959, with Hanson Martin coeditor in the years 1954 to 1960; Mary Stegner in 1960; Richard Poirier from 1961 to 1966, with assistance from and coeditorship with William Abrahams from 1964 to 1966. William Abrahams became editor of the series in 1967.

In 1970, Doubleday published under Mr. Abrahams's editorship *Fifty Years of the American Short Story*, and in 1981, *Prize Stories of the Seventies*. Both are collections of stories selected from this series.

The stories chosen for this volume were published in the period from the summer of 1988 to the summer of 1989. A list of the magazines consulted appears at the back of the book. The choice of stories and the selection of prizewinners are exclusively the responsibility of the editor. Biographical material is based on information provided by the contributors and obtained from standard works of reference.

INTRODUCTION

The state of the American short story, entering the 1990s, justifies a good deal of optimism—no sense of the story trailing off from the 1980s, but instead, blazing new trails, new paths, and aiming toward new destinations. So it would seem fair to assume from the twenty stories in the present collection. They show among them a richness of language, a yielding to the seductive powers of the imagination, and a willingness to explore and reinvigorate traditional forms and styles that would not have been anticipated as recently as the day before yesterday. Truly we are at a new point in the continuing and evolving history of the story. Joyce Carol Oates speaks for more than herself when she tells us, "Each story I write seems to me a new departure."

To understand how this present, very promising situation has come about, one might start by taking into account the rise of an American institution: the creative writing program—or course, or workshop—at universities and colleges and in private enclaves and conferences all over the country. It has proved itself, for better or worse, the most enduring influence upon the short story in the past twenty-five years. By now it is safe to say that a vast majority of our writers have participated, full-time or part-time, in some form of these programs as students or teachers, and not infrequently in a progression from one role to the other. Despite the occasional carping of critics (myself included), I think it has to be acknowledged that the effect of these programs and courses has been significantly to the good.

Skills have been learned, techniques have been acquired—evidently writing can be taught (and, of course, also *self*-taught) —at least to the point where Craft ends and Art begins. The risk attendant upon apprenticeship in groups is an over-reliance on craft, the model that reassures even as it restrains. It would be unduly severe to write off the story that aspires to and achieves no more than a mastery of craft, something recognizable and enjoyable at a first read, content to make no further claim upon our attention. But the stories to which we return and return are those where with each new reading we discover qualities and meanings that were not apparent immediately: in short, the rewards of art. It would be disingenuous to declare that there has been a sudden generous burgeoning of such stories (now, no more than ever) but they do exist, and I like to think they are represented in this year's collection.

Certainly they justify an optimistic view of the future of the story as a new decade begins. The bright view darkens, however, when one looks beyond the first step in the familiar, essential equation—the story must be written—to the second step —the story must be published—and so to the third—the story must be read. It is that second step that has become increasingly worrisome. For purposes of comparison, let me go back a decade, to *Prize Stories 1980: The O. Henry Awards*, a vintage year, it seems in retrospect, with "A Silver Dish" by Saul Bellow and "The Men's Club" by Leonard Michaels, and "The Old Forest" by Peter Taylor, to name only a few. There were twenty-two stories chosen that year, twelve from eight magazines of large circulation (four from *The New Yorker*, two from *Esquire*), ten from magazines of small circulation, the little magazines (literary journals, quarterlies, etc., including two from *Antaeus*). Now to the present collection: there are twenty stories, five from magazines of large circulation (two from *The Atlantic Monthly*), fifteen from the little magazines (two from *The Paris Review*, two from *The Kenyon Review*). The contrasting numbers between 1980 and 1990 seem significant, and I feel compelled to say that this change in representation—the ascendancy of the little magazines—did not happen because I wanted to make an editorial point. It *has* happened, though, and at the least it suggests a direction for the future.

When a large-circulation magazine buys a story, the author will be rewarded not only with a handsome fee but also with a vast audience, more potential readers for a single story than a serious, talented author is likely to have for a whole shelf-ful of books. No wonder, then, that so many aspiring writers send off their stories, thousands in the course of a year, to the editors of such magazines, and no wonder, also, that most of them must make do with a printed or scribbled rejection. Having said that, I should add that I don't believe a single serious author has abandoned a career after being turned down by one or another celebrated magazine. As for potential readers, the greater number will skip the token story on the way to the indispensable nonfiction that is the magazine's true *raison d'être*. We hear of "service" magazines, and it is surely the case that most magazines, addressed to a large audience, do serve their readers, supplying them with everything they think they want to know: the cornucopia overflows . . . but they don't (and why should they?) feel a need to serve the story.

Hence the ever-increasing importance of the little magazines for the future of fiction, providing a welcome—and space—that too many "big" magazines can no longer afford. Their value to writers and readers promises to be inestimable in the decade ahead.

At what point does an innovation become a tradition? The introduction of biographies and comments by the authors represented an experiment last year. This year, expanded and enriched, they have become an essential part of the collection, and we trust will continue so hereafter.

I am happy to acknowledge very great assistance from John M. Dean in California, and from Sally Arteseros and Ellen Corey in New York.

—William Abrahams

PRIZE STORIES
1990
THE O. HENRY
AWARDS

◆ *Leo E. Litwak* ◆

THE ELEVENTH EDITION

I came to Detroit from Iron Mountain, Michigan, a poor boy with nothing to lose and a world to gain. Iron Mountain winters were terrible but no season gave me relief. I escaped as soon as I finished high school. I left nothing behind. There was only Dad, who was bitter and alcoholic, and by the time I left we had exhausted each other. We were no longer even joined by dislike. He shrugged when I told him I was taking off.

"You can always come back, but that's nothing to look forward to."

I arrived in Detroit, eighteen years old, entirely free, eager for a new life. And there it was, at Wayne University, available to all comers.

Two nights a week I entered a private home converted to college use. A once-elegant parlor had been painted light green and unsparingly illuminated with overhead fluorescent lighting. I listened to the scraping of iron and plywood chairs, the squeal of wooden arms unfolded, briefcases unsnapping, notebooks and texts thumped down. We waited for the magician who would transform this plain room and its ordinary sounds into our land of dreams.

His coming was heralded by the brisk rap of his cane on the outside stairs. He began lecturing while at the parlor door. He hung his cane on the lip of the blackboard and kept talking while arranging his notes on Renaissance Florence.

Professor Diekman was a bent little man. He was slightly twisted to the right, as if he were lecturing on the run, hurling words back at his pursuers.

We learned about Guelphs, Ghibellines, Dante, Machiavelli, the painters, the sculptors, the craftsmen, the poets, the guilds.

He operated in great swoops. He lighted on a detail, developed it, then leaped elsewhere. Over the weeks the direction of his narrative became clear.

The Florentine bankers lent to monasteries, took the sheep as collateral, traveled Europe without regard for boundaries, and finally controlled the wool market. Diekman followed the vagaries of capitalism from its beginnings in fourteenth-century Florence to its consummation on the Detroit assembly line.

There was nothing so odd that he couldn't find a link to our experience. He clarified what was opaque, made coherent what seemed alien and terrifying.

I studied with Diekman for three years, then entered the graduate program. I enrolled in whatever he taught. I took his three-semester history of philosophy sequence, his course in esthetics, dabbled at Homeric Greek to become eligible for his *Iliad* seminar, learned German in preparation for his lectures on Goethe.

During those years I was employed at Brant's Import and Export. Each morning I reported to the warehouse and checked inventory. I counted slabs of Italian marble. I unwrapped delicate wall sconces, examined them for defects, rewrapped them. I counted boxes of cut crystal to make sure that Brant had received the full order. I measured bolts of English linen, stacked Polish carpets, opened crates of Mexican glassware. By late af-

ternoon I had finished. The rest of my time belonged to
Diekman.

*   *   *

I lost all connection to Iron Mountain. I was no longer that boy.
But who was I and where was I? I was out of touch. I didn't
allow myself to touch. There was no ground under my feet. I
felt that I belonged nowhere until I established myself on campus.

I moved whenever I found a cheaper room and finally ended
at Tuchler's place, a few blocks from the Wayne campus. I had a
room on the second floor, next to the bath. I was utterly concentrated on my studies. My vision narrowed. My hearing, though,
became omnivorous. I devoured sound, greedy for it, straining
like a hungry fledgling for any word that could bring me ease.

All I heard was old Walsh coughing in the room next to mine.
He desperately harrumphed, trying to clear his throat of a death
that was already beyond his throat.

His memory was erratic and he sometimes forgot that we'd
met. The wispy old fellow would knock on my door to introduce himself again.

"Hi, there. My name is Frank Walsh. I'm your neighbor."

We met regularly but no use clarifying matters, so once more
I'd say, "Russell Hansen."

"What?"

"Hansen."

"Hansen. That's a good simple name. I didn't catch the first
name."

"Russell."

"Russell? I had a partner named Russell. I was in the seed
business, you know. Volunteer Seed." And he was off. Till the
moment when he could again describe the one agony that remained fresh and unforgotten. "My wife died last year. We
were married fifty-three years. And when you lose a companion

of fifty-three years, oh golly," he said, "oh, golly. You don't get over it in a day."

More than a day had elapsed; in fact, more than a year. His wife was long dead. The old man couldn't distinguish days and years. He was a retired pensioner. He slept when sleep came. He once knocked at my door after midnight. "Sorry, sir. I thought I heard you dining. I wonder if you could use this bottle of wine. It was a gift to me but I don't touch the stuff." It was an ancient bottle, opened years ago, and long since become vinegar. I thanked him, took the bottle, but didn't allow him to stay.

His radio sputtered out at night and then self-ignited in a jarring burst of breakfast music at five in the morning. I heard the confused old man call out, "Yes? Yes? What time is it?"

He wasn't the neighbor I'd have chosen. I avoided distraction. Professor Gerard Diekman ruled my life. The austere little man didn't suffer fools. I labored to stay in his good graces. When he mentioned a text during class, I checked it out. At his beckoning I entered deep waters. I floundered but learned to swim. When he wrote a critique of my paper and concluded, "Very good," I felt confirmed. But his disapproval, displayed in that same precise, crabbed script, could take the ground from under my feet. Four years his student and I was still unacknowledged. He called my name at the beginning of each semester but there was no further recognition. I had no idea where I stood, and there were times when I choked on books.

I was as desperate as Walsh for human connection. Even the old man would sometimes serve.

I knocked on his door, beat hard to penetrate the sound of his radio. He finally called out, "Hello? Is someone there?"

When he opened up I reminded him that I was his neighbor, Russell Hansen.

"Of course you're Russell Hansen. I know that."

His room was crammed with furnishings gathered over a lifetime. I noticed a Seth Thomas pendulum clock, a massive oak wardrobe, a glass-enclosed bookcase containing a leatherbound edition of the *Encyclopedia Britannica.* The room was dominated by a radio phonograph console, tuned to the news.

He invited me to sit. He told me again of his arrival in Detroit at the turn of the century. He came by steamer from Buffalo with his bride, Louise. He landed at a slip later occupied by an excursion boat. He rented a duplex on Bagley Street and started the Volunteer Seed Company.

Everyone loved Louise, he said. She had the best heart in the world. This was the preliminary of a story I heard him tell more than once. They were young. Louise was expecting. The business struggled but prospects were good. It would have been paradise except for the man next door who had converted a backyard toolshed into a machine shop. He made a terrific racket but Walsh was reluctant to complain. The fellow was skinny as death and clanged away with intimidating earnestness. Louise urged her husband to talk to the man.

" 'Tell the gentleman I can't get to sleep, Frank. He's disturbing the neighborhood.' "

Walsh told Louise it was his policy to live and let live and he did nothing about the noise until one night the racket went on and on—steel on steel—and it was too much. He put on a buffalo-plaid robe over his pajamas. The man was in his garage, working at his lathe. Walsh pleaded with him.

" 'Have a heart, sir. I have to be up at five in the morning and it's already ten-thirty.'

"This fellow pulls away from the lathe. He pushes back his goggles. 'Ten-thirty, you say? It can't be ten-thirty. Only a loony would be out at ten-thirty in his pajamas. And you don't look like a loony to me.' I didn't want to make a fuss. I admired his industry. If it was only a case of my pleasure I'd say, 'Go on till the rooster crows.' But I told him my Louise was expecting and she wasn't having an easy time of it.

" 'Well, sir,' this skinny gentleman said to me, 'I know your missus and if she wants me to shut down business—' He turned

off the lathe, took off his gloves, stuck out his hand and introduced himself.

" 'Henry Ford of the Edison Illuminating Company.'

"Yessir! Henry Ford. Isn't that a piece of history, young man?
He was working on a model of the internal combustion engine
in that shed. We became friends. Not so much me and Henry—
no one ever called him Hank—but his wife Clara and my Louise. Everyone loved Louise. It was the easiest thing in the world.
Henry told me, 'You got yourself a princess. More than a dumb
mick has a right to.' And I said to him, 'Mr. Ford, I couldn't
agree with you more.'

"Oh, golly," Frank Walsh said. "Oh, golly. When you lose a
companion of fifty-three years you don't get over it in a day."

I once asked about the *Encyclopedia Britannica*, Eleventh Edition.
Was he aware of its achievement?

"A salesman came to our door. Louise was at home. She mis-
carried, you see, and we tried again. But the years went by and
we knew we couldn't have kids. She handled the correspon-
dence for Volunteer Seed. The best secretary in the world. Still,
that wasn't her life. That salesman told her the *Encyclopedia* was
the way out. It was an education. 'How can we afford it, honey?'
We were trying to make a go of it and it was no cinch. Who was
going to read it? Twenty-nine volumes. I'm not much of a
reader. We publish a seed catalog, you know. One of the largest
in the Midwest. But she'd set her heart on the *Encyclopedia.* He
was a darned fine salesman. With an item as expensive as his,
why cut corners?"

He bought the leatherbound version, not the cloth. And not
the diminutive Handy Volume Issue, but the full-sized deluxe
set, easy on the eyes. For a time she would come home from
Volunteer and fix dinner and afterwards sit with the *Encyclopedia*
and unfold the delicate tissue maps and, for instance, consider
the state of Michigan. Population in 1900, 90 percent white.
About 15,000 Negroes. 6,000 Indians. And exactly 9 Japanese.
The state of Michigan produced the bulk of the peppermint

crop in the United States. "Did you know that, Russ?" The statistics read to him by Louise were never forgotten. But she gave up reading after a few tries. The *Encyclopedia* wasn't what she expected. Volunteer Seed went bankrupt in 1930. Louise took a job as a saleslady at Hudson's, Walsh as a bookkeeper for the Briggs Bodyworks in Highland Park.

They never owned a home. They could have bought a Chicago Boulevard mansion in the days when the seed company flourished. But they had no need for it without kids. They always rented fine, large apartments until the last. Now one room was enough. He had a decent landlady and good neighbors.

But, oh, golly, to lose a companion of fifty-three years—

Mrs. Tuchler had to remind him each week to pay the rent. She retained a German accent and delivered her cautions to Walsh with the spirit of a Prussian sergeant. I heard her repeat the rules with special addenda for Walsh. Prompt payment on Monday. Clean the tub after you bathe. Each resident was responsible for his own room. She did the hallways and bathroom. No loud music. No loud parties. All calls reported on the pad by the phone. She warned that excessive use of electricity or gas would bring a rent increase.

The rules, hand-lettered on green matting paper, were mounted next to the phone. She told us she didn't apologize for being strict. It was a declining neighborhood and she meant to hold the fort. She kept after the old man. He was hard of hearing, his memory dimmed. She spoke at full-volume in an accent that refused to acknowledge *w*'s. She came upstairs, hitting every tread with authority, disciplining the wood beneath her.

"Mr. Walsh? Mr. Walsh?" (Pronounced "Valsch.") Hard raps, then letting herself in. I heard her clearly through the wall. "You must raise the toilet seat. The other roomers complain." I hadn't complained, nor, I'm sure, had Betty McCarthy. "You get the seat dirty, you get the floor dirty. You don't clean the tub neither."

Walsh was abject. "Sorry," he said. Sorry wasn't enough. He

said again, "I'm sorry, Missus." She occupied an apartment directly below. When she heard the nighttime pacing and the radio at full-volume she stepped into the vestibule, braced on the newel post, and shouted, "Quiet!" Then the trek upstairs to discipline him face-to-face.

She called me "Professor." I corrected her a few times. "Only a student, Mrs. Tuchler." Perhaps she imagined that if a professor were in residence the encroaching ghetto would stop a block away and not incorporate her house.

"The Professor is preparing his lessons," she warned Walsh. "He wants quiet."

I told her the old man didn't bother me. "Old age is our destiny, too, Mrs. Tuchler."

"Ah," she said. "What would you know from old age? You learn it in books? You think I am the hard-hearted landlady, but do you know, for three months that man has not paid his rent? His pension check doesn't come. I write for him and they promise to send new checks. Maybe it will come. Maybe not. My bills come for sure."

He'd been with her for five years. His wife was already dead when he arrived. He said she died last year but his memory was jumbled. He had no one. Who was he to Mrs. Tuchler? Not her kin. She knew there was no pleasure growing old. She knew far better than I that there were no happy endings. She was preparing for her own bad time. She began by hardening her heart. If he didn't pay the rent—out! If he continued bothering other tenants, he had to go.

Walsh usually managed to soften her. When she stomped upstairs to demand quiet and to threaten eviction, he endured the scolding. Sorry, he said. Sorry. And when her anger ebbed he reminded her that Louise was also of German origin. He insisted that she sit while he played a favorite record of Louise's, Richard Tauber singing, *"Du, du liegst mir im Herzen."* The song always touched her. She urged the old man to stay alert. If he lost his wits he was doomed.

"Don't you worry, Missus. I'm fine. Don't you worry."

He sometimes lured me to his room to hear his records. He had an old recording of Bing Crosby singing "Pennies from Heaven." He played a scratchy record of a thin tenor voice singing "Poor Butterfly" and "Ramona." He turned up the volume, his ear pressed to the speaker. "They sure knew how to write songs in those day, Russ."

Betty McCarthy was the other lodger on our floor. She had the room across the hall. She was a new tenant, a Wayne drama student. She worked nights in a cabaret. She was plump and attractive, a cheerful, busy young woman but it was fortunate for my peace of mind that she didn't spend much time at Tuchler's. She was always in hurried transitions. She moved at full speed and set off waves of turbulence. Her high heels click-clicked on the outer stone stairs. She rattatattatted up the wooden stairway. When she reached the first landing the phone invariably began ringing. She came down full force in her rush to be there and then a breathless, "Hiiii," and I overheard the dumb, flirty exchange that followed. "I can't," she said, drawing out the "can't" so that it meant she wanted to, she'd love to, but, regrettably, she was unable to. "Maybe next week. If I can get away. No, I can't say for sure." Then an almost orgasmic, "Me, too! Oh, yes!"

Then rush, rush, rush. I heard the frantic sound of her across the hall. Drawers jerked open and slammed shut, a rush to the bath ahead of me, a chipper, "Be right out!" and the sound of faucets, the toilet flushing, emerging with hair in pink rollers, "All yours!" Back to her room, the rattle of hangers, all that scurrying in behalf of projects I couldn't imagine as anything but trivial. When she finally slammed the door on her way out (Tuchler yelled, "Don't slam the door!") and Walsh was, for the moment, subdued, I could again pursue my obligations to Professor Diekman without distraction. I wanted nothing more.

* * *

Diekman weeded his classes ruthlessly and it was a triumph to survive his selection. If you didn't have the prerequisites he said, "Sorry." If you came to class unprepared, he invited you to drop the course. If you were loyal but without promise, he let you know—in a generous manner, true—that it made no sense for you to persist. But if you persisted, as I did, you might find the everyday world transformed into Homer's or Goethe's.

I was in the last year of the MA program when I summoned up the nerve to approach him. I asked him to supervise my thesis. I should have consulted him at an earlier stage. I waited for him to choose me, but he gave no sign. I couldn't stall off the interview and finally made the appointment.

He was a small man, further diminished by a spinal curvature arrested at an eleven-degree tilt to the right. The slant was a perfect orientation for a point of view always on the bias toward irony.

"What are you after, Mr. Hansen?"

I hoped for an academic career.

"Surely not in philosophy."

Did he think that was so absurd? I knew I was too young to have that large an ambition. Still, I hoped some day to be worthy.

"You hope . . ." His off-center look spared me a direct gaze but lent emphasis to the sardonic tone. "Mr. Hansen, I am obliged to try to discourage you. You impose a terrible responsibility on me."

"How is that, sir?"

No doubt I was bright enough. He liked my written work. I would probably make a decent teacher. "But to what purpose, Mr. Hansen? What reward do you expect?" Honor? Who would honor me? Students would pass out of my life. The university had no more regard for a professor's achievement than a landlord had for his lodger's. What reward then? Association with the wise? Was that the basis for my hope? I'd discover knuckleheaded colleagues, venal superiors, moronic students.

Did I have the illusion of a handsome salary? It was his duty to thwart the philosopher and encourage the entrepreneur. Better a car dealer or a realtor than a philosopher.

All I wanted, I said, was the good opinion of Professor Diekman. That was reward enough.

"Are you of sound mind, Mr. Hansen? Do you know my reputation? A martinet. Notorious for holding students back for unacceptable thesis work. You'll have an easier road with others in the department." If I insisted on working with him he'd hold me to a high level of performance. There would be no perfunctory acceptance of a manuscript. Nothing shoddy would pass his supervision.

I wanted to stretch and he was the man to draw me out. I would accept no one but Professor Diekman.

It was then he used my first name. "What is your topic, Russell?"

" 'Descartes's Dream of a Demon.' "

I was, of course, familiar with Descartes's famous dreams that preceded the Meditations, wasn't I?

I was.

There was no dream of a demon.

I referred to the demon whom Descartes invited us to dream, the subverter of the material world.

Wasn't that too labored a topic? Did I have something new to add? But we would talk, he said, and agreed to supervise my thesis.

He invited me to join a circle of students who met at his home Friday nights. "It means giving up more robust Friday night pleasures, Russell. I'll understand perfectly if you find that's too great a sacrifice."

I was delighted to make the sacrifice. I was more than delighted. Ecstatic. And I joined the Diekman circle.

There were six of us, all graduate students, all male. I was the youngest and the least schooled. We met in Diekman's apartment Friday evening for supper. A topic emerged while we were eating, apparently at random. Then for several hours Diekman guided us along the path we had chosen.

We read for him. We adopted his aloof ironic style. Perhaps I even began tilting to the right.

On Friday night I'd leave my barren, mildewed room and the sound of Walsh harrumphing and the cascade of Betty's heels and enter the formality of Diekman's apartment off Jefferson Avenue. Diekman was heir to a Grand Rapids stove factory and very well off. There was a uniformed doorman in the plush lobby. I rose in a gilded elevator to the fifth floor. The apartment was furnished with old family pieces—eighteenth-century pine cabinets, hefty armoires, leather-topped desks, copper lamps hooded by steeply sloped silk shades with beaded fringes. Everything was placed with a precision that was the signature of one ordering sensibility. No wife, no mother, no decorator, only Diekman. There were walls of graphics, one room specializing in Orientals, elsewhere Rembrandt miniatures, Italian views, French contemporaries.

He prepared careful suppers. He himself ate little. Eating was for him a matter of discipline rather than appetite.

One night he watched a portly graduate student, Jules Vincenti, lavish preserves on Breton crepes, then take the pancakes in a few massive bites, his chewing thoughtful and bovine. Diekman asked, "Do you like sweets, Mr. Vincenti?"

"They're my undoing."

Vincenti stopped eating while Diekman mused on sweets. Could a world open on a tea-softened madeleine? A coffee-dunked cruller? He didn't think so. Sugar wasn't a thoughtful food. The gratification was too immediate and conclusive. A subtle cuisine carried with it the threat of decay, an ambiguous texture, the tongue made cautious, the pace of eating slowed, all our senses marshalled as we carefully ventured into the next bite. The French and Chinese offered a metaphysical cuisine whose purpose wasn't merely to gratify the palate but to chasten it. The sauces that lingered on the edge of decay reminded the palate that it masticated death, not only the death of what was ingested, but the death of the chewing machine itself —teeth, tongue, palate.

"When we're children we have the blissful conviction that there is nothing beyond the heaven of distilled sweetness. But as we age, Mr. Vincenti, we begin to taste our dying and our appetite matures. We are on the treadmill of generation and decay and if we are to become wise there's no return to the simple connection to sugar."

He formalized the needs of his body. He transformed such necessities as eating into an artful practice. He dressed with great care, not to hide his crookedness—that was out of the question—but to make it irrelevant, to establish that he was the author of himself and not the mere effect of his scoliosis.

Stripped of his tailored tweeds and striped shirt and red bow tie and built-up oxfords he would have appeared as grotesque as a crab without its carapace. He didn't allow himself to be stripped. He maintained austere control. He called us by first name. We would never think of calling him "Gerard." It was always "Sir" or "Professor Diekman."

His aloofness veiled a passionate nature that he could expose in the safety of the Diekman circle.

He once began a reading from *Faust.* He was powerfully moved. He trembled, the verse barely audible. He was obviously having trouble continuing. There were only the six of us to see him make a fool of himself, but these six were his entire dominion. He stopped, closed his eyes, then rushed for his Baldwin Grand. He weaved back and forth as he played. He sang Gretchen's song in German. Her peace is gone, she's heartweary, and she'll never find peace again. Never again. *Nimmermehr.*

A high tenor voice. He was first Marguerite, then stepped into the shoes of Faust. He observed the mad Gretchen. He grieved, but there was no going back. The compact was made. Her madness was the price he paid en route to power.

I was at first embarrassed by the release of his voice. He stretched to the breaking point to accommodate the final *NIM-mermehr*, hovering near an uncontrolled tremolo. What idea did he have of himself? But then, entirely composed, he went on to observe how Faust, shaken by pity, is tempted to give up the struggle for transcendence. He is kept on track by the necessary devil. To live is to sin for to live is to strive and the striving will not be arrested. Poor lunatic Gretchen is the sacrifice to the God he unwittingly serves. As the mocking devil says of Faust, "He serves you in peculiar ways *(besondre Weise)."*

He came from Grand Rapids. His origins were Dutch Reform. He'd long since abandoned the creed but retained a sense of a grievous past and an apocalyptic future. This was the position that structured his courses: we were inextricably embedded in history, fixed there by our station and its duties, doomed whatever our struggles to consummate the destinies of our fathers. The past was fossilized in our character and language: nothing new under the sun. And then, for those elected, a release from bondage through the miracle of art. Grace conferred, not by God in heaven, but by Homer and Mozart and Rembrandt and Goethe.

Our crooked Mephisto led us to the Detroit Institute of Art, prepared to go to any length to open our eyes. He once stood in front of a Mondrian, tucked his cane under his arm and made surprising staccato motions like an East Indian dancer. A group of passing teenagers giggled. A museum guard moved toward us. The dapper little man, tilted off-center, flapped his arms, shuffled his feet, danced his response to Mondrian, scorning a dogmatic formalism that insisted on the sufficiency of the painting within its frame. He didn't care who saw or heard. He spoke in full voice.

"I reflect the force in the painting. The tension between line and color is in me. I experience the stress. It is resolved inside me. The harmony in the Mondrian I find in myself. Where it is hot, I am hot. Where the line thickens, I thicken. I experience the thickening."

He broke into a peculiar jig, his cane fell, his arms mimed vectors working through the Mondrian checkerboard, his pace regulated by the intensity of color. He ignored the gigglers. He didn't allow the possibility of our embarrassment. The guard saw that it was Professor Diekman and withdrew.

"When you face the work of art your obligation is to experience the work, not make judgments. Risk yourselves. Be fools if necessary."

I was tremendously excited by these sessions. The ordinary world seemed illuminated and transformed.

Wasn't the luminous vision worth any sacrifice? Even family? Even Gretchen's? There was no Gretchen for Diekman. He had his Rembrandts, his Utamaros, his Wunderlichs, his Hundertwassers. Above all, his library.

He had turned a large parlor into a cylinder of books. A 180-degree arc was occupied by philosophy. There was a large segment for classics. There were leather-bound collections and massive art books. The middle shelf above his desk featured the *Encyclopedia Britannica,* Eleventh Edition.

I mentioned that my neighbor owned the same edition.

One of the grand human achievements, Diekman said. The world orchestrated by an extraordinary assembly of scholars, acting in concert, as if there were a single author with a single vision and a single voice and that voice offered a universal design, history unrolling, purposefully directed. Was there any need for updating? All that had happened since the 1911 publication could be extrapolated. Was there any novelty? The scale of events had changed. Otherwise the Eleventh Edition was sufficient.

From the fifth floor at Diekman's, I glimpsed Canada across the Detroit River. At this height—the windows closed—we couldn't hear traffic. We had no inkling of neighborhoods in convulsion. When Diekman went to his piano and illustrated

Apollonian grace with a phrase of Mozart, the turbulence below disappeared. I forgot my mornings at Brant's warehouse and the sound of death in Frank Walsh's throat.

But then down the elevator, out into the street, winter coming, a sharp edge in the air, and back to the commonplace world of Tuchler's rooming house.

*   *   *

One night, returning from Diekman's, traffic seemed especially dense. There was a tie-up at the intersection of Woodward and Warren. Horns were blaring. And there was Frank Walsh at the center of it. He had stepped off the curb. Instead of crossing he turned in every direction. Drivers stopped to allow the old man to fix on a course. Those who couldn't see what caused the tie-up blew their horns. I led him to the walk. He wasn't dressed for the weather. He wore a summer suit of black poplin. He was too disoriented to recognize me.

"Russ Hansen," I said. "Your neighbor."

"Russ!" He caught my hand. "This is terrible! I've lost my car!"

I didn't know he had a car.

"A 1940 Plymouth coupe, a two-seater. You can't miss it. Dark green, a big trunk, whitewalls. She's old but she's never failed me. I seem to have lost her." He'd gone to the neighborhood grocery earlier in the day. Parked his car on Forest near Cass. And somehow forgotten it. He'd walked home, listened to the radio, opened a can of soup for dinner. Dozed off. Then, suddenly awakened, he remembered his car. He couldn't find it. He feared it had been stolen. He walked down Forest to Second. He returned via Warren. "It must be stolen."

"Did you leave your keys in the car?"

He searched his pockets. He flapped his arms in dismay. "I'm sorry, Russ."

I told him we'd have to awaken Mrs. Tuchler. He pleaded

with me not to wake her up. But he couldn't find his license or registration and she might have the information.

"Don't wake the poor lady. Morning is soon enough."

She was still up and despite his pleading I knocked on her door. Orange hair in curlers, a robe over a flannel nightie, chins gathering, thin lips pursed in outrage.

"Are you crazy, Mr. Walsh? You don't have a car for three years now. They took away your license." She explained to me that he'd had a series of accidents. "One after another. He bumps the car in front. He bumps the car in back. He bumps the car on the side. Then he drives away." She said to Walsh, "And what do you mean, a Plymouth? It was a Buick you owned. A big car. Don't you remember? They took away your license and you sold it to the Russian housepainter who lived on the third floor. Georgie. You don't remember Georgie, for godsakes, Mr. Walsh?"

"He had a wife Masha."

"Yes, Masha. You sold him your Buick. The Plymouth was your car maybe when your missus was alive. You're losing your head, Mr. Walsh. You made the professor walk up and down the street for nothing."

"Oh, dear, I'm sorry." It must have been a dream. He'd awakened suddenly, recalling that he'd gone to the grocery and left his car. He hurriedly dressed, rushed over, and it was gone. Of course. He sold his car to the Russian housepainter who lived upstairs with Masha. Georgie. Completely forgotten. Could it have been a dream? It was so vivid. He was so sure. The Buick and not the Plymouth? The Plymouth long gone?

He came to my door before dawn and woke me up. "Something's happening, Russ. I'm sure I parked the Plymouth outside the A&P. I know it's there."

He faded fast. Not even memories held him in place. A week later I heard him cry out in the hall. "No," he shouted. "Oh, no!" He shrunk away from me. He was in his pajamas, a trail from the middle of the hallway to his door. The hall carpet was a mess. I smelled death in his spoor. It was an awful smell. "I'm sorry," he groaned, "I'm so sorry," then started weeping and ran to his room.

I knocked on the door. "It's O.K., Mr. Walsh. Anybody can have an accident. Let me help you clean up."

I walked in. He was standing with his pajama bottoms around his ankles. He begged me to leave.

"It could happen to anyone. We'll clean up before Mrs. Tuchler finds out."

"Please! Please!"

I stooped to get his pajama bottoms. He tried to push me away.

"No reason to be embarrassed," I told him. There was every reason and I struggled to keep disgust out of my voice. I bundled his pajama bottoms and lifted them gingerly.

"I got lost," he mourned.

I assured him it could happen to anyone.

I led him to the bathroom and ran a tub. His legs were smeared. I helped him into the tub. I talked to keep down the disgust. "It's O.K. It's not so terrible." And, in fact, as I worked it stopped being terrible.

His feet and hands seemed huge because the rest of him had dwindled to skin and bones. He leaned on my shoulder. I held him around the waist and mopped him with a washcloth hanging on the rack, probably Betty McCarthy's. I drained the tub, then filled it again. I told him to sit and relax while I cleaned the hallway.

I went downstairs to the utility closet beneath the stairs, looking for a mop and bucket. Mrs. Tuchler heard and came out in her robe. I told her there had been an accident.

"What kind of accident?"

"Mr. Walsh got lost on the way to the toilet."

She charged upstairs. I heard her shout, *"Gott im Himmel!* You were lost? From your room to the toilet?"

"I was lost." He imagined himself in another home, another time, utterly confused. A few feet from succor, but lost.

"You cannot be lost! They'll put you in the crazy house!" She looked at the mess. *"Schrecklich! Schrecklich!"* She warned Walsh he was on thin ice. If he didn't take care he was done for. "Do you understand? Can you hear me?"

"I was lost."

"Ach. It's no use."

I offered to clean the floor.

"Don't trouble yourself, Mr. Hansen. The old fellow is no good anymore."

I told her not to be hard on him. He was only confused.

"Only confused? Only? He got nothing. He got nobody. He'll end in the crazy house."

She toweled the old man and we led him to bed. She insisted that I go to my room. She was still working at midnight, scrubbing the carpet, mopping the floor, the bucket clanging. I heard her, *"Gott im Himmel!"* out in the hallway.

Betty McCarthy, returning from her late stint as a cabaret waitress, knocked on my door.

"I saw your light. Listen. Mr. Walsh is crying."

I told her what happened.

"Oh, gee, the poor old guy."

She knocked but he refused to answer. She coaxed him to open the door. Did he need anything? Wasn't he hungry? She bet he hadn't eaten.

"Please, Miss. Don't trouble yourself. I'm fine."

"It's no trouble. There's an all-night place only a couple blocks away."

He didn't mean us to hear his weeping. He meant to swallow his death without troubling anyone but couldn't remember his resolve for courage.

She located a Chinese restaurant that was open and brought him a container of wonton soup. "It's delicious. You'll feel better if you eat."

We found the container still untouched when we entered his room several days later.

*　　　*　　　*

Betty McCarthy suggested we meet to discuss arrangements for Mr. Walsh. We went downstairs to see Mrs. Tuchler. She had just finished eating and was still in her apron. Her living room smelled of onions and chicken.

"Arrangements? What do you mean arrangements?"

"The old man needs help," Betty said. "We could see to it that he gets regular meals. We could take care of his laundry, help with his bath."

"His bath? We should wash him and dry him? Like his baby-sitters?"

"I wouldn't put it that way."

"A baby-sitter is part-time. The parents show up. They pay the sitter. They drive the sitter home. Who is it that drives me home, Miss McCarthy?"

"That's not what I had in mind."

"Even if he was my own family I would have problems. I got something more to do with my time than to be a baby-sitter. Maybe you can afford such charity—"

"I don't look at it as charity."

"What else? You give up your time for a man who is nobody to you."

"He's a human being, Mrs. Tuchler."

"I am also a human being. You'll take care of me, also?"

"I hope there'll be someone for you, Mrs. Tuchler."

"I don't count on it. I take care of myself."

I suggested we think of our obligation to Mr. Walsh as a temporary arrangement while we inquired about relatives.

"You don't think I asked? There is nobody. He is alone. I warned him—you heard me, Professor—he shouldn't lose his head, it will be the end for him."

Betty said she could bring food before she left for work.

"Tell me. How long will you keep up such an arrangement? One week, maybe? I give it no more."

"Don't you have any feeling for him, Mrs. Tuchler?"

"Feelings I got. Feelings I got plenty. Feelings cost nothing."

I went to his room in the morning.

The container of soup was unopened on his table.

I asked if he wanted breakfast.

He shook his head.

No orange juice? No coffee?

He shook his head.

Toast?

He didn't answer.

He sat in his Morris chair.

"Do you want me to read you the morning paper?"

He shook his head.

"Shall I read something from the *Encyclopedia?*"

He looked up.

"Shall I find something to read?"

He nodded.

Only the pages of Volume 18 were cut, MED to MUM, where Louise had read the statistics of Michigan and found nine forlorn Japanese in that peppermint-growing state.

I pulled out the tissue map of Michigan.

I brought him his spectacles. I drew my finger up Lake Erie and the Detroit River into Lake St. Clair. I traveled up Lake Huron through the Straits of Mackinac into Lake Michigan. We hugged the shore all the way to Chicago. I called out the beach towns and offshore islands.

"Leland," he repeated after me.

"Do you know Leland?"

He spoke in a rusty, abraded voice. "We stayed in Leland one summer. There was an Indian family. Potawatomies. One of them named Archie brought us white fish. They treated them like colored people."

I offered him juice and toast and a banana and he ate with good appetite.

I opened POL-REE and cut pages with a paring knife.

Potawatomi, derived from the Indian word for fire-maker. Algonquian stock. Settled in lower Michigan. They were allied with the French in their wars against the Iroquois and took part in the conspiracy of Pontiac.

Pontiac. A chief of the Ottawas. On May 7, 1763 he tried to occupy Fort Detroit and failed. He besieged the fort until October 30th.

The city of Pontiac, named in honor of the Indian chief, is the county seat of Oakland County, Michigan, on the Clinton River, about 26 miles N.W. of Detroit. The Eastern Michigan Asylum for the Insane (1878), with grounds covering more than 500 acres, is located in Pontiac. The name "Eloise" was derived from the official name.

MOTOR VEHICLES.

In 1910. The total number in the United Kingdom was 183,000. There were 46,000 vehicles in France and 42,000 in Germany. The United States of America with 225,000 cars was foremost.

"Old Henry," he said. "Good old Henry. Nobody ever called him Hank."

There was no mention of Ford in 1910. The invention of the internal combustion engine was attributed to a German, Gottlieb Daimler.

"Henry worked on the internal combustion engine in a garage on Bagley Street. He was with the Edison Illuminating Company."

I opened DEM-EDW and located Detroit, founded in 1701 by Antoine de la Mothe Cadillac (c.1661–1730). Cadillac arrived on the 24th of July with about 1600 followers. They at once built a palisade fort about 200-feet-square south of what is now Jefferson Avenue between Griswold and Shelby Street. Cadillac named it Fort Pontchartrain in honor of the French Colonial Minister.

*   *   *

Betty called to say she might be late and I told her not to rush. The old man seemed back to his ordinary state of unworldliness.

"I'll bring him a bite to eat."

"No wonton soup," I told her. "He's well-stocked."

I checked again that evening before leaving for Diekman's and he was in his chair, nodding off with the radio on.

*   *   *

At Diekman's that night I mentioned the old man and the tragedy of old age and the apparent failure of community.

There was a time, Diekman said, when old age was no tragedy.

The monastery town of St. Gall thrived in an age of walls. Walls around the monastery, walls around the castle, walls around the town. And beyond the walls a girdle of fields and then forest. Everything necessary for the complete life was inside the walls or just beyond.

There were goldsmiths, silversmiths, blacksmiths, potters, weavers, bakers, brewers. The monks had flocks of sheep and goats and herds of cattle and horses. Their gardens were designed for year-around sustenance. The ten thousand people within the walls served under the benign rule of the abbot. It was a way of life that came about as a consequence of the Saracen invasion. The barbarians had destroyed all connections. Language itself was at risk. Spoken utterance coarsened. The written language became exclusively the province of clerics. The abbot stood at the center of a world that had otherwise lost its center.

The discipline imposed by the abbot secured the walled paradise.

How tentative was our link to the past. How easy to break the chain of tradition that bound us to our origins and safeguarded the knowledge needed for survival.

The good father was the salvation. The abbot supervised life within the walls. Every moment had its definition. Time was marked by the seasons and the sacraments and the holy days. There was no confusion of estates. Every position was clear and distinct.

Diekman said that if he could have arrested history he would have chosen a time before Henry Ford bound us together in a chain of highways and made us one. Divisions were overcome, boundaries removed. Making us one, Ford made us nothing. Letting everyone in, he breached the walls of community, destroyed the distinction between inside and outside, hastened the entropy that would in its final stage bring us again to chaos.

The university should have been our tower, our fortress, our St. Gall. But Wayne was penetrated by city streets, everyone allowed to enter, the university turned from its vocation to safeguard the life of the spirit.

Diekman saw himself, I suppose, as our abbot and Friday nights in his apartment a recreation of St. Gall.

I was ready to settle for a good father.

*   *   *

I put my ear to the wall and didn't hear any coughing or rattling. The radio was off. I knocked on his door and he didn't answer. I called Mrs. Tuchler.

I feared what we might find when she opened his door but he wasn't in. We waited past midnight and he didn't show up and Mrs. Tuchler called the police.

Betty returned at two in the morning.

"You said he was back to normal and there was no reason to stick to the schedule."

"Normal in his case does not mean in full possession of his wits."

The next morning we walked the neighborhood and asked if anyone had seen Frank Walsh. The old man was well-known. Everyone seemed to know he'd been married for fifty-three years and was a friend of Henry Ford. The postman reported seeing Walsh get on the Woodward streetcar at Warren.

A couple days later Mrs. Tuchler received a call from a social worker at the Eastern Michigan Asylum, once explicitly designated for the insane and known as Eloise. The old man had somehow managed the twenty-six miles to Pontiac and checked himself in. He was unable to identify himself but Mrs. Tuchler's phone number was in his wallet.

Perhaps he'd gone there because the name sounded like "Louise."

*   *   *

Betty borrowed a 1950 powder-blue Ford coupe and we drove to Pontiac to visit Walsh.

I didn't find out until we were underway that she was a novice driver with only a temporary permit. She leaned forward, clenched the wheel.

"Are you sure you can drive?"

"What's to it?"

I had never learned, myself.

Her chatter ebbed and flowed with the conditions of traffic. She became more confident as we drove out Woodward beyond the zoo. We passed the Wigwam restaurant, the Shrine of the Little Flower where Father Coughlin once presided. She relaxed as traffic diminished. Her conversation steadied. She was a drama student at Wayne. She had played Irina in *The Three Sisters*. She had been Miriam in *Winterset*. She'd been enthusiastically reviewed in the college newspaper. Philosophy wasn't her thing and she'd never heard of Professor Diekman.

She rattled on and I pretended to listen.

The asylum came into view off the road, a red-brick castle, steep pitched roof clutched by gables, towers with witches' hats. It was the kind of redness you'd get if the brick clay never dried. Inside that red building you felt as if you were underground, even on the top floor in the tiny rooms beneath the plunging roof.

"Well, we're here. Shall we go in?"

Smoke curled from the chimneys of Eloise. The day was cold and the brittle grass cracked when we stepped on it.

The smell of the place must have come from a desperate effort to purge what had been in the red clay from the beginning and could never be removed unless the site were leveled and the remains either carted off or buried.

We were stopped at Reception and told we couldn't see the old man since we weren't relatives but Betty led the way down a corridor. We drifted with visitors and crazy people and old folks. We mingled with the robed and the pajama-ed and those in overcoats and mufflers. We walked up broad stairways illuminated by dull globes, past red lights marking exits, through wards of the ambulant. We came to a corridor where the old folks were seated on cane benches in a glassed-in porch. We found old Walsh in a wheelchair. He wore a threadbare robe. He was so faded and withered we would have passed without recognizing him. A custodian told us, "That's him. That's your grandpa."

"It's Russ Hansen," I told him, "and Betty McCarthy." His lips fluttered, his eyes wouldn't focus.

Betty, who had hardly spoken more than words of greeting to the old man, tried to prod him into response.

"How do you like it here, Mr. Walsh? Do they feed you O.K.? I bet the food's terrible. Do you remember that soup I brought you, Mr. Walsh?" On and on, as if she imagined she could talk him out of senility.

I think he said, "Russ?" The voice was unused and choked and the sound not coherent. I'm not sure he spoke my name.

"We're holding your things for you."

The pale blue eyes didn't record a thing.

I asked if he wanted the picture of Louise in his room. It might make the room more like home. He didn't respond.

I held his hand for a few moments then placed it on the arm of the chair. He took no further notice and I had nothing to say.

Betty whispered, "Let's go."

Outside her breath frosted. Her long muffler came loose. She furled it securely. She tugged down on her green tam-o'-shanter. "Well," she said, "at least someone saw him."

"What did we see? There's no one there."

*　　*　　*

He bequeathed Eloise his shadow. The substance remained with Mrs. Tuchler.

There was the Seth Thomas pendulum clock, the wardrobe with the lion's claw feet, his Zenith console, an oak highboy, a gilt-framed photo of himself as a young Irishman—tinted blond, red-cheeked—a companion photo of a corseted Louise with splendid curls and a firm sensible mouth. There were other items that Mrs. Tuchler disposed of—a paperweight with a Currier and Ives snow scene, a signed Maxfield Parrish "Dawn," a hand-crocheted bedspread. And so on. The treasure for me was the Eleventh Edition, in pristine condition.

An Eloise doctor said that Walsh would never be back. He walked when set in motion but the spirit had left the machine. Tuchler said she'd have to get rid of his things. She had no place to store them. Betty wanted the old man's room with its exterior windows. There was already a prospective tenant for the vacancy. There weren't any relatives to assume debts or assets. He owed Mrs. Tuchler several months' back rent. A lawyer advised her she could sell the "junk"—the clock, the wardrobe, the bedstead, the chest of drawers, the dresser with the oval mirror. The sale would cover her expenses. As for the *Encyclopedia*, any dealer would be glad to pay a few dollars, but why not keep it in the family?

"You take it, Professor. Give me ten dollars and it is done."

We stalked his dying, and now closed in to feed.

I arranged the *Encyclopedia* on my windowsills, ten volumes to a window and entered its pages.

REF-SAI was still uncut.

The town of St. Gall owes its origin to St. Gall, an Irish hermit, who in 614, built his cell in the thick forest which then covered the site of the future monastery, and lived there, with a few companions, till his death in 640. Many pilgrims later found their way to his cell, and about the middle of the eighth century the collection of hermits' dwellings was transformed into a regularly organized Benedictine monastery. For the next three centuries this was one of the chief centers of learning and education in Europe. About 954 the monastery and its buildings were surrounded by walls as a protection against the Saracens, and this was the origin of the town.

The Encyclopedia offered whatever anyone wanted in the way of towns, cities, continents, even the starry universe. Walsh wanted nothing. He only claimed a bed in a ward at Eloise.

Mrs. Tuchler gave Betty the photographs of Walsh and Louise, valuable for the elaborate, gilt frames.

The poor old guy, Betty said. No one cared. And we were already divvying up the spoils.

*   *   *

I came across the final words imputed to Descartes, dying in Sweden of pneumonia. I offered them to the Diekman circle:

" 'My soul, you have been captive for a long time, now the

hour has come when you must leave your prison, this body; you must bear this separation with joy and courage.' "

The words were reported by Ambassador Charcut, who was in attendance.

I found the speech repellent.

"Why?"

"It's too rehearsed."

Diekman didn't take Descartes's statement at face-value. "My soul? This body?" Whose voice was it that addressed the soul and referred to the body? Someone named René Descartes who distinguished himself from his soul and body? "Where is the voice housed that speaks to 'my soul'? Who is the third man who intrudes between body and soul?"

Vincenti suggested that the voice of Ego occurs at a higher level of language than the mention of body and soul and so doesn't intrude between them.

Diekman dismissed this solution. "It's simpler to not accept the speech at its face-value. Though clearness and distinctness are everything to Descartes, he doesn't have time to make his meaning clear when he's dying. His language becomes condensed, ambiguous, poetic. Surely he doesn't mean to say that the soul of René Descartes will survive disembodiment as a ghost of himself. Who would the ghost resemble? There is no single Descartes. He has passed—as we all do—through a series of transformations, from youth to age, from health to illness. So even if there were cameras available, no single representation would serve. There's no fixing him once and for all. Isn't he simply foretelling what in fact turns out to be the case? Descartes tells us, as he's dying, that he welcomes his disembodiment and his coming immortality. Cartesianism will survive, he tells us."

I offered a simpler explanation. Descartes didn't make the deathbed speech. A man dying of pneumonia wouldn't have had enough wind for that speech. It must have been composed by Charcut, an avid Cartesian.

"That, too," Diekman said, "is irrelevant. The separation of body and soul is a fable. The fable holds that we are victims of our appetites and only free when appetite diminishes. Cephalus, for example, welcomes old age and the ebbing of desire. We have other uses for a fable than to question its truth."

"The truth about dying," I said, "is that it leaves you speech-less."

I was hooted down for offering "the truth about dying." They weren't tempted to move the discussion in a morbid direction. It was raining; snow was on the way; we were cozy inside, dining by candlelight, a fire crackling in a frame of ceramic tiles.

The supper that night featured a seafood pasta, served in a porcelain tureen. Prawns and scallops and crabmeat were added to each portion of pasta and the dish topped with sautéed peas and carrots.

Vincenti asked for grated cheese but the Professor told him grated cheese was not served with seafood pasta.

Diekman's bathroom was a large, tiled room, entered through a dressing alcove. I opened a cabinet and saw thick towels rolled in the shape of loaves of bread in hues of red, blue, green, yellow. Above the double basin of pink porcelain there was a large mirror circled by fluorescence. The medicine cabinet revealed a man who must have suffered in every part. There were capsules for muscle spasm. He used sedatives and laxatives. There were medicines for eyes, skin, feet, rectum.

He clearly took great care before presenting himself. There was a tub with an aluminum railing and a separate shower stall. A shelf, straddling the bath, contained bath oil, skin lotion, pumice stone. On the lip of the tub there were shampoos and moisturizers. On the marble commode there were soaps in a variety of shapes, little balls in gaudy wrappers, rounds of soap, rectangles of soap, a green-flecked soap in the form of a fish, another shaped from transparent, pink gel into the form of a cupid. A basket of potpourri on the water tank shed a cinnamon, ginger odor.

*   *   *

There was little evidence of shit in that room and hardly any evidence in the Eleventh Edition. I opened SAI-SHU and didn't find a listing. There were no entries for excreta or feces in EVA-FRA.

The encyclopedia contained the world in almost every feature but only a Latinate mention of shit under sewage where there was a discussion of the use of "excreta" as manure and the storing of excreta in middens and cesspools. The method for disposing of feces in 1910 was the same as ours today, dilution and defecation through pipes four to six inches in diameter.

*   *   *

I shoved open the bathroom door. Either the latch didn't hold or she was neglectful. Betty was poised at the sink in an open kimono, her left leg extended, foot in the basin, leaning forward soaping painted toes, red hair floating down over her eyes, a glimpse of freckled breasts, the rusty thatch below, the tensed right leg sturdy and muscular. "Sorry," I said and shut the door.

I apologized when she came out.

"No problem. I should have made sure the door was locked."

"Anyway," I said, "it's a gorgeous view."

She moved into Walsh's room, her bed against the wall dividing us. We were separated by six inches of lathe and air and plasterboard. I could hear the rustle of her sheets and the squeal of springs.

One early morning before dawn I knocked at her door.

"Who is it?"

I whispered, "Russ," and she opened to me.

*   *   *

I knew that the charges I brought against Diekman in the court of my mind wouldn't hold. Was his john too lavish? Was he to blame for the way Vincenti ate, for Descartes's foolish death, for the absence of any reference to Iron Mountain or lost fathers or shit in the Eleventh Edition? The grievances were trivial but suddenly his walled city closed in on me and I felt entombed and couldn't bear listening to him tidy up the world.

I dropped out of the Diekman circle. I left without saying a word to Diekman. I had nothing to say. I couldn't give an account of a defection I didn't understand. I abandoned campus. I didn't answer Vincenti's messages. I prepared to move from the neighborhood. I was with Betty so it's not entirely true that I was in despair.

I met him again, possibly for the last time, shortly after Christmas. Trees were still up, stars still in windows, there was new snow on the ground. I was shopping at the Kroger's Market. I walked down the soup aisle and there he was in overcoat, muffler, gloves, a basket in his hand, his cane hooked on an arm, wearing a Russian-style fur hat.

It wasn't his neighborhood or his kind of store and I didn't expect to meet him there.

Yes, he said, a surprising place to meet. He didn't ordinarily shop here. He was careful about food, as he was sure I knew, but he felt a cold coming on and didn't have time or energy for refined shopping. At any rate, the objects he carried were only apparently trivial. He held up the soup can glorified by Andy Warhol. He spoke in full voice, no evidence of a cold. He praised Warhol for transforming banality and demonstrating that food had become something other than food. A citizen of mid-twentieth-century America was free of the necessity imposed by brute hunger and didn't have to spend a major effort tracking down the next meal. The package was now more important than the soup.

He had once scorned salesmen as purveyors of kitsch and schlock. Now he understood that they were, in fact, visionaries

of the commonplace, true esthetes who awakened us to neglected beauty and enlarged our world. We could enter Kroger's
as we once entered a gallery of art.

He denied the food he craved and passed off the denial as art.

I was outraged by the show he put on for random shoppers
who had stopped traffic in the aisle to listen. He didn't ask me
where I'd been. He didn't give me a chance to make excuses.

"Food isn't a priority with me and I don't care how it comes
wrapped."

He nodded, smiled. It was the betrayal he expected. He offered me a slanted, mocking look. "We welcome the moment
when our children instruct us so we can cut them free."

*   *   *

He acknowledged me as his child and there are times when I can
imagine pleading, "Take me back. I've lost my way."

*   *   *

She's pinned photos of stars to the walls. Dietrich and Hepburn
and Harlow and Gable nourish her dream of stardom. I saw her
at the World Theater in "My Sister Eileen." She played perky
Eileen. It was herself she played, without subterfuge, almost
artlessly. She was charming and likable and received an ovation
from the mainly college audience.

I told her, "Everyone pulls for you. You're really liked."

She wanted honest feedback that would help in her work.
What didn't I like about her performance?

I enjoyed the evening. She was a fine Eileen. Still, I wasn't
sure about her range. Her voice lacked timbre and occasionally
faded. There was actually something appealing in this, something naive and childlike that disarmed criticism. But how deep
could she go?

"I'm not deep, Russ. I never said I was."

*   *   *

Her dream of stardom will pass. She's buoyant and good-hearted and believes any condition is alterable, even grievous old age. It's typical that she would offer Frank Walsh wonton soup.

I've said goodbye to the Diekman circle and it terrifies me when I think I've set myself on the trail of Frank Walsh, headed toward a red-brick grave among the living dead. I warn Betty— no mausoleums, no walls, no ill health, no old age. We live young and die happy. I want that in the contract.

Agreed, she says, confident that enthusiasm and buoyancy can manage anything.

◆ *Peter Matthiessen* ◆

LUMUMBA LIVES

1

He comes by train out of the wilderness of cities, he has come from abroad this very day. At mid-life he has returned to Arcadia-on-Hudson, where he knows no one.

The train tugs softly, slides away, no iron jolt and bang as in his childhood, no buck and yank of couplings, only a gathering clickety-click away along the glinting track, away along the river woods, the dull shine of the water, north and away toward the great bend in the Hudson.

Looking north, he thinks, the river has lost color. The track is empty, the soft late summer sunshine fills the bend, the day is isolate.

He is the one passenger left on the platform, exposed to the bare windows of Arcadia. He might be the one survivor in a cataclysm, emerging into the flat sun of the river street at the foot of this steep decrepit town fetched up against the railroad tracks on the east slope of the Hudson River Valley. What he hasn't remembered in the years he has been gone are the hard bad colors of its houses, the dirtied brick and the fire bruises of the abandoned factory, the unbeloved dogs, the emptiness.

On this railroad street, a solitary figure with a suitcase might attract attention. To show that his business is forthright, he crosses the old cobbles quickly to the salesmen's hotel at the bottom of the downhill slide of human habitation. The dependent saloon has a boarded-up side door marked "Ladies Entrance," and the lobby reminds him, not agreeably, of looted colonial hotels in the new Africa that he supposes he will never see again.

The stranger's soft voice and quiet suit, his discreet manner, excite the suspicion of the clerk, who puts down a mop to shuffle behind the desk and slap out a registration form. This dog-eared old man spies on the name as it is being written. "We got a park here by that name," he says.

The man shakes his head as if shaking off the question. Asked where he's from, he says he has lived abroad. The foreign service. Africa.

"Africa," the clerk says, licking a forefinger and flicking the sports pages of a New York daily. "You'll feel right at home, then." He reads a while as if anticipating protest. "Goddam Afros overflowing right out of the city. Come up this way from Yonkers, come up at night along the river."

The clerk looks up. "Rape and steal, y'know. You have a wife?"

"I saw them," the stranger says. At Spuyten Duyvil, where the tracks emerged from the East River and turned north up the Hudson, black men had watched his train from the track sidings. The stranger's fingertips lie flat upon the counter as if he meant to spring into the air. "They were fishing," he says.

He is a well-made man of early middle age and good appearance, controlled and quiet in his movements. Dry blond hair is combed across a sun-scarred bald spot.

"I guess you learned to like 'em over there."

The man says nothing. He has shallow and excited eyes. He awaits his key.

Irritable and jittery under that gaze, the clerk picks out a key with yellowed fingers. "How many nights?"

The man shrugs. Who knows? Asked if he wishes to see the room, he shrugs again. He will see it soon enough. When he produces a thick roll of bills to pay the cash deposit in advance, the old man inspects the bills, lip curled, checking the stranger's face at the same time. Still holding the cash as if in evidence, he leans over the desk to glare at the large old-fashioned leather suitcase.

The stranger says, "I'll take it up. It's heavy."

"I'll bet," says the clerk, shaking his head over the weight he had almost been asked to hump up the steep stair. He snaps open the next page of his paper. "Bathroom down the hall."

On the floor above, the man listens a moment, wondering briefly why he sets people on edge even before trouble occurs. Their eyes reflect the distemper he is feeling.

He opens, closes, bolts the transomed door.

*   *   *

The room is penitential, it is high-ceilinged and skinny, with defunct fire pipes, no pictures, a cold-water sink, a scrawny radiator, a ruined mirror on the wall. The water-marked walls are the color of blue milk. The bedside table is so small that there is no room for a lamp. The Gideon Bible sits in the chipped washbasin. A rococo ceiling fixture overhead, a heavy dark armoire, an iron bed with a stained spread of slick green nylon.

The pieces stand in stiff relation, like spare people whom no one is concerned to introduce.

His reflected face in the pocked mirror is unforgiving.

The room has no telephone, and there will be no visitors. He has no contacts in this place, which is as it should be. Checking carefully for surveillance devices, he realizes the precaution is absurd, desists, feels incomplete, finishes anyway.

Big lonesome autumn flies buzz on the windowsill. The high bare window overlooks the street, the empty railroad station, the river with its sour burden of industrial filth carried down from bleak ruined upstate valleys. Across the river the dark cliffs of the Palisades wall off the sky.

*   *   *

His mother had not felt well enough to see him off, nor had his father driven him down to the station. The Assistant Secretary for African Affairs had wished to walk his English setter, and had walked his son while he was at it.

We want you to gain the Prime Minister's confidence. He may trust you simply because you are my son.

Unfortunately the more . . . boyish? . . . elements in our government want another sort of man entirely. They are sure to find some brutal flunky who, for a price, will protect Western interests.

He had not waited for the train.

Make the most of this opportunity, young man.

By which the Assistant Secretary meant, *You have this chance to redeem yourself, thanks to my influence.*

The gardener had brought the leather suitcase. From the empty platform they watched his father stride away. At the north end of the street, the tall straight figure passed through the iron gate into the park.

The gardener cried, *So it's off to Africa ye are! And what will ye be findin there, I'm askin?*

*   *   *

Turning from the window, he removes his jacket, drapes it on a chair; he does not remove the shoulder holster, which is empty.

He contemplates the Assistant Secretary's ancient suitcase as if the solution to his life were bundled up in it.

He unpacks his clothes, takes out a slim chain, locks and binds the suitcase, chains it to the radiator.

On the bed edge he sits upright for a long time as if expecting something. He has trained himself to wait immobile hour after hour, like a sniper, like a roadside African, like a poised hawk, ready for its chance, thinking of nothing.

A dying fly comes to his face. It wanders. Its touch is weak and damp. He does not brush it away.

*　　　*　　　*

By the river at the north end of town is a public park established by his grandfather, at one time a part of the old Harkness estate. His father's great-uncle, in the nineteenth century, had bought a large tract of valleyside and constructed a great ark of a house with an uplifting view of the magnificent Palisades across the river, and his descendants had built lesser houses in the park, in one of which, as an only child, he had spent the first years of his life.

Not wishing to hurry, he does not go there on the first day, contenting himself with climbing the uphill street and buying a new address book. He must make sure that each day has its errand, that there is a point to every day, day after day.

Soon he visits the real-estate agent's office. The agent, a big man with silver hair slicked hard and puffy dimpled chin, concludes that the old Harkness property will have just the "estate" that Mister . . . ? might be looking for.

"Call me Ed," the agent says, sticking out his hand. The client shakes it after a brief pause but does not offer his name.

All but the river park presented to the village was sold off for development, the agent explains, when the last Harkness moved away some years before. But the big trees and the big stone houses—the "manor houses," the agent calls them—are still there, lending "class" to the growing neighborhood.

*   *   *

Mother says you are obliged to sell the house. I'd like to buy it.
   Absolutely not!

*   *   *

The narrow road between high ivied walls was formerly the service driveway, and the property the realtor has in mind is the gardener's brick cottage, which shares the river prospect with "the big house" on the other side of an old stand of oak and hickory.

As a child he fled his grandmother's cambric tea to take refuge in this cottage full of cooking smells. His nurse was married to the gardener, and he knows at once that he will buy the cottage even if the price is quite unreasonable. So gleeful is he in this harmony of fate that his fingers work in his coat pockets.

He has no wish to see the rooms until all intervening life has been cleaned out of them. Before the agent can locate the keys, he says, "I'll take it."

When the agent protests—"You don't want to look inside?"— he counts off five thousand dollars as a deposit and walks back to the car, slipping into the passenger seat, shutting the door.

Not daring to count or pocket so much cash, the agent touches the magic bricks in disbelief. He pats the house as he might pat a horse and stands back proudly. "Nosir, they don't make 'em like this, not anymore."

The one thing missing here is burglar lights, the agent says—a popular precaution these days, he assures his client, climbing back into the car. Like the man at the hotel, he evokes the human swarm emerging from the slums and coming up along the river woods at night. "Engage in criminal activity," he emphasizes when the other man, by his silence, seems to question this.

"Ready to go?" the client says, looking out the window.

On the way home he inquires about New York State law in regard to shooting burglars, and the agent laughs. "Depends on his color," he says, and nudges his client, and wishes he had not. "Don't get me wrong," he says.

*   *   *

Back at the office the agent obtains the buyer's name to prepare the contract. "You've come to the right place, all right! Any relation?"

The man from Africa ignores the question. He will reveal that he belongs here in his own good time. First he wants everything to be in place, the little house, its furnishings, his history. The place will be redone in the style of the big house across the hedge, with English wallpapers, old walnut furniture, thick big towels and linen sheets, crystal and porcelain, such as his parents might have left him, setting off the few good pieces he had put in storage after their death. The inside walls will be painted ivory, as the house was, and the atmosphere will be sunny and cheerful, with an aura of fresh mornings in the spring.

Once the cottage is ready, his new life will commence, and the names of new friends will flower in his address book.

*   *   *

To his childhood house he wishes to return alone, on foot. Since he means to break in, he makes sure that he leaves the hotel unobserved, that he is not followed. Not that there is anyone to follow him, it is simply a good habit, sound procedure.

He enters the park by the iron gate beyond the railroad station, climbing transversely across a field, then skirting an old boxwood border so as not to be seen by the unknown people who have taken over his uncle's house. He trusts the feel of things and not his sight, for nothing about this shrunken house looks quite familiar. It was always a formal, remote house, steep-roofed and angular, but now it has the dark of rottenness, of waterlogged wood.

He hurries on, descending past the stables (no longer appended to his uncle's house or frequented by horses, to judge from the trim suburban cars parked at the front). In the old pines stands a grotesque disc of the sort recommended to him by his would-be friend the agent, drawing a phantasmagoria of color from the heavens.

He is seeking a childhood path down through the wood, across the brook, and uphill through the meadow.

From the trees come whacks and pounding, human cries.

*   *   *

The trouble was, he had not liked Lumumba.

In a letter to his parents in Arcadia he had wondered if the Prime Minister might be unstable. Lumumba's hostility toward Europeans, flaring and dying like a fire in the wind, was unmistakable. He ate distractedly in small brief fits, growing thinner and thinner. He was moody, loud, self-contradictory, he smoked too much hemp, he drank a lot, he took one woman after another despite his devotion to his wife, he could not stop talking or stand still.

*   *   *

A paddle-tennis court has spoiled the brook, which is now no more than an old shadow line of rocks and broken brush. Wary of his abrupt appearance, his unplayful air—or perhaps of a stranger not in country togs, wearing unsuitable shoes for a country weekend—the players challenge him. Can they be of help?

He says he is looking for the Harkness house.

"Who?" one man says.

Calling the name—*Harkness!*—through the trees, hearing his own name in his own voice, makes him feel vulnerable as well as foolish, and his voice is thickened by a flash of anger. He thinks, I have lost my life while soft and sheltered men like these dance at their tennis.

He manages a sort of smile, which fails to reassure them. They look at each other, they look back at him. They do not resume playing.

"Harkness," one man says finally, cocking his head. "That was long ago. My grandfather knew your father. Something like that."

Dammit, he thinks. Who said that was my name!

Now the players bat the ball, rally a little. He knows they watch him as he skirts the court and leaves the trees and climbs the lawn toward the stone house set against the hillside at the ridge top.

His father's house has a flagstone terrace with a broad prospect of the Hudson. It is a good-sized stone house, with large cellar rooms, a downstairs, upstairs, and a third story with servants' rooms and attic. Yet even more than his uncle's place it seems diminished since his childhood. Only the great red oak at this south end of the house seems the right size, which confuses him until he realizes that in the decades he has been away it has grown larger.

In a snapshot of himself beneath this tree, in baggy shorts, he brandishes a green garden stake shoved through the hole of a small flower pot, used as a hand guard. He is challenging to a duel the Great Dane, Inga.

The oak stands outside the old "sun room," with its player piano and long boxes of keyed scrolls, and a bare parquet floor for children's games and tea dancing. The world has changed since a private house had a room designed for sun and dancing.

The weather-greened cannon are gone from the front circle.

Once this staid house stood alone, but now low dwellings can be seen, crowding forward like voyeurs through what is left of the thin woods farther uphill.

Completing the circuit of the house, he arrives at the formal garden—"the autumn garden," his mother called it, with its brick wall and flowered gate, its view down across the lawn to the woods and river. The garden is neglected, gone to weeds. Though most are fallen, his mother's little faded signs that identified the herb species still peep from a coarse growth of goldenrod, late summer asters.

In other days, running away, he had hidden past the dusk in the autumn garden, peering out at the oncoming dark, waiting for a voice to call him into the warm house. They knew his ways, and no one ever called. Choked with self-pity, a dull yearning in his chest, he would sneak up the back stairs without his supper.

The boiler room has an outside entrance under the broad terrace, on the downhill side. He draws on gloves to remove a pane, lever the lock. He crosses the spider-shrouded light to the cellar stair, and enters the cold house from below, turning the latch at the top of the stair, edging the door open to listen. He steps into the hall. The house feels hollow, and white sheets hide the unsold furniture. In the kitchen he surprises an old cockroach, which scuttles beneath the pipes under the sink.

The silence follows him around the rooms. On his last visit before his father sold the house, faint grease spots still shone through the new paint on the ceiling of his former bedroom. Sometimes, sent up to his room for supper, he had used a banged spoon as catapult to stick the ceiling with rolled butter pats and peanut-butter balls.

From his parents' bedroom, from the naked windows, he gazes down over the lawn, standing back a little to make sure he is unseen. The court is empty. He is still annoyed that the paddle-tennis players have his name. Possibly they are calling the police. To be arrested would reflect badly on his judgment, just when he has asked if there might be an assignment for him someplace else.

Hearing a car, he slips downstairs and out through the cellar doors.

"Lookin for somebody?"

The caretaker stands in the service driveway by the corner of the house. He wears a muscle-tight, black T-shirt and big sideburns. He is wary, set for trouble, for he comes no closer.

Had this man seen him leave the house?

He holds the man's eye, keeping both hands in his coat pockets, standing motionless, dead silent, until uneasiness seeps into the man's face.

"I got a call. The party said there was somebody lookin for someone."

"Can't help you, I'm afraid." Casually he shrugs and keeps on going, down across the lawn toward the brook.

"Never seen them signs?" the man calls after him, when the stranger is a safe distance away. "What do you want around here, Mister?"

2

With some idea of returning to the hotel by walking south beside the tracks, he makes his way down along the brook, his street shoes slipping on the aqueous green and sunshined leaves.

Whenever, in Africa, he thought of home, what he recalled most clearly was this brook below the house and a sandy eddy where the idle flow was slowed by his rock dam. Below this pool, the brook descended through dark river woods to a culvert that ran beneath the tracks into the Hudson. Lit by a swift sun that passed over the trees the water crossed the golden sand— the long green hair of algae twined on bobbing stems, the clean frogs and quick fishes and striped ribbon snakes—the flow so clear that the diadem of a water skater's shadow would be etched on the sunny sand glinting below. One morning a snake seized a small frog—still a tadpole, really, a queer thing with new-sprouted legs and a thick tail—and swallowed it with awful gulps of its unhinged jaws. Another day, another year, perhaps, peering into the turmoil in a puff of sunlit sand of the stream bottom, he saw a minnow in the mouth and claws of a mud-colored dragon. The dragonfly nymph loomed in his dreams for years thereafter, and he hated the light-filled creature it became, the crazy sizzle of the dragonfly's glass wings, the unnatural hardness of this thing when it struck the skin.

For hours he would hunch upon a rock, knees to his ears, staring at the passages and deaths. Sometimes he thought he would like to study animals. How remote this dark brook was from the Smiling Pool in his Peter Rabbit book up in the nursery, a meadow pool all set about with daffodils and roses, birds, fat bumblebees, where mirthful frogs, fun-loving fish, and philosophical turtles fulfilled their life on earth without a care.

Even then he knew that Peter Rabbit was a mock-up of the world, meant to fool children.

*   *   *

Nearing the railroad, the old brook trickles free from the detritus, but the flow is a mere seepage, draining into a black pool filled with oil drums. An ancient car, glass-shattered, rust-colored, squats low in the thick Indian summer undergrowth where once—or so his father said—an Algonkin band had lived in a log village.

In the sun and silence of the river, he sits on the warm trunk of a fallen willow, pulling mean burrs from his city trousers. From here he can see across the tracks to the water and the Palisades beyond. Perhaps, he thinks, those sugar-maple yellows and hot hickory reds along the cliffs welcomed Henry Hudson, exploring upriver with the tide four centuries before, in the days when this gray flood—at that time blue—swirled with silver fishes.

Hudson's ship—or so his father always claimed—had an elephant chained on the foredeck, an imposing present for the anticipated Lord of the Indies. Turned back at last by the narrowing river from his quest for the Northwest Passage, fed up with the task of gathering two hundred pounds of daily fodder for an animal that daily burdened the small foredeck with fifteen to twenty mighty shits—his father's word, in its stiff effort at camaraderie, had astonished and delighted him—Henry the Navigator had ordered the elephant set free in the environs of present-day Poughkeepsie. Strewing its immense sign through the woods, blaring its longing for Africa to the silent pines, the great beast surely took its place in Algonkin legend.

Misreading his son's eager smile, his father checked himself, sighed crossly, and stood up. *A vigorous Anglo-Saxon term, not necessarily a dirty word to be leered and giggled at. You should have outgrown all that by now.* He left the room before the boy found words to undo such awful damage.

*   *   *

Beyond the misted trees, upriver, lies Tarrytown—had someone tarried there, his mother asked his father, purling demurely. Why his father smiled at this he did not know. From Tarrytown one might see across the water to the cliffs where Rip Van Winkle had slept for twenty years. As a child he imagined a deep warm cleft full of autumn light, sheltered from the northeast storms and northwest winds. He peers across the mile of water, as if that shelter high up in clean mountains were still there.

In the Indian summer mist the river prospect looks much as he remembered it—indeed, much as it had been portrayed by the Hudson River School of painters so admired by his maternal grandmother. Her small landscape of this stretch of river—was

that in the crate of family things he had in storage? How much
he has lost track of, in those years away.

He places a penny on the railroad track.

He longs to reassemble things—well, not "things" so much as
continuity, that was his mother's word. Her mother had been
raised on the west bank of the Hudson, and she could recall,
from her own childhood, her great-aunt relating how *her* grandmother had seen Alexander Hamilton sculling downriver one
fine morning just below their house—"Good day, Mr. Hamilton!"—and how Mr. Hamilton had never returned, having lost
his life to Mr. Burr in a duel that day at Weehawken.

His father loved this story, too, the more so because that
reach of river cliff had changed so little in the centuries between. For both of them, the memory of Mr. Hamilton had an
autumnal melancholy that reached far back across the nation's
history, to the Founding Fathers.

It seemed he had not responded to it properly.

I suppose you find it merely quaint, his mother said.

*   *   *

At one time he attended Sunday school here in Arcadia, and he
thinks he will rejoin the Episcopal Church. On sunny Sundays
in white shirt and sober suit he will find himself sustained and
calmed by stained-glass windows and Bach organ preludes. Afterward he will return to the garden cottage with its antique
furniture, blue flowers in white rooms, fine editions, rare music,
and a stately dog thumping its tail on a warm rug. He envisions
an esoteric text, a string quartet, a glass of sherry on a sunlit
walnut table in the winter—his parents' tastes, he realizes, acquired tastes he is determined to acquire.

In this civilized setting, smoking a pipe, he will answer questions from young women about Africa, and the nature of Africans, and how to deal judiciously with these Afro-Americans,
so-called. (He would condemn any ignorant use of the word

"nigger.") Those who imagined that Africans were inferior did not know Africans, he'd say. Africans had their own sort of intelligence, they were simply not interested in the same things we were. Once their nature was understood, he would say, Africans are Africans, wherever you find them, never mind what these bleeding-hearts might tell you.

* * *

A train comes from the north, clicketing by, no longer dull coal black, as in his childhood, but a tube of blue-and-silver cars, no light between. In his childhood he could make out faces, but with increased speed the human beings were pale blurs behind the glass, and nobody waves to the man on the dead tree by the railroad tracks.

The wind and buffet of the train, the sting of grit, intensify his sense of isolation. To his wave, the train responds with a shrill whistle that is only a signal to the station at Arcadia, a half mile south.

He gets up, stretching, hunts the penny. It glints at him among the cinders. Honest Abe, tarnished by commerce, has been wiped right off the copper, replaced by a fiery smooth shine.

Looking north and south, he picks his way across the tracks. The third rail—if such it is—is a sheathed cable between pairs of rails marked "Danger Zone 700 Volts." Has the voltage increased since his childhood? *If you so much as point at that third rail,* explained his mother, who worried about his solitary expeditions to the river, *you'll be electrocuted, like one of those ghastly criminals up at Sing-Sing!* He hesitates before he crosses, stepping over this rail higher than necessary.

The tracks nearest the river are abandoned, a waste of rusted rails and splintered oaken ties and hard dry weeds. Once across, he can see north to the broad bend where a shoulder of the Palisades juts out from the far shore into the Tappan Zee. A thick new bridge has been thrust across the water, cutting off the far blue northern mountains. In his childhood, a white steamer of the Hudson River Day Line might loom around that bend at any moment, or a barge of bright tomato-red being towed by a pea-green tug, both fresh as toys. His father would evoke the passage of Robert Fulton's steamship *Claremont,* and the river trade on this slow concourse, flowing south out of the far blue mountains.

In his own lifetime—is this really true?—the river has changed from blue to a dead gray-brown, so thickened with inorganic silt that a boy would not see his own feet in the shallows. The agent, not a local man but full of local lore, asserts that the Atlantic salmon have vanished from the Hudson, and that the striped bass and shad are so contaminated by the poisons dumped into these waters by the corporations that people are prohibited from eating them. Only the blacks, says he, come out to fish for them, prowling the no-man's-land of tracks and cinders.

A grit beach between concrete slabs of an old embankment is scattered with worn tires. He wonders, as his father had, at the sheer number of these tires, brought by forces unknown so very far from the roads and highways and dumped in low woods and spoiled sullen waters all across America, as if, in the ruined wake of the course of empire, the tires had spun away in millions down the highways and rolled off the bridges into the rivers and down into deep swamps of their own accord.

But the horizon is oblivious, the clouds are white, the world rolls on. Under the cliffs, the bend is yellow in the glow of maples, and the faraway water, reflecting the autumn sky, is gold and blue. Soiled though they are, the shining woods and glinting water and the bright steel tracks, the high golden cliffs across the river, seem far more welcoming than the valley slope above, with its tight driveways, cars, vigilant houses.

For a long time, by the riverside, he sits on a drift log worn smooth by the flood, withdrawn into the dream of Henry Hudson's clear blue river, of that old America off to the north toward the primeval mountains, off to the west under the shining sky.

3

The real-estate agent has persuaded him to come to dinner, to celebrate his move into the cottage, and a van has delivered a large crate containing what is left of the family things. On a journey home after his father's death, he had got rid of everything else, glad to have Arcadia behind him. But when his years in Africa were ended, and he was faced with a return to the United States, where he knew no one, this crate, in his imagination, had overflowed with almost everything from childhood. However, all he finds are a few small antiques that could not be sold quickly yet had seemed too valuable to abandon. There are also a few unaccountable small scraps—a baby-blue bathroom rug with faded bears, the Peter Rabbit book, the photograph of his duel with the Great Dane Inga.

His grandmother's riverscape is jammed in carelessly, its gold frame chipped. Wrapped around his father's Hardy reels and .410 Purdy shotgun is the Assistant Secretary's worn-out hunting jacket, the hard brown canvas and scuffed corduroy irrevocably stained with gun oil and bird blood, whiskey, and the drool of setter dogs.

The riverscape is hung over the mantel, with the Purdy on oak dowel pins beneath. He likes the feel of the quick gun, with its walnut stock and blue-black finish, its fine chasing. He will keep it loaded, as a precaution against looters and marauders. Agent Ed has advised him to emulate the plump homes of his neighbors, which are wall-eyed with burglar lights, atremble with alarms.

However, he hates all that night glare, he feels less protected than exposed. As soon as his pistol permit is restored—he concocts this plan over his evening whiskeys—he'll use a silencer to extinguish every burglar light in the whole neighborhood.

Why scare off marauders, he asks Mrs. Ed at supper, when the death of one burglar at the hands of a private citizen would do more to prevent crime than all the floodlights in Westchester County? He has said this for fun, to alarm this upstate couple. Poor Ed loves this dangerous talk, having no idea that his guest means it, and as for the hostess, the woman is agog, her eyes loom huge and round behind her spectacles.

"You're such a . . . well, a *disturbing* man!" she says.

"Disturbed *me* from the very first day I met him!" Ed cries jovially to soften his wife's inadvertent candor. "I suppose you're waiting for a new assignment?"

"There won't be any new assignment," he says, abruptly angry, as if admitting this to himself for the first time.

He drinks the whiskey he has carried to the table. That these folks want a Harkness for a friend is all too plain. He picks up the wine, sips it, blinks, pulls his head back from it, sets his glass down again. "A bit sweet," he explains, when her stare questions him.

Ed jars the table and his face goes red with a resentment that he has avoided showing until now. "Well, shit," he says. "You're a damn snob," he says.

"Oh my." The woman does not take her round eyes off their guest.

Ed scrapes his chair back and goes to the front door and opens it. "We just thought you might be kind of lonely," Mrs. Ed mourns.

"Probably likes it that way," the agent says.

Things are awry again. Afraid of something, he takes a large swallow of wine and nods approvingly. "Not bad at all," he says, with a poor smile.

"It's not just the wine," the agent warns his wife. The woman has crossed her bare arms on her chest in the cold draft that wanders through the opened door.

"I was hoping you'd call me Henry," he says, drinking more wine. "Very nice," he says. She turns her face away, as if unable to look upon his desperation. "Forgive me," he says.

"Nosir," the voice says from the door. "Nosir, I don't think we will."

4

Not wanting his new house to be finished, leaving things un-done, he takes long walks along suburban roads and drives. People stare to let him know they have their eye on him. Bad dogs run out. Even so, the walks are dull and pointless. More and more often he returns to the low river woods, the endless iron stretch of tracks, the silent river, flickered over by migrat-ing swallows.

One day in October, he crosses the tracks and sits on a dock piling with twisted bolts, wrenched free by some upriver devas-tation. The piling's faint creosote smell brings back some child-hood boat excursion, upriver through the locks of Lake Cham-plain.

The breeze is out of the northwest, and has an edge to it. With a fire-blackened scrap of siding, he scrapes out a shelter under the old pilings, partly hidden from the woods by the pale sumac saplings that struggle upward from the cinders.

In the early autumn afternoon, out of the wind, he is warmed by the westering sun across the river. If the beach litter were piled in front of him, he thinks, he would be unseen even from the water. Not that there is anyone to see him, it is just the sheltered feeling it would give him. The freighters headed up to Albany, the tugs and barges, an occasional fat white motor cruiser with its nylon Old Glory flying from the stern, pass too far offshore to be aware of a hat-shadowed face in a pile of flotsam.

He hunches down a little, squinting out between his knees.

He is safe and secret, sheltered from the world, just as he had been long ago in his tree houses and attic hideouts, in the spruce hollow in the corner behind the lode of packages under the Christmas tree, in warm nests in the high summer grass, peeping out at the Algonkin Indians. *Delawares,* his father said. *Algonkin is the language family.* In the daytime, at least, no one comes along the tracks. He has the river kingdom to himself. As to whether he is content, he does not know.

He has packed dry sherry in his father's silver flask, a sandwich, a hard apple, and also a new bleeding-heart account of modern politics in the former Belgian Congo. His name receives harsh passing mention. He thinks, To hell with it. I did what was asked of me. I did my duty. Having the courage to dirty one's hands, without glory and at great risk of ingratitude, may become one's higher duty to one's country. Wasn't that true?

Wild ducks pass by within gun range, flaring away from his little cove with hard quacks of alarm. He swings his arms as if holding a gun, and they crumple and fall in a downward arc as he follows through. Watching them fly onward, he feels an exhilaration tinged with loss that wild fowl still tried to migrate south along this shore of poisoned mud and rust and cinders. On a northeast wind, in rain, his hiding place would serve well as a duck blind, for in order to land into the wind the birds would hook around over the open water and come straight in to the gun.

More ducks appear farther upriver where the black stumps of an old dock jut from the surface. The long rust heads and silver-white bodies are magically unsullied in the somber water. There are five.

Needing something to look forward to, he decides upon a sacramental hunt. A hunter's stiff whiskey by the fire, the wild-duck supper with wild rice, the red Bordeaux from his mother's old colonial crystal decanter—thus will he consecrate the return of the Harkness family to Arcadia. Since it will happen only once, he can't be bothered with decoys, waders, far less a retriever. The river is too swift and deep to wade in, and in the unlikely event that a duck falls, the current is bound to carry it ashore.

To acquire a license to kill ducks he goes to Yonkers, not wishing to excite local curiosity. It seems absurd to bother about a license for one bird, when to shoot on the railroad right-of-way will be illegal in the first place. He applies for the permit for the same reason that he would feel obliged to retrieve and eat any bird he shot, rather than waste it. His father had been strict about licenses, bag limits, and using what one killed, even in the days when ducks were plentiful. To offend this code would violate the hunt ceremony in some way, make the supper pointless.

He has no proof of U.S. residence in the previous year—in the previous two decades, if it comes to that. He does not say this, lest his very citizenship be challenged by the hostile young black woman, who says he will have to identify himself, submit proof of residence, proof of citizenship. But he has no driver's license or certificate of birth, and can't tell her that his passport has been confiscated.

"Next!"

As for the huge hunting license, it looks nothing like the duck-stamp badge his father had worn upon his fishing hat. The new license is worn on the back, to facilitate identification by the game warden. Though he knows it is foolish, he feels he is being tricked into the open. One might as well wear a bull's-eye on one's back.

"Next!"

Are the authorities suggesting, he inquires, that the duck hunter is stupid as well as lawless, that he will shoot over his limit and make off with his booty, yet neglect to remove this grotesque placard from his back?

"We ain't suggesting nothing. That's the law." She waves him aside. "Next!"

He is surprised that the man behind him in the line is black.

"Move along please! Next!"

His stalling has permitted him to fold a twenty-dollar bill into his application form and ease it back across the counter, at the same time requesting her to be more careful how she talks to him. Raising her eyebrows at his tone, then at the money, she heaves around as if to summon her superior, giving him a chance to withdraw the bill. He does so quickly, winking at the black man, asking this female if he really requires proof that he is an American—doesn't he look like one?

With the back of her hand, she brushes away his application form, which flutters to the floor.

"I could bust you, Mister. You just watch your step."

She is already processing the next application.

"Everybody looks American," she is saying. *"I* look American. And you know what, Mister?" She looks up at him. "I *am* American. More than you." She points at the incomplete form in his hand. "I haven't lived in Africa for half my life."

*   *   *

Please do not confuse your activities in Africa with the foreign service, far less true service to your country, less still an honorable career that would make you a credit to this family.

When he raised his eyes, his mother averted hers. He flipped his father's note back at her, in a kind of spasm. The letter struck her at the collarbone and fell into her lap. She looked down at it for a long moment, then picked it up between two fingers and set it on the table. Her eyes glistened.

You've changed so, Henry, dear. When you went off to war, you grew so hard. It wasn't your fault, of course. Seeing all those dreadful things—it's enough to confuse anyone, *I'm sure!*

Before he could protest, she had slipped away from him.

You were such a lonely boy. How I wish you'd found somebody. Or become a naturalist! she added brightly. *Animals are so much easier, aren't they?*

Inappropriately, she tried to smile, as if to soothe him.

We shall always love you, dear.

His rivals killed him! he insisted. *Mother?* He had wanted to seize her, to shake from her frail body some pledge of loyalty. *Patrice was the Soviets' little macaque!*

She opened her eyes wide in mock astonishment—Patrice? *And your little Mr. Mobutu, dear? The dictator? Whose macaque is he?*

*   *   *

He decides he will need decoys after all. His father's hand-carved balsa ducks, close-etched with wild colors, had been rigged with cedar keels and fine-smelling tarred cod line and square lead anchors on which the line was wrapped, leaving just enough room in the open center so that line and weight fitted neatly over bill and head. But sturdy wood decoys are no longer available, or not, at least, in these seedy river towns.

What are offered instead are swollen plastic mallards, drake mallards only, with heads the dead green of zinc alloy and the rest a bad industrial brown fit to attract those mongrel ducks that inhabited the dirty waters of the city parks and the pilings of old river docks in Yonkers. By means of gaudy plastic twine that would cut the hands in winter weather each duck is rigged to a scrap of pig iron, sure to drag in any sort of wind.

He cannot bring himself to acquire more than three *(Always set an odd number,* his father had said, *in case of a lone bird),* since he would not harbor such horrors in his house, and does not intend to hunt ever again. So irritated is he by wasting money on such rubbish that he feels justified in commandeering a rain parka in its slim packet and also a handful of shotgun shells.

At the cottage he finds a burlap sack for carrying and concealing the decoys, the dismantled gun, the shells, and a thermos of coffee in its leather case. That evening, he rigs a treble-hooked surf-casting lure on a length of line—a makeshift retrieval gear of his own devising.

Within a few days comes a forecast of northeast wind, with

rain. Since his days are his own—the one activity left to him, now that the house is finished, is phoning for groceries, which are delivered daily—he will go hunting with the first change in the weather.

*   *   *

Bearing his sack over his shoulder like a burglar, he makes his way down toward the river. In the darkness, each house is fortified by its hard pool of light, and he half expects that his flashlight, spotted at the wood edge by some nosy oldster out of bed to pee, will bring police from all directions, filling the suburban night with whirling red white and blue beacons—the Nigger Hunters, as the hotel clerk referred to them, conveying contempt for cops and blacks alike.

In the woods he descends wet shadow paths, his sack catching and twisting in the thorns. At the track edge he peers north and south through a grim mist that hides him entirely from the world, then crosses the railroad to the river.

He lobs the decoys out upon the current, and the wind skids them quickly to the end of their strings, which swing too far inshore. In daybreak light, in choppy water, they in no way resemble three lorn ducks yearning for the companionship of a fourth.

He yanks his blind together, scrunching low as a train sweeps past toward the city. He feels clumsy, out of place, not nearly so well hidden as he had imagined. The upstate passengers, half-dozing in the fetid yellow light, cannot have seen him, though they stare straight at him through the grit-streaked windows. He breaks the light gun, loads two shells, and snaps it to, then sips his cup of coffee, peering outward.

As forecast, the wind is out of the northeast. Pale gulls sail past. But there is no rain, and the mist lifts, and the sun rises from the woods behind, filling the cliff faces across the river with a red-gold light.

The eerie windshine of the first day of a northeaster exposes the decoys for the poor things they are; the unnatural brightness of their anchor lines would flare a wild bird from five gunshots away. His folly is jeered at by clarion jays that cross back and forth among the yellow maples at the wood edge.

*   *   *

BANG

He has whirled and with a quick snap shot extinguished one of the jays, which flutters downward in the river woods like a blue leaf. He sinks back, strangely out of breath. And he is about to break his gun, retreat, slink home—he wants to drink—when there comes a small whispery sound, a small watery rush.

A black duck has landed just beyond the decoys. Struggling to make sense of its silent company, it quacks softly, turning back and forth. It rides the gray wavelets, wheat-colored head held high in wariness.

He has one shell left and no time to reload.

The gentle head switches back and forth, one eye seeking, then the other. In the imminence of the morning sun, in the wild light, the bird's tension holds the earth together.

The duck springs from the surface with a downward buffet of the wings. In one jump it is ten feet in the air, drops of water falling, silver-lined wings stretched to the wind that will whirl it out of range.

BANG

The dark wings close. The crumpled thing falls humbly to the surface, scarcely a splash, as the echo caroms from the cliffs across the river.

In the ringing silence, the river morning is resplendent. Time resumes, and the earth breathes again.

The duck floats upside down, head underwater, red legs on the bronze-black feathers twitching.

Not a difficult shot, his father would have said. *The trigger is*

*squeezed when the bird levels off at the top of the jump, for just at that moment
it seems almost motionless, held taut by wires—not a difficult shot.*

How often in his boyhood he had missed it, turning away so
as not to see his father's mouth set at the corners. Then one day
he outshot his father, finishing up with a neat double, trying not
to grin.

With that second barrel he overshot his limit. He had known
this but could not resist, his father's good opinion had seemed
more important. The Assistant Secretary's nod acknowledged
the fine shot, but his voice said, *You've always been good at things,
Henry. No need to be greedy.* It was no use blustering that he had
followed through the double as his father had taught him. His
father had no patience with excuses.

Often his mother felt obliged to say, *Your father's standards are so
high, you see.*

When he tried to ask just what she meant, she cut him off.
She smiled. *Sometimes what I think you lack is a sense of humor.*

He whirls his retrieval rig around his head and lets it go,
looping the casting plug out beyond the duck, then tugging it
back across the line of drift. On the third try it catches in the
tail feathers and turns the bird around before pulling free. The
next two tries are rushed, the last falls short.

The current has taken the diminished thing, it is moving more
rapidly now, tending offshore.

Alone on the riverbank, peering about him, he takes a deep
breath and regrets it, for the breath displaces his exhilaration,
drawing into his lungs intuitions of final loneliness and waste
and loss. That this black duck of the coasts and rivers should be
reduced to a rotting tatter in the tidal flotsam, to be pulled at by
the gulls, to be gnawed by rats, is not bearable, he cannot bear
it, he veers from this bitter end of things with a grunt of pain.
Or is it, he wonders, the waste that he cannot bear? Something
else scares him: he dreads going home alone and empty-handed,
to the life still to be lived in the finished cottage. If the hunt
supper does not take place, nothing will follow.

Sooner or later, the black duck must enter an eddy and be brought ashore. Hiding the shells and thermos under the driftwood, abandoning the decoys to the river, he hurries down the tracks toward the city, gun across his shoulder.

The bird does not drift nearer, neither does it move out farther. Wind and current hold it in equilibrium, a dull dark thing like charred deadwood in the tidal water. Far ahead, the cliffs of both shores come together at the George Washington Bridge, and beyond the high arch the sinking skyline of the river cities.

*   *   *

The world is littered with these puppet dictators of ours, protecting our rich businessmen and their filthy ruination of poor countries, making obscene fortunes off the misery of the most miserable people on this earth!

The old man shifted his bones for a better look at his impassive son, as if he had forgotten who he was. He considered him carefully in a long mean silence. *Who do you really work for these days, Henry? What is it that you do, exactly?*

When his son was silent, the old man nodded. *I gather they pay you well for what you do.*

Mother says you are obliged to sell the house. I'd like to buy it.

Absolutely not! I'd sooner sell it to Mobutu!

Didn't you warn me once against idealism? The Cold War is not going to be won by the polite and passive intrigues of your day—

Stop that at once! Don't talk as if you had standards of your own—you don't! You're some damn kind of moral dead man! You don't know who the hell you are, and I don't either! You probably should have been an undertaker!

The old man rummaged his newspaper. When his son sat down by him, he drew his dressing gown closer. Stricken, he said, *Forgive me. Perhaps you cannot help what you have become. I asked too much of you, your mother says, I was too harsh.* He paused for a deep breath, then spoke shyly. *I'm sorry, Henry. Please don't come again.*

*   *   *

The mist has lifted, the sun rises.

Trudging south, he is overtaken by the heat, the early trains. In his rain parka with the stiff canvas beneath, lugging the gun, his body suffocates. It is his entire body, his whole being, that is growing angry. The trains roar past, they assail him with bad winds, faces stare stupidly. He waves them off, his curses lost in the trains' racketing. His jaw set in an iron rage, he concentrates on each railroad tie, tie after tie.

The dead bird is fifty yards offshore, bound for the sea. In the distance, the silver bridge glints in the mist. Nearer are the cliffs at Spuyten Duyvil, where the tracks turn eastward along the East River. Cut off by that channel, he could only watch as the bird drifted by its mouth and on down the west shore of Manhattan.

He trots a little. He can already see the rail yard and trestle where the tracks bend away under the cliffs.

5

There they are.

Perched on concrete slabs along the back, thin dark-skinned figures turn dark heads to see this white man coming with a gun. Though the day is warm, they are wearing purple sweatshirts with sharp, pointed hoods drawn tight, as in some archaic sect in Abyssinia.

They pretend to ignore him, he ignores them, too. "Hey," one says, more or less in greeting. Rock music goes loud then soft again as he moves past paper bags, curled orange peels.

In painted silver, the purple sweatshirts read:

LUMUMBA LIVES

On a drift log lies a silver fish, twenty pounds or more, with lateral black stripes from gills to tail. In the autumn light, the silver scales glint with tints of brass. Should he tell these Africans that this shining New World fish carries cancer-causing poison in its gut?

Beyond the Africans, on the outside of the tracks between rails and river, is a small brick relay station. The wrecked windows are boarded up with plywood, and each plywood panel is marked with a single word scrawled in harsh black:

NAM COKE RUSH

Crouched behind the station, he hides the gun under a board, slips his wallet into a crevice, then his shoulder holster. He fits a shard of brick.

The plaint of a train, from far upriver. The Africans teeter on their slabs, craning to see where he has gone. The sun disappears behind swift clouds.

He strips to his shorts and picks his way across dirtied weeds and rocks, down to the water edge.

Where an eddy has brought brown scud onto the shore lie tarred scrap wood and burnt insulation, women's devices in pink plastic, rusted syringes, a broken chair, a large filth-matted fake-fur toy, a beheaded cat, a spent condom, a half grapefruit.

Ah shit, he says aloud, as if the sound of his own voice might be of comfort. He forces his legs into the flood, flinching in anticipation of glass shards, metal, rusty nails through splintered wood.

The hooded figures shout, waving their arms. They yell again, come running down the bank.

His chest is hollowed out, his lungs yawn mortally. He hurls himself outward, gasping as the hard cold strikes his temples, as a soft underwater shape nudges his thigh. In his thrash, he gasps up a half mouthful of the bitter water, losing his breath as he coughs it out, fighting the panic.

Rippling along his ear, the autumn water whispers of cold deeps, green-turning boulders. The river is tugging at his arms, heavy as mercury, entreating him to let go, to sink away. Through the earth's ringing he can hear his arms splash, as the surface ear hears the far whistle of a train, as yells diminish.

Cold iron fills his chest, and desolation. It is over now—this apprehension of the end comes to him simply, as if body and soul were giving up together. The earth is taking him, he is far out on the edge, in the turning current.

The duck floats belly up, head underwater, droplets of Adirondack water pearled on the night blue of its speculum, drifting downriver from the sunny bend, from the blue mountains.

His cold hand is dull as wood on the stiffened duck.

The cold constricts him and his throw is clumsy. The effort of the throw takes too much strength. The duck slides away downstream. He swallows more water, coughs and spits, and overtakes it, rolling over on his back to get a breath.

A rock nudges him. He sees bare trees whirl on the sky. The point-head purple hoods loom up, dark faces break.

"Yo, man! Lookin good, man! You all right?"

From the shallows, he slings the duck onto the litter. He crawls onto the rocks, knocks away a hand.

"Easy, man! We tryin to help!"

"Yay man? What's happenin? How come you jumpin in the river?"

"October, man! *Bad* river, man!"

"Never catch no *nigger* swimmin! Not out there!"

They yell with laughter.

"Goodbye cruel world, look like to me!"

"Cruel world!" Another hooted with delight. "That's about it!"

His wet underwear is transparent. He feels exposed, caught in the open. Rage grasps him, but he has no strength. He fights for breath.

"Hey man? You hearin me? Next time you need duck bad as that, you let me know. Go walkin in the park, toss me some crumbs, noose all you want! Two bucks apiece! Yeah man! I give you my card!"

They laugh some more. "Give him his *card,* that nigger say!"

"Like to eat fish? We gone fry fish!"

He gazes from one black man to another, trying to bring the turmoil in his head under control. Four are middle-aged, in old suit trousers and broken street shoes. The fifth might be a son, and wears new running sneakers.

LUMUMBA LIVES

They smile at him. He knows these Africans, he knows how well they feign subservience and admiration, laughing at someone when they have him at their mercy. He gets slowly to his feet.

"Who's Lumumba?" he inquires, playing for time.

"Who Lumumba *is?*"

This man looks down, he spreads his lettering with all eight fingers, then looks up at the younger man, who must be twenty.

"My boy Junius our Lumumba man. Who Lumumba, Junius?"

"Frag!"

"Who Lumumba, Frag?" The white man coughs. Wasn't that the problem? That he had not liked Lumumba? Wasn't that it?

Ashamed of his elders, Frag rolls his eyes. Frag is feverish and skinny, wild-eyed, angry. "Have Lumumba on your fuckin shirt, don't know who he *is?"*

"Who he *was,* Lumumba Man. He's dead."

Frag shrieks, "You makin fun? You makin fun with me?"

"Wholumumba, wholumumba, wholumumba, WHO!" The

white man does a stiff shuffle, almost falling. He is foot-numb, goosefleshed, shuddering with cold. Nothing seems real to him.

The faces in the purple hoods look mystified. He thinks, Come on, get it over with.

He starts out along the rail bed for the relay station, on the dead city stones and broken glass and metal litter.

At a sharp whistle he turns. Frag pitches the duck underhand, too hard, straight at his gut. He lets it fall.

"Shot it and swam for it, almost got drownded," one man says. "So why you *leavin* it? Ain't got no license?"

He points toward their fishing poles, upriver. They have no license, either. And possession of striped bass, he says, is against the law.

They exchange looks of comic disbelief. One raises both hands. "Whoo!" he says.

"Ol' fish washed up out of the river!"

"Yessir, that fish *all* washed up!"

They hoot, delighted, then frown and mutter when he will not laugh with them.

"Hey, we ain't gone *possess* that fish!"

"No man! We gone *eat* him! You *invited!*"

When he tells them that their fish is poisoned, they stare back in mock outrage.

"Shit, man! Ain't niggers poisoned it!"

He goes on, knowing they will follow. They are after his wallet, and the gun.

"Where's that gun at, Whitey?"

There it is. They have come up fast, they are right behind him.

"None of your business, Blacky," he says, and keeps on going. He feels giddy.

"Blacky" is repeated, bandied about. He hears a whoop, a cry of warning, and he turns again.

An older man with silver grizzle at the temples, dark wet

eyes, has his hand on Frag's arm. In Frag's hand is a large rock. The others jabber.

"What's happenin, man? What's up wit' you?"

"Come downriver see if we can help, and you just don't do right."

He resumes walking, paying no attention to the rock. Hauteur, he thinks, will always impress Africans. All the same, he feels confused, and tries to focus. On impulse he admits over his shoulder that he hid the gun, since they know this anyway.

"Scared we steal it, right?" Frag's voice is a near-screech. "Seen niggers hangin around, right?" Frag bounces his big rock off a rail.

He wants to shout "Right!" but restrains himself.

An older voice says, "Easy, Junius, don't excite yourself."

"Frag!"

"Easy, Frag, don't excite yourself. You okay, Frag?"

At the relay station, his clothes are undisturbed. He sees the corner of his wallet in the crevice.

NAM COKE RUSH

He pulls the pants on over his wet underwear, realizes that he does this out of modesty, stops himself, strips. They whoop and whistle. When he reaches for his pants a second time, Frag snaps them from his hand.

"Don't like niggers, right? Scared of 'em, right? We smell it! Oh, we *hate* that honky smell, man!"

His foot is right beside the board, he slides his toe beneath it.

"Mister? Frag excites his self, okay?"

"Truth!" Frag yells. "Fuckin truth, man! We can take it! Don' like niggers, right?"

"Right," he says, because the timing is so satisfying. He doesn't care whether or not it's true. Five blacks, one white—a clear case of self-defense. He flips the board, stoops quick, brings up the gun.

"Let's have those pants," he says. "I'm tired of this."

The black men back away, form a loose circle neither out of range nor close enough to threaten him. Breathing raggedly, beside himself, Frag stays where he is, as if transfixed by the twin black holes of the gun muzzle.

"Don' point that mothafucka, man!" he gasps at last.

"Toss the man his damn pants, Junius! Go ahead, now!"

"Man might do it, Junius! See them eyes?"

"Fuck!" Frag yells, beside himself. "L'il popgun!"

The father's soft voice is a plea. "Easy Mister, please, what's up wit' you? That boy can't help his self."

He sees their fear of what they take to be his naked craziness.

At the train whistle, the black men look relieved. Frag jabs his finger, furious and scared. He keeps staring at the gun, he will not back off.

"Toss the man them pants now, Junius."

The train is coming down the track toward the city, loud as a riveting machine, as a machine gun.

"Train comin, man."

But he makes no move to hide himself. He steps farther out onto the tracks. What the engineer must see is a naked white man surrounded and beset by a gang of blacks.

The train blows three shrill whistles, lurches, and begins to slow.

"Junius? Trouble, boy! You got enough!"

"Shit!" the boy snarls. "Ain't us done nothin!"

He slings the pants. The older man grabs him from behind, spins him away. The boy curses in a vicious stream, angling out across the tracks toward the woods on the river slope behind the train, ready to run if anyone on the train starts to descend. He yells, "You ain't done with Frag yet, shithead! Honky mothafuck!"

The train eases to a stop. A hiss of steam. High cirrus clouds come out over the trees, over the river.

"Put them pants on, Mister! Folks is *lookin* at you!"

"Back up," he says, lifting the gun. And right now, remembering that both shells in the gun have been expended, he feels a sharp tingle at the temples.

A voice from the train calls, "You all right?" He waves his hand, then lays the gun down and begins to dress.

Sullen and sad, the black men shake their heads. They mutter, but they do not speak, they will not meet the stares from the train windows. They watch him dress, watch him take his wallet from the crevice in the wall. When he straps on the empty shoulder holster, they groan and retreat still farther.

The train departs. He starts away, walking upriver.

He wonders now if they meant him any harm, but he takes no chances. Every little while he turns to be sure he is not followed.

The figures stand in silhouette. Three wave and point as the fourth raises the wild duck, bill pointed against the city. They seem to entreat him, but it is too late. What are they calling?

The hurled duck arches on the sky, falls fast, and bounces, coming to rest in the junk along the river.

When he goes back for it, they scatter, abandoning their fish. He puts the gun down, raises both his arms. "Wait a minute!" he calls. "Listen!"

"Get outta here!" they holler back. "You jus' get *outta* here!"

*   *   *

At his blind he retrieves his equipment, leaving the three decoys to the river. With his burlap sack, he starts across the tracks toward the woods. Near the mouth of the old brook, he spins, recoiling from a clip of wind right past his ear.

A purple hood sinks back behind the auto body in the

swamp. He circles the auto, crouching and running, but the rock-thrower has vanished, and the woods are silent.

He hunts quickly through the woods, chasing scared footfalls, then retreats half backward, swinging the gun. Moving slowly so that Frag can tail him without difficulty, he climbs the steep lawn below his father's house. Someone is shouting.

Inside, the cottage seems to enclose him. He listens to the clock tick. The house creaks. He pours himself a whiskey.

No one answers at the real-estate office. To the answering machine he whispers, "This is Henry Harkness. I have a wild duck here, and some wild rice and good wine. I was hoping you and . . ." He doesn't want to say "your wife," but he cannot recall the round-eyed woman's name. He puts the phone down. Somewhere his life took a turning without his knowledge.

The duck drips blood and water from its bill onto the white enamel of the kitchen table.

He slips out the back door and through the trees to the autumn garden. From here he can spot the purple hood coming up along the woods. The running, the game of it, the ambush are exhilarating, but the excitement dies quickly with the whiskey flush and does not return.

He settles down to wait behind the wall.

The light has gone wrong in some way. The sky is darkening in the noon sun, the dusk is waiting in the trees, and nowhere is there any shelter.

The African will come, perhaps at dark. Even now that face is peering from the trees, a menace to society. Neighbors will come to pay respects once it is over.

A police car comes and goes, lights flashing slowly, humping around the drive on its fat tires. The caretaker rides in the front seat.

No one comes up from the woods, the glinting river. Still he waits there in the autumn garden, cooling his forehead on the night-blue metal, in the haunted sunlight, in the dread of home.

◆ *Lore Segal* ◆

THE REVERSE BUG

"Let's get the announcements out of the way," said Ilka, the teacher, to her foreigners in Conversational English for Adults. "Tomorrow evening the institute is holding a symposium. Ahmed," she asked the Turkish student with the magnificently drooping mustache, who also wore the institute's janitorial keys hooked to his belt, "where are they holding the symposium?"

"In the New Theatre," said Ahmed.

"The theme," said the teacher, "is 'Should there be a statute of limitations on genocide?' with a wine-and-cheese reception—"

"In the lounge," said Ahmed.

"To which you are all invited. Now," Ilka said in the bright voice of a hostess trying to make a sluggish dinner party go, "what shall we talk about? Doesn't do me a bit of good, I know, to ask you all to come forward and sit in a nice cozy clump. Who would like to start us off? Tell us a story, somebody. We love stories. Tell the class how you came to America."

The teacher looked determinedly past the hand, the arm, with which Gerti Gruner stirred the air—death, taxes, and Thurs-

days, Gerti Gruner in the front row center. Ilka's eye passed
over Paulino, who sat in the last row, with his back to the wall.
Matsue, a pleasant, older Japanese from the university's engi-
neering department, smiled at Ilka and shook his head, meaning
"Please, not me!" Matsue was sitting in his usual place by the
window, but Ilka had to orient herself as to the whereabouts of
Izmira, the Cypriot doctor, who always left two empty rows
between herself and Ahmed, the Turk. Today it was Juan, the
Basque, who sat in the rightmost corner, and Eduardo, the
Spaniard from Madrid, in the leftmost.

Ilka looked around for someone too shy to self-start who
might enjoy talking if called upon, but Gerti's hand stabbed the
air immediately underneath Ilka's chin, so she said, "Gerti
wants to start. Go, Gerti. When did you come to the United
States?"

"In last June," said Gerti.

Ilka corrected her, and said, "Tell the class where you came
from, and, everybody, please speak in whole sentences."

Gerti said, "I have lived before in Uruguay."

"We would say, *'Before that I lived,'* " said Ilka, and Gerti said,
"And *before that* in Vienna."

Gerti's story bore a family likeness to the teacher's own su-
perannuated, indigestible history of being sent out of Hitler's
Europe as a little girl.

Gerti said, "In the Vienna train station has my father told to
me . . ."

"Told me."

"Told me that so soon as I am coming to Montevideo . . ."

Ilka said, *"As* soon as I *come,* or more colloquially, *get* to Montevideo . . ."

Gerti said, *"Get* to Montevideo, I should tell to all the people . . ."

Ilka corrected her. Gerti said, *"Tell* all the people to bring my
father out from Vienna before come the Nazis and put him in
concentration camp."

Ilka said, "In 'the' or 'a' concentration camp."

"Also my mother," said Gerti, "and my Opa, and my Oma, and my Onkel Peter, and the twins, Hedi and Albert. My father has told, 'Tell to the foster mother, "Go, please, with me, to the American Consulate." ' "

"*My* father went to the American Consulate," said Paulino, and everybody turned and looked at him. Paulino's voice had not been heard in class since the first Thursday, when Ilka had got her students to go around the room and introduce themselves to one another. Paulino had said that his name was Paulino Patillo and that he was born in Bolivia. Ilka was charmed to realize it was Danny Kaye of whom Paulino reminded her—fair, curly, middle-aged, smiling. He came punctually every Thursday. Was he a very sweet or a very simple man?

Ilka said, "Paulino will tell us his story after Gerti has finished. How old were you when you left Europe?" Ilka asked, to reactivate Gerti, who said, "Eight years," but she and the rest of the class, and the teacher herself, were watching Paulino put his right hand inside the left breast pocket of his jacket, withdraw an envelope, turn it upside down, and shake out onto the desk before him a pile of news clippings. Some looked sharp and new, some frayed and yellow; some seemed to be single paragraphs, others the length of several columns.

"You got to Montevideo . . ." Ilka prompted Gerti.

"And my foster mother has fetched me from the ship. I said, 'Hello, and will you please bring out from Vienna my father before come the Nazis and put him in—*a* concentration camp!' " Gerti said triumphantly.

Paulino had brought the envelope close to his eyes and was looking inside. He inserted a forefinger, loosened something that was stuck, and shook out a last clipping. It broke at the fold when Paulino flattened it onto the desk top. Paulino brushed away the several paper crumbs before beginning to read: "La Paz, September 19."

"Paulino," said Ilka, "you must wait till Gerti is finished."

But Paulino read, "Señora Pilar Patillo has reported the disappearance of her husband, Claudio Patillo, after a visit to the American Consulate in La Paz on September 15."

"Gerti, go on," said Ilka.

"The foster mother has said, 'When comes home the Uncle from the office, we will ask.' I said, 'And bring out, please, also my mother, my Opa, my Oma, my Onkel Peter . . .'"

Paulino read, "A spokesman for the American Consulate contacted in La Paz states categorically that no record exists of a visit from Señor Patillo within the last two months. . . ."

"Paulino, you really *have* to wait your turn," Ilka said.

Gerti said, " 'Also the twins.' The foster mother has made such a desperate face with her lips."

Paulino read, "Nor does the consular calendar for September show any appointment made with Señor Patillo. Inquiries are said to be under way with the Consulate at Sucre." And Paulino folded his column of newsprint and returned it to the envelope.

"O.K., thank you, Paulino," Ilka said.

Gerti said, "When the foster father has come home, he said, 'We will see, tomorrow,' and I said, 'And will you go, please, with me, to the American Consulate?' and the foster father has made a face."

Paulino was flattening the second column of newsprint on his desk. He read, "New York, December 12 . . ."

"Paulino," said Ilka, and caught Matsue's eye. He was looking expressly at her. He shook his head ever so slightly and with his right hand, palm down, he patted the air three times. In the intelligible language of charade with which humankind frustrated God at Babel, Matsue was saying, "Calm down, Ilka. Let Paulino finish. Nothing you can do will stop him." Ilka was grateful to Matsue.

"A spokesman for the Israeli Mission to the United Nations," read Paulino, "denies a report that Claudio Patillo, missing after a visit to the American Consulate in La Paz since September 15, is en route to Israel. . . ." Paulino finished reading this column also, folded it into the envelope, and unfolded the next column. "U.P.I., January 30. The car of Pilar Patillo, wife of Claudio Patillo, who was reported missing from La Paz last September, has been found at the bottom of a ravine in the eastern Andes. It is not known whether any bodies were found inside the wreck," Paulino read with the blind forward motion of a tank that receives no message from any sound or movement in the world outside. The students had stopped looking at Paulino; they were not looking at the teacher. They looked into their laps. Paulino read one column after the other, returning each to his envelope before he took the next, and when he had read and returned the last, and returned the envelope to his breast pocket, he leaned his back against the wall and turned to the teacher his sweet, habitual smile of expectant participation.

Gerti said, "In that same night have I woken up . . ."

"That night I *woke* up," the teacher helplessly said.

"*Woke* up," Gerti Gruner said, "and I have thought, What if it is even now, this exact minute, that one Nazi is knocking at the door, and I am here lying not telling to anybody anything, and I have stood up and gone into the bedroom where were sleeping the foster mother and father. Next morning has the foster mother gone with me to the refugee committee, and they found for me a different foster family."

"Your turn, Matsue," Ilka said. "How, when, and why did you come to the States? We're all here to help you!" Matsue's written English was flawless, but he spoke with an accent that was almost impenetrable. His contribution to class conversation always involved a communal interpretative act.

"Aisutudieddu attoza unibashite innu munhen," Matsue said.

A couple of stabs and Eduardo, the madrileño, got it: "You studied at the university in Munich!"

"You studied acoustics?" ventured Izmira, the Cypriot doctor.

"The war trapped you in Germany?" proposed Ahmed, the Turk.

"You have been working in the ovens," suggested Gerti, the Viennese.

"Acoustic ovens?" marvelled Ilka. "Do you mean stoves? Ranges?"

No, what Matsue meant was that he had got his first job with a Munich firm employed in soundproofing the Dachau ovens so that what went on inside could not be heard on the outside. "I made the tapes," said Matsue. "Tapes?" they asked him. They figured out that Matsue had returned to Japan in 1946. He had collected Hiroshima "tapes." He had been brought to Washington as an acoustical consultant to the Kennedy Center, and had come to Connecticut to design the sound system of the New Theatre at Concordance University, where he subsequently accepted a research appointment in the department of engineering. He was now returning home, having finished his work— Ilka thought he said—on the reverse bug.

Ilka said, "I thought, ha ha, you said 'the reverse bug'!"

"The reverse bug" was what everybody understood Matsue to say that he had said. With his right hand he performed a row of air loops, and, pointing at the wall behind the teacher's desk, asked for, and received, her O.K. to explain himself in writing on the blackboard.

Chalk in hand, he was eloquent on the subject of the regular bug, which can be introduced into a room to relay to those outside what those inside want them not to hear. A sophisticated modern bug, explained Matsue, was impossible to locate and deactivate. Buildings had had to be taken apart in order to rid them of alien listening devices. The reverse bug, equally impossible to locate and deactivate, was a device whereby those outside were able to relay *into* a room what those inside would prefer not to have to hear.

"And how would such a device be used?" Ilka asked him.

Matsue was understood to say that it could be useful in certain situations to certain consulates, and Paulino said, "My father went to the American Consulate," and put his hand into his breast pocket. Here Ilka stood up, and, though there was still a good fifteen minutes of class time, said, "So! I will see you all next Thursday. Everybody—be thinking of subjects you would like to talk about. Don't forget the symposium tomorrow evening!" She walked quickly out the door.

*   *   *

Ilka entered the New Theatre late and was glad to see Matsue sitting on the aisle in the second row from the back with an empty seat beside him. The platform people were already settling into their places. On the right, an exquisite golden-skinned Latin man was talking, in a way people talk to people they have known a long time, with a heavy, rumpled man, whom Ilka pegged as Israeli. "Look at the thin man on the left," Ilka said to Matsue. "He has to be from Washington. Only a Washingtonian's hair gets to be that particular white color." Matsue laughed. Ilka asked him if he knew who the woman with the oversized glasses and the white hair straight to the shoulders might be, and Matsue said something that Ilka did not understand. The rest of the panelists were institute people, Ilka's colleagues—little Joe Bernstine from philosophy, Yvette Gordot, a mathematician, and Leslie Shakespere, an Englishman, the institute's new director, who sat in the moderator's chair.

Leslie Shakespere had the soft weight of a man who likes to eat and the fine head of a man who thinks. It had not as yet occurred to Ilka that she was in love with Leslie. She watched him fussing with the microphone. "Why do we need this?" she could read Leslie's lips saying. "Since when do we use microphones in the New Theatre?" Now he quieted the hall with a grateful welcome for this fine attendance at a discussion of one of our generation's unmanageable questions—the application of justice in an era of genocides.

Here Rabbi Shlomo Grossman rose from the floor and wished

to take exception to the plural formulation: "All killings are not murders; all murders are not 'genocides.' "

Leslie said, "Shlomo, could you hold your remarks until question time?"

Rabbi Grossman said, "Remarks? Is that what I'm making? Remarks! The death of six million—is it in the realm of a question?"

Leslie said, "I give you my word that there will be room for the full expression of what you want to say when we open the discussion to the floor." Rabbi Grossman acceded to the evident desire of the friends sitting near him that he should sit down.

Director Leslie Shakespere gave the briefest of accounts of the combined federal and private funding that had enabled the Concordance Institute to invite these very distinguished panelists to take part in the institute's Genocide Project. "The institute, as you know, has a long-standing tradition of 'debriefings,' in which the participants in a project that is winding down sum up their thinking for the members of the institute, the university, and the public. But this evening's panel has agreed, by way of an experiment, to talk in an informal way of our notions, of the history of the interest each of us brings to this question—problem—at the point of entry. I want us to interest ourselves in the *nature of inquiry:* Will we come out of this project with our original notions reinforced? Modified? Made over?

"I imagine that this inquiry will range somewhere between the legal concept of a statute of limitations that specifies the time within which human law must respond to a specific crime, and the Biblical concept of the visitation of punishment of the sins of the fathers upon the children. One famous version plays itself out in the 'Oresteia,' where a crime is punished by an act that is itself a crime and punishable, and so on, down the generations. Enough. Let me introduce our panel, whom it will be our very great pleasure to have among us in the coming months."

The white-haired man turned out to be the West German ex-mayor of Obernpest, Dieter Dobelmann. Ilka felt the prompt conviction that she had known all along—that one could tell from a mile—that that mouth, that jaw, had to be German. Leslie dwelled on Dobelmann's persuasive anti-Nazi credentials. The woman with the glasses was on loan to the institute from Georgetown University. ("The white hair! You see!" Ilka whispered to Matsue, who laughed.) She was Jerusalem-born Shulamit Gershon, professor of international law, and longtime adviser to Israel's ongoing project to identify Nazi war criminals and bring them to trial. The rumpled man was the English theologian William B. Thayer. The Latin really was a Latin—Sebastian Maderiaga, who was taking time off from his consulate in New York. Leslie squeezed his eyes to see past the stage lights into the well of the New Theatre. There was a rustle of people turning to locate the voice that had said, "My father went to the American Consulate," but it said nothing further and the audience settled back. Leslie introduced Yvette and Joe, the institute's own fellows assigned to Genocide.

Ilka and Matsue leaned forward, watching Paulino across the aisle. Paulino was withdrawing the envelope from his breast pocket. "Without a desk?" whispered Ilka anxiously. Paulino upturned the envelope onto the slope of his lap. The young student sitting beside him got on his knees to retrieve the sliding batch of newsprint and held onto it while Paulino arranged his coat across his thighs to create a surface.

"My own puzzle," said Leslie, "with which I would like to puzzle our panel, is this: Where do I, where do we all, get these feelings of moral malaise when wrong goes unpunished and right goes unrewarded?"

Paulino had brought his first newspaper column up to his eyes and read, "La Paz, September 19. Señora Pilar Patillo has reported the disappearance of her husband, Claudio Patillo . . ."

"Where," Leslie was saying, "does the human mind derive its expectation of a set of consequences for which it finds no evidence whatsoever in nature or in history, or in looking around its own autobiography? . . . Could I *please* ask for quiet from the floor until we open the discussion?" Leslie was once again peering out into the hall.

The audience turned and looked at Paulino reading, "Nor does the consular calendar for September show any appointment . . ." Shulamit Gershon leaned toward Leslie and spoke to him for several moments while Paulino read, "A spokesman for the Israeli Mission to the United Nations denies a report . . ."

It was after several attempts to persuade him to stop that Leslie said, "Ahmed? Is Ahmed in the hall? Ahmed, would you be good enough to remove the unquiet gentleman as gently as necessary force will allow. Take him to my office, please, and I will meet with him after the symposium."

Everybody watched Ahmed walk up the aisle with a large and sheepish-looking student. The two lifted the unresisting Paulino out of his seat by the armpits. They carried him reading, "The car of Pilar Patillo, wife of Claudio Patillo . . ."—backward, out the door.

The action had something about it of the classic comedy routine. There was a cackling, then the relief of general laughter. Leslie relaxed and sat back, understanding that it would require some moments to get the evening back on track, but the cackling did not stop. Leslie said, "Please." He waited. He cocked his head and listened: it was more like a hiccupping that straightened and elongated into a sound drawn on a single breath. Leslie looked at the panel. The panel looked. The audience looked all around. Leslie bent his ear down to the microphone. It did him no good to turn the button off and on, to put his hand over the mouthpiece, to bend down as if to look it in the eye. "Anybody know—is the sound here centrally controlled?" he asked. The noise was growing incrementally. Members of the audience drew their heads back and down into their shoulders. It came to them—it became impossible to not know—that it was not laughter to which they were listening but somebody yelling. Somewhere there was a person, and the person was screaming.

Ilka looked at Matsue, whose eyes were closed. He looked an old man.

The screaming stopped. The relief was spectacular, but lasted only for that same unnaturally long moment in which a howling child, having finally exhausted its strength, is fetching up new breath from some deepest source for a new onslaught. The howl resumed at a volume that was too great for the small theatre; the human ear could not accommodate it. People experienced a physical distress. They put their hands over their ears.

Leslie had risen. He said, "I'm going to suggest an alteration in the order of this evening's proceedings. Why don't we clear the hall—everybody, please, move into the lounge, have some wine, have some cheese while we locate the source of the trouble."

Quickly, while people were moving along their rows, Ilka popped out into the aisle and collected the trail of Paulino's news clippings. The young student who had sat next to Paulino found and handed her the envelope.

Ilka walked down the hall in the direction of Leslie Shakespere's office, diagnosing in herself an inappropriate excitement at having it in her power to throw light.

*   *   *

Ilka looked into Leslie's office. Paulino sat on a hard chair with his back to the door, shaking his head violently from side to side. Leslie stood facing him. He and Ahmed and all the panelists, who had disposed themselves about Leslie's office, were screwing their eyes up as if wanting very badly to close every bodily opening through which unwanted information is able to enter. The intervening wall had somewhat modified the volume, but not the variety—length, pitch, and pattern—of the sounds that continually altered as in response to a new and continually changing cause.

Leslie said, "We know this stuff goes on whether we are hearing it or not, but this . . ." He saw Ilka at the door and said, "Mr. Patillo is your student, no? He refuses to tell us how to locate the screaming unless they release his father."

Ilka said, "Paulino? Does Paulino *say* he 'refuses'?"

Leslie said to Paulino, "Will you please tell us how to find the source of this noise so we can shut it off?"

Paulino shook his head and said, "It is my father screaming."

Ilka followed the direction of Leslie's eye. Maderiaga was perched with a helpless elegance on the corner of Leslie's desk, speaking Spanish into the telephone. Through the open door that led into a little outer office, Ilka saw Shulamit Gershon hang up the phone. She came back in and said, "Patillo is the name this young man's father adopted from his Bolivian wife. He's Klaus Herrmann, who headed the German Census Bureau. After the Anschluss they sent him to Vienna to put together the registry of Jewish names and addresses. Then on to Budapest, and so on. After the war we traced him to La Paz. I think he got into trouble with some mines or weapons deals. We put him on the back burner when it turned out the Bolivians were after him as well."

Now Maderiaga hung up and said, "Hasn't he been the busy little man! My office is going to check if it's the Gonzales people who got him for expropriating somebody's tin mine, or the R.R.N. If they suspect Patillo of connection with the helicopter crash that killed President Barrientos, they'll have more or less killed him."

"It is my father screaming," said Paulino.

"It's got nothing to do with his father," said Ilka. While Matsue was explaining the reverse bug on the blackboard the previous evening, Ilka had grasped the principle. It disintegrated as she was explaining it to Leslie. She was distracted, moreover, by a retrospective image: Last night, hurrying down the corridor, Ilka had turned her head and must have seen, since she was now able to recollect, young Ahmed and Matsue moving away together down the hall. If Ilka had thought them a curious couple, the thought, having nothing to feed on, had died before her lively wish to maneuver Gerti and Paulino into one elevator just as the doors were closing, so she could come down in the other.

Now Ilka asked Ahmed, "Where did you and Matsue go after class last night?"

Ahmed said, "He wanted to come into the New Theatre."

Leslie said, "Ahmed, forgive me for ordering you around all evening, but will you go and find me Matsue and bring him here to my office?"

"He has gone," said Ahmed. "I saw him leave by the front door with a suitcase on wheels."

"He is going home," said Ilka. "Matsue has finished his job."

Paulino said, "It is my father screaming."

"No, it's not, Paulino," said Ilka. "Those screams are from Dachau and they are from Hiroshima."

"It is my father," said Paulino, "and my mother."

*   *   *

Leslie asked Ilka to come with him to the airport. They caught up with Matsue queuing, with only five passengers ahead of him, to enter the gangway to his plane.

Ilka said, "Matsue, you're not going away without telling us how to shut the thing off!"

Matsue said, "Itto dozunotto shattoffu."

Ilka and Leslie said, "Excuse me?"

With the hand that was not holding his boarding pass, Matsue performed a charade of turning a faucet and he shook his head. Ilka and Leslie understood him to be saying, "It does not shut off." Matsue stepped out of the line, kissed Ilka on the cheek, stepped back, and passed through the door.

*   *   *

When Concordance Institute takes hold of a situation, it deals humanely with it. Leslie found funds to pay a private sanitarium to evaluate Paulino. Back at the New Theatre, the police, a bomb squad, and a private acoustics company from Washington set themselves to locate the source of the screaming.

Leslie looked haggard. His colleagues worried when their director, a sensible man, continued to blame the microphone after the microphone had been removed and the screaming continued. The sound seemed not to be going to loop back to any familiar beginning, so that the hearers might have become familiar—might, in a manner of speaking, have made friends—with one particular roar or screech, but to be going on to perpetually new and fresh howls of pain.

Neither the Japanese Embassy in Washington nor the American Embassy in Tokyo had got anywhere with the tracers sent out to locate Matsue. Leslie called in a technician. "Look into the wiring!" he said, and saw in the man's eyes that look experts wear when they have explained something and the layman says what he said in the beginning all over again. The expert had another go. He talked to Leslie about the nature of the sound wave; he talked about cross-Atlantic phone calls and about the electric guitar. Leslie said, "Could you look *inside* the wiring?"

Leslie fired the first team of acoustical experts, found another company, and asked them to check inside the wiring. The new man reported back to Leslie: He thought they might start by taking down the stage portion of the theatre. If the sound people worked closely with the demolition people, they might be able to avoid having to mess with the body of the hall.

*   *   *

The phone call that Maderiaga had made on the night of the symposium had, in the meantime, set in motion a series of official acts that were bringing to America—to Concordance—Paulino Patillo's father, Claudio/Klaus Patillo/Herrmann. The old man was eighty-nine, missing an eye by an act of man and a lung by an act of God. On the plane he suffered a collapse and was rushed from the airport straight to Concordance University's Medical Center.

*   *   *

Rabbi Grossman walked into Leslie's office and said, "Am I hearing things? You've approved a house, on this campus, for the accomplice of the genocide of Austrian and Hungarian Jewry?"

"And a private nurse!" said Leslie.

"Are you out of your mind?" asked Rabbi Grossman.

"Practically. Yes," said Leslie.

"You look terrible," said Shlomo Grossman, and sat down.

"What," Leslie said, "am I the hell to do with an old Nazi who is postoperative, whose son is in the sanitarium, who doesn't know a soul, doesn't have a dime, doesn't have a roof over his head?"

"Send him home to Germany," shouted Shlomo.

"I tried. Dobelmann says they won't recognize Claudio Patillo as one of their nationals."

"So send him to his comeuppance in Israel!"

"Shulamit says they're no longer interested, Shlomo! They have other things on hand!"

"Put him back on the plane and turn it around."

"For another round of screaming? Shlomo!" cried Leslie, and put his hands over his ears against the noise that, issuing out of the dismembered building materials piled in back of the institute, blanketed the countryside for miles around, made its way down every street of the small university town, into every back yard, and filtered in through Leslie's closed and shuttered windows. "Shlomo," Leslie said, "come over tonight. I promise Eliza will cook you something you can eat. I want you, and I want

Ilka—and we'll see who all else—to help me think this thing
through."

*   *   *

"We . . . I," said Leslie that night, "need to understand how
the scream of Dachau is the same, and how it is a different
scream from the scream of Hiroshima. And after that I need to
learn how to listen to the selfsame sound that rises out of the
Hell in which the torturer is getting what he's got coming. . . ."

His wife called, "Leslie, can you come and talk to Ahmed?"

Leslie went out and came back in carrying his coat. A couple
of young punks with an agenda of their own had broken into
Patillo/Herrmann's new American house. They had gagged the
nurse and tied her and Klaus up in the new American bathroom.
Here Ilka began to laugh. Leslie buttoned his coat and said, "I'm
sorry, but I have to go on over. Ilka, Shlomo, please, I leave for
Washington tomorrow, early, to talk to the Superfund people.
While I'm there I want to get a Scream Project funded. Ilka?
Ilka, what is it?" But Ilka was helplessly giggling and could not
answer him. Leslie said, "What I need is for you two to please
sit down, here and now, and come up with a formulation I can
take with me to present to Arts and Humanities."

The Superfund granted Concordance an allowance, for scream
disposal, and the dismembered stage of the New Theatre was
loaded onto a flatbed truck and driven west. The population
along Route 90 and all the way down to Arizona came out into
the street, eyes squeezed together, heads pulled back and down
into shoulders. They buried the thing fifteen feet under, well
away from the highway, and let the desert howl.

◆ Joyce Carol Oates ◆

HEAT

It was midsummer, the heat rippling above the macadam roads. Cicadas screaming out of the trees and the sky like pewter, glaring.

The days were the same day, like the shallow mud-brown river moving always in the same direction but so slow you couldn't see it. Except for Sunday: church in the morning, then the fat Sunday newspaper, the color comics and newsprint on your fingers.

Rhea and Rhoda Kunkel went flying on their rusted old bicycles, down the long hill toward the railroad yard, Whipple's Ice, the scrubby pastureland where dairy cows grazed. They'd stolen six dollars from their own grandmother who loved them. They were eleven years old, they were identical twins, they basked in their power.

Rhea and Rhoda Kunkel: it was always Rhea-and-Rhoda, never Rhoda-and-Rhea, I couldn't say why. You just wouldn't say the names that way. Not even the teachers at school would say them that way.

We went to see them in the funeral parlor where they were waked, we were made to. The twins in twin caskets, white, smooth, gleaming, perfect as plastic, with white satin lining puckered like the inside of a fancy candy box. And the waxy white lilies, and the smell of talcum powder and perfume. The room was crowded, there was only one way in and out.

Rhea and Rhoda were the same girl, they'd wanted it that way.

Only looking from one to the other could you see they were two.

The heat was gauzy, you had to push your way through like swimming. On their bicycles Rhea and Rhoda flew through it hardly noticing, from their grandmother's place on Main Street to the end of South Main where the paved road turned to gravel leaving town. That was the summer before seventh grade, when they died. Death was coming for them but they didn't know.

They thought the same thoughts sometimes at the same moment, had the same dream and went all day trying to remember it, bringing it back like something you'd be hauling out of the water on a tangled line. We watched them, we were jealous. None of us had a twin. Sometimes they were serious and sometimes, remembering, they shrieked and laughed like they were being killed. They stole things out of desks and lockers but if you caught them they'd hand them right back, it was like a game.

There were three floor fans in the funeral parlor that I could see, tall whirring fans with propellor blades turning fast to keep the warm air moving. Strange little gusts came from all directions making your eyes water. By this time Roger Whipple was arrested, taken into police custody. No one had hurt him. He would never stand trial, he was ruled mentally unfit, he would never be released from confinement.

He died there, in the state psychiatric hospital, years later, and was brought back home to be buried, the body of him I mean. His earthly remains.

Rhea and Rhoda Kunkel were buried in the same cemetery,

the First Methodist. The cemetery is just a field behind the church.

In the caskets the dead girls did not look like anyone we knew really. They were placed on their backs with their eyes closed, and their mouths, the way you don't always in life when you're sleeping. Their faces were too small. Every eyelash showed, too perfect. Like angels everyone was saying and it was strange it was *so*. I stared and stared.

What had been done to them, the lower parts of them, didn't show in the caskets.

Roger Whipple worked for his father at Whipple's Ice. In the newspaper it stated he was nineteen, he'd gone to DeWitt Clinton until he was sixteen, my mother's friend Sadie taught there and remembered him from the special education class. A big slow sweet-faced boy with these big hands and feet, thighs like hams. A shy gentle boy with good manners and a hushed voice.

He wasn't simpleminded exactly, like the others in that class. He was watchful, he held back.

Roger Whipple in overalls squatting in the rear of his father's truck, one of his older brothers drove. There would come the sound of the truck in the driveway, the heavy block of ice smelling of cold, ice tongs over his shoulder. He was strong, round-shouldered like an older man. Never staggered or grunted. Never dropped anything. Pale washed-looking eyes lifting out of a big face, a soft mouth wanting to smile. We giggled and looked away. They said he'd never been the kind to hurt even an animal, all the Whipples swore.

Sucking ice, the cold goes straight into your jaws and deep into the bone.

People spoke of them as the Kunkel twins. Mostly nobody tried to tell them apart. Homely corkscrew-twisty girls you wouldn't know would turn up so quiet and solemn and almost beautiful, perfect little dolls' faces with the freckles powdered over, touches of rouge on the cheeks and mouths. I was tempted to whisper to them, kneeling by the coffins. Hey Rhea! Hey Rhoda! Wake *up!*

They had loud slip-sliding voices that were the same voice. They weren't shy. They were always first in line. One behind you and one in front of you and you'd better be wary of some trick. Flamey-orange hair and the bleached-out skin that goes with it, freckles like dirty raindrops splashed on their faces. Sharp green eyes they'd bug out until you begged them to stop.

Places meant to be serious, Rhea and Rhoda had a hard time sitting still. In church, in school, a sideways glance between them could do it. Jamming their knuckles into their mouths, choking back giggles. Sometimes laughing escaped through their fingers like steam hissing. Sometimes it came out like snorting and then none of us could hold back. The worst time was in assembly, the principal up there telling us that Miss Flagler had died, we would all miss her. Tears shining in the woman's eyes behind her goggle-glasses and one of the twins gave a breathless little snort, you could feel it like flames running down the whole row of girls, none of us could hold back.

Sometimes the word "tickle" was enough to get us going, just that word.

I never dreamt about Rhea and Rhoda so strange in their caskets sleeping out in the middle of a room where people could stare at them, shed tears and pray over them. I never dream about actual things, only things I don't know. Places I've never been, people I've never seen. Sometimes the person I am in the dream isn't me. Who it is, I don't know.

Rhea and Rhoda bounced up the drive behind Whipple's Ice. They were laughing like crazy and didn't mind the potholes jarring their teeth, or the clouds of dust. If they'd had the same dream the night before, the hot sunlight erased it entirely.

When death comes for you you sometimes know and sometimes don't.

Roger Whipple was by himself in the barn, working. Kids went down there to beg him for ice to suck or throw around or they'd tease him, not out of meanness but for something to do. It was slow, the days not changing in the summer, heat sometimes all night long. He was happy with children that age, he was that age himself in his head, sixth grade learning abilities as the newspaper stated though he could add and subtract quickly. Other kinds of arithmetic gave him trouble.

People were saying afterward he'd always been strange. Watchful like he was, those thick soft lips. The Whipples did wrong, to let him run loose.

They said he'd always been a good gentle boy, went to Sunday school and sat still there and never gave anybody any trouble. He collected Bible cards, he hid them away under his mattress for safekeeping. Mr. Whipple started in early, disciplining him the way you might discipline a big dog or a horse. Not letting the creature know he has any power to be himself exactly. Not giving him the opportunity to test his will.

Neighbors said the Whipples worked him like a horse in fact. The older brothers were the most merciless. And why they all wore coveralls, heavy denim and long legs on days so hot, nobody knew. The thermometer above the First Midland Bank read 98° F. on noon of that day, my mother said.

Nights afterward my mother would hug me before I went to bed. Pressing my face hard against her breasts and whispering things I didn't hear, like praying to Jesus to love and protect *her* little girl and keep *her* from harm but I didn't hear, I shut my eyes tight and endured it. Sometimes we prayed together, all of us or just my mother and me kneeling by my bed. Even then I knew she was a good mother, there was this girl she loved as her daughter that was me and loved more than that girl deserved. There was nothing I could do about it.

Mrs. Kunkel would laugh and roll her eyes over the twins. In that house they were "double trouble"—you'd hear it all the time like a joke on the radio that keeps coming back. I wonder did she pray with them too. I wonder would they let her.

In the long night you forget about the day, it's like the other side of the world. Then the sun is there, and the heat. You forget.

We were running through the field behind school, a place where people dumped things sometimes and there was a dead dog there, a collie with beautiful fur but his eyes were gone from the sockets and the maggots had got him where somebody tried to lift him with her foot and when Rhea and Rhoda saw they screamed a single scream and hid their eyes.

They did nice things—gave their friends candy bars, nail polish, some novelty key chains they'd taken from somewhere, movie stars' pictures framed in plastic. In the movies they'd share a box of popcorn not noticing where one or the other of them left off and a girl who wasn't any sister of theirs sat.

Once they made me strip off my clothes where we'd crawled under the Kunkels' veranda. This was a large hollowed-out space where the earth dropped away at one end, you could sit without bumping your head, it was cool and smelled of dirt and stone. Rhea said all of a sudden, Strip! and Rhoda said at once, Strip!—come *on!* So it happened. They wouldn't let me out unless I took off my clothes, my shirt and shorts, yes and my panties too. Come *on* they said whispering and giggling, they were blocking the way out so I had no choice. I was scared but I was laughing too. This is to show our power over you, they said. But they stripped too just like me.

You have power over others you don't realize until you test it.

Under the Kunkels' veranda we stared at each other but we didn't touch each other. My teeth chattered because what if somebody saw us? Some boy, or Mrs. Kunkel herself? I was scared but I was happy too. Except for our faces, their face and mine, we could all be the same girl.

The Kunkel family lived in one side of a big old clapboard house by the river, you could hear the trucks rattling on the bridge, shifting their noisy gears on the hill. Mrs. Kunkel had eight children, Rhea and Rhoda were the youngest. Our mothers wondered why Mrs. Kunkel had let herself go—she had a moon-shaped pretty face but her hair was frizzed ratty, she must have weighed two hundred pounds, sweated and breathed so hard in the warm weather. They'd known her in school. Mr. Kunkel worked construction for the county. Summer evenings after work he'd be sitting on the veranda drinking beer, flicking cigarette butts out into the yard, you'd be fooled almost thinking they were fireflies. He went barechested in the heat, his upper body dark like stained wood. Flat little purplish nipples inside his chest hair the girls giggled to see. Mr. Kunkel teased us all, he'd mix Rhea and Rhoda up the way he'd mix the rest of us up like it was too much trouble to keep names straight.

Mr. Kunkel was in police custody, he didn't even come to the wake. Mrs. Kunkel was there in rolls of chin fat that glistened with sweat and tears, the makeup on her face was caked and discolored so you were embarrassed to look. It scared me, the way she grabbed me as soon as my parents and I came in. Hugging me against her big balloon breasts sobbing and all the strength went out of me, I couldn't push away.

The police had Mr. Kunkel, for his own good they said. He'd gone to the Whipples, though the murderer had been taken away, saying he would kill anybody he could get his hands on, the old man, the brothers. They were all responsible he said, his little girls were dead. Tear them apart with his bare hands he said but he had a tire iron.

Did it mean anything special, or was it just an accident, Rhea and Rhoda had taken six dollars from their grandmother an hour before? Because death was coming for them, it had to happen one way or another.

If you believe in God you believe that. And if you don't believe in God it's obvious.

Their grandmother lived upstairs over a shoe store downtown, an apartment looking out on Main Street. They'd bicycle down there for something to do and she'd give them grape juice or lemonade and try to keep them a while, a lonely old lady but she was nice, she was always nice to me, it was kind of nasty of

Rhea and Rhoda to steal from her but they were like that. One was in the kitchen talking with her and without any plan or anything the other went to use the bathroom then slipped into her bedroom, got the money out of her purse like it was something she did every day of the week, that easy. On the stairs going down to the street Rhoda whispered to Rhea what did you *do?* knowing Rhea had done something she hadn't ought to have done but not knowing what it was or anyway how much money it was. They started in poking each other, trying to hold the giggles back until they were safe away.

On their bicycles they stood high on the pedals, coasting, going down the hill but not using their brakes. *What did you do! Oh what did you do!*

Rhea and Rhoda always said they could never be apart. If one didn't know exactly where the other was that one could die. Or the other could die. Or both.

Once they'd gotten some money from somewhere, they wouldn't say where, and paid for us all to go to the movies. And ice cream afterward too.

You could read the newspaper articles twice through and still not know what he did. Adults talked about it for a long time but not so we could hear. I thought probably he'd used an ice pick. Or maybe I heard somebody guess that who didn't know any more than me.

We liked it that Rhea and Rhoda had been killed, and all the stuff in the paper, and everybody talking about it, but we didn't like it that they were dead, we missed them.

Later, in tenth grade, the Kaufmann twins moved into our school district. Doris and Diane. But it wasn't the same thing.

Roger Whipple said he didn't remember any of it. Whatever he did, he didn't remember. At first everybody thought he was lying then they had to accept it as true, or true in some way, doctors from the state hospital examined him. He said over and over he hadn't done anything and he didn't remember the twins there that afternoon but he couldn't explain why their bicycles were where they were at the foot of his stairway and he couldn't explain why he'd taken a bath in the middle of the day. The Whipples admitted that wasn't a practice of Roger's or of any of them, ever, a bath in the middle of the day.

Roger Whipple was a clean boy, though. His hands always scrubbed so you actually noticed, swinging the block of ice off the truck and, inside the kitchen, helping to set it in the ice box. They said he'd go crazy if he got bits of straw under his nails from the ice house or inside his clothes. He'd been taught to shave and he shaved every morning without fail, they said the sight of the beard growing in, the scratchy feel of it, seemed to scare him.

A few years later his sister Linda told us how Roger was built like a horse. She was our age, a lot younger than him, she made a gesture toward her crotch so we'd know what she meant. She'd happened to see him a few times she said, by accident.

There he was squatting in the dust laughing, his head lowered watching Rhea and Rhoda circle him on their bicycles. It was a rough game where the twins saw how close they could come to hitting him, brushing him with the bike fenders and he'd lunge out not seeming to notice if his fingers hit the spokes, it was all happening so fast you maybe wouldn't feel pain. Our back of the ice house where the yard blended in with the yard of the old railroad depot next door that wasn't used any more. It was burning hot in the sun, dust rose in clouds behind the girls. Pretty soon they got bored with the game though Roger Whipple even in his heavy overalls wanted to keep going. He was red-faced with all the excitement, he was a boy who loved to laugh and didn't have much chance. Rhea said she was thirsty, she wanted some ice, so Roger Whipple scrambled right up and went to get a big bag of ice cubes!—he hadn't any more sense than that.

They sucked on the ice cubes and fooled around with them. He was panting and lolling his tongue pretending to be a dog and Rhea and Rhoda cried, Here doggie! Here doggie-doggie!

tossing ice cubes at Roger Whipple he tried to catch in his mouth. That went on for a while. In the end the twins just dumped the rest of the ice onto the dirt then Roger Whipple was saying he had some secret things that belonged to his brother Eamon he could show them. Hidden under his bed mattress, would they like to see what the things were?

He wasn't one who could tell Rhea from Rhoda or Rhoda from Rhea. There was a way some of us knew, the freckles on Rhea's face were a little darker than Rhoda's. Rhea's eyes were just a little darker than Rhoda's. But you'd have to see the two side by side with no clowning around to know.

Rhea said okay, she'd like to see the secret things. She let her bike fall where she was straddling it.

Roger Whipple said he could only take one of them upstairs to his room at a time, he didn't say why.

Okay said Rhea. Of the Kunkel twins Rhea always had to be first.

She'd been born first, she said. Weighed a pound or two more.

Roger Whipple's room was in a strange place—on the second floor of the Whipple house above an unheated storage space that had been added after the main part of the house was built. There was a way of getting to the room from the outside, up a flight of rickety wood stairs. That way Roger could get in and out of his room without going through the rest of the house. People said the Whipples had him live there like some animal, they didn't want him tramping through the house but they denied it. The room had an inside door too.

Roger Whipple weighed about one-hundred ninety pounds that day. In the hospital he swelled up like a balloon, people said, bloated from the drugs, his skin was soft and white as bread dough and his hair fell out. He was an old man when he died aged thirty-one.

Exactly why he died, the Whipples never knew. The hospital just told them his heart had stopped in his sleep.

Rhoda shaded her eyes watching her sister running up the

stairs with Roger Whipple behind her and felt the first pinch of
fear, that something was wrong, or was going to be wrong. She
called after them in a whining voice that she wanted to come
along too, she didn't want to wait down there all alone, but
Rhea just called back to her to be quiet and wait her turn, so
Rhoda waited, kicking at the ice cubes melting in the dirt, and
after a while she got restless and shouted up to them—the door
was shut, the shade on the window was drawn—saying she was
going home, damn them she was sick of waiting she said and
she was going home. But nobody came to the door or looked out
the window, it was like the place was empty. Wasps had built
one of those nests that look like mud in layers under the eaves
and the only sound was wasps.

Rhoda bicycled toward the road so anybody who was watching would think she was going home, she was thinking she
hated Rhea! hated her damn twin sister! wished she was dead
and gone, God damn her! She was going home and the first
thing she'd tell their mother was that Rhea had stolen six dollars
from Grandma: she had it in her pocket right that moment.

The Whipple house was an old farmhouse they'd tried to
modernize by putting on red asphalt siding meant to look like
brick. Downstairs the rooms were big and drafty, upstairs they
were small, some of them unfinished and with bare floorboards,
like Roger Whipple's room which people would afterward say
based on what the police said was like an animal's pen, nothing
in it but a bed shoved into a corner and some furniture and
boxes and things Mrs. Whipple stored there.

Of the Whipples—there were seven in the family still living
at home—only Mrs. Whipple and her daughter Iris were home
that afternoon. They said they hadn't heard a sound except for
kids playing in the back, they swore it.

Rhoda was bent on going home and leaving Rhea behind but
at the end of the driveway something made her turn her bicycle
wheel back . . . so if you were watching you'd think she was
just cruising around for something to do, a red-haired girl with

whitish skin and freckles, skinny little body, pedaling fast, then slow, then coasting, then fast again, turning and dipping and criss-crossing her path, talking to herself as if she was angry. She hated Rhea! She was furious at Rhea! But feeling sort of scared too and sickish in the pit of her belly knowing that she and Rhea shouldn't be in two places, something might happen to one of them or to both. Some things you know.

So she pedaled back to the house. Laid her bike down in the dirt next to Rhea's. The bikes were old hand-me-downs, the kickstands were broken. But their daddy had put on new Good-year tires for them at the start of the summer and he'd oiled them too.

You never would see just one of the twins' bicycles anywhere, you always saw both of them laid down on the ground and facing in the same direction with the pedals in about the same position.

Rhoda peered up at the second floor of the house, the shade drawn over the window, the door still closed. She called out Rhea? Hey Rhea? starting up the stairs making a lot of noise so they'd hear her, pulling on the railing as if to break it the way a boy would. Still she was scared. But making noise like that and feeling so disgusted and mad helped her get stronger, and there was Roger Whipple with the door open staring down at her flush-faced and sweaty as if he was scared too. He seemed to have forgotten her. He was wiping his hands on his overalls. He just stared, a lemony light coming up in his eyes.

Afterward he would say he didn't remember anything— didn't remember anything. Big as a grown man but round-shouldered so it was hard to judge how tall he was, or how old. His straw-colored hair falling in his eyes and his fingers twined together as if he was praying or trying with all his strength to keep his hands still. He didn't remember anything about the twins or anything in his room or in the ice house afterward but he cried a lot, he acted scared and guilty and sorry, they decided he shouldn't be put on trial, there was no point to it.

Mrs. Whipple kept to the house afterward, never went out not even to church or grocery shopping. She died of cancer just before Roger died, she'd loved him she said, she always said none of it had been his fault really, he wasn't the kind of boy even to hurt an animal, he'd loved kittens especially and was a good sweet obedient boy and religious too and whatever happened it must have been because those girls were teasing him, he'd had a lifetime of being teased and taunted by children, his heart broken by all the abuse, and something must have snapped that day, that was all.

The Whipples were the ones, though, who called the police. Mr. Whipple found the girls' bodies back in the ice house hidden under some straw and canvas.

He found them around nine that night, with a flashlight. He knew, he said. The way Roger was acting, and the fact the Kunkel girls were missing, word had gotten out. He knew but he didn't know what he knew or what he would find. Roger taking a bath like that in the middle of the day and washing his hair too and shaving for the second time and not answering when his mother spoke to him, just sitting there staring at the floor as if he was listening to something no one else could hear. He knew, Mr. Whipple said. The hardest minute of his life was in the ice house lifting that canvas to see what was under it.

He took it hard too, he never recovered. He hadn't any choice but to think what a lot of people thought—it had been his fault. He was an old-time Methodist, he took all that seriously, but none of it helped him. Believed Jesus Christ was his personal savior and He never stopped loving Roger or turned His face from him and if Roger did truly repent in his heart he would be saved and they would be reunited in Heaven, all the Whipples reunited. He believed, but none of it helped in his life.

The ice house is still there but boarded up and derelict, the Whipples' ice business ended long ago. Strangers live in the house and the yard is littered with rusting hulks of cars and pickup trucks. Some Whipples live scattered around the county but none in town. The old train depot is still there too.

After I'd been married some years I got involved with this man, I won't say his name, his name is not a name I say, but we would meet back there sometimes, back in that old lot that's all weeds and scrub trees. Wild as kids and on the edge of being drunk. I was crazy for this guy, I mean crazy like I could hardly think of anybody but him or anything but the two of us making love the way we did, with him deep inside me I wanted it never to stop just fuck and fuck and fuck I'd whisper to him and this went on for a long time, two or three years then ended the way these things do and looking back on it I'm not able to recognize that woman as if she was someone not even not-me but a crazy woman I would despise, making so much of such a thing, risking her marriage and her kids finding out and her life being ruined for such a thing, my God. The things people do.

It's like living out a story that has to go its own way.

Behind the ice house in his car I'd think of Rhea and Rhoda and what happened that day upstairs in Roger Whipple's room. And the funeral parlor with the twins like dolls laid out and their eyes like dolls' eyes too that shut when you tilt them back. One night when I wasn't asleep but wasn't awake either I saw my parents standing in the doorway of my bedroom watching me and I knew their thoughts, how they were thinking of Rhea and Rhoda and of me their daughter wondering how they could keep me from harm and there was no clear answer.

In his car in his arms I'd feel my mind drift. After we'd made love or at least after the first time. And I saw Rhoda Kunkel hesitating on the stairs a few steps down from Roger Whipple. I saw her white-faced and scared but deciding to keep going anyway, pushing by Roger Whipple to get inside the room, to find Rhea, she had to brush against him where he was standing as if he meant to block her but not having the nerve exactly to block her and he was smelling of his body and breathing hard but not in imitation of any dog now, not with his tongue flopping and lolling to make them laugh. Rhoda was asking where was Rhea? —she couldn't see well at first in the dark little cubbyhole of a room because the sunshine had been so bright outside.

Roger Whipple said Rhea had gone home. His voice sounded scratchy as if it hadn't been used in some time. She'd gone home he said and Rhoda said right away that Rhea wouldn't go home without her and Roger Whipple came toward her saying yes she did, yes she *did* as if he was getting angry she wouldn't believe him. Rhoda was calling, Rhea? Where are you? Stumbling against something on the floor tangled with the bedclothes.

Behind her was this big boy saying again and again yes she did, yes she *did,* his voice rising but it would never get loud enough so that anyone would hear and come save her.

I wasn't there, but some things you know.

◆ *Carolyn Osborn* ◆

THE GRANDS

The ground mist eddied around the mule's legs. He walked
slowly toward a farmhouse as if aware that the man on his back
was asleep. Behind the hills the moon set casting long shadows
on rows of cotton already stripped. Leftover bits dotted the dark
earth, fluttered from the bolls' dry hulls, caught the eye of the
mule's rider as he woke. Rising slightly, he touched the fiddle
tied to the back of his saddle. As he reached the front porch
steps, he shook his head then shouted.

"Hal-loo! Hal-loo!"

The front door opened quickly, but he could not make out the
figure holding the lamp.

"Can you tell me where Edgar Moore lives?"

"Edgar Moore?" a woman's voice answered.

"Yes."

"Mr. Moore, this is your own house, you fool. Get off that
mule and come inside."

He slid off the mule, untied his fiddle, pulled the girth free,
and with the same hand wrestled the saddle and blanket to the
porch. Tucking the fiddle under one arm, he moved to the

mule's head, already lowered, slid the bridle off, tossed it, reins dragging, on top of the saddle. For a moment he considered the steps. Five, or were there six? He took every other one in defiant leaps. As he fell over the doorsill, he held the fiddle up in his right hand, then gently both arm and fiddle sank to the carpet.

Kate Moore looked down at him. She had on a new night-dress which she saw he would not notice. Her long, dark hair was covered with a paisley scarf to keep it unmussed till church time tomorrow. She turned away and put the lamp down on a table by the door. Gathering the white dress around her legs, she sat down on the third step of the stairs. For ten minutes she waited. The figure at her feet did not stir. She stood up, carefully curved his legs out of the way, and pushed the door to. Moving deliberately, she stepped over to pick up the lamp, then carrying it before her, she walked to their bedroom. A mule loose on the front lawn, her husband so drunk he couldn't move out of the entry hall. Such depravity stopped at her threshold. She locked the door.

* * *

It was 1906. My grandmother Moore told me this incident—part of it—long after Grandpa was dead, long after I'd left Tennessee, had married and gone to New Mexico. Part of it she may have imagined. Mine is a family of tale tellers, anecdote swappers, believers in the word, for we have used the word to know each other's lives. But the word often fails. There are lapses, year long pauses, lies perhaps. And who's to set matters straight? Whoever is left. There are not many of us.

* * *

Leaning back in her chair fifty-four years later, my grandmother drifted away for a moment as old people do when telling a story they know well, yet at these times she seemed to be musing over some fragment she did not choose to reveal.

"And the fiddle wasn't broken?" I asked.

"No, would have served him right if it had been. Would have served him right if I'd never opened the front door. He'd been at a country dance right after harvest. Big, noisy gatherings. I seldom went. Mr. Moore always wanted to go so he rode off to play the fiddle for them. In those days they paid the fiddler with liquor, moonshine most likely. That's why Mr. Moore came home, rather the mule brought him home, in that disgraceful condition."

"Miss Kate," Grandpa called her, twenty-two in 1906, seventy-six when she decided to tell me the tale, remained a formidably respectable woman. A churchgoer, organizer of Sunday Schools, a housecleaner, and a collector of cut-glass and porcelains which stood on what-not shelves, a piece of furniture all children were forbidden to approach, she was described by everyone in the family with one word—particular. Though reputedly the best cake baker in the country, she detested cooking. Her ideas about what ladies did and did not do led her away from the farm to her house in town as often as possible. She knew how to make lye soap and wring a chicken's neck but she preferred, as she grew older, to forget such skills. She continued, however, to call Grandpa, dead thirty years before her, "Mr. Moore" all her life.

Did the formality mark the distance between them? He was ten years older. Or was it merely the custom at that time for women to refer to their husbands as "Mr." in public while reserving first names for private conversations? Both of these I suspect. And there was yet another reason—inverse snobbery. By continual use of this title and by other means—she insisted he should wear a suit rather than overalls to town—Grandmother tried to reconstruct Grandpa. He would, she was determined, become a gentleman, an act of will bound to fail. Grandpa's friends called him "Sog," a name given to him as a child after he fell into a half-empty barrel of sorghum molasses. When told that his station in life demanded a suit he said, "Miss Kate, I will cover myself with a suit for weddings, funerals, going to the bank for a loan, and other great occasions but I will not ruin my business by wearing one. Mule traders wear overalls like mule buyers do."

It was a spurious argument since he had many other occupations; however, it served his purpose. She gave up on the suit but not the "Mr." Though she never said so, it was apparent Grandmother felt she had married beneath her. She was an Allen from Virginia, a designation involving, as far as we could tell, contriving to act as if one's breeding and social position were more important than money, especially when the family fortune had fallen to the poverty level.

Some of "the other Moores," alas, included a distant uncle in an equally distant penitentiary and a brother who made moonshine in one of the local hollows. Grandmother never uttered their names, nor did anyone else in her presence. In fact I did not know of their existence till I was thirty-two, and Uncle Phillip, an in-law, told me Miss Kate had pruned the family tree, lopsidedly as it turned out. She continued to visit her own brother who beside working as a circus roustabout and running the Silver Slipper Saloon somewhere in Oklahoma later opened a liquor store in the Texas Panhandle. He was excused because it was a legitimate business located at a safe distance from Allen territory. Texas, to her mind, was the wild west, a suitable place for a wild brother.

Grandpa also still went to see his brother, privately we supposed. Except for lineages of mules, horses, and birddogs, Mr. Moore did not care about breeding. Somewhere during their marriage, early I'd venture, Grandpa gave up discussing asses, mares, stallions, and bitches when Grandmother dropped the Allens of Virginia. By the time I was old enough to notice such omissions, she seemed to have lost interest in ancestry altogether.

*   *   *

Grandpa Moore died in 1938 when he was sixty-three and I was three, too young to ask him the truth of those surmises or any others that were passed on to me. Only a few of the immediate family are left. Age, accident, and illness carried off Grandmother, my mother, the only son George. Aunt Lucy, her husband Phillip, and their son Fergus remain in Tennessee. I married and moved first to Texas, then to New Mexico, but I fly back to visit my relatives, compelled, I imagine, by the almost atavistic instinct of kinship that knots some families together. Air hours are short; movement through time is long. The moment I leave New Mexico I know I'm flying into a sepia-tone world peopled with beloved though elusive ghosts. Certain characteristics remain distinct while others are exaggerated, softened, forgotten, or changed entirely depending on who's telling the story. What is it we are after? No one seems to desire the whole truth, whatever that may be.

*   *   *

We have never ceased speculating about Grandpa's death, which was admittedly strange. He was run over by the Interurban, an electric trolley which ran from Nashville to Franklin, a nearby county seat. Part of the tracks bordered his farm, so he often rode home from the fields. What was he doing on those well-known tracks? Could he possibly have gotten stuck? He was diabetic. Did he fall into a coma right there? Did he get drunk and fall asleep on the tracks? Uncle Phillip brought this up, but nobody else agreed with his theory. Was Grandpa suicidal? Why would he have been? None of these questions have ever been answered to anyone's satisfaction. In 1938 autopsies were seldom performed to settle family curiosity. The suggestion of

one would have, no doubt, shocked my grandmother. The Interurban had run over Grandpa. That was enough.

He is so much alive in everyone's imagination that I cannot
imagine his death. During childhood summers at the farm I'd
seen the trolley swerving along making clicking noises on the
tracks. Since then I've seen those abandoned tracks. I've seen
the place Grandpa Moore lay across them. Where was the mus-
tachioed villain? The peril was evident. Oh, it was absurd! Like
drowning in two feet of water, or choking to death on a fish
bone, or dying from a concussion after slipping in a bathtub.
Nevertheless, the Interurban ran over Grandpa Moore.

                    *   *   *

His farmhouse was two-story, faded red brick. The sloping roof
of the long front porch divided the front of the house in half.
Inside, underneath the stairs, was a closet with a fake floor and
space enough between it and the cellar ceiling for a man to hide,
a secret place never revealed to children of the family for fear
something might happen to one of us if we used it. When
Grandmother finally told me, I was twenty-eight and had children of my own to protect, yet I felt cheated.

"What a grand place for hide-and-seek it would have been."

"You might have gotten stuck. The hinges were rusty. Anyway you most certainly would have been afraid in that small
dark space. You would have been hysterical. Screaming and crying."

"I wouldn't have."

"Some other child would've."

"I wonder who built it?"

"We never knew. Perhaps it was added. The farmhouse was
old. I forget when it was built exactly, sometime before the Civil
War though."

"Perhaps Confederate soldiers were hidden there."

"Aren't you the romantic!"

"Or it was part of the underground railway."

"More than likely it was meant to hide valuables. Silver, and jewelry, and such."

Wasn't it just as likely that Grandpa hid his whiskey there, and she knew it though she wasn't supposed to? I stared at her. She had dark eyes, a small staunch figure. No matter what the season she wore a full corset. Her composure, her certainty about all matters of opinion, was broken only by laughter. I cannot remember seeing her cry until she was in her eighties and had had a cerebral hemorrhage. Yet I was not there to witness every moment of her life.

There were many secrets in the family, things not told for years. Grandmother never told anyone where she met Mr. Moore, not even her own children. My cousin Fergus said he bet they met on a train. Fergus is "a little wild" his mother says, but he's my only first cousin. He drove our grandmother out to Santa Fe to my oldest child's christening, so naturally I like him. And I like his idea. Everybody rode trains then.

*   *   *

"How do you do, Miss—? My name is Edgar Moore. I farm down around Franklin, Tennessee." Mr. Moore sat in the seat across from her.

"I don't know a thing about agriculture. I could hardly tell you if that was corn or cotton growing out there." She folded her white gloved hands on her lap and looked out the window.

"Ladies needn't know about farming. Where are you from?"

"Virginia. Most of my family lives in Richmond. I have an aunt in Tennessee."

"Where?"

"Franklin." She twisted her fingers together. She had never ridden on a train alone before, much less spoken to a man while riding on one, but it seemed uncivil not to speak when he was sitting just across from her. Of course she would not give him

her name. Fortunately Mr. Moore recognized the aunt when he
and Miss Kate arrived at the station. In time, allowing a few
days for her to recover from her journey, he came calling.

*   *   *

If they were both on the train from Richmond to Nashville in
1904, it was as innocent as that, I believe. How easy it is to
believe one's own fictions. Perhaps they were not riding the
train. Perhaps they met on some other occasion. He was an eligible bachelor, and she was a young woman in need of a husband. I'm certain they did not meet in church. Grandpa was a
backslidden Methodist, one of those who attended Easter services if he went at all, while Grandmother was a Campbellite, a
member of the Church of Christ, one of the fiercer fundamen-
talist groups. Drinking, smoking, dancing, gambling, and card
playing were forbidden. So were musical instruments in church.
To tune the congregation for hymn singing, the minister blew
on a pitchpipe. The only amusement during the service was
reading the hymnal or lugubrious funeral parlor advertisements
on one side of the cardboard fans.

Invariably the picture was of a long-haired, extremely gentile
Christ dressed in a white robe vaguely reminiscent of garments
worn by the choir in other churches. He was standing in a
highly idealized garden of Gethsemane alone except for a number of rose bushes in the foreground and cypress trees in the
background. I used to wonder about those heavy, red, symmet-
rical roses. They were like no others I'd seen. Finally I decided
they were supposed to be heavenly flowers. The message beneath ran: Your Friend In Your Hour Of Need. Then there was
the name and phone number of the funeral parlor. As a child
with a wide experience in visiting family churches—all kinds of
Protestants plus Catholics were represented—I found Grandmother's the most dour. However, it suited her astringent needs
which were most apparent in her sense of decorum. To her the

simplest act such as meeting a man could be dangerous. One had to have a proper introduction by some family member or, lacking that, by a trusted friend. Over-trained in social conventions, she had no training at all in being a farmer's wife. How did she adapt? I wish I'd asked her during her lifetime, still the question isn't difficult. So much is already known it's easy for me to intuit her answers.

"At the farm the front porch was a good deal of trouble because children wanted to play out there. I would be in the kitchen and Mr. Moore would come in carrying George. He was about two then."

Both Grandpa's and George's faces were red. Grandpa's from the sun, George's from bawling.

"Miss Kate, he's fallen off the porch again. Why can't you watch this child?" he shouted.

She shouted back, "I can't watch George and cook dinner at the same time. There are too many dangerous places around here. Watch him yourself."

"I'm hiring you a cook."

"High time!" Miss Kate turned her own reddened face back to the wood stove, a large black cast iron monster she despised every day all day every summer.

She was expecting my mother then. 1908. Pregnant, hot, often exhausted, she was in no humor to accommodate. George did not fall off the porch again. She sat on the porch swing, fanned herself, and watched him while Minnie took over the kitchen.

My grandmother and I never looked in the least alike. Our opinions seldom matched. Though I cry easily, perhaps our temperaments are somewhat the same. Children are easily influenced. I lived in the town house with her, Uncle George, and my mother during part of WW II. I wish I had a cook.

In his photograph Grandpa, curly-headed and long-nosed, looked like a sober, industrious squire. In many ways he was. A gold watch chain stretched across a large belly. He had three hundred acres of rich Middle Tennessee land where he raised cotton, corn, alfalfa, tobacco, and the usual barnyard produce, hogs and chickens. He also had mules to trade and property in town to tend. Until Miss Kate made him take it down, he had a sign on his front gate reading *Trade In Your Old Mules For New.* After he died my grandmother lived for thirty years on his investments and had some money left over to leave to their children. In part he was another sort of person which accounted for a barely suppressed smile and definite laughter in his eyes in that photograph. As a child I simply thought he looked jolly. Fergus, five years older, knew better.

"Grandpa was a rascal. He taught me to chew tobacco when I was seven."

"Didn't you hate the taste of it?"

"Yes, but he convinced me it was something a man needed to know how to do. He taught me how to spit too. Put me up on a wagon seat with him, took me off to town to trade mules. On the way there and back he gave me cussing lessons. We had a wonderful time."

"What did Aunt Lucy say about that?"

"Mama didn't know until too late. There was a whole side to Grandpa he didn't show to women."

Fergus has Grandpa's long nose and curly hair. He was working on the belly, said it came naturally since he had to stay up all night eating and drinking with his clients, country musicians who swept into Nashville to play at the Grand Ole Opry or hoped to play there. Like so many bats out of a cave blinded by light, they weren't really comfortable until dark, so Fergus kept his recording studio open till two or three in the morning. We were talking in his office, the single messiest place I've ever entered—this includes the slums of Naples and my children's bedrooms. Over two desks a hanging basket of red plastic geraniums dangled from a set of longhorn steer horns partially hiding a five foot print of a tiger serenely marching through his jungle. A round table pushed to one side held stacks of poker chips, cards, a cluster of dirty glasses and ashtrays. File boxes sat on all but one seat of a couch. Next to them was a charro hat somebody had brought Fergus from Mexico. Plastic ferns caught dust in front of a window that was never opened.

Behind me in the next room was a well-stocked bar equally in shambles. People, most of them wearing bluejeans, wandered through the office to the bar to replenish drinks. Fergus nodded or waved as they came and went. Grandpa's gold watch, suspended under a glass globe, shone amid the chaos of papers, calculators, hunting knives, and one villainous looking carved coconut rolling around between the phones on his desk. The coconut had on an eyepatch, a bit of blue bandana, and an earring, all attempts to transform it into a pirate's head. I counted three broken guitars in two corners; a busted drum took up one chair. In order to sit down, I had to prop my feet on a large carton of toilet paper, not that I minded. Fergus has always been like this, a collector and a keeper. The office was his version of Grandpa's barn, a jumble of harness, buggies, and everything that ever was a piece of farm equipment. Strictly his territory. No one disturbs Fergus's clutter but him. He lives in it like a bandit chief surrounded by his spoils.

"You know, Marianne, the only woman who ever caught sight of Grandpa's carrying on was Miss Kate, and she didn't know the half of it."

"How did they stay together all those years? Of course there were three children. But he was ten years older than she was—"

"People did then," said Fergus. He'd been divorced once and seemed perpetually on the edge of marrying again though he could never quite make up his mind to it. Compared to Fergus, I've lead a sedate life, married for twenty-five years to the same man, mother of three. My husband, a lawyer, and I run a horse ranch, a place near Santa Fe where we breed and raise quarter horses. Like Grandmother we have a house in town also.

"Of course," Fergus reminded me, "Miss Kate was his perfect opposite. He honored her quirks—built her that house in Franklin, paid for all kinds of help—and she put up with his . . . his good times."

And the bad times? Do we forget them too easily? "Sufficient unto the day is the evil thereof." Well, yes. We don't like to think of our grandparents as pitiable. They were though. For all her bossiness, my grandmother loved men, yet for thirty years she was a widow. During her last years she was quite mad. In her senility she confused me with my mother, another of her sorrows, a daughter dead in a plane wreck—the reason why Fergus drove her to New Mexico. She wouldn't fly. She had allergies, arthritis, her share of aches, fevers, and anxiety attacks which she called "nerves."

As for Grandpa? I do know a mean old sow bit him in the calf of his leg, and he had to use a cane for six months. He was aware that his only son George hated farming. He was not fond of either one of his sons-in-law. Hail flattened entire alfalfa crops. Drought destroyed the cotton. Every kind of pest invaded his fields. To the forces of nature, he remained a stoic. ("The earth survives all weather," he said.) To the forces within he was, I think, largely a stranger. He often drank too much when he wasn't supposed to drink at all. Diabetes made him melancholy. Some days he sat alone on the steps to the hay loft and cursed. I never saw him there, still I'm sure he must have done it, slumped there in the dark barn, fanned his face with his hat, and cursed repetitively, dully.

*   *   *

"Why didn't I ever hear Grandpa play the fiddle?" Aunt Lucy is the only one I can ask.

"Oh, you were too young. No, let me think. He quit playing for the family sometime in the thirties. He'd go to his room to play or sit out under a tree in the yard. I don't know what made him do it, some argument he and Mother had, I guess . . . something to do with fiddling and drinking. They seemed to go together. But he used to play for us all on Saturday nights—when we'd stay home to listen. He was the only one in the family who knew how to play a musical instrument. Mother had a player piano. Remember?"

I did. It stood in a corner of the living room out at the farm and was as forbidden to children as the what-not shelves. Field mice had invaded it, eaten all the felt off the hammers, chewed through rolls of paper. My grandmother's mute cultural pretension; it might as well have been a broken hay mower.

"Your mother and father—before they married—Uncle Phillip, and I used to dance on the front porch in the summers. No rugs were ever rolled up for dancing in Mother's houses. George joined in when he was courting a girl. He was always the caller. It wasn't the kind of music we wanted in the twenties. Papa only knew square dance tunes, things like 'Cotton-Eyed-Joe,' 'The Virginia Reel,' 'Shoofly.' We wanted saxophones, drums, trumpets . . . jazz."

It was easy to see them. Grandpa in a vest and shirt sleeves, tapping his foot just outside the front screen door, light from the entryway falling on his fiddle under his chin, moths fluttering toward the light. Three young men, three young women dancing.

"Promenade all," George called, and they pranced all the way to the swing, heels clattering on the wooden porch floor. An owl hooted. The moon rose. At a distance the lawn's familiar elms, maples, magnolias were outlined in black, and the tops of the men's cars shone in the driveway. Grandpa played while his children square danced before him wearing flapper clothes. That was the only kind of dancing Miss Kate allowed. The Charleston, the shimmy, the blackbottom, even the foxtrot were as religiously banned as the hip flask.

"Your father generally had some whiskey with him. Or if he didn't your Uncle Phillip did. I suspect George did too only he couldn't very well offer his papa a drink. When we were finished the men would go out to the cars and—"

"Where was Grandmother?"

"In the kitchen unpacking ice-cream. She had Minnie to make it and George to crank it. She made the cake . . . chocolate with a fudge icing or lemon with bits of shredded peel in a white seven minute icing." She smiled. "Makes me hungry to think about them. Your father and Phillip and Papa sat on the porch steps chewing mints till she called them in."

Aunt Lucy is white-headed and slight. Fluttery as a small, nervous bird. Uncle Phillip is short, pink-cheeked, white-headed also. He likes the nostalgic tales but he insists, sensibly as usual, "You're forgetting the bad years."

"Yes," Aunt Lucy sighed. "There were those Papa would plant, we'd have a drought, and there would be nothing to reap. Mother hated those times. She'd have to rent the town house and she couldn't go to Saratoga. Oh Lord, how she loved going to Saratoga Springs! So we'd just be stuck there on the farm gathering eggs and waiting for the weather to change. That's when Papa took off. I never knew where he went exactly. He'd be gone over a week sometimes." She drifted back to the kitchen to bring us some coffee.

"Hunting," Fergus winked at me and his father. "He went off hunting I expect."

We were sitting in another room full of Grandmother's dark Victorian furniture Aunt Lucy had inherited. Carved leaves, nuts, fruit protruded from the backs and arms; unyielding upholstery held us upright. The cut-glass shone on the sideboard and the what-not shelves were full of fussy porcelain figurines; a milkmaid, a shepherd, a harlequin, and men and women covered with lace who appeared to be engaged in a court dance sometime in the 1700s somewhere in Europe. There wasn't a single chicken, dog, pig, horse, or mule, no figure from my grandparents' daily lives. Naturally Grandmother wouldn't have wanted a figurine of the hired man or the cook, and the idea of a porcelain pig or mule in her parlor would have offended her. Propriety and beauty were Made In Dresden. Meanwhile Grandpa slopped hogs, traded mules, tilled the soil, bought property in town, and every once in a while, broke loose.

"I don't see any reason to disturb Mother's . . . um, view of the world. She's happy with it. But I'll tell you, Grandpa didn't do much hunting. He had a shack out in the wood where he went to do his serious drinking. One time he took the sheriff with him." Fergus laughed.

"Why?"

"Marianne," said Uncle Phillip, "You remind me of your mother, always wanting to know why this and why that. Until you came along she asked more questions than anybody in the family. No one knows why exactly. He thought the sheriff was working too hard maybe. Mr. Moore and some fellow were having an altercation on the square. The sheriff's office was right there. He stepped out to ask them to quiet down. Mr. Moore talked him into getting in the buggy with him. You wouldn't remember his horses. He had a fine pair of matched bays. Before the sheriff knew it, your grandpa had taken him out of the county. They spent three or four days in the woods eating country ham, biscuits, and redeye gravy, and drinking whiskey. Country ham creates a powerful thirst. Probably they did a little dove hunting too. Finally the sheriff mentioned he had to get back to town."

I sat in that upright chair thinking for a few minutes about a three or four day diet of country ham, redeye gravy, biscuits, and whiskey. There is absolutely nothing anybody can do to vary the taste of Tennessee country ham. Smoke cured, with hickory usually, heavily salted, it's first boiled for hours, baked, cooled, then cut into the thinnest possible slices which are eaten cold or fried in ham fat. After the first day maybe the whiskey helped. Or maybe Grandpa and the sheriff stumbled to the nearest farm and bought some eggs. Oh, it's not hard at all to search the country for groceries, not for me. I know that country, know what a hungry farmer and a sheriff might eat.

"Sog, I can't eat eggs."

"Can't?"

"Never could look a fried egg in the eye."

"Scrambled?"

"Them neither. My mama used to cook them with brains. With or without they still look suspicious to me."

The woman at the back door waited holding a bowl in her hands. Her hair was gray, her figure slack. She had on a loose brown shift. Miss Kate wouldn't have given her the time of day if she'd seen her in the country or in town.

"What about turnip greens, Ma'm. You got any turnip greens you'll sell us."

"Out there in the garden if you'll pick 'um. You won't be wanting the eggs then?"

"Let's cut that to a dozen 'stead of two."

"How you going to carry 'um?"

"I'll figure that out."

He wrapped the eggs in some turnip green leaves and put them in his hat. The sheriff stuck the rest of the greens under the buggy's seat.

"Ain't we dandies, by God!" Sog roared as they took off.

"You're going to think so when one of them eggs breaks in your hat," said the sheriff.

*   *   *

"I wonder what Grandmother said when he got back?"

"I don't think she said anything much. They understood each other. He'd toe her mark just so long, then he'd rip off," Uncle Phillip said. He must have wished sometimes that he'd ripped more himself. Most of his life he sold insurance and when he retired he kept on looking after anyone who needed looking after, which amounted to nearly all the Moores—Grandmother, Uncle George, Aunt Lucy, and elderly cousins that everyone else had forgotten. He was a man naturally inclined toward benevolence, but can't such an inclination become a burden too?

"Miss Kate would leave when she pleased," Fergus reminded me. "Don't forget her hayfever."

Grandmother's hayfever dictated a trip every fall. She got on a train and left the state for some other where ragweed wasn't pollinating. Her family had scattered by then. She visited a sister in Pennsylvania, the brother in the Texas Panhandle. More often she went to a spa like Saratoga or Red Boiling Springs in Arkansas. And she travelled alone. A few years after Grandpa died she announced she'd cured herself of hayfever by eating the local honey.

Fergus's comment was, "She would have had to have eaten about fifty gallons of it. Miss Kate lost her reason for going. She didn't have to get away from the farm anymore."

"But she usually spoke of Grandpa as if she adored him."

"Sure. Sure she did. They admired each other. He did everything she wouldn't have dared to do and she . . . she was such a model of respectable behavior he couldn't help but admire her."

"You keep throwing the old opposites theory at me."

Fergus took a long puff on his cigar. He often used it to underline his opinions in the same way that pipesmokers pointed the stems of their pipes or made people wait while they puffed and considered an important question.

"Honey, I can't come up with nothing no better."

This was another of Fergus's tricks, to switch to bad English when he wanted to make a point. In the country music business to be able to talk "country" was a necessity. It was also an effective way of disparaging someone else's opinion. By playing the ignoramus, he could at the same time play the sage, plainspoken hick. At times like this I thought I saw Grandpa's influence coming through again, or maybe it was just the cigar that made me think of him and tobacco.

Aunt Lucy floated back in just as I spoke of seeing tobacco in his fields.

"Now, you have that wrong. Papa only raised tobacco once. He said it was too much worry."

"It wasn't just worry about the crop," Uncle Phillip interrupted. "He said it was too hard on his barn. Curing, the way he did it, required a hardwood fire burning slow on the floor of the barn and lasted nearly three weeks. You never saw that done did you, Marianne?"

I hadn't. I knew almost nothing about the real business of farming. Grandpa's only son Uncle George didn't like what he knew. He was far more interested in buying and selling land than he was in plowing and harvesting, so in 1941, four years after Grandpa died, Uncle George sold the farm, moved into town with Miss Kate, and took up auctioneering first, then real estate. I wondered briefly what Grandpa would have thought about that.

"Well, he was a trader himself," said Fergus.

"Papa wasn't sentimental about farming. He liked the look of the land, the way certain fields lay, and he took pride in what he could raise but he always planned for us to leave the place—all of us. He insisted on college educations, girls included. Papa was a great believer in education." Aunt Lucy got up again and went to the dining room.

"I want to show you something. You haven't seen it in years." She held up a wax apple with teeth marks on it.

For an instant I was seven years old again tasting wax instead of the tart apple I'd expected, and Fergus was laughing just as he laughed then. Of course he was the one who had dared me to take the fruit from Grandmother's cut-glass bowl on her dining table. Of course I chose the apple; I liked it best. It was a strong primary red, darker on one side than the other.

"Did you keep the rest of it, Aunt Lucy?" Once there was a bunch of grapes, a banana, a pear, two plums, two peaches, and an orange. All were wax, all beautifully colored and shaded to ripe perfection, or so they appeared to me in those pre-plastic days. By some childish twist of logic I had not thought to wonder why the fruit never spoiled. Perhaps I unconsciously assumed everything in my grandmother's house stayed quietly perfect in the way old people seem always the same age to children.

"That kind of thing went out of style, and Mother put them in the attic. One hot summer they must have collapsed. Only the apple kept its shape. When we cleared out the house I threw the rest away."

The truth is sometimes a poor, sad thing—wax fruit melted in an attic, a lone mule wandering on the front lawn, a mute player piano—a few insubstantial fragments. All we could to was grab hold and make something more of them. I turned the apple in my hands.

"It's a grief, clearing out a house after someone's gone. But you can't keep everything. You'd never believe that though looking at Fergus's office."

"The ghost of Miss Kate flies through there on white angel wings around four every morning. Sometimes people hear her screaming." Fergus grinned.

"And Grandpa's ghost?"

"Oh, his is still riding through the Arcade on a mule."

The arcade is a short covered passageway through the middle of a block in downtown Nashville. Small stores used to face pedestrians on either side. I don't know what's there now or if it's even still used.

"Why did he do that?"

"He'd been up to Nashville to see some friends," Fergus said and looked at the ceiling as if he wished I hadn't asked.

"You mean he'd been up all night drinking," Aunt Lucy intervened. "I know he did that kind of thing. I swear, the way he treats me, you'd think I was Mother. She'd hardly let anybody say 'whiskey' in front of her."

"Yes," Fergus went on, "Well . . . he rode through the

Arcade and found a policeman waiting for him on the other side. And the policeman said, 'I'm fining you five dollars for disorderly conduct.'

"Grandpa pulled some money out of his pocket, 'Here's ten dollars. I'm going back the same way.' He turned the mule around and rode through again, went on back to the farm I reckon."

I saw him with the sun rising over the stubby green hills, a portly squire, his jacket rumpled, his face reddened, his watch chain strained against his belly. He was a little sleepy. He let the mule settle into a slow walk, then shook himself awake and trotted off into the countryside through the perpetual mist that surrounds mythical figures.

♦ *James P. Blaylock* ♦

UNIDENTIFIED OBJECTS

In 1956 the downtown square mile of the city of Orange was a collection of old houses: craftsman bungalows and tile-roofed Spanish, and here and there an old Queen Anne or a gingerbread Victorian with geminate windows and steep gables, and sometimes a carriage house alongside, too small by half to house the lumbering automobiles that the second fifty years of the century had produced. There were Studebakers at the curbs and Hudsons and Buicks with balloon tires like the illustrations of moon-aimed rockets on the covers of the pulp magazines.

Times were changing. Science was still a professor with wild hair and a lab coat and with bubbling apparatus in a cellar; but in a few short years he would walk on the moon—one last ivory and silver hurrah—and then, as if in an instant, he would grow faceless and featureless and unpronounceable. There would come the sudden knowledge that Moon Valley wasn't so very far away after all, and neither was extinction; that the nation that controlled magnetism, as Diet Smith would have it, controlled almost nothing at all; and that a score of throbbing bulldozers could reduce the jungle wilds around Opar and El Dorado to desert sand in a few short, sad years. The modern automobile suddenly was slick and strange, stretched out and low and with enormous fins that swept back at the rear above banks of superfluous taillights. They seemed otherworldly at the time and were alien reminders, it seems to me now, of how provincial we had been, balanced on the back edge of an age.

The pace of things seemed to be accelerating, and already I could too easily anticipate stepping out onto my tilted front porch some signifying morning, the wind out of the east, and seeing stretched out before me not a shaded avenue of overarching trees and root-cracked sidewalks but the sleek, desertlike technology of a new age, a new suburbia, with robots in vinyl trousers sweeping fallen leaves into their own open mouths.

*   *   *

There is a plaza in the center of town, with a fountain, and in the autumn—the season when all of this came to my attention —red-brown leaves from flowering pear trees drift down onto the sluggish, gurgling water and float there like a centerpiece for a Thanksgiving table. On a starry evening, one November late in the Seventies, I was out walking in the plaza, thinking, I remember, that it had already become an artifact, with its quaint benches and granite curbs and rose garden. Then, shattering the mood of late-night nostalgia, there shone in the sky an immense shooting star, followed by the appearance of a glowing object, which hovered and darted, sailing earthward until I could make out its shadow against the edge of the moon and then disappearing in a blink. I shouted and pointed, mostly out of surprise. Strange lights in the sky were nothing particularly novel; I had been seeing them for almost twenty years. But nothing that happens at night among the stars can ever become commonplace. At that late hour, though, there was almost certainly no one around to hear me; or so I thought.

So when she stood up, dropping papers and pencils and a wooden drawing board onto the concrete walk, I nearly shouted again. She had been sitting in the dim lamplight, hidden to me beyond the fountain. Dark hair fell across her shoulders in a rush of curl and hid her right eye, and with a practiced sweep of her hand she pulled it back in a shock and tucked it behind her ear, where it stayed obediently for about three quarters of a second and then fell seductively into her face again. Now, years later, for reasons I can't at all define, the sight of a dark-haired woman brushing wayward hair out of her eyes recalls without fail that warm autumn night by the fountain.

She had that natural, arty, blue-jeans-and-floppy-sweater look of a college girl majoring in fine arts: embroidered handbag, rhinestone-emerald costume brooch, and translucent plastic shoes the color of root beer. I remember thinking right off that she had languorous eyes, and the sight of them reflecting the soft lamplight of the fountain jolted me. But the startled look on her face implied that she hadn't admired my shouting like that, not at eleven o'clock at night in the otherwise deserted plaza.

There was the dark, pouting beauty in her eyes and lips of a woman in a Pre-Raphaelite painting, a painting that I had stumbled into in my clodlike way, grinning, I thought, like a halfwit. I too hastily explained the shooting star to her, gesturing too widely at the sky and mumbling that it hadn't been an ordinary shooting star. But there was nothing in the sky now besides the low-hanging moon and a ragtag cloud, and she said offhandedly, not taking any notice of my discomfort, just what I had been thinking, that there was never anything ordinary about a shooting star.

I learned that her name was Jane and that she had sketched that fountain a dozen times during the day, with the blooming flowers behind it and the changing backdrop of people and cars and weather. I almost asked her whether she hadn't ever been able to get it quite right, but then, I could see that that wasn't the point.

Now she had been sketching it at night, its blue and green and pink lights illuminating the umbrella of falling water against night-shaded rosebushes and camphor trees and box-wood hedges.

It was perfect—straight out of a romantic old film. The hero stumbles out of the rain into an almost deserted library, and at the desk, with her hair up and spectacles on her nose, is the librarian who doesn't know that if she'd just take the glasses off for a moment . . .

I scrabbled around to pick up fallen pencils while she pro-tested that she could just as easily do it herself. It was surely only the magic of that shooting star that prevented her from gathering up her papers and going home. As it was, she stayed for a moment to talk, assuming, although she never said so, that there was something safe and maybe interesting in a fancier of shooting stars. I felt the same about her and her drawings and her root beer shoes.

She was distracted, never really looking at me. Maybe the image of the fountain was still sketched across the back of her eyes and she couldn't see me clearly. It was just a little irritating, and I would discover later that it was a habit of hers, being distracted was, but on that night there was something in the air and it didn't matter. Any number of things don't matter at first. We talked, conversation dying and starting and with my mind mostly on going somewhere—my place, her place—for a drink, for what? There was something, an atmosphere that surrounded her, a musky sort of sweater and lilacs scent. But she was dis-tant; her work had been interrupted and she was still half lost in the dream of it. She dragged her hand in the water of the foun-tain, her face half in shadow. She was tired out, she said. She didn't need to be walked home. She could find her way alone.

*   *   *

But I've got ahead of myself. It's important that I keep it all straight—all the details; without the details it amounts to nothing. I grew up on Olive Street, southwest of the plaza, and when I was six and wearing my Davy Crockett hat and Red Rider shirt, and it was nearly dusk in late October, I heard the ding-a-linging of an ice cream truck from some distant reach of the neighborhood. The grass was covered with leaves, I remember, that had been rained on and were limp and heavy. I was digging for earthworms and dropping them one by one into a corral built of upright sticks and twigs that was the wall of the native village on Kong Island. The sky was cloudy, the street empty. There was smoke from a chimney across the way and the cloud-muted hum of a distant airplane lost to view. Light through the living room window shone out across the dusky lawn.

The jangling of the ice cream bell drew near, and the truck rounded the distant corner, the bell cutting off and the truck accelerating as if the driver, anticipating dinner, had given up for the day and was steering a course for home. It slowed, though, when he saw me, and angled in toward the curb where I stood holding a handful of gutter-washed earthworms. Clearly he thought I'd signaled him. There were pictures of frozen concoctions painted on the gloss-white sides of the panel truck: coconut-covered Neapolitan bars and grape Popsicles, nut and chocolate drumsticks, and strawberry-swirled vanilla in paper cups with flat paper lids. He laboriously climbed out of the cab, came around the street side to the back, and confronted me there on the curb. He smiled and winked and wore a silver foil hat with an astonishing bill, and when he yanked open the hinged, chrome door there was such a whirling of steam off the dry ice inside that he utterly vanished behind it, and I caught a quick glimpse of cardboard bins farther back in the cold fog, stacked one on top of another and dusted with ice crystals.

I didn't have a dime and wouldn't be allowed to eat ice cream so close to dinnertime anyway, and I said so, apologizing for having made him stop for nothing. He studied my earthworms and said that out in space there were planets where earthworms spoke and wore silk shirts, and that I could fly to those planets in the right sort of ship.

Then he bent into the freezer and after a lot of scraping and peering into boxes found a paper-wrapped ice cream bar—a FLYING SAUCER BAR, the wrapper said. It was as big around as a coffee cup saucer and was domed on top and fat with vanilla ice cream coated in chocolate. He tipped his hat, slammed his door, and drove off. I ate the thing guiltily while sitting beneath camellia bushes at the side of the house and lobbing sodden pink blooms out onto the front yard, laying siege to the earthworm fortress and watching the lamps blink on one by one along the street.

*   *   *

There are those incidents from our past that years later seem to us to be the stuff of dreams: the wash of shooting stars seen through the rear window of the family car at night in the Utah desert; the mottled, multilegged sun star, as big as a cartwheel, inching across the sand in the shallows of a northern California bay; the whale's eyeball floating in alcohol and encased in a glass fishing float in a junk store near the waterfront; the remembered but unrecoverable hollow sensation of new love. The stars vanish in an instant; the starfish slips away into deep water and is gone; the shop with its fishing float is a misty dream, torn down in some unnumbered year to make room for a hotel built of steel and smoked glass. Love evaporates into the passing years like dry ice; you don't know where it's gone. The mistake is to think that the details don't signify—the flying saucer bars and camellia blooms, rainy autumn streets and lamplight through evening windows and colored lights playing across the waters of a fountain on a warm November evening.

All the collected pieces of our imagistic memory seem sometimes to be trivial knickknacks when seen against the roaring of passing time. But without those little water-paint sketches, awash in remembered color and detail, none of us, despite our airy dreams, amount to more than an impatient ghost wandering through the revolving years and into an increasingly strange and alien future.

*   *   *

I came to know the driver of the ice cream truck. We became acquaintances. He no longer sold ice cream; there was no living to be made at it. He had got a penny a Popsicle, he said, and he produced a slip of paper covered with numbers—elaborate calculations of the millions of Popsicles he'd have to sell over the years just to stay solvent. Taken altogether like that it was impossible. He had been new to the area then and hadn't got established yet. All talk of money aside, he had grown tired of it, of the very idea of driving an ice cream truck—something that wouldn't have seemed possible to me on the rainy evening of the flying saucer bar, but which I understand well enough now.

He had appeared on our front porch, I remember, when I was ten or eleven, selling wonderful tin toys door-to-door. My mother bought a rocket propelled by compressed air. It was painted with bright, circus colors, complete with flames swirling around the cylindrical base of the thing. Looking competent and serious and very much like my ice cream man was a helmeted pilot painted into a bubblelike vehicle on the top of the rocket, which would pop off, like a second stage, when the rocket attained the stupendous height of thirty or forty feet. I immediately lost the bubble craft with its painted astronaut. It shot off, just like it was supposed to, and never came down. I have to suppose that it's rusting in the branches of a tree somewhere, but I have a hazy memory of it simply shooting into the air and disappearing in a blink, hurtling up through the thin atmosphere toward deep space. Wasted money, my mother said.

Our third meeting was at the Palm Street Market, where I went to buy penny candy that was a nickel by then. I was thirteen, I suppose, or something near it, which would have made it early in the sixties. The clerk being busy, I had strayed over to the magazine shelves and found a copy of *Fate,* which I read for the saucer stories, and which, on that afternoon, was the excuse for my being close enough to the "men's" magazines to thumb through a couple while the clerk had his back turned. I had the *Fate* open to the account of Captain Hooton's discovery of an airship near Texarkana, and a copy of something called *Slick* or *Trick* or *Flick* propped open on the rack behind. I read the saucer article out of apologetic shame in between thumbing through the pages of photographs, as if my reading it would balance out the rest, but remembering nothing of what I read until, with a shock of horror that I can still recall as clearly as anything else in my life, I became aware that the ice cream man, the tin toy salesman, was standing behind me, reading over my shoulder.

What I read, very slowly and carefully as three fourths of my blood rose into my head, was Captain Hooton's contempt for airship design: "There was no bell or bell rope about the ship that I could discover, like I should think every well-regulated air locomotive should have." At the precise moment of my reading that sentence, the clerk's voice whacked out of the silence: "Hey, kid!" was what he said. I'd heard it before. It was a weirdly effective phrase and had such a freezing effect on me that Captain Hooten's bit of mechanical outrage has come along through the years with me uninvited, pegged into my memory by the manufactured shame of that single moment.

Both of us bought a copy of *Fate.* I *had* to, of course, although it cost me forty cents that I couldn't afford. I remember the ice cream man winking broadly at me there on the sidewalk, and me being deadly certain that I had become as transparent as a ghost fish. Everyone on Earth had been on to my little game with the magazine. I couldn't set foot in that market without a disguise for a solid five years. And then, blessedly, he was gone, off down the street, and me in the opposite direction. I stayed clear of the market for a couple of months and then discovered, passing on the sidewalk, that the witnessing clerk was gone, and that went a long way toward putting things right, although Captain Hooton, as I said, has stayed with me. In fact, I began from that day to think of the ice cream man as Captain Hooton, since I had no idea what his name was, and years later the name would prove strangely appropriate.

*   *   *

It was in the autumn, then, that I first met Jane on that November night in the plaza, and weeks later when I introduced her to him, to Captain Hooton. She said in her artistic way that he had a "good face," although she didn't mean to make any sort of moral judgment, and truthfully his face was almost inhumanly long and angular. She said this after the three of us had chatted for a moment and he had gone on his way. It was as if there were nothing much more she could say about him that made any difference at all, as if she were distracted.

I remember that it irritated me, although why it should have I don't know, except that he had already begun to mean something, to signify, as if our chance meetings over the years, if I could pluck them out of time and arrange them just so, would make a pattern.

"He dresses pretty awful, doesn't he?" That's what she said after he'd gone along and she could think of nothing more to say about his face.

I hadn't noticed, and I said so, being friendly about it.

"He's smelly. What was that, do you think?"

"Tobacco, I guess. I don't know. Pipe tobacco." She wasn't keen on tobacco, or liquor either. So I didn't put too fine a point on it because I didn't want to set her off, to have to defend his smoking a pipe. It was true that his coat could have used a cleaning, but that hadn't occurred to me, actually, until she mentioned it, wrinkling up her nose in that rabbit way of hers.

"I keep thinking that he's got a fish in his pocket."

I smiled at her, suddenly feeling as if I were betraying a friend.

"Well . . ." I said, trying to affect a dropping-the-subject tone.

She shuddered. "People get like that, especially old people. They forget to take baths and wash their hair."

I shrugged, pretending to think that she was merely trying to be amusing.

"He's not that old," I said. But she immediately agreed. That was the problem, wasn't it? You wouldn't think . . . She looked at my own hair very briefly and then set out down the sidewalk with me following and studying my shadow in the afternoon sun and keeping my hands away from my hair. It looked neat enough there in the shadow on the sidewalk, but I knew that shadows couldn't be trusted, and I was another five minutes worrying about it before something else happened, it doesn't matter what, and I forgot about my hair and my vanity.

Her own hair had a sort of flyaway look to it, but perfect, if you understand me, and it shone as if she'd given it the standard hundred strokes that morning. A dark-red ribbon held a random clutch of it behind her ear, and there was something in the ribbon and in the way she put her hand on my arm to call my attention to some house or other that made me think of anything but houses. She had a way of touching you, almost as if accidentally, like a cat sliding past your leg, rubbing against you, and arching just a little and then continuing on, having abandoned any interest in you. She stood too close, maybe, for comfort—although *comfort* is the wrong word because the sensation was almost ultimately comfortable—and all the while that we were standing there talking about the lines of the roof, I was conscious only of the static charge of her presence, her shoulder just grazing my arm, her hip brushing against my thigh, the heavy presence of her sex suddenly washing away whatever was on the surface of my mind and settling there musky and soft. There hasn't been another man in history more indifferent to the lines of a roof.

*   *   *

In the downtown circular plaza each Christmas, there was an enormous Santa Claus built from wire and twisted paper, lit from within by a spiral of pin lights, and at Halloween, beneath overcast skies and pending rain, there were parades of school-children dressed as witches and clowns and bed-sheet ghosts. Then in spring there was a May festival, with city dignitaries riding in convertible Edsels and waving to people sitting in lawn chairs along the boulevard. One year the parade was led by a tame ape followed by fezzed Shriners in Mr. Toad cars.

Twice during the two years that Jane studied art, while the town shrank for her and grew cramped, we watched the parade from a sidewalk table in front of Felix's Café, laughing at the ape and smiling at the solemn drumming of the marching bands. The second year one of the little cars caught fire and the parade fizzled out and waited while a half-dozen capering Shriners beat the fire out with their jackets. It was easy to laugh then, at the ape and the Edsels and the tiny cars, except that even then I suspected that her laughter was half cynical. Mine wasn't, and this difference between us troubled me.

In the summer there was a street fair, and the smoky aroma of sausages and beer and the sticky-sweet smell of cotton candy. We pushed through the milling crowds and sat for hours under an ancient tree in the plaza, watching the world revolve around us.

It seems now that I was always wary then that the world in its spinning might tumble me off, and there was something about the exposed roots of that tree that made you want to touch them, to sit among them just to see how immovable they were. But the world couldn't spin half fast enough for her. You'd have thought that if she could get a dozen paintings out of that fountain, then there would be enough, even in a provincial little town like this one, to amuse her forever.

Captain Hooton always seemed to be turning up. One year he put on a Santa costume and wandered through the shops startling children. The following year at Halloween he appeared out of the doorway of a disused shop, wearing a fright wig and carrying an enormous flashlight like a lighthouse beacon, on the lens of which was glued a witch cut out of black construction paper. He climbed into a sycamore tree in front of Watson's Drugs and shined the witch for a half hour onto the white stone facade of the bank, and then, refusing to come down unless he was made to, was finally led away by the police. Jane ought to have admired the trick with the flashlight, but she had by then developed a permanent dislike for him because, I think, he didn't seem to take her seriously, her or her paintings, and she took both of those things very seriously indeed, while pretending to care for almost nothing at all.

He ate pretty regularly for a time at Rudy's counter, at the drugstore. It was a place where milk shakes were still served in enormous metal cylinders and where shopkeepers sat on red Naugahyde and ate hot turkey sandwiches and mashed potatoes and talked platitudes and weather and sports, squinting and nodding. Captain Hooton wasn't much on conversation. He sat alone usually, smoking and wearing one of those caps that sports car enthusiasts wear, looking as if he were pondering something, breaking into silent laughter now and then as he watched the autumn rain fall and the red-brown sycamore leaves scattering along the street in the gusting breeze.

There was something awful about his skin—an odd color, perhaps, too pink and blue and never any hint of a beard, even in the afternoon.

A balding man from Fergy's television repair referred to him jokingly as Doctor Loomis, apparently the name of an alien visitor in a cheap, old science-fiction thriller. I chatted with him three or four times when Jane wasn't along, coming to think of him finally as a product of "the old school," which, as Dickens said, is no school that ever existed on Earth.

There were more sightings of things in the sky—almost always at night, and almost always they were described in slightly ludicrous terms by astonished citizens, as if each of them had mugged up those old issues of *Fate.* The things were egg-shaped, wingless, smooth silver; they beamed people up through spiraling doors and motored them around the galaxy and then dropped them off again, in a vacant lot or behind an apartment complex or bowling alley and with an inexplicable lapse of memory. The *City News* was full of it.

Once, at the height of the sightings, men in uniforms came from the East and the sightings mysteriously stopped. Something landed in the upper reaches of my avocado tree one night and glowed there. Next morning I found a cardboard milk carton smelling of chemicals, the inside stained the green of a sunlit ocean, lying in the leaves and humus below. It had little wings fastened with silver duct tape. The bottom of it had been cut out and replaced with a carved square of pumice, a bored-out carburetor jet glued into the center of it.

*   *   *

It happened that Captain Hooton lived on Pine Street by that time, and so did I. I rented half of a little bungalow and took walks in the evening when I wasn't with Jane. His house was deceptively large. From the street it seemed to be a narrow, gabled Victorian with a three-story turret in the right front corner, and with maybe a living room, parlor, and kitchen downstairs. Upstairs there might have been room for a pair of large bedrooms and a library midway up in the turret. There was a lot of split clinker brick mortared onto the front in an attempt to make the house look indefinably European, and shutters with shooting stars cut into them that had been added along the way. Old newspapers piled up regularly on the front porch and walk as if he were letting them ripen, and the brush-choked flower beds were so overgrown that none of the downstairs windows could have admitted any sunlight.

Jane seemed to see it as being a shame—the mess of weeds and brush, the cobbled-together house, the yellowing papers. Somehow I held out hope that it would strike her as—what?— original. Eccentric, maybe. At first I thought that they were too much alike in their eccentricities. I considered her root beer shoes and her costume jewelry and her very fashionable and practiced disregard for fashion and her perfectly disarranged hair, and it occurred to me that she was art, so to speak—artifice, theater. And although she talked about spontaneity, she was a marvel of regimentation and control, and never more so than when she was being spontaneous. The two of them couldn't have been more unalike.

He was vaguely alarming, though. You couldn't tell what he was thinking; his past and his future were misty and dim, giving you the sort of feeling you get on cheap haunted-house thrill rides at carnivals, where you're never quite sure what colorful, grimacing thing will leap out at you from behind a plywood partition.

I could see the rear of his house from my backyard, and from there it appeared far larger. It ran back across the deep lot and was a wonder of dormers, gables, and lean-to closets, all of it overshadowed by walnut trees and trumpet flower vines on sagging trellises and arbors. Underneath was a sprawling basement, which at night glowed with lamplight through aboveground transom windows. The muted ring of small hammers and the hum of lathes sounded from the cellar at unwholesomely late hours.

The double doors of his garage were fastened with a rusted iron lock as big as a man's hand, and he must have had a means by which to enter and leave the garage—and perhaps the house itself—without using any of the visible doors. I rarely saw him out and about. When I did, he sometimes seemed hardly to know me, as if distracted, his mind on mysteries.

Once, while I was out walking, I came across him spading up a strip of earth beneath his kitchen window, breaking the clods apart and pulling iron filings out of them with an enormous magnet. I recalled our distant meeting behind the ice cream truck, but by now he seemed to remember it only vaguely. I took him to be the sort of eccentric genius too caught up in his own meanderings to pay any attention to the mundane world.

He'd started a winter garden there along the side of his house, and a dozen loose heads of red-leaf lettuce grew in the half-shade of the eaves. We chatted amiably enough, about the weather, about gardens. He gave me a sidewise squint and asked if I'd seen any of the alleged "saucers" reported in the newspaper, and I said that I had, or at least that I had seen some saucer or another months ago. He nodded and frowned as if he'd rather hoped I hadn't, as if the two of us might have sneered at the notion of it together.

A spotted butterfly hovered over the lettuce, alighting now and then and finally settling in "to eat the lettuce alive," as he put it. He wouldn't stand for it, he said, and very quietly he plucked up a wire-mesh flyswatter that hung from a nail on the side porch, and he flailed away at the butterfly until the head of lettuce it had rested on was shredded. He seemed to think it was funny, particularly so because the butterfly itself had got entirely away, had fluttered off at the first sign of trouble. It was a joke, an irony, a metaphor of something that I didn't quite catch.

He gave me a paper sack full of black-eyed peas and disappeared into the house, asking after the "young lady" but not waiting for an answer, and then shoving back out through the door to tell me to return the sack when I was through with it, and then laughing and winking and closing the door, and winking again through the kitchen window so that it was impossible to say what, entirely, he meant by the display.

*   *   *

There wasn't much I could have told him about the "young lady." Much of what I might have said would already be a reminiscence. The thing that mattered, I suppose, was that she made me weak in the knees, but I couldn't say so. And she was entirely without that clinging, dependent nature that feeds a man's vanity at first but soon grows tiresome. Jane always talked as if she had places to go to, people to meet. There was something in the tone of her voice that made such talk sound like a warning, as if I weren't invited along, or weren't up to it, or were a momentary amusement, like the May parade, perhaps, and would have to suffice while she was stuck there in that little far-flung corner of the globe.

She wanted to travel to the Orient, to Paris. I wanted to travel, too. It turned out that her plans didn't exclude me. I would go along—quit work and go, just like that, spontaneously, wearing a beret and a knapsack. And that's just what I did, finally, although without the beret; I'm not the sort of a man who can wear a hat. I'm too likely to affect the carefree attitude and then regret the hat, or whatever it is I'm wearing, and then whatever it is I'm not wearing but should have. It's a world of regrets, isn't it? Jane didn't think so. She hadn't any regrets, and said so, and for a while I was foolish enough to admire her saying so. I don't believe that Captain Hooton would have understood her saying such a thing, let alone have admired it.

I brought around his paper sack, right enough, two days later, and he took it from me solemnly, nodding and frowning. At once he blew it up like a balloon—inflated it until it was almost spherical—and then, waving a finger in order to show me, I suppose, that I hadn't seen anything yet, he pulled a slip of silver ribbon out of his vest pocket, looped it around the bunched paper at the bottom, and tied it off. He lit a kitchen match with his fingernail and held it to the tails of the ribbon. Immediately the inflated sack began to glow and rocketed away through the curb trees like a blowfish, the ribbons trailing streams of blue sparks. It angled skyward in a rush and vanished.

I must have looked astonished, thinking of the milk carton beneath my tree. He pretended to smoke his pipe with his ear. Then he sighted along the stem as if it were a periscope, and made whirring and clicking sorts of submarine noises with his tongue. Then waggling his shoulders as if generally loosening his joints, he blew softly across the reeking pipe bowl, dispersing the smoke and making a sound uncannily like Peruvian panpipes. He was full of tricks. He suddenly looked very old—certainly above seventy. His hair, which must have been a transplant, grew in patterns like hedgerows, and in the sunlight that shone between the racing clouds, his skin was almost translucent, as if he were a laminated see-through illustration in a modern encyclopedia.

*   *   *

And so one evening late I knocked on the cellar window next to his kitchen door, then stood back on the dewy lawn and waited for him. He was working down there, tinkering with something; I could see his head wagging over the bench.

In a moment he opened the door, having come upstairs. He didn't seem at all surprised to see me skulking in the yard like that but waved me in impatiently as if he had been waiting for my arrival, maybe for years, and now I'd finally come and there was no time to waste.

The cellar was impossibly vast, stretching away room after room, a sort of labyrinth of low-ceilinged, concrete-floored rooms. I couldn't be certain of my bearings any longer, but it seemed that the rooms must have been dug beneath the driveway alongside his house as well as under the house itself—

maybe under the house next door; and once I allowed for such a thing, it occurred to me that his cellars might as easily stretch beneath my own house. I remembered nights when I had been awakened by noises, by strange creaks and clanks and rattles of the sort that startle you awake, and you listen, your heart going like sixty, while you tell yourself that it's the house "settling," but you don't believe it. And all this time it might have been him, muffled beneath the floor and perhaps a few feet of earth, tapping away at a workbench like a dwarf in his mine.

All of this filled my head when I stood on the edge of his stairs, breathing the musty cellar air. It was late, after all, and a couple of closets with lights casting the shadows of doorways and shelves might have accounted for the illusion of vast size. We wandered away through the clutter, with me in my astonishment only half-listening to him, and despite all the magical debris, what I remember most, like an inessential but vivid element in a dream, was his head ducking and ducking under low, rough-sawn ceiling joists that were almost black with age.

I have a confused recollection of partly built contrivances, some of them moving due to hidden, clockwork mechanisms, some of them sighing and gurgling, hooked up to water pipes curling out of the walls or to steam pipes running in copper arteries toward a boiler that I can't remember seeing but could hear sighing and wheezing somewhere nearby. There were pendulums and delicate hydraulic gizmos, and on the corner of one bench a gyroscope spun in a little depression, motivated, apparently, by nothing at all. The walls were strewn with charts and drawings and shelves of books, and once, when we bent through a doorway and into a room inhabited by the hovering, slowly rotating hologram of a space vehicle, we surprised a family of mice at work on the remains of a stale sandwich. What did they make, I wonder, of the ghost of the spacecraft? Had they tried to inhabit it, to build a nest in it? Would it have mattered to them that they were inhabiting a dream?

What did I make of it? *Here's Captain Hooton's airship,* I remember thinking. *Where's the bell rope?* But it wasn't his airship, not exactly; the ship itself was in an adjacent room.

The whole thing was a certainty in an instant—the lights in the sky, the odd debris beneath the avocado tree, even the weird pallor of his see-through skin. It had all been his doing all these years. That's no surprise, I suppose, when it's taken altogether like this. When all the details are compressed, the patterns are clear.

He had come from somewhere and was going back again. With the lumber of mechanical trash spread interminably across bench tops, and the cluttered walls and the mice, and him with his pipe and hat, he seemed so settled in, so permanent. And yet the continual tinkering and the lights on at all hours made it clear that he was on the edge of leaving—maybe in a week, maybe in the morning, maybe right now; that's what I thought as I stood there looking at the ship.

It was nearly spherical, with four curved appendages that were a hybrid of wings and legs and that held the craft up off the concrete floor. Circular hatches ringed the ship, each covered with lapped plates that looked as if they'd spiral open to expose a door or a glassed-over window. The metal of the thing was polished to the silver shine of a perfect mirror that stretched our reflections like taffy as I stood listening to him tell me how we were directly under the backyard, and how he would detonate a charge, and one foggy night the ship would sail up out of the ground in a rush of smoke and dirt and be gone, affording the city newspapers their last legitimate saucer story.

*   *   *

I didn't tell Jane about it. There were a lot of things I couldn't or wouldn't tell her. I wanted some little world of my own, which was removed from the world we had together, but which, of course, could be implied now and then for effect, but never revealed lest it seem to her to be amusing. One day soon the papers would be full of it anyway—the noise in the night, the scattered sightings of the heaven-bound craft, the backyard crater. There would be something then in being the only one who knew.

And he no doubt wasn't anxious that the spaceship became general knowledge. There was no law against it, strictly speaking, but if they'd jailed him for the trick with the flashlight and the paper witch, or rather for refusing to come down out of a tree, then who could say what they might do if they got wind of a flying saucer buried in a cellar?

Then there was the chance that I might be aboard. He was willing to take me along. We talked about it all that night, about the places I'd see and the people I'd meet—a completely different sort of crowd than Jane and I would run into in our European travels.

It was then, about two years after I'd met Jane, that I gave up the house on Pine Street and moved in with her. She was free of school at last and was in an expansive, generous mood, which I'll admit I took advantage of shamelessly, and when, in early July, she received money from home and bought a one-way ticket to Rome, I bought one, too, only mine was a round-trip ticket with a negotiable return date. That should have bothered her, my having doubts, but it didn't. She didn't remark on it at all. From the start it had been my business—another aspect of her modern attitude toward things, an attitude I could neither share nor condemn out loud.

*   *   *

The rest is inevitable. I returned and she didn't. Captain Hooton was gone, and there was a crater with scorched grass around the perimeter of it in the backyard of his empty house. I might have gone along with him. But I didn't, and what I get to keep is the memory of it all—the hologram, so to speak, of the ship and of faded desire, having given up the one for the already fading dream of the other.

There's the image in my mind of a card house built of picture postcards pulled from a rusting wire rack of memories—the sort of thing that even a mouse wouldn't live in, preferring something more permanent and substantial. But then, nothing is quite as solid as we'd like it to be, and the map of our lives, sketched out across our memory, is of a provincial little neighborhood, crisscrossed with regret and circumscribed by a couple of impassable roads and by splashes of bright color that have begun to fade even before we have them fixed in our memory.

◆ *Jane Brown Gillette* ◆

SINS AGAINST ANIMALS

In 1965, a few months before graduation, a man from the Job Corps penetrated to the upper floors of Main, the building at Vassar College where the seniors lived, a presumably impregnable niche. There he found corridors lined with astonished women who were more than willing to go teach remedial English, math, and social studies to high school dropouts: tender long-legged birds bred to serve, stuffed with good intentions and an amazing amount of useless knowledge, eager to fly the coop.

"Lambs to the slaughter," Diana teased her friend Eleanor. Diana was engaged to a student at Yale Law School and had been accepted as a graduate student in Art History. Her future was assured, but for a moment she felt inadequate, even wrong, because Eleanor, who had no plans at all, had graciously accepted the kind invitation of the man from the Job Corps.

To Diana's eyes, it was all too typical that Eleanor would fall for this offer. She was forever going off on blind dates with boys who managed to break her heart within six hours, or crying her eyes out over somebody's brother at Hamilton who hadn't asked her out for a second date, or mooning around for months over some jerk from home who had never asked her out in the first place. Still, the Job Corps was clearly a worthy cause, a chance to do some real good in the world, and so for a day or two Diana felt guilty that she was too cynical to give it a try.

For a year and a half, Eleanor taught reading and grammar to boys from the ghetto who were getting a second chance—or sometimes a third or a fourth. Eleanor's family—prosperous Quakers and liberal Democrats, who had named their eldest daughter after their heroine—approved of her job; the boys were by and large appreciative; and at first every small gain counted for a lot. Many of her Vassar friends who were working for the Job Corps seemed to fall in love with the other instructors; they were all the age for marriage. Eleanor fell in love with nobody and, faced with melioration on a day-to-day basis, rapidly grew disenchanted. At the end of the second year, she left the Job Corps to join a project in New York called Neighborhoods Inc.

Neighborhoods (cynics joked about capitalizing the second "h") was an offshoot of a drug-treatment program called Resurrection, which—flush with hopeful funding—used the relatively new technique of group dynamics to break down the old personality of the drug addict and replace it with a new, nonaddictive self. Although the group therapy was admittedly brutal, the reconstruction was complete, and—in theory—once the addict lost his old destructive defenses in Resurrection, he was free to use his new self to help others in Neighborhoods. And he would do so with the zeal of the converted, which burns by abandoned shame. In practice, Neighborhoods sent the ex-addict out with a conventional social worker to live on a deteriorating street in Harlem. Together, they would gradually rehabilitate the block. They would begin with their own building, for example, by organizing an entry way clean-up. Then they would bully the relevant city agency into picking up the trash or find pro-bono lawyers to sue the landlord. Next, gradually, they would urge people to form tenant associations to do more complex things like neighborhood patrols against drug-trafficking. Along the way, the ex-addict would gain confidence and self-esteem and recruit other addicts into the Resurrection treatment program.

The success of this venture depended heavily on the quality of the social workers, and these were in short supply, perhaps because Neighborhoods demanded that they undergo the same group therapy as the addicts. Soon Neighborhoods had to abandon the requirement of conventional degrees. Not with alarm, however, because what they really needed were not social workers, but responsible, well-educated, middle-class individuals—like Eleanor, who had, nevertheless, majored in sociology in college.

No one worried about what the self of a reconstructed social worker would amount to. For example, would it continue to be responsible, well-educated, and middle-class? Certainly if Eleanor ever considered this issue, she forgot it in the press of learning how to organize neighborhoods. For three months, she studied in the main Resurrection-/Neighborhoods office in the East Sixties; and then she had her group therapy session. Five quasi social workers and ten ex-addicts locked themselves in a room for 72 hours. No one was allowed to sleep; food was delivered through a crack in the door; the room filled with smoke as each social-worker type was criticized in turn. Nothing was off-limits. In Eleanor's case, everyone focused on her middle-class background and education, although a few raised their voices against her dowdy clothes, her gently whining voice, and what one ex-addict called her "bourgeois sentimental romantic attitude about fucking."

Eleanor had always accepted guilt readily, readily deferring to others, especially men. This attitude aided in her speedy self-destruction by the group. Her old personality was obliterated in tears of self-hatred, and after 12 hours of sleep she awoke feeling reborn and thoroughly capable of reforming the --th block of ---st Street.

With two ex-addicts, Fred and Goose, Eleanor moved into a run-down building, where, in spite of the '68 riots, they enjoyed a productive season. Both the entryway and the alley were cleaned up; a bake-sale earned more than a hundred dollars; an Anti-Rat Day was projected for the fall. And in July Eleanor fell in love with the star of the whole program, Addison, an ex-addict who'd worked his way up the ladder to become one of the directors of Resurrection itself.

Fred and Goose moved into the building next door, and Addison moved in with Eleanor, who walked around all day on the cusp of significance. Her life had achieved its form, and no matter what happened to her in the future, she knew she would always remember this summer: her work was important, this was true love! For the first and last time in her life, she reported her doings to the *Vassar Alumnae Magazine*.

2

Meanwhile, Diana finished her course work, passed her orals, started her dissertation, and made wedding plans. The two women seldom saw each other, but they occasionally talked on the phone and once in a great while exchanged letters. Even in sporadic context, they were important to each other. They came from the same small industrial city, a grimy ash heap dumped on the green Ohio countryside. Diana's family was Republican and Presbyterian instead of Democratic and Quaker, significant cause for all sorts of divergences of taste and opinion. Diana, the two women agreed, was in thrall by birth to a sterner vision of humanity; Eleanor, they likewise agreed, was free to improve the human lot. With so much symbolism at hand, they needed just a very little of each other's actual presence to feel themselves friends for life. Diana loved Eleanor's easily dejected idealism; Eleanor admired Diana's free-ranging skepticism. Diana felt a little more solid and real having Eleanor as a friend, while

Eleanor felt a little more savvy and energetic knowing that Diana admired her. Neither felt substantially more self-confident and less to blame, but—as they frequently pointed out to each other—there was nothing in either of their backgrounds that encouraged *those* feelings.

And so, it was not surprising that when the drug dealers murdered Addison in the entryway of the apartment building that Eleanor called Diana to come help her with his funeral.

Diana was so reluctant that it took her almost 24 hours to get herself onto the mid-morning train to New York. The bright sunlight on the dirty windows seemed to point a finger at the misfit who rode the rails outside the dawn-and-dusk structure of commuting. The air had the superfluous metallic aftertaste of vitamin pills with iron. It was early May, yet hot as midsummer, and the dirty plush upholstery of the seats reminded Diana that the last time she'd visited Eleanor she'd broken out in a rash.

During that visit, six months before, Diana had, at first, found Eleanor much the same as ever: a C+ student whose highest goal was to be a wife and mother; a nonjudgmental sort who still believed in good manners as the outward signs of virtue. Her slum apartment featured cloth napkins and a guest bedroom. Soon, however, Diana found herself wondering if Eleanor hadn't really changed, for as she spoke of her work on the block, of the people she'd met, of the injustice of their lives, she ignored Addison's antics, which in earlier times would have immediately reduced her to tears.

Eleanor hardly seemed to notice the glass Addison threw at her early in the evening, nor did she seem particularly upset when he called her a rich white bitch and then stormed out to spend the night with an old girl friend. Eleanor seemed not to notice his absence; she continued to talk about the embryonic tenants' association. Diana eventually concluded that radical political conviction had overtaken Eleanor's former emotional liberalism. The women sat there all night, smoking, drinking, Eleanor calmly going into some detail about the dynamics of the entry clean-up, Diana scratching and waiting nervously for Addison's return. She could only wonder at the political wisdom that promoted indifference to such manipulation, an invulnerable wisdom that made her feel utterly inadequate.

Now, on the train, Diana itched in anticipation, as if the dirty plush and the dusty glass were vehicles through which the spirit of history conveyed to a worn-out civilization the gospel of a revolution to come.

3

After the murder, Eleanor decided to stay with some friends on the Upper West Side. Mrs. Berke edited a glossy women's magazine, while Mr. Berke was legal counsel to an enormous labor union. Their living room was full of objects signifying culture, wealth, and beauty without in the least suggesting the traditional or the exclusive. Diana knew this was no mean feat, and Eleanor sat in the midst of it all, pale, calm, unusually confident. The Berkes were nowhere in sight. Addison hung in the air like the smile of the Cheshire Cat.

Eleanor explained what had happened: she had been lying in bed reading, waiting for Addison, who'd been out at some meeting, she wasn't sure where. About three in the morning she thought she heard him come in. Since their apartment was on the second floor at the front corner of the building she could hear things in the entryway—but only if she already more or less knew what she was listening to. She thought she'd heard him come in—didn't she hear her name?—but he didn't come up, and so, at first, she assumed she'd been mistaken. Then, after ten minutes or so, she decided that the sound she'd heard had most certainly been "Eleanor." And so she put on her robe and slippers and went down—even though she knew this was not a safe thing to do. The entryway was clean now, but it was still Harlem and three in the morning.

She found Addison dead. In his arm, a hypodermic needle bobbled up and down like the stinger of a gigantic mosquito. She pulled out the needle and tried to revive him. Apparently the murderer had waited in the shadowy entryway and stabbed Addison with the needle as he walked in the door. Unused as Addison now was to the drug, he had died almost immediately of an overdose with just time enough to shout out her name—and now she wasn't even sure about that.

Diana couldn't believe it. "It seems so risky. Don't you have to hit a vein or something?"

"Oh, it happens all the time," Eleanor assured her. "It's the way drug dealers handle people who interfere with business. Addison's death shows we're having some effect. He's a real hero."

Diana resigned herself to this interpretation. "What can I do to help?"

The funeral, it seemed, was already arranged. Addison had been raised by a great aunt, who had firm ideas, to which Eleanor—given the aunt's age, poverty, and race—felt bound to accede. Only innumerable details remained. Could Diana go back to the apartment and pack? Eleanor had no desire to live there anymore. If Diana could get everything ready tonight, then tomorrow, after the memorial service, the Mass, the burial, and the Resurrection/Neighborhoods party, Eleanor would move into a different apartment on a new block where—all that work gone to waste!—she could start over.

4

Two hours later, a taxi driver helped Diana carry some empty boxes to the entryway of Eleanor's apartment building. Outside, the streets of Harlem looked untouched by Neighborhoods. The entryway, however, showed signs of improvement. The 12 mailboxes were still broken; a dangling bare bulb still tenuously provided light; the elevator was still boarded against use—but the tile floor was clean and the walls recently painted. The scene of the crime, and yet it looked no different for that. Was this because places are impervious to the events that take place in them? or because murder is so common that its mark is indistinguishable to the eye? The art historian in Diana considered edifices temporal and sacred, modern and ancient, vernacular and monumental, ugly and beautiful: was any without its crime? Although no drug dealer had reason to murder her, she felt a certain relief when she had locked herself safely in Eleanor's apartment. The door had two deadbolts and a chain.

As she remembered from her other visit, Eleanor had taken pains to set a good example: lots of paint, new linoleum, curtains—yet it wouldn't take all that long to dismantle. Brick and board bookcases full of Eleanor's college paperbacks, the minimum number of dishes, a few old dresses in the closet. Eleanor's clothes could go into her suitcases; Addison's things, into a box for the aunt, who could also have the furniture, such as it was. Wouldn't it just be easier to open the door and commit the contents to the neighborhood? This wasn't her decision, however, so she started to pack.

Diana had actually cleared one closet before she noticed the cat. Orange and white, pink nose, calm yellow eyes, a young altered male: the quintessential Ohio cat. Back home, he would sleep in the window box among the geraniums. Here, he sat on top of the icebox, patiently waiting for cockroaches? rats? Investigation revealed a litter box in the shower (of all places!) and a box of Friskies. The cat ate with some eagerness and offered a purr to Diana's caressing hand. After eating, he took up a new position on top of the bookcase.

A call to Eleanor reached Mrs. Berke, who said that the sedative had taken effect and Eleanor was out cold for the night. She *had* mentioned something about getting rid of the cat. Mrs. Berke suggested the Animal Shelter.

Well, not tonight, thought Diana. She would call him Joe until

Eleanor told her his real name. The Animal Shelter. Wasn't that the same as the Pound?

The apartment was hot and airless, so Diana opened the window onto the fire escape. The window lacked a screen, and as she packed she began to hope that Joe would take this occasion to claim his freedom and his life. The Animal Shelter, indeed! But Joe hunkered down into the shape of a casserole, paws neatly folding in front of him, totally uninterested in escaping into Harlem: I am your responsibility, he seemed to say. She quickly grew used to his presence and, around eight, rather than venture out onto the streets, shared a can of tunafish with him. By midnight, when she was down to the odds and ends, she was sorry to see Joe accept self-determination and disappear through the window and down the fire escape, leaving her alone.

Alone. She thought about where she was and shut and locked the window. If Addison saw Eleanor as a rich white bitch, how would his neighbors see *her*? Would they be predisposed to mercy on individual grounds? What grounds could these possibly be? Perhaps she had sweated so much that her electrolytes were out of order, for suddenly she was sick with fear. She draped towels over the front windows to protect herself from prying eyes, checked the locks, and almost decided that she was safe, when her anxieties suddenly veered in Joe's direction.

He was out there on the streets, alone. Wouldn't he be lost? Freedom was all very well, but who would feed him and take him to the vet when he got sick? This is not reasonable, Diana told herself, but she couldn't keep herself from wondering if life were worth living for Joe on the streets. Who would love him? Where would he sleep at night? Prey to what dogs and ruthless children, large rats, faceless violence, random cars? How would he feel if he climbed back up the fire escape and found the window locked against him? She unlocked the window and raised it a cat-sized crack.

It was late. Leaving her clothes on, she turned out the light and lay down on the bare mattress, face to the fire escape. Anyone could climb up that fire escape, crawl in that window, murder her. Stomach churning with apprehension, afraid to open her eyes, Diana lay in the darkness until she couldn't bear it any longer. She jumped up and closed the window.

Then all she could imagine was Joe, his calm yellow eyes staring hopelessly in through the window, abandoned. . . . It was at least three in the morning. She must try to be sensible. She must get control of herself. She got up and opened the window. When her mother had had Diana's cat Snowball put to sleep—at the vet's, surely; not the Pound—she had told Diana that Snowball had gone to live in the country. Remembering this, Diana again felt betrayed and sick with helplessness and rage. She thought of the black man who would climb the fire escape, climb through the window, and stand above her bed, looking down on her in a long meditative moment of revenge and uttering a prayer to the hungry god, before he strangled her and dragged her twitching body to the bathtub where he set to work dismembering her and throwing gobbets of her body all over Harlem, like that argument—or was it a poem?—about the ceiling of the Sistine Chapel: divided up so that everyone could have an equal share, it amounted to less than a grain of salt. No matter how much they hated her, no matter how wrong she was, there wasn't enough to go around. No loaves and fishes, she, and so doomed to be inadequate.

When she woke up just before dawn, she found Joe in her arms like a teddy bear, his head on her shoulder, purring away with all the satisfaction of the prodigal returned. His fur was cold and slightly damp. After an adventure he'd come home to stay. Diana fell back to sleep without a care in the world. She did not bother to get up and close the window, for who in the world would climb through a window after her?

In the morning, she gave Joe the last can of tuna, cleaned out the icebox, assembled the garbage, and watched the rooms—stripped of their trappings—rejoin themselves to the slum that shimmered outside the windows. Joe ate his tunafish, used his pan, and took a prolonged and thorough bath, biting into the spaces between his clear pink toe-pads, chewing down a rough claw, and finally sharpening the whole set on the black and white striped, brown-puddled mattress. Shortly thereafter, Eleanor arrived with Mr. Berke, who loaded up his station wagon with Eleanor's belongings and drove off, leaving the women to deal with Joe, whose name turned out to be Brahms.

Brahms was a problem because he was Addison's cat. He slept on Addison's side of the bed. Addison had loved him. Eleanor had never taken to Brahms, nor he to her. Like Diana, she was not intrinsically fond of cats so that Siamese elegance or black and white wit was necessary to seize her fancy. Eleanor had asked Addison's great aunt to take Brahms, but she had refused, hinting at darker responsibilities. "You don't want him, do you?" Eleanor asked with a thoughtlessness that almost made Diana lose her temper.

"I'm going to Italy for a year! He's not my boyfriend's cat! Isn't there anybody at Resurrection who can take him? What about one of your *neighbors?* Look! why don't you send him home to Ohio? Your mother can always find room for a cat." Snowball went to live in the country; why not a real version of an old lie?

"He would always remind me of Addison."

"You really don't think you're going to forget him, do you?" Diana saw, nevertheless, that this was no time to press a point, and so the women took a taxi to the Animal Shelter, which looked unavoidably like a gigantic oven from which Joe/ Brahms had but a 72-hour reprieve. Handing him over, Diana couldn't bring herself to meet his eyes; even so she could feel his purr. A good animal, he made himself easy to dispose of, unlike Addison, who would require the next six hours to make his adieux.

Diana gave in: O.K., O.K., I'll come back. Even though I don't really like cats. You can stay in Ohio with *my* mother until I get back from Italy. Then you can live with me.

Finally she could look into his calm yellow eyes and prepare herself for the next ordeal.

5

At eleven, there was an open-casket viewing at the funeral home in the Bronx—round one for the grieving aunt, a wizened sorceress complete with turban and mumbling false teeth. She was accompanied by two small brown boys in little black suits and white shirts, whose overpowering resemblance to Addison spelled trouble. Diana dismissed them with "different mores," but she could tell that Eleanor was hurt as well as surprised.

A record player, hidden somewhere underneath the casket, played Vivaldi's Four Seasons over and over and over again as Addison contemplated eternity with smug pleasure, like the cat —Diana unavoidably thought—who had swallowed the canary. For a solid hour the bigwigs of Resurrection praised Addison to the skies. Under Diana's gaze, his expression turned to one of polite disbelief: this was me? You've got to be kidding! Eleanor sat in the front row by the aunt and the little boys, who laughed, squirmed, hit each other, and looked more like Addison by the minute.

At one o'clock, round two for the aunt, an hour-long Mass echoed through a Catholic church half a block from the funeral home. The church dwarfed both coffin and mourners, who had already shrunk in number, about half going off in search of lunch. Had Addison been christened and confirmed here? Certainly none of the mourners were Catholics—not even the aunt, it would seem for she neither rose nor kneeled nor took Communion but sat solidly at Eleanor's side, while the little boys took a well-deserved nap. Diana herself struggled to stay awake. The priest called Addison Edison.

At two-thirty they left the church for the cemetery, which was far away on Long Island—round three for the aunt.

Eleanor climbed into a silver gray limousine directly behind the hearse. Since she was then joined by the aunt and the boys, Diana abruptly ducked into the next limo, and so near was her escape that it took a few moments before she could calm down and focus on the other passengers, five more or less reformed addicts, one of whom had the shakes. By the time she took them in—braids, elf locks, turbans, beads, dashikis, bells, caftans, and eyes incapable of meeting hers—the cortege was off and they were stuck with each other.

No one uttered a sound, and Diana was struck with the wild impulse to apologize for her shoes. These were plain white pumps with two-inch heels—and Memorial Day was a full three weeks away! They were the only shoes she had that went with the only dress she owned that was long enough to wear to a funeral; everything else was mini. Still, she knew they were wrong; her feet looked enormous; and their whiteness kept catching her eye, and she also wanted to apologize for drinking spirits before dinner unmixed with wine or juice, for wearing nylon underwear, for eating egg salad in restaurants, for loving a man with a mustache, for smoking in public, for chewing gum even in private, for never really loving anyone or anything, for doing all these things her mother had told her never to do, but even though she wished to apologize, she had actually done none of these things, except wear white shoes and fail to love, and so, instead of apologizing, she fell asleep.

As she slept she heard the men talk about what a hero Addison was. She heard because of the translating power of the unconscious, for when she woke up, she couldn't understand a word they were saying; it was English, but not to her ear. Accustomed to her presence, they talked on among themselves, while she stared out the window at a cemetery so big it threatened to swallow up everyone in the world.

Traffic was heavy. Their cortege passed four funerals, clusters of cars waiting at the side of the road. Two other funerals passed in the opposite direction, going home for the night, funerals no longer. A dark green army truck whizzed past and pulled off to the side of the road. A group of soldiers jumped out, guns at the ready, and ran off toward a hidden ceremony, the bugle player trotting along behind.

Ten minutes later, their cortege pulled over to the side of the road. At the grave, a short walk away, Eleanor stood with Addison's aunt and the little boys, who stood still for once, quiet in a daze. The ex-addicts and social-worker types arranged themselves in twos and threes. Struck by the sight of the open grave, no one talked.

Diana stood alone on the edge of the mourners and watched the green truck drive up. The troops jumped out and charged up to the grave, late as usual, behind in their work, the bugler still lagging in the rear, a fat boy about 20. The soldiers were all young, with smooth blank faces that suggested boredom. Were they thinking of the battles they were missing and the heroes who were falling in them? They did not look at the bizarre crowd that faced them across the grave: voodoo spirits, the ghosts of ancient tribesmen. Their eyes stuck to the middle distance as the priest rushed through his lines, calling down mercy on Addison, whom he continued to call Edison. The soldiers fired their salute, listened to the final Taps—how many times today?—then ran back to the truck. If they only hurried, might they not catch up with that elusive war halfway around the world?

Eleanor threw a single red rose in the grave, and Diana leaped forward to claim her firmly by the elbow. She steered her back to the gray limo, told the driver to make it snappy, and left the aunt and children to the priest. Never had she been so hungry in her life.

6

At first the women sat in apprehensive silence as the chauffeur
tried to make his way through the worst of rush hour with
something passing for speed. At last, Diana told him to slow
down, or to feel all right about going so slowly, for they were in
fact going almost nowhere, only sitting in the middle of six
lanes of cars surrounded by acres of houses that looked like
more cars.

When Eleanor said, in a perfectly serious tone, "Wasn't that
beautiful?" Diana raised the window that cut them off from the
driver and waited in silence until Eleanor came to her senses.
"Actually, I suppose it was pretty ridiculous." As yellow as the
flowers in her dress, Eleanor no longer looked like her old self.

"Well, it's hard to stage a funeral that pleases everyone. You
did a great job, given the aunt and all. We're probably the only
ones who think it was ridiculous. Everybody else probably
thinks it was the perfect funeral for a hero. But, *really*, Eleanor—"

"Weren't the soldiers a stitch?"

"Does the cemetery just throw them in free?"

"Oh, no. They're the real thing. Addison's aunt wants to get
benefits for the children. I guess she thought a military funeral
would establish her claims. He might have been in the Army,
but I'm sure he never actually fought in anything. And he
wasn't a Catholic either. And the little boys don't even have the
same mother. I didn't know about them. About the children. I
knew about the other women."

"Maybe she's counting on help from the Church?"

"The whole thing was a fraud." Eleanor began to cry again.

In disgust the chauffeur turned off the highway. Now around
them endlessly stretched something that was not Manhattan.
"Now, now. Symbols are everything. Maybe it's best to think of

the whole thing as a sign of good intentions. Addison probably
believed in something, and if he didn't, he probably wished he
did." Twaddle, Diana thought, a language I speak fluently.
"And as for his not being a real soldier, he's a real hero. You
should have heard the men in my car."

"I can't go to this party."

"Thank God; let's not. Why don't—"

"He wasn't murdered. He killed himself. Maybe by accident.
Maybe not. We had a fight. I told him I was tired of his stunts,
tired of him. I wanted him to move out. I told him I'd only put
up with him for so long because he loved me more than I loved
him and I've never had that happen before. He started crying.
He said he was a failure at everything. He said he might just as
well go back on drugs. I told him I was tired of his threats. He
stormed out, and I went to bed. I was so relieved to get rid of
him and his . . . his *stupidity* that I felt I could sleep forever. My
whole life, all I've wanted was to be loved, and he even made
me tired of that."

"How did he die?"

"The rest of what I said was more or less true. I heard him in
the entryway. He woke me up shouting my name. I think. Eleanor, or Dirty Whore. Who knows? Anyway, when I got downstairs he was dead. He'd taken an overdose, I don't think on
purpose. I think it was just to say, see what you made me do. I
don't know. I pulled out the needle and tried to get as many of
my fingerprints on it as possible."

"Stop the car!" Diana demanded. They were probably somewhere in Brooklyn, not that it mattered. They were trapped
somewhere in an endless city, and this corner was as good as
any. In fact, after they got out, they discovered both a Chinese
restaurant and a movie theater.

They decided to see the movie first to calm down. Science
fiction, Diana had trouble getting into it: Charleton Heston
crashes his space ship onto a planet that turns out to be run by
apes; not a thoroughly bad lot, they view the subjected human

species with a mixture of pity and disgust. About the time, Diana understood that this was New York City after the nuclear holocaust, she also noticed that the apes bore a strong facial resemblance to the ex-addicts in the limo. It was Eleanor, however, who actually said, "Is this movie as racist as I think it is?"

"I don't know," answered Diana, "but it's certainly anti-simian. Perhaps we should leave?"

Next door, at the Chinese restaurant, the menu was elaborate, and the women tried all sorts of strange things, for in the long run what did they have to lose? After two bottles of a wine that tasted of moth balls, Eleanor told Diana that Addison had been wonderful in bed; he'd made her feel that she was the most exciting person in the world. Maybe she *had* loved him. Maybe he *had* been murdered— No, she didn't love him. He was just a manipulator—always trying to protect a self he didn't have. He bored her. He betrayed her. All the time. How did he have the nerve to bore her *and* betray her? She didn't love him, and, exciting or not, she'd gotten tired of having him love her.

Diana felt relieved. No matter who loved whom, it was just love after all. Not politics, not a new self, just bourgeois sentimental romantic love. If group dynamics had eradicated Eleanor's personality, Nature had issued a near-perfect duplicate. Diana felt so much better about her friend that she didn't allow herself the additional luxury of self-disgust. So *she* had never loved anyone. So what? Instead she suggested that they borrow Mr. Berke's station wagon and drive home.

Eleanor agreed, and before dawn the next morning, they set out, Diana so elated that she drove all the way, back to Ohio, where the city didn't go on forever, but stopped at the edge of the country so that you had to drive out through fields of soybeans and corn and hogs just to get to the country club; back to Ohio, where Addison's ghost could be laid to rest in no time.

7

Eighteen years later, Eleanor is the head of a progressive school in Chicago. She has had many lovers, but none whom she felt like marrying, although last year she adopted an orphan from El Salvador and is now thinking that the divorced head of a local boys' school might do as a stepfather. He is wild about her, passion's eternal response to indifference. Eleanor has fallen into a bad habit.

She thinks about Addison from time to time and wonders what would have happened if she'd managed to love him more than he loved her. Would she have gone on loving all her life? But she hadn't. And what if he had been murdered? Would she have been frightened enough to marry a dull accountant as soon as possible after his death? Would she have had three children just to be safe? Would she still lie awake at night feeling relieved that Addison died—and feeling guilty that she feels relieved?

Diana is divorced and no longer close to Eleanor—time and distance have intervened—and she never thinks of Addison if she remembers him at all. And yet—as she is fond of telling her students—there is a God in Heaven, and He is a just God, and so Diana has terrible nightmares every year in the late spring, a time of year that is very hard for animals. It is worse than early spring when nameless eggs splash, unidentifiable, on the sidewalk. The young are just as vulnerable in the late spring, but by then everyone has gotten to know one another.

A little starling trembles on the edge of his nest and breaks his neck when he hits the concrete. His brother lands back down, beak upwards. The old Siamese cat remembers better days and eats them both while entertaining the fantasy that he has actually hunted them down. He enjoyed watching the nest

from the bedroom window, and all day he feels vaguely dissat-
isfied: something is coming; what is it?

Paths cross in troubling ways. A mother duck leads her brood
across a major thoroughfare in rush hour, heading toward the
nearest body of water. She is hit by a taxi, but loses only one
duckling and a wing. Mother squirrels dash across the traffic,
fetching hidden nuts to their babies in the nest. One is hit in the
hindquarters but drags herself across the rest of the street and
disappears into the bushes. Is it for the best if she makes it back
to the nest? A raccoon lies twitching in the road until a carful of
teenagers swerves to hit the body. Blood spurts, parts scatter,
crows gather, raccoon flattens. Soon there is only a hairy pelt;
then, only a grease spot.

Diana dreams the cat dream and wakes up screaming from
something she can't remember. A grin forgives her, fades away
into the hanging fern at the window, not a cat at all. The lights
in the bedrooms of the neighboring apartment houses accuse
her of betrayal and breach of trust. She sits there in bed, exhausted and weeping, sweating, shaking, trying her best to remember what it is she has forgotten to do.

◆ *Julie Schumacher* ◆

THE PRIVATE LIFE OF ROBERT SCHUMANN

Before Mr. Zinn came to teach us music, we were bored every Wednesday and Friday afternoon. We'd had to study with a woman named Miss Fox, who scratched herself with a pointer, and who died of a heart attack one day in the coatroom, clutching the sleeves of a dozen jackets in her arms. With Miss Fox we'd had to learn "This Land Is Your Land" and the national anthem on two different instruments: we had a choice of the autoharp, the recorder, the triangle, and a pair of blocks. The blocks had sandpaper stapled to their sides. If you couldn't play you had to sing, so most of us banged and strummed away, while Miss Fox counted time at the front of the room, her worn heart pounding like a tired drum.

We had one week free of music after she died, and then the district hired Mr. Zinn. He was only the third male teacher in the middle school, and he didn't look like Mr. Hickman, who taught phys. ed., or like Mr. Vandeveer, who wore a suit and had a white goatee. Mr. Zinn was young: he had short, wavy black hair and sideburns, and watery eyes that protruded farther than they should. They were round like the eyes of a lizard or a frog.

The first day back we noticed instantly that the autoharps were gone. The recorders and triangles and blocks were missing too; the music table held only a record player and an enormous pile of books.

"Sit," Mr. Zinn said. You'd think he was talking to a dog, but we heard nothing cruel in his voice, so we sat down. On the board we saw his name, Francis J. Zinn, and the date, March 3. "How many of you know anything about music?" No one raised a hand. "That's what I expected," he said. "That's why you aren't going to play. There's no use trying to play an instrument if you don't know anything about music's *source,* its fountainhead. Who's been to Europe?"

Few of us had left Delaware, except for occasional trips to the Jersey shore.

"To understand music," Mr. Zinn said, raising himself on tiptoe and slowly lowering himself back down, "you need to understand Vienna, Leipzig, Schiller. Who knows what I mean by *strophic* and *durchkomponiert?"*

No one spoke, and Mr. Zinn began to fill the board with words. We learned that Vienna crossed the Danube like a bridge, that Beethoven went deaf, and that almost everyone related to Johann Sebastian Bach had the same first name. By the end of class we still hadn't said a thing. Mr. Zinn turned to Valerie Kenny. "Tell me something about music that you'd like to know."

Of the twenty-one kids in the class, probably twenty of us would have been stumped for what to say. I would have tried for something correct, because that's what I do. But Valerie was strange.

"I'd like to know if you knew Miss Fox."

"We were acquaintances," Mr. Zinn said.

"Were you sad when she died?" Valerie was pale and thin and feverish, and we made fun of her for the veins that shone through her skin. We didn't yet understand that she was pretty: she had long tangled hair the color of almonds, a reddish mouth, and fingertips that glowed.

"That's an unusual question." Mr. Zinn folded his arms across his chest in a gesture that seemed borrowed from a book. "I suppose I'd have to say that I was. Yes, I was sad. Any other questions?"

Lois and Chuckie and I were laughing at the back of the room. "I'd like to know if Valerie's retarded," Lois said.

Mr. Zinn blushed. We'd never seen a grown man blush, the color rising up his neck like juice in a glass, and blooming when it reached the level of his ears. "Thank you," he said. Clearly, he'd never taught school before.

                    *   *   *

I knew Mr. Zinn already, because he directed our choir at church. Not because he was Methodist, my mother explained, but because he earned money from the service every week. Whenever I dropped a dime in the collection tray, I imagined it going straight to Mr. Zinn.

Our church, as vast as a cavern, was left from the time when the city wasn't a slum, when it held white doctors and their families instead of the poor. Now the church was seldom filled, but it was still white, the stubborn doctors and their wives driving in from the suburbs to spend an hour beneath the massive gold-leaf dome and think of God. They could *believe* more easily in the presence of matching marble fonts and leaded glass, a hundred pipes for the organ, an immaculate burgundy carpet, and wooden doors that two men together had to push to admit the sun. The back of the church held a balcony, the front a gigantic stained-glass window showing Jesus, hands tipped out as if he'd heard of crucifixion, surrounded by children twice my size, and enormous lambs.

I was in the confirmation class that spring. We had to study

the parable of the good Samaritan and sing in front of the congregation in a special program at the end of the year. Methodists
—the ones I knew—loved to sing. They tapped their feet impatiently through the sermon, browsed the hymnal during
prayers, and sang *Amen* in twelve-part harmony as if God himself directed from the floor. My lack of enthusiasm for hymns
was a family trial. My mother would push the hymnal toward
me, point to the verse (we sang them all), and sing in a voice as
high and perfect as a dream. I had a scratchy alto voice that
sometimes buzzed. It was always lost between octaves and I
used it sparingly, whispering along with the choir on refrains.

Every Sunday for half an hour the confirmation class practiced two short hymns: "O for a Thousand Tongues" and something about sheep that we sang as "mutton" just for fun. Mr.
Zinn directed us with an atheist's determination. We hummed
with our mouths half open, snoring the words, while he blinked
and pressed his lips together, as if struggling to overcome with
his own effort our lack of it. On especially bad days he'd set
down his baton, run a hand through his wavy hair, and approach the line. "Keep singing," he'd say, and we'd try another
verse while he drew near, his red tie flapping over his shoulder.
He'd start in the second row and walk past each of us, head bent
low as if in prayer, to find out who was singing out of tune.
Sometimes he'd pause at a single mouth for quite a while, coming so close to our lips with his well-scrubbed ear that we
couldn't sing above a whisper, afraid of damaging the parts that
lay within. We didn't know where to look when he hovered
close: breathe, and his inner ear was moist; sniff, and the hair at
his sideburns brushed your nose. I dreamed of shrinking to the
size of a crumb and climbing in, exploring the hammer, anvil,
stirrup, and shell: it was pink and barren there, and my voice,
when I let it go, spun cascading through the arcs and tunnels,
sweet and clear.

*   *   *

The autoharps and the recorders never reappeared. By the second week we were building instruments of our own. He called it "Musicshop": we made banjos from oatmeal boxes and rubber bands, whistles from pens, drums from aluminum cans and Playtex gloves. While we worked, Mr. Zinn played records and told us stories about the music we listened to.

"Schumann was a true romantic," he explained. "He liked to read Byron. He was Schubert's successor as the master of the German *Lied*."

"That's World War Two," Chuckie said. He was building a flute. He took it home every few nights and got his father to fix it up with a welding torch.

I was working with Lois, who had asked me to be her partner because she wasn't capable of doing anything alone. "Forget it," I said, when I looked up from my plans and saw her bushy yellow hair, the constellation of freckles on her skin.

"What do you mean, forget it? You and me are building a trumpet. Just like this." She showed me a wrinkled magazine picture of a black man playing an instrument with at least a hundred metal parts.

I looked at the picture of the trumpet and then at Lois. "What do we make it from?" I asked. I'd finally decided to build a xylophone with sticks.

"I've got these." She showed me a plastic bag full of cardboard toilet rolls and mismatched copper wire. "Once we're done we can paint it gold."

I didn't ask her how she expected it to sound. Lois got mad fairly easily, and I didn't want her yelling at me in class. That's how our friendship worked: when she wanted something from me, I always said yes; when I wanted something back, Lois said she wasn't sure. I admired her for her confidence and style.

*   *   *

Mr. Zinn liked to sing during class. He paced the room with his hands carving gestures in the air: *"Nun hast du mir den ersten Schmerz getan. . . ."* He had a beautiful tenor voice; when he took a breath and spread his hands, tilting back his head so the veins in his neck stood out like string, we knew he imagined himself in another place and time, dressed in leotards and a blouse on a moonlit stage.

He rarely looked at our projects. He spent most of his time filling the board with scales and notes we couldn't read, or brooding by the window at the back of the room. He smelled of chalk dust and shampoo, and we learned to pinpoint his location by his odor as he paced between the coatroom and the window. We craved his recognition and his words. When he did stop to check the progress of our work, throwing his tie over his shoulder as he squatted down, we had the impression he was studying our lives, that he held our souls, and not a cigar box or a hammer, in his hands. He didn't treat us the way the other teachers did; I wondered if he realized we were young, or if he even understood what children were.

"The world is full of mediocrity," he said, sometimes to himself and sometimes to us. "Nothing is worse. Failing is better than being simply good at what you do." He picked up Chuckie's flute. "Failure's a virtue, next to undistinguished skill."

"Practice makes perfect," Chuckie said.

"No, unfortunately, it doesn't. Practice breeds *competence*, not perfection." Mr. Zinn examined the flute, by far the best-looking instrument in class. "Look at Schubert. He wrote symphonies, some of his best, at the age of eighteen. He suffered depressions all his life, but in a single year he wrote almost a hundred and fifty songs. He died of typhoid at thirty-one, a physical wreck. He was utterly ruined."

"It's just a saying," Chuckie said.

"Perfection comes from genius, or from God." Mr. Zinn turned to me. "Doesn't it, Jane?" It was the first time he'd singled me out. I had glue on the tips of my fingers, shreds of cardboard in my teeth. I wanted desperately to say something clever and uplifting, something that would cause him to bring up my name in the teachers' lounge.

"Yeah, I guess," I said, smiling so that he would know I understood my limitations, that if I was dumb it was through no fault of my own.

Mr. Zinn put the flute on the desk. "What are you smiling at?" he asked.

"Great move," Lois said, when he walked away.

*   *   *

We noticed the ring on Valerie's hand at the end of March. Lois and I sat together in science class, with our desks pushed close so that she could cheat, and when she kicked me, I looked up and saw Valerie rubbing the stone on her dress to make it shine. It was a dark-green gem in a wad of gold, with a square insignia on either side. It was much too big for her finger; it slid up and down over her knuckle, as bright as chrome.

"Where'd you get it?" Lois asked, poking Valerie in the neck with a felt-tip pen.

"Don't, you'll stain me." Valerie lifted her hair and revealed the ink. Her neck was petite, a perfect stem. The ring was visible through the woods of her tangled hair.

"That's just a school ring," Chuckie said. "Everyone buys one when they graduate, that's all."

"Where'd you get it?" Lois asked again. She wasn't whispering anymore, and Mrs. Hardimer, the teacher, gave us a look.

"It's probably her dad's," Chuckie said.

We tried to pretend we didn't care, but Lois couldn't let a problem go unsolved. During gym we trapped Valerie in the bathroom and asked again. She was using the middle stall, so we stood on the toilet seats on either side and leaned over the top. "Tell us whose," Lois said.

Valerie let the top of her gym suit fall, and we saw her chest, as smooth and flat and white as ours. She didn't cover herself with her arms as we would have done.

"We're going to start spitting when I count to two." Lois draped an arm across the door to block escape.

Valerie flashed the ring. The stone was as green as a parrot's eye. "Okay," she said, "it's Mr. Zinn's. He gave it to me Friday afternoon."

"He didn't *give* it to you," Lois said.

Valerie shrugged and pulled up her gym suit, showing the name tag with her name embroidered upside down.

"He probably just let you see it. Friday you'll have to give it back."

"I don't think so." Valerie sat down on the toilet, fully dressed. When we looked down at her from above, she seemed tiny and pure.

"Look how small," I said to Lois. But Lois was running through the double doors, racing with the other kids outside.

*   *   *

He didn't ask for it back on Friday, even though Valerie wore it around her neck on a silver chain.

"We aren't positive it's his," I said to Lois after school. We were riding bikes in the parking lot between the teachers' cars.

"Are you saying Valerie's a liar?"

I came around the side of a VW bus; we were face to face. "Maybe not on purpose. I mean, not like you or me." I looked at the gap between Lois's teeth, big enough for a coin. "Maybe she wishes it was his. Maybe she has a crush on Mr. Zinn."

"That's disgusting." Lois made a narrow passage by a Plymouth, scraping the yellow paint with her handlebar.

"Careful," I said, and she kicked a dent in one of the hubcaps with her shoe.

"We have two more years of this place, and I think it stinks.

I'm going to be a rifle girl in high school." She put her kickstand
down and twirled an imaginary rifle, taking aim.

"You don't get to shoot," I said. "Those rifles probably aren't
real."

"Nothing's real." She pulled the trigger. "Not even you." We
rode the long way home through the empty lots, bruising our
tires on tree roots and jagged stones. A block from our neighborhood Lois stopped. "Here's where Valerie lives," she said. "I
came here on Halloween last year." She pointed to a house that
wasn't like any of the rest. It didn't have shutters or a sidewalk
or a porch or a basketball court. It looked like a pile of wooden
boxes stacked on top of each other so that some of them jutted
out. The yard was overgrown with raspberry bushes and weeds.

Lois wanted to spy on Valerie through the first-floor windows, so we parked our bikes and crept through the neighbors'
yard to station ourselves in the brush at the side of the house.
As soon as we took our positions, Valerie's mother, Mrs. Kenny,
appeared with a folding chair and a sunhat and a camera, turning the lens on us where we stood.

"I thought I'd get a look at who was breaking into the house,"
she said, focusing on our hands on the windowsill. Seeing Mrs.
Kenny was always scary: she dressed like us, in pants and
T-shirts, with her hair in a ponytail or a braid, while all the
other mothers dressed in skirts. At one of the parents' days at
school she showed up with a paintbrush in her jeans and her
hair full of dirt. She was disconcerting—she made us feel as if
we might just get larger instead of older when we grew up.

"We were looking for Valerie," Lois said.

"Oh, I see." Mrs. Kenny nodded. "Did you try the door?"

"We thought it was stuck."

"Try it again," Mrs. Kenny said. "I'll watch from here. You
can turn the handle and go right in."

We traipsed to the door like zombies.

"Second left," Mrs. Kenny called, and we went inside.

Valerie sat on the bed in her room, holding a wooden box

between her knees. "I've told my mom not to do that," she said. "She hijacks kids my age and sends them in."

"Your mom is cracked," Lois said. She looked at the box.

"No, but she thinks I ought to have visitors," Valerie said. She lifted the lid and we saw the folded squares of paper, as tempting as cream. "Do you want to know what I have in here?"

"It doesn't matter," Lois said. "We don't really care."

"I'm not supposed to show you." Valerie chose a note from the top, easing it open fold by fold. "Do you want to see?" We craned our necks as she smoothed the paper against her thigh. "This one's the first."

It was a drawing in black. It showed a flute with a person's face where the mouthpiece was. The eyes were closed, and around the head was a mass of hair.

"Where'd you get it?" Lois asked.

"Here's the next." Valerie unfolded another square. The second was a drawing of a harp, like the prow of a ship, but again with a face and hair. It was drawn very lightly, the eyes of the harp half closed and the mouth half open in a smile. She showed us a violin, a guitar, a drum, and several instruments we'd never seen. All had the same dreamy eyes and tangled hair, and not a word appeared on any page.

"Mr. Zinn gave you these," I said. I recognized the paper from his desk.

Valerie looked pleased, and some of the pallor disappeared from her face and arms. "That's what I thought." She folded the notes and stashed the box in her underwear drawer. I saw the ring still dangling from its chain around her neck. "I'm taking lessons. I'm learning to play the piano after school."

"This is stupid," Lois said. "You don't know they're from him."

Valerie smiled, showing her gums. "At first I found them in my desk. But the last one I found in my jacket pocket, so he must have put it there during lunch."

"Still, you don't *know*," Lois said. "You aren't sure."

"He's going to teach me about the composers. Private things. He says I remind him of Clara Schumann."

"You don't even brush your hair," Lois said.

"He called me Clara once," Valerie said, not even listening anymore. When we left, she thanked us for coming. "It makes my mother happy," she explained.

*   *   *

That night at dinner I wanted to talk. I had something to say.

"What," my mother said. She finally put down her knife and fork. "What's so important that you have to interrupt?"

I felt the weight of what I knew on the back of my tongue. I had all of it there: Valerie was getting notes from the teacher, we never played music in music class, and on Sundays Mr. Zinn was a different man. I had all of the knowledge ready, and felt certain that if I phrased it right it would be of interest to anyone. But when my mother and father turned to me, I forgot which part came first; I couldn't remember how it all made sense, the way I'd figured it out before.

"I'm not going to eat these carrots," I said. "They stink." My parents ignored me and went on talking, as if I were someone else's child or had never been born.

*   *   *

Lois ignored me too. Something was lost: she refused to answer the phone at her parents' house, and at school she sat by herself at a broken desk. When I tore our trumpet into shreds, letting the cardboard glide and settle in the trash, she didn't care.

Though she wouldn't talk to me anymore, she sent two notes. The first was from the library encyclopedia. I knew it was from Lois because of the smudgy fingerprints and the fact that the page was torn out of the book. Under the heading "Robert Schumann" was a blurb about Clara Wieck: the name was underlined in blue. It said that Clara was Schumann's wife, that she was the daughter of Schumann's teacher, and that Schumann had met her when he was eighteen and she was nine. The difference in ages, it said, didn't matter to the two, who finally married, despite objections, when Clara turned twenty-one.

The second note Lois wrote herself. "Everything makes me sick. That includes you." I found it in my jacket pocket after school.

I blamed Mr. Zinn for everything that went wrong. Now when I sang in his ear in church, I thought of Catholics, the way they whispered through a wall to a waiting priest. I thought about humming softly in his hair, so softly that he'd put his ear against my mouth. I thought of whispering in that pink and marbled maze, *I've seen the notes. You told her not to show us but she did.* But I sang "O for a Thousand Tongues" and waited for the opportunity to speak.

Chuckie said it wasn't possible—no one Valerie's age had a boyfriend half that old. "He must be thirty or forty," Chuckie said. "You guys are nuts. Is that what you've been fighting about all this time?"

We were riding bikes at the top of the block; Lois was trying to jab a stick through the spokes of our wheels. "You wait," she said. "Just wait one minute or two."

"I've got to go in and take a bath," Chuckie said, but he didn't go. Lois had called both of us on the phone and told us to meet at the top of the hill, at the dead end over the highway that we weren't allowed to cross. It was seven o'clock, and the shadows of our bikes had thinned and gone. We circled a few more times, listening to a pair of beagles down the block, and then Lois braked. We saw Valerie and Mr. Zinn in a light-blue Ford on the highway. The car slowed down on the opposite shoulder, and from the embankment we saw only their arms and legs beneath the roof: Mr. Zinn was wearing a sweatshirt, not a tie, but Chuckie recognized his watch. We saw him reach across

Valerie's lap and open the door. When she got out, he pulled away, without waiting to see where she'd go.

"Hey," Chuckie yelled, and Valerie looked up. The air was thick with mosquitoes and lightning bugs, and we seemed to be looking at Valerie through a screen. She made a dash across two lanes to the yellow line and stood between streams of traffic, shifting from one foot to the other, small and pale. When she finally crossed the other lanes and reached the bank, pulling on reeds as she clambered up, each of us extended a hand to help her climb.

Valerie continued on her own. Her knee socks were balled around her ankles and her sweater was buttoned wrong. She reached the top and brushed herself off and immediately started down the street.

"Were you at school all that time?" Chuckie asked. We began circling on our bikes.

"I had my music lesson." She walked with tiny shuffling steps to avoid our tires.

"Your lesson's on Tuesday," Lois said. "From four to five." We expected Valerie to cry. We needed her to: her tears would tell us who was right and who was not, they would reconfirm our places in the world.

"He isn't a boyfriend," I said, "or a friend. If it was me, I'd make him drive me to the door."

"It wouldn't *be* you," Valerie said, not angrily but as if stating a simple fact. We stood in the darkness of the trees for a little while.

"Mr. Zinn's married, you know," Lois said. "Jane sees him every Sunday in the choir."

In fact I hadn't said he was married; I only said he was old enough.

"She's seen them kiss," Chuckie said, making a smooching noise with his lips against his arm.

"That isn't true," Valerie said.

All three of them turned to me. I was the tallest and heaviest;

I felt the stature of my flesh, the heft and decisiveness of my organs, busy at their work beneath the bones.

"She can prove it," Lois said. And I said I would.

*   *   *

My parents were surprised I'd invited friends to confirmation, but I told them we were supposed to bring guests, so they didn't care. We picked Valerie up—she was wearing a sun-colored dress and a bright straw hat—and drove to Lois's, down the street. Lois sat on the stoop wearing a pair of jeans and roller skates instead of shoes. "I can't go," she said. "I have to help my mother clean the house."

"How are you going to help if you're wearing roller skates?" I said. I leaned out the window and threatened to pull out her teeth with pliers if she wouldn't come.

Lois turned and skated down the walk, making an *rrrrrr-clack-clack* sound as she rolled away.

My parents dropped us off in front of the huge oak doors of the church. Walking in was a vision: you took a program from the usher and entered the floodlit stained-glass air of the center aisle. Valerie started for the doors, but I pulled her back.

"You can't go in that way if you're not a member."

She looked surprised. "I thought anyone could come."

"You can visit, but you have to use the entrance over here." I led her into the basement, down a narrow, dusty hall away from the church, to the choir's practice rooms and the vestry, where the sound of handbells and the scent of heavy robes dulled the click of our footsteps on the tiles. We walked up a flight of stairs to the treasurer's office, past the custodians and the gift shop on the left. Valerie pulled my arm. "The altar's down there."

I shook her off. She could barely follow me up the narrower steps to the tower; I let myself run, I let my clumsy legs unfold and carry me through the DO NOT ENTER door and down the dead-end passage above the sanctuary. Valerie had dirt on her dress;

she was breathing hard. She nearly tripped around the final corner, slamming into me where I'd stopped at the secret place.
Above our heads the massive stained-glass window bulged like
the side of a balloon. It was five or six times our height, pressing
outward toward the wall. The first time I saw it, I was shocked:
the colored panes were lit not by sunlight but by a hundred
ordinary bulbs. But most disturbing, the people in the window
faced you. I had expected to see the backs of their heads, but
their eyes, in brilliant topaz and aqua blue, met your gaze on
either side.

I peered through a broken pane at the window's edge. The
pews were filling up; the ushers collected their silver plates, and
the organist cracked her knuckles on the rail. Mr. Zinn stood off
in the corner, wearing a robe, not white like the minister's but
black, with enormous flowing sleeves. His wingtips gleamed in
the yellow light from the chandeliers.

Valerie still gazed above her head. The organ hummed a pro-
cessional, sending vibrations through our shoes.

"Tell me," I said. "At your lesson. What do you do with Mr.
Zinn?" It was time for me to line up with the rest of the class.

"He pulls the shades," Valerie said.

"But what do you do?"

The glare of the lights made the hallway warm. "Different
things."

"Show me what they are."

Valerie squinted when she looked my way. I must have been
haloed by the bulbs on every side. She reached up around my
neck with her blue-veined arms and unbuttoned my dress.
"Sometimes like this." She laid her palm, warm and sweaty, on
my chest. The convocation began below.

"What else?" I said, and Valerie showed me where he
touched. She was hiccuping, sending nervous bubbly echoes
down the hall.

"You can't tell anyone," she whispered, her pointed chin
against my chest.

Through the crack in the window I saw my class lining up in a pew.

"It's partly your fault, now that you've done it." She was warm against me, glowing like a coal. "You'll never tell."

I buttoned up as best I could.

Valerie helped me straighten my collar. "He isn't married, you know," she said, and I felt the tears welling up in my eyes. "I knew he wasn't all along." Her yellow dress held pieces of color from the window, and in its light she seemed to be broken into shards.

I turned the corner at a run, plugging my fingers in my ears so that I wouldn't hear.

* * *

I walked up to the altar disheveled, out of breath, from a direction opposite that of everyone else in the class. Mr. Zinn blinked his limpid, startled eyes when I took my place; the other kids nudged one another and whispered until he lifted his baton.

Through the whole first song I didn't sing. I knew that the world was constructed solely for humiliation, that nothing was fair, and that being right would never matter in the end. I still felt the press of Valerie's hands on my neck and chest.

Between the hymns we were supposed to count to ten. On eight Mr. Zinn looked up. He was listening, hand suspended in the air, baton tip pointing straight to God. We had our mouths half open, ready to sing, but the baton stayed fixed. Mr. Zinn tilted his head to the side. In the quiet that followed, we heard a noise barely audible, coming from just above our heads, or from the vents, or the organ pipes, or from the dome. It was a small, desperate sound, barely a whisper, but clear and distinct: *Don't tell.*

Mr. Zinn could have kept right on, but he was a man attuned to sound, and the voice that repeated *Don't tell* had a certain music, like a chant or a primal song. The organist took off her glasses; the minister scratched his head, revealing a bold striped shirt beneath his robe. People in the farthest aisles began to stir.

I thought I knew how the moment would end. I would be denied, they'd pass the cup above my head, the wafer would burn a hole through the flesh of my tongue. Valerie would be rescued, starved and tear-stained in her dress, and I would be left in the church alone, with the treasurer loading coins into blue felt bags and the janitor pushing his oblong broom between the rows. Mr. Zinn was pale. He was combing the window with his eyes, searching for Valerie, looking through the holy faces for her own.

I knew I had seconds before he found her, before the three of us were called on to explain the things we'd done.

I took a breath and began to sing.

◆ *Joanne Greenberg* ◆

ELIZABETH BAIRD

She had been born with a very slight cerebral lesion and it produced brief pauses in her speech and the movements of her body, so that she seemed always to be hesitating, fawnlike, before the disclosure of her thought or will. This shy-gentle quality was much commented on and much praised during her childhood in Ionia, South Carolina. When the heat of summer had only fans to move it and women wore softly floating dresses of lawn and dimity, there were pictures taken of her standing by a snowball bush. The picture was of a lovely little girl, but the photographer had no way to get that little wait, the arm halted before rising, the voice stopped, not like a stammer —like the halt of a small animal before venturing into an open field. The townspeople made much of that delicacy of hers. Dr. Baird's girl was what a girl should be. Her beauty wasn't dramatic like her mother's; it offered no challenge. Her ways were lovely, womanly and modest, and she was tiny as an elf.

No one knew about the lesion then. It wasn't found until she was in the hospital in California where doctors were trying to sort out the ravages all the prisoners had sustained from beatings, malnutrition, jungle diseases, parasites, and untreated wounds. When one of the doctors came to see Elizabeth at the place on the sun porch she had staked out as her own, he moved slowly, sat slowly, spoke slowly. The prisoners often fainted at fast moves. They were all like Elizabeth, now, stopped still, unable to think or speak or hear for the small seconds that seemed lifetimes.

She didn't take in what he said at first. Later she thought she had been dreaming. Still later, she got Sue Garland to show her the records and there it was in the neurologist's scrawl. She went back to the ward and thought long, slow thoughts about the years of her difference. It had been more than the unknown imperfection in her brain. She had been taught her caution well all her childhood long.

Dr. Baird had been the only pediatrician in a hundred miles. He, too, was watchful of his surroundings because chairs and the corners of furniture seemed to catch and trip him when he came home tired in the evenings, and often a general morning pain made him very cautious where he put his feet.

Elizabeth's mother was Alicia Powell Baird. She had been a celebrated beauty with auburn hair whose braids were thick as yacht cables, a table-dancer with rolled stockings and a fashionable boyish body. In the days of bobbed hair she danced the Charleston with hers long and loose and cascading down her shoulders. What a sad awakening to come to consciousness every morning and find herself the mother of a dream-struck little girl, wife of a gin alcoholic doctor in a small, hidebound town, mistress of a house that fronted the main street and so had to be kept looking nice all the time and of three mumbling, snuff-dipping Negro servants who lied, stole, and did as little as possible because they had no respect for her.

So, in addition to the hesitancy imposed on her by nature, Elizabeth learned her caution until it was bone deep. She seldom laughed and she was the most silent of the children in school, the most tentative of any group at play.

Life changed suddenly when she was fourteen. Her father

died. She stood in the hot, flower-cloying church in her pink voile dress dyed black, among the stranger-kin to hear him described in ways she had not experienced him. His mounded grave was not to be given a stone because there was no money. As she examined her life with the new knowledge in it, Elizabeth lay quietly in bed and saw the grave in her mind, the slow town, the grown-over ground that Alicia was too hurried to tend. She wondered now if she could even find the place. Years ago. It was to be years also before Mrs. Agnew would say to her, "Why, honey, everyone knew he drank. The better people didn't trust their children to him and the poorer ones couldn't afford a baby doctor. That's why there was no money, but he was a good man for all that, and don't forget his goodness in your need."

It had made Elizabeth all the more cautious, made all the more necessary the stopping her condition imposed.

In the early years of the widowhood, Alicia was frantic with poverty. Everywhere the depression cramped possibility. Even the work she might have done did not exist in Ionia or anywhere nearby.

Elizabeth did better. She worked in the five and dime and later at the bank. Scrimping and saving and renting out rooms to the occasional traveler, the two of them got up the money for Elizabeth's tuition in nurse's training.

*　　　*　　　*

They were separating, going home. Because of what had happened in the camp, Elizabeth kept apart from the others, women with whom she had spent the three years of her imprisonment. When they all said goodbye, the tears and hugs were not for her. This difference had not been missed by the hospital people but no one spoke of it. Elizabeth was put on a train, a sleeper, and she was given many medications she was to take for the diseases and weakness she still had. The porter had been told about her, mercifully not about the differences between her and the others. To him she was one of them, that famous group of army nurses, heroines now, who had lived those years in the Japanese prison camp in the Philippines. "I'm gonna see you rest good all the way to Savannah," he said, "rest good and eat good, too, all the way."

She was exhausted still, and dazed with illness. It was a relief to get into her berth and lie down, but she did not sleep. She needed time with the knowledge that there was a secret cleaving, which she saw as being something half-moon shaped, folded in the shining gray folds of her brain.

Had she known in childhood what she now knew, would it have changed anything? Probably not. She had been praised for it in Ionia, loved for it, and she had, in the arid, cruel years of nurse's training, as undeservedly been cursed and castigated for it.

Her first year at Savannah General had been a sudden shock followed by a drawn out misery. Students were expected to be lightning quick. Her teachers seemed to think her pauses before action and speech were caused by stupidity or unwillingness. Miss Martin cried at her, "Do I wait forever!" Mrs. Templeman: "Is this a home for the feeble-minded?" And in the long pause, Elizabeth couldn't bring up the simple, "No, ma'am." It amazed her that some of her teachers were bitter about their profession. Amazement silenced her even more; more silence, more singling out. "Here's a procedure even Miss Baird can do." "Zombies and the slow-witted, that's what they're sending us now." Had she had a place of escape, Elizabeth would have fled. As there was none, she stayed and slowly, first among the other students, then waiting out the teachers year by year, she gained a gradual, grudging acceptance. She was pretty. One or two of the girls asked her to double date with them. She was grateful but said no. She wrote to her mother, "I want to be independent, to be free. Girls around here talk about snagging some rich old man they get as a private patient. I'll take low wages but I'll choose my place and my conditions." Later she wrote, "Ionia's not for single women. There are places we can both work and have a good life. Can you ever sell that house?" She was working and learning and she spent no money. She tried not to hate the weakness of her stopped motion and sudden stillness; she tried to compensate for her tiny stature that made the patients call her "dear" and "cute" and "doll-like," like a doll who must click into action only after the pause in winding before its mechanism engaged.

It occurred to her now that had they known about what was going on in her brain, they wouldn't have accepted her into nurse's training and certainly not into the army, and if she hadn't gone into the army, she might have—she began to chuckle in her berth, quietly, facing the metal wall. She might have been able to be of some help in the war effort.

She graduated in 1939 and two days later, she joined the army. It was the first duty then available. "Why?" cried Alicia from Ionia, "I thought you wanted independence!" "I want to find a place for us and that means looking around." Unfortunately, it also meant a whole new chain of icy-faced superiors to convince that she was neither stupid nor unwilling. "Good God! What are they sending us!" Major Bradema had cried the first time, the first of many, and always worse in the tension of meetings with superiors.

She was posted to New Jersey. She was posted to San Diego. She was studying possibilities and places looking for somewhere she and Alicia could settle, work, and be quiet, and owe no one and draw no one's attention. Late in 1941, she was posted to the large hospital on Oahu, near Pearl Harbor, and studying that, it looked as though she had found such a place. She wrote to Alicia with a plan. If Hawaii was good, she would try for something permanent there. Alicia would sell the house for whatever it would bring and join her. Alicia wrote back, labile with hope. "Do you really think we could do it? When you get there see if it would work; I hardly dare to dream!"

During her training there had been rumors of war, but Elizabeth's personal case had been too urgent for her to give any thought to them. Her own life was so near the bone, her arguments with tradesmen over half-soles and cleaning bills so intense, there was no room for other struggles. They were two days out of San Francisco when the captain of their ship told them what the world had been up to while their private struggles had been occupying them: the Japanese had bombed American installations on Hawaii. The nation was at war.

At the first shock of hearing everyone behaved with Elizabeth's breath-caught silence, stopped motionless, speechless for the endless catchbreath which was only seconds. Then a roar went up, a roar of rage in which she did not partake. She and the other nurses, caught in mid-passage, were suddenly traveling too slowly. Army nurse now had another meaning than it had a day ago. They were forefront, cutting edge. Silence, stillness, hiding—all the cloaks of it had been blown and burned away.

No one on the ship had experienced war. Elizabeth listened to the other nurses, and they seemed to know the world better than she. They were frightened but also excited in a way that she was not. No longer would they have to hope for challenge and purpose; and suddenly, nothing was routine.

At Honolulu, some of them were ordered to stay; most of the nurses were dispatched to other stations. Elizabeth was sent to the Philippines where the need was greatest. They experienced the need, but none of the nurses served it long. They were overwhelmed by the invading armies, taken, and brutalized. Those who lived, lived in the hand of the unreadable, incomprehensible enemy. They were marched—starved, beaten, parched, and sick—into long captivity at a women's camp near Luzon.

The camp was in miasmic jungle. Their captors did not function well in such an environment. They felt it a monstrous loss of face to be used for this lowest of all purposes—the guardianship of women, and in the beginning they took out their resentment on the prisoners. Major Naohito Nishimura was the camp's commander. He had been injured in training—no dishonor, but. . . ."

Not for the first two years would Elizabeth know why Major Nishimura chose her. Simply, at first, she thought that it was because Ionia, South Carolina, was twelve miles from Savannah, and that it lay low and humid and marshy. This had given her an advantage in her adaptation to the tropical heat, to the dampness and fetor of the jungle prison. She had borne up better than most of the others. Nishimura had been looking for someone as liaison. His eye had run over the gathered female prisoners. They appeared hideous to him. They were over-large, physically; their size revolted and oppressed him; it was unwomanly; their limbs were too long, their faces protruded in a very unattractive way. They were also dirty, listless, lankhaired, and stinking. That one there, though. . . .

Elizabeth had been standing in a posture as close to attention as she could manage but she had not been attending. It was enough, this first day in the camp, to be standing still, quiet, under the palm hat she had made for herself, not having to be alert for kicks and blows from the soldiers who had driven them on and on like an animal herd. She had received more abuse than most of the others because of that hesitation of hers, the half-second it took her to begin to move. Time and again she had been threatened with death. Luck had been with her, there. So far. . . . She felt a stir beside her and raised her eyes slightly. The woman beside her hissed, "He wants *you!*" Elizabeth had learned about bowing early in her captivity; they seemed to want it as prelude to anything, even death. She bowed. The interpreter was a Sergeant Akimoto. He explained something, but his English was poor. Elizabeth did not understand. Again, more slowly. This time she did understand but fear and exhaustion made her unable to react at all. Her cursed body, never eager as other people's, had stopped working entirely under the new challenge. A question: "Name, you!"

Another long moment. They might kill her. Another bow. "Elizabeth Baird, Otaii San." (This had been learned at the cost of a torn ear and a tooth.) There was laughter from all the Japanese, but for once it was not angry or vengeful laughter; it was playful, almost. "Ebisu," the sergeant said. They laughed again. Looking up from under her lids at them, she saw that her captors' eyes had changed momentarily. Later she was to understand that they could not catch *Elizabeth,* but that *Ebisu* was a well-loved nursery figure in Japan—a sea god; all the soldiers knew of his exploits and a section of Tokyo had been named for him. The sound of her name made the soldiers remember home, a home shining above the stench of exile—not their lust but their humanity had been stirred. Rapists and killers, deniers of water to the dying—now they had the look of school boys: Ebisu.

And it had been her hesitation, her shyness, her lowered eye, her quick intake of breath before speech, everything that had caused Elizabeth pain and shame through school and the army, that represented for these lonely men the qualities they longed for in woman.

*   *   *

Day time. The train stopped at the stations of prosperous cities and at each one there was a tug, gentle and insistent as a child at his mother's skirts: no one knows me here—there wouldn't be the shackling gentility of her town. . . . Elizabeth knew she was still too sick to go back to work. The doctors had said it might be months, but the quiet of Ionia didn't represent rest but hopelessness to her. If only she could find a place, she and Alicia. . . . She tried to let the trip calm her; the train was passing land that was nothing like jungle or camp. Once she had yearned to see it; now it seemed unsheltered, fearful, featureless. She turned back to the comforting metal wall. The doctors had told her to try to forget everything that had happened, but they had known only of the suffering, not of the puzzles attending it. Elizabeth—Ebisu. In the interrogations they all had had, others must have spoken of her as a collaborator. The accusation had not been proved, and the doctors had tried, foolishly, she thought, to pave over what they could not understand. . . .

In the camp after the first week of routine, the community began to differentiate itself. A social world emerged. There were Mothers and Bosses and Givers and Takers, Housekeepers and Gossips, Liars, Toadies, and the too ill to care exiles. Ebisu, unique among them, found herself with few friends and many enemies. At first she tried to reason with their scorn. "I have no extra privileges; *they* picked me." It did no good. Everyone knew that the few improvements depended on Elizabeth's good relations with the guards and the major. It was obvious, too, that the more and better Japanese she learned, the easier things would be for everyone, but they were sick and starving and the feelings were strong and ugly and they persisted: anger at their dependence on Ebisu and the enemy and a terrible, despairing rage as supplies dwindled further and new diseases came. Later they were too tired for rage and settled into a dull, intractable resentment.

To Nishimura and the other guards, Ebisu became dearer. She had, at first, unwittingly learned Men's abrupt Japanese instead of the gentler feminine tongue. Sergeant Akimoto had to take her education in hand. Many of her manners had to be corrected and of course there were her looks: a face too florid and the fox-colored hair; fox-witch hair was unnerving, but her size and that hesitant grace, that stillness above all, ritual pause in speech and movement, reminded them achingly of the women at home. It was difficult to keep from mistreating the other prisoners; most of them were over-large and ugly red, they stared, and had no civilized ways. Ebisu was like a loved, slightly retarded little sister, and thus to be protected and furtively given gifts.

*   *   *

It was the third day of travel. They had crossed Texas from the baked plains of the west to what Elizabeth could now identify as being the landscape of the south; she was moving toward home. As the train neared Savannah, the combination of eagerness and fear she dreaded, mounted in her. Suddenly she was hit with the tremors of a malarial attack. She carried medication that was supposed to ease the fever and chill that followed it, but even when she took the pills, the paroxysms left her exhausted, sweat-drenched, and weepy. She had been sitting up, dressed. Now she went back to the berth and lay in the fever dream remembering the last days of captivity; eagerness and fear, and the tremors of fever, like the fever now.

*   *   *

Day after day, inexorably, the old rules were ending. The camp felt the subtle anarchy grow and became terrified of Nishimura and the rage of his men. Everyone knew that shipments of food and weapons were coming later and scanter and then not at all. The planned deployment of landing forces near the camp, the arming for further conquests and then for defense, never materialized. Less and less often were the planes flying overhead Japanese planes. Fewer of Sergeant Akimoto's radio transmissions were getting through.

In the camp there had been more dysentery, more fever. The water supply, barely adequate at the beginning, had become polluted. They caught rainwater which soon soured and grew slime. Rank growth was everywhere. Every morning had to be spent brush cutting—if the brush were not cut back constantly, it overgrew every trail and would even choke the compound. The prisoners noticed that Nishimura and his men were uncomfortable in heavy forest. While crowding people did not bother them—no American would have packed the barracks as close or full as they had, crowding vegetation made them almost panicky. They demanded the exhausted prisoners burn or cut off large swaths at the edges of the compound to give themselves vistas and open views. This was not to prevent escape; the jungle and the sea were more dangerous than the camp, even with its fever and dysentery.

One day at brush cutting, the prisoners were startled by noise above them, noise that did not immediately pass over. Looking up, they saw above them, airplanes, first one, then another, wheeling and sputtering like huge wasps. They were the fighter planes of . . . in her darkened berth, Elizabeth lay trembling and relived the dogfight, seeing it again in the lurid colors of fever. The planes did not stay parallel with the ground long enough to be identified by their shapes, as everyone had learned to do, and they were too high and quick to be read for insignia by the dulled women. For three minutes nothing moved in the camp; machetes were not raised, bodies were still, prisoners and guards all looked up, held breathless by the sight in the air. Neither knew any more than that The War, which had brought them all to loneliness and suffering in this fetid place, was being waged in miniature, beautifully aloft, like a dance.

There was one plane that had the capacity, it seemed, to drop without needing any lateral or forward distance, and this plane kept getting under the others, and would come up spitting sound that was almost like cursing; words, then silence, then words again. On one of these maneuvers, the two planes that were above him parted and turned like doors opening, and the clever plane went up between them, and they turned and shot, and Clever Plane wobbled and at the same time, one of those planes turned away and shot and another plane burst into fire that made a blot against the sky and from which they could see bits falling. Still, no one moved because no one knew which had gone down and from which side victory was announcing itself. Clever Plane seemed to be drowning in the air; it struggled to right itself. The three others circled it and the prisoners caught a glimpse of the underside of one of them. It looked . . . it was, a P-40, ours. No one believed it. It was too easy to hallucinate, starved and sick, in the gassy miasma of this jungle. Clever Plane was losing altitude but like a leaf, fluttering down. One of the others moved away and came up at a bank turn and spoke the words out of the guns, and a black scarf of smoke spewed out of Clever Plane and Clever Plane turned sharply but could not lose the smoke and came roaring down straight for them unmistakable now, to eyes that blinked to blink away any doubt; they saw the red ball of Japan's totem sun.

The prisoners cheered. In spite of the obvious danger, a ragged cry went up. The soldiers were always more nervous when brush was being cut when they were surrounded by the forests they hated and the prisoners held machetes in their hands. The prisoners felt their guards' anxiety. There were always guns pointed at them, then. Clever Plane dove as though willing it, into the ground beyond the edge of the camp. There was no fire or explosion but there was a rending, a tearing sound, and a crash. The sound was cut off then, as it was eaten by the jungle. At the crashing sound, the prisoners threw up their arms and cheered.

Elizabeth was with one of the brush groups. She, too, had gaped at the beauty and grace of the dogfight; she had seen the underside of the P-40 and was shamed at her weakness lest it be a hallucination. She had heard her heart pounding out of control when she saw and blinked and saw again, the enemy's red ball: zero. She had put her head back and opened her mouth to cheer, but as the moment came, she was overtaken by that terrible, choking feeling, her head came forward and dropped, the word throttled, while her body trembled and her hands were caught in a bizarre splay at her thighs. It saved her life. Corporal Abé saw the prisoners raising their machetes in hands suddenly unconscious of them; he heard the dry shout of triumph from their parched throats. Hating the cheer, hating them, he had opened fire, raking across the line of them, stopping where he saw Ebisu, head down, standing frozen.

Nishimura, who had come from his office to watch, also saw. He had cried out to Abé, but the corporal had been carried away and was beyond the reach of his voice. He saw the bullets hit and the women go down. And in all of it, Ebisu had not moved or spoken. Nishimura had seen her, had stopped in wonder at her infinite courage, standing, ready to endure whatever came. He began to run toward her to stop Abé. Then Abé stopped. The last bullet must have fluttered the rice sack prison shirt she wore. There was dead silence. Nishimura turned and walked back to his office. If he offered her protection, the others were sure to kill her at the end, and he no longer doubted what that end would be. He called Abé into his office and slapped him for his loss of control. He did not approach Ebisu then or later.

It was the merest chance that saved Elizabeth from being killed by the zealots for collaborating. The lucky accident was that the small group of brush cutters under Abé's gun had been separated from the others by a fallen tree. They had not been visible to the others who had been watching the dogfight and had then heard the shooting. Two women near Elizabeth had also been spared because in their panic they had fallen and had not seen Elizabeth as Abé's stopping point. The ones who had seen her sudden freezing, her clutching silence, her inability to share the risk and glory of the cheer, had been killed. Abé had seen her, and Nishimura. The major ordered the women buried decently. Their food rations were now shared among the living, and because of this, the others lived. Elizabeth continued as the necessary, hated liaison between the commandant and the camp. She was the one who bowed deep and, in the high indrawn breath whose climax was a silence, begged the honorable sergeant, beseeched the exalted lieutenant. . . .

The prisoners were liberated in the retaking of the Islands. One morning they woke without the whistle to wake them and after moments of confusion realized that the Japanese were no longer there. Panic ensued. Five women who had endured years of starvation and abuse died in the three days before the first Marines came.

*   *   *

Now she was going back to Ionia a heroine. National magazines had written stories about the nurses, their capture and years in the women's camp. There was to be a town ceremony: the mayor—amazingly, it was still Mayor Seddon—was to greet her at the station. There was to be a band, dignitaries, speeches. She had tried, had begged to refuse the honor, but Alicia had written that the ceremony was on and Elizabeth might simply sit quietly through it. She was too tired and too long out of the habit of demanding or refusing anything, to object. As in the jungle, escape was beyond her. There was only what there had been for three years: power to endure. The train pulled up to a strangely bustling and crowded station at Savannah. Where had all these people come from? Elizabeth was led carefully to a seat and waited with until the local train pulled in. Her head was pounding and she felt dizzy and sick. She was seated carefully for the short trip. "You'll soon be home," they said, as though to comfort her.

Even travel-dulled, ill with a dozen diseases, Elizabeth could tell that the land here, the farms and roads and people had greatly changed. When she had left, the traveler to Ionia had had to go to Marshall and get a jitney bus. Now, the town had its own station, they told her. As she came closer and the land became home-familiar, Elizabeth saw that the well-remembered Negro tenant-fields and poor-white farms were sprucer, more prosperous. At first she thought that she was seeing the old place with prisoner's eyes, that compared to the abjectness of the camp, any American scene looked splendid, but she soon realized that what she was seeing was far more than the difference between the wealth of America and the poverty in which she had lived in the camp. Off the roads the train was passing, the close-in tenant shacks had been replaced by comfortable, painted houses, and there were cars and buses coming and going and new roads, paved roads, cutting through the dark green land. There were many more cars, many more people, fewer mule and cart teams. There had been change here, great change. They came to the Ionia station, a large and spacious structure, roofed over and newly painted. There were flowers planted around it in large painted pots.

Her mother came into the car where she sat, to lead her to the welcoming dignitaries. Elizabeth had seen Alicia at the hospital in California when she had first come there, but she had been too ill to notice how much her mother had changed. Now the differences leaped out at her. The stunned and struggling widow had become a fashionable matron. Her clothing was expensive and severe. She wore a suit and the wonderful hair was rolled at the back of her neck. The change was in her manner, too; there was authority in her voice, command in her gestures. She led Elizabeth out to the doorway and down the steps. When the crowd saw them, the band started. The war's opportunities for martial music had been no help to Ionia. Elizabeth bit her lip and thought of train wrecks. She watched the mayor and others defer to Alicia. This seemed to be in far more than her position as mother of a war heroine. There were speeches through which the old Alicia would have squirmed and even giggled. This woman kept her jaw clamped on whatever rebellious word might rise from her throat.

Heroine. American Courage. Mayor Seddon and Pastor Aycroft spoke ringingly of it. They praised all the wrong things in all the wrong ways. Elizabeth sat, stood, bowed her head, outwaiting them. Eventually the ceremony was over and Alicia guided her to a car. When the mayor and the pastor made moves to join them, Alicia smoothly, deftly forestalled them. "She's still sick, and very tired—you can see. I want to ride her around town for a look and then take her home and put her to bed."

"Whose car is this?"

"It's mine. See the sticker? Unlimited gas ration."

"Aren't we going home?"

"We certainly are going home, honey, but not to that mausoleum your father left us. It's a boarding house now—most of those houses are. . . ." They turned down a new, paved road, a road that had once meandered along the river. They were traveling to some place that had not existed when she had lived here. The road was straight now, the river banked, walled off, and the thickets and woods on the other side, cleared to make a swath 100 feet wide. "The army built this road and the barracks I live in. . . ."

"Barracks?" Elizabeth had a sudden wave of dizziness. For a moment she had a picture of the bamboo-grass. "Barracks—"

"We're coming, you'll see." Alicia went on, driving competently, not aware of her daughter's panic.

They went up the road and Elizabeth saw the reason for the changes in Ionia. They were coming to a huge factory, a complex of buildings big as a town. "Food," Alicia said, "there's a cannery and a drying plant and a processing plant and a slaughter house and a packaging plant. We produce field rations and now that the war is winding down, we're going to be feeding all those refugees in Europe."

"You work here?"

"I'm in charge, darlin'. Personnel. I hired everyone who works here."

Alicia stopped the car and both the women sat still and looked at the pile of buildings. People were coming and going from them, moving quickly, energetically. There were white and colored together and the colored people whom Elizabeth had thought slow by nature were moving with the same kind of vigorous purpose. She felt utterly lost in everyone's speed and energy. For three years as she and the other camp people had moved into and away, washing, cutting brush, eating, rebuilding storm wrecked barracks, all dreamy with starvation and illness—like walkers under water, all the while, back here, the gears of the normal world had been turning faster, faster, leaving the prisoners even further and further behind. Elizabeth felt herself shrinking away almost to disappearance.

Alicia was talking. "I always wanted to *get out* of this town; you remember all our plans; but then the war came and I found out about this plant coming, and I caught my chance and held on. Ionia is rich now and going to get richer, and that means more modern. You wait and see. There'll be more stores and schools and entertainment and more professional people will come to live here. Right now, I live over yonder in a quonset, but I've got money, lots of it, saved and when the war's over, we'll build something nice. I have the land picked out already. . . ."

She went on as Elizabeth dwindled away. Her sound was so confident, so competent, as she threw abbreviations and neologisms into a speech already changed, a tone and speed and sweep beyond Elizabeth's understanding.

"Honey, the whole south has gone *forward.* There's no room any more for shuffling Negroes and mint juleps on the verandah. The new south is going to *produce,* to outproduce the north. We have the people now, people are beginning to come *here,* not go there. Once we change our system politically . . ." and she went on talking about money and manpower, electrification, coal, energy. It flowed past Elizabeth who was sitting, eyes lowered, stopped still in the momentary neurological shutdown that had been read as stupidity, laziness, demureness, innocence, and most recently, as Japanese feminine modesty. At two periods in her life that body silence had been accepted and praised. She was aware, with a wry feeling almost like a laughter from the deepest places in herself, that such acceptance and praise would never come again unless, of course, she visited the land of the enemy.

◆ *Alice Adams* ◆

1940: FALL

"Hasn't anyone noticed those clouds? They're quite incredibly beautiful." These words were spoken with some despair, for indeed no one had noticed, by a woman named Caroline Gerhardt, on a late evening in September, 1940. Caroline Coffin Gerhardt, actually, or so she signed the many letters that she wrote to newspapers, both local and further afield: *The Capitol Times,* right there in Madison, Wisconsin, and Colonel Mc-Cormick's infamous (Caroline's word) *Chicago Tribune.*

The ponderously shifting, immense white clouds contemplated by Caroline were moving across an enormous black sky, above one of Madison's smaller lakes. This house, Caroline's, was perched up on a fairly high bluff, yielding views of the dark water in which the reflected clouds were exaggerated, distorted by the tiny flicker of the waves. There was also a large full moon, but full moons at least to Caroline seemed much less remarkable than those clouds.

No one else in the room noticed anything remarkable because almost all of them, all much younger than Caroline, were dancing slowly, slowly, body to body, to some slow, very sexy recorded music. The "children," as Caroline thought of these steamy adolescents, especially her own two girls, have only taken romantic notice of the moon. Beautiful raven-haired Amy Gerhardt, who resembles her absent father rather than smaller, pale and somewhat wispy Caroline—Amy's perfectly painted lips have just grazed her parent's ear as she whispered, "You see? Another full moon. That makes seven since February." The boy pressed her more tightly into his own body. All those tall boys and smooth-haired, gardenia-smelling girls danced too closely, Caroline had observed, with pain. Hardly dancing at all. Six or eight couples, two or three stags, in the big, low-ceilinged, pine-panelled room—the game room. Dancing, their eyes half closed, not looking out to the lake, to the moon and sky.

Caroline's letters to the papers had to do with the coming war, with what Caroline saw as its clear necessity: Hitler must be stopped. The urgency of it possessed her, what Hitler was doing to the Jews, the horror of it always in her mind. And the smaller countries, systematically devastated. There in the isolationist Midwest she was excoriated as a warmonger (small, gentle, peaceable Caroline). Or worse: more than once—dirty toilet paper in the mail.

She also received from quite other sources pictures that were just beginning to be smuggled out of the camps. Buchenwald, Dachau.

She was actively involved in trying to help the refugees who had begun to arrive in Madison with housing, jobs, sometimes at the university.

There was in fact a refugee boy at the party in Caroline's game room that night. Egon Heller, the son of an anti-Nazi editor, now dead in Auschwitz. Egon and his mother had arrived from England. Hearing of them, going over to see them and liking the mother (able in fact to help her with a translator job), Caroline impulsively invited the boy. "If you're not busy tonight, there's a little party at my house. My daughters—about your age. They're both at Wisconsin High. Oh, you too? Oh, good."

Egon seemed more English than German. "The years of formation," his mother explained. Tall and shy, long-nosed and prominent of tooth, he seemed much younger than he was, younger that is than American boys his age. Not adolescent, more childlike. One of the three young people not dancing just then, Egon stood near the record player, in the proximity of Caroline's younger daughter, Julie—plump and brilliant and not yet discovered by boys (Caroline's idea being that she surely would be, and soon)—although Julie was extremely "well-liked," as the phrase then went, in high school. By boys and girls, and teachers.

Caroline's secret conviction about her daughter was that within Julie's flesh were embedded her own genes, her sensuality. The intense dark impulses that had enmeshed her with Arne Gerhardt and landed her with three children—the youngest, now upstairs asleep, embarrassingly born only a year ago, when Caroline was already over forty.

Caroline felt with Julie a sensual kinship and consequent cause for alarm far more than with more overtly sexy Amy, the oldest. Caroline too had once been plump and brilliant and shy.

Maybe this Egon will be the one, romantic Caroline thought, looking toward the corner to Egon and Julie, who so far seemed to have in common only the fact of not dancing. He's so tall and thin and toothy, Julie now so unsmiling, so matter-of-fact. Still, it would be very nice, thought Caroline. English-Jewish-New England-Swedish grandchildren—she would like that very much.

The other young person not dancing in the early part of that evening was a new girl in town, from Julie's class, invited by generous Julie (who would later be strongly maternal, Caroline knew). A strange-looking girl from Oklahoma, with an odd accent and a funny name: Lauren. Most striking of all about Lauren, right off, was her hair—very pale, more white than blond, it stood out all over her head in tiny fine soft ringlets.

She looked younger than the rest of the girls, perhaps partly because she did not wear lipstick. Her mouth was long and finely drawn, and pale, in that roomful of girls. Even Julie had dark blood-red lips. A very tall, very thin girl, her neck was long and she moved her head about uncertainly, watching the dancers. Her smile was slightly crooked, off.

Someone should ask her to dance, thought Caroline. How rude these children are, how entirely selfish. Perhaps Egon will, that would be very nice, two strangers finding each other. But maybe he is too polite to ask Lauren with Julie standing there; he doesn't know that Julie wouldn't mind in the least being left alone. She will probably be going up soon to see about Baby.

Seeing no way out of this social dilemma, but fated always to feel responsible, Caroline herself began to move in Lauren's direction—not easy, as the music had become more lively, people hopping about and arms and legs thrust out. Slowly making her way, Caroline tried to think of social-welcoming-maternal conversation.

"So, you and Julie are taking Latin together?" Reaching Lauren at last, this breathless, silly remark was all she had been able to summon up, finally.

"Yes. Cicero. There's only five of us in the class." Lauren laughed apologetically, as though abashed at the small size of the Latin class. But then, her huge eyes on Caroline, she said earnestly, "This is the most beautiful room I've ever seen. The view—"

Unprepared for intensity, Caroline was flustered. "Well, it's a funny old house. Not exactly practical. But it is nice, being here on the lake."

"I love it in Madison." Lauren's voice was rapt, those huge pale eyes burned. Caroline sensed that the girl had not said this before, to anyone. It was not a remark to be made to contemporaries, other children.

"Well yes, it is a very nice town," Caroline agreed. "Especially the lakes, and the university." Some flicker of intelligent response across Lauren's face made her add, "A very conservative place, though, on the whole."

"Try Enid, Oklahoma," Lauren laughed quickly. "More backward than conservative. But I know what you mean. The whole Midwest. Especially now."

Was the girl simply parroting remarks overheard at home, or were those ideas of her own? Impossible to tell, but in any case Caroline found herself liking this Lauren, wanting to talk to her.

However, just at the moment of Caroline wanting to speak, in her mind forming sentences, the two of them were interrupted by a tall, fair thin boy—Caroline knew him, knew his parents, but could not for the moment recall his name. Thick light hair, distinctively heavy eyebrows above deepset dark blue eyes. To Lauren he said, "Care to dance this one?" And then, somewhat perfunctorily (still, he did say it), "Okay with you, Mrs. Gerhardt?" He was staring at Lauren.

And they were gone, off and out into the room, lost among other couples, Lauren and Tommy Russell (his name had just come to Caroline, of course). And before she could collect herself or even could turn to watch them, from far upstairs she heard Baby's urgent cry. Bottle time. Glancing toward Julie, observing that she and Egon had at last begun to talk, Caroline signalled to her daughter that she would go up. "I want to get to bed early anyway," Caroline mouthed above the music, smiling, as she headed for the kitchen. For milk, a clean bottle, a heating saucepan.

Good Baby, the easiest child of the three, subsided as soon as she heard her mother's footsteps on the stairs. Smiling up from her crib, she grasped the proferred bottle, clamped it into her mouth, as Caroline settled into the adjacent battered easy chair.

From here, upstairs, she had an even better view of the lake, and the moon and the marvelous white clouds, and Caroline then felt an unaccustomed peace possess her. She thought, it *is* easier with Arne away (a fact hitherto not quite acknowledged). Generally his absences were only troubling: *would* he come back? That year he had a visiting professorship at Stanford, two years before at Virginia.

Now, as she peacefully crooned to the milk-smelling, half asleep fair child, she thought that this time even if Arne decided to take off for good, she would really be all right, she and her three girls, who themselves were more than all right, they were going to be great women, all three. She could cope with the house, the good big lake front place bought so cheaply ten years back. They would all be perfectly okay, Amy with her heady romances and her disappointing grades, Julie with her perfect grades, and perhaps a new beau in this nice English-German boy, this Egon. And maybe a nice new friend in this Lauren Whitfield, from Enid, Oklahoma. And Baby will always be fine, thought Caroline, sleepily.

And Roosevelt will win the election and declare war on Germany within the year, and we will win that war in a matter of months. Hitler defeated. Dead. Maybe tortured in a concentration camp.

Caroline thought all that, still crooning to Baby, and smiling secretly, somnolently to herself.

*   *   *

Lauren Whitfield, the new girl with the funny hair, and Julie Gerhardt did indeed become friends, though not quite of the sort that Caroline had envisioned. They began going to lunch at the Rennebohm's drugstore across from the school, and Julie, sensing Lauren's extreme interest in what was to her a glamorous new place, became a sort of balladeer, a chronicler of high school love affairs, past and present. Disastrous breakups, the occasional betrayal. Along with a detailed run-down on the current situation, who was going with whom as this new season began, this warm and golden fall.

Over thick chocolate malteds and English muffins Julie told Lauren everything she wanted to know, or nearly, including the story of Julie's own sister, Amy the beautiful, with whom boys quite regularly fell in love. "She was just having a good time, her sophomore year, really getting around. But the phone calls! My mother was going crazy, and Arne threatened to have the phone cut off, he has a pretty short temper. And then during spring vacation she went dancing with someone out at the Hollywood, and she met Nelson Manning, he was home from Dartmouth, much too old for her, about nineteen. But they fell absolutely madly in love, flowers all the time and after he went back to school those letters. And more flowers, and phone calls! Poor Amy spent that whole spring fighting with Caroline and Arne. But she sort of won, I think mostly just wearing them down, and of course Caro was busy with Baby, just born. So that when Nelson came home in June she got to see him. Under certain conditions. Well, she sneaked out and saw him a lot more than they ever knew about. Nelson was entirely insane over Amy, he wanted to quit school and get married right away. But of course Amy wasn't about to do that, and so in the fall he went back to Dartmouth and she moped around and then suddenly no more letters. No flowers. Another girl back there, probably someone at Vassar or one of those places, we're sure it must have been. Well, a really horrible winter, Caro and I were truly worried about her. Moping all day, not eating. But gradually she began to go out a little, and then over Christmas she got sort of serious about Jeff, and they started going steady in February. Full moon time. But there are still certain songs she can't hear without crying. 'All The Things You Are' is one. She's not *really* over Nelson."

Nothing like that had ever gone on in Enid, not that Lauren had ever heard about.

And then, "I think Tommy Russell is really interested in you," Julie told Lauren.

So much for the intellectual friendship that Caroline Gerhardt had envisioned between her brilliant middle daughter and Lauren Whitfield, the bright new girl in town. But even had she been aware of the content of those endless conversations Caroline would really not have cared, so entirely absorbed was she in her own despair: her desperation over what was going on, still, in Germany.

She was worried too about Arne, in California, but to herself she said: I would give up Arne and every thought of him if that would save one Jewish family from Hitler.

*   *   *

Even the Midwestern press had by now conceded that Roosevelt would win the election, and would get the country into that European war—wasteful, unnecessary. But Caroline often felt that it would be too late, too late for murdered Jews, for devastated Poland. Holland. Fallen France.

She continued her impassioned but well-reasoned letters to the press, along with occasional gay (she hoped for gaity) small notes to Arne, in response to his occasional cards from California.

*   *   *

Caroline Coffin, from Vermont, and Arne Gerhardt, from northern Wisconsin, Door County, met at Oberlin College in the early Twenties, and both at that time were filled with, inspired by, the large-spirited ideals of that institution. Big, dark, clumsy (but very brilliant, Caroline thought) Arne, enthusiastic about the new League of Nations, and smaller, fairer Caroline, who was then as now dedicated to peace, the abolition of war. Young and passionately in love, together they read Emma Goldman, Bertrand Russell—and moved into an apartment together. Caroline became pregnant, and a week before the birth of Amy they yielded to their parents and got married.

"Lauren Whitfield is going steady with Tommy Russell," Julie reported to her mother, at breakfast on Saturday morning. They were both feeding Baby, alternating spoonfuls of cereal with scrambled eggs, which was Baby's preferred method. Amy slept upstairs, on into the day.

"Isn't that rather sudden?" Caroline was a little surprised at the censoriousness with which she herself spoke.

"Oh yes, everyone thinks it's terribly romantic. He asked her on their first date."

Impossible for Caroline to gauge the content of irony in her daughter's voice. "I somehow thought she was more—" Caroline then could not finish her own sentence, and she realized that she had to a considerable degree already lost interest in this conversation, a thing that seemed to happen to her far too often.

"You thought she was more intelligent?" Knowing her mother well, Julie supplied the missing bias. "Actually she's extremely smart, but she's sort of, uh, dizzy. Young. Her parents are breaking up, that's why she's here with her grandparents. They drink a lot, her parents."

"Poor girl."

"Yes. Well, anyway, she's bright but she's not all intellectual. Yet."

*   *   *

Julie herself did not go out a lot with boys, that year. But she seemed both busy and contented. She studied hard and read a lot, at home she helped Caroline with Baby. She also functioned as a sort of occasional secretary for her mother, opening mail and often shielding Caroline from extreme isolationist vituperation.

And Julie and Egon Heller, the German-English refugee boy, did become friends, of sorts, if not in the romantic way that Caroline had hoped. Their friendship was in fact remarked upon, so unusual was it in those days of rigidly coded adolescent behavior. Simply, they spent a lot of time together, Egon and Julie. They could be seen whispering over their books in study hall, though very possibly about assignments. Never holding hands, no touching, nothing like that. Sometimes they went to the movies together, but usually on a Saturday afternoon, sometimes with Baby along. Not at night, not a date.

Very odd, was what most people observing them thought. But then exceptionally bright children were often odd; psychologists said so.

*   *   *

Caroline heard from Arne in a somewhat longer than usual postcard that he would not, after all, be coming home to Madison for Christmas, for a number of reasons; money, time and work were cited. Nothing very original by way of an excuse.

*   *   *

But Caroline, who had painful premonitions of just this announcement reacted with a large sense of relief. To her own great surprise. Oh *good,* is what she thought. I won't have to make a lot of Christmas fuss—or, not Arne's kind of fuss. No big parties, and I won't have to try to look wonderful all the time. And worry that he's drinking too much and making passes at undergraduate girls. I can just do the things I like, that he thinks are dumb: I can bake cookies, maybe run up a new formal for Amy. (Caroline had a curious dramatic flair for making certain clothes. Highly successful with evening things, she had never done well with the small flannel nightgowns, for example, that other women did in no time.) I can read a lot, she thought. And I'll go for a lot of walks in the snow.

*   *   *

The snows had come somewhat earlier than usual, to Madison, that year. Soon after the first of November (just after the election) serious snowfalls began, blanketing the steeply sloped university campus, causing traffic trouble in the streets—and making life far more wonderful for all children, including those in high school.

Couples on dates went toboganning on the vast golf course of the Black Hawk Country Club, an endless hill, just dangerous enough to provide a long intensely satisfying thrill. And couples who had parked on other hills to neck, in the marvelous privacy of deep snow banks, could emerge to observe a curious pink light on all the surrounding miles of white, reflected in all the lakes.

Lauren Whitfield and Tommy Russell spent considerable time in his car, in that way. They marvelled both at each other (so much in love), and at the loveliness of snow, which Lauren had never really seen before.

*   *   *

Caroline's kitchen was hung with rows of copper pots, enthusiastically bought in Paris, in the flea market, on Arne and Caroline's honeymoon (with baby Amy in tow). Never polished, they were now all dark and dull, black-grimed. The blue Mexican tile around the sink, from an attempted second honeymoon, this time without Amy but on which Julie was conceived—the tile had fared somewhat better; though cracked, it retained a bright brave color.

On the afternoon that Caroline had chosen for Christmas cookie baking, by the time the children arrived from school there were already smells of burned sugar, and spilled flour on the floor into which Baby continually crawled. Julie had brought both Lauren Whitfield and Egon Heller.

"Egon, and Lauren! How very nice to see you. These days I hardly ever." Floury, flustered Caroline made effusive welcoming gestures, to which Egon responded with one of his curious stiff bows (he actually bowed), and a smile.

Julie took over the problem of keeping Baby out of the general mess, and Caroline divided her attention between the cookies, which she judged still salvageable, and an intense old argument with Egon, about Roosevelt.

"But he's always—"

"But what you fail to grasp—"

"People of his social class—"

Lauren seemed very quiet, preoccupied and sad, Caroline observed, with a certain impatience. Adolescents are simply very, very self-absorbed, she thought.

To Egon she said, very positively, "Roosevelt will soon declare war on Germany, and he will be able to win it very quickly. And I know a man who's in a position to know things who tells me that the Nazi-Soviet pact can't last, not possibly. The Russians will come in on our side. Our strongest allies."

*   *   *

"Lauren and Tommy Russell have broken up," Julie told her mother one night in February, as together they did the supper dishes, Baby being asleep and Amy out.

"Wasn't that rather quick? You just told me, I thought—" Caroline heard her own voice trail off into vagueness.

"Quick and strange. She can't quite say what happened, or she won't. She just cries a lot. Like when Amy and Nelson broke up."

"That's too bad," Caroline began to say, and then did not, as she recognized that in truth she had almost no sympathy for the broken hearts of the very young. "That girl seems to be rushing through her life at quite a rate," was her more sincere comment.

"I think she'll be okay eventually. It may just take a while." Judicious Julie.

*   *   *

"When I think of Tito's brave Partisans," wrote Caroline to the *Capitol Times* (Madison) with copies to the *Chicago Tribune,* the *Des Moines Register,* and the *Moline Dispatch.* She thought of the *San Francisco Chronicle* or even the *Palo Alto Times* (where Arne was) but she censored that impulse as frivolous. Also, they would probably not print letters from an unknown woman in Wisconsin. And anyway, California went for Roosevelt.

Actually, Caroline was managing considerable detachment from Arne these days, this early and acutely beautiful spring.

Long walks were a reliable cure for her troubled sleep, she found, and so every afternoon for an hour or so she walked around the lake, noting pussywillows at the muddy edges of the water, where small gentle waves lapped, very slowly. And sudden secret wildflowers, in what had been a small neglected meadow. And, at the bottom of her garden (also neglected) early iris, wild and bright.

She began to sleep better. Or, if she should wake up she could read. One of the joys of singleness, she told herself: you don't have to worry about the other person's sleep, along with your own.

*　　　　*　　　　*

June 22, 1941, was the day on which Hitler's troops attacked Soviet Russia. No more Nazi-Soviet pact. The Russians were now our valiant allies. (It was also Lauren Whitfield's last day in Madison. Back to Enid, Oklahoma.)

Possibly more than anyone else in Madison, Caroline Coffin Gerhardt was moved to celebrate this clear beginning of the end of Hitler. She wanted a party, but from the beginning nothing worked out, in terms of this festive impulse. No one even remotely appropriate was available. Vacations had begun, varieties of other plans. Even her children failed her: Amy was off dancing with her beau, and Julie was to have an early farewell supper with Lauren and her grandparents.

Caroline's happy day was further marred by news from Arne: a postcard (so typical) announcing his imminent arrival. "I've missed all my girls." Well, I'll bet he has, was Caroline's sour reaction. Who else would put up with such a selfish bastard?

We will have to work out a much more independent life from each other, Caroline thought, over the small steak that she had bought for her solitary celebration (not black market: her month's ration), as she sipped from the split of beaujolais, an even greater treat.

I should not even have Arne so continually in my mind, she told herself. That's what the children do, they think only of themselves and their impassioned sexual lives.

The important fact is that the end of Hitler's evil has now begun.

* * *

Epilogue: San Diego, California. The middle Eighties.

The man at the next table at this almost-empty semi-Polynesian restaurant is not even slightly interested in her, thinks Lauren Whitfield, now a tall, gray-blonde, very well-dressed woman, a psychologist, well known for several books.

She is in fact on a tour for her latest book, having to do with alcoholic co-dependency. She reached San Diego a day early, hoping for a rest. On her way to her room, across a series of tropically planted lawns she observed an Olympic pool, and she thought, Oh, very good. And seated next to the pool, though fully dressed, she saw this same tall man, whom she had also seen at the reservation desk. Coming into the dining room just now he smiled very politely, if coldly, acknowledging these small accidental encounters.

Lauren is quite used to book tours, by now. Living alone in New York after the lengthy demise of her second marriage, she rather likes the adventure of trips, the novelty of unfamiliar scenery, new faces. She quite often falls into conversation with other single travelers, such encounters providing at the worst only a few bored hours. More frequently she has felt warm stirrings of interest, of possible friendship. On far rarer occasions, sex.

But this tall, too-thin, near-sighted and not-well-dressed European intellectual keeps his large nose pushed clearly into his book. Lauren has observed him with some care, over all of their small encounters, and is quite sure that they could find areas of common interest, some shared opinions. Their political views, she would bet, would be similar.

Sex is out, in a sexual way she is not drawn to him in the least. But so often men are slow to perceive that overtures of any sort are not necessarily sexual in nature. Lauren ponders this sad and trouble-causing human fact, as she also thinks, Well, hell, I'd really like an hour or so of conversation. Coffee. Damn his book.

And then, as she stares (he is so entirely unaware of her that she is able to stare with impunity), a small flash goes off within the deep recesses of her mind, so that she is able, with great confidence, and a smile that she knows is appealing, slightly crooked and not *too* self-assured, to tap his elbow and to say, "Excuse me, but aren't you Egon Heller?"

Perfectly calm, as though used to being thus accosted (possibly he is somewhat famous too, used to being recognized? or, a professor, with old students sometimes showing up? or both?) Egon lowers his book very patiently, and very politely he tells her that yes, that is his name. And then, with the very slightest English-German accent he asks her, "But have we met?"

"Yes, but terribly long ago. At the Gerhardts'. In Madison, Wisconsin."

Now Egon does look quite startled, and confused, so much so that he drops his book as he stands and extends a smooth cool strong hand to Lauren. "At the Gerhardts'! Extraordinary."

"Yes, in the fall of 1940. You'd just got there, I think, and I had just moved to Madison. But do sit down. Coffee?"

"Yes, thank you." He does sit down, now smiling warmly, attractively.

Lauren asks him, right off, "Do you ever go back to Madison? I always wonder what happened to Julie Gerhardt. My favorite friend."

At this quite startlingly Egon begins to laugh, in a choking, ratchety way that reddens his face, and it is some minutes before he is able to say, "Well, one of the things that happened to her is that she married me, in 1947. And another thing, or five other, is our children. We have five, the last one thank God just out of graduate school. And another, I know I should have said this first, she has her doctorate in math. From the University of Chicago. Very hard on her, doing all that at once." Egon smiles with such sympathy, such unambivalent admiration that Lauren is more than a little envious (neither of her husbands had much use for her work). As well as touched.

She says, "Well, I love that news, that's wonderful. And it's so amazing that I ran into you. By the way, I'm Lauren Whitfield, I just lived in Madison that one year."

Obviously not remembering her (if he noticed her at all he must have thought her just another blonde, boy-crazy American girl, which Lauren will now concede that she was), Egon politely says, "Oh, of course," and proceeds to tell her more Gerhardt news.

Amy has been married three times but seems at last to have settled down with a man whom Egon describes as a really nice fellow (Lauren has the sense, though, that Egon, so visibly nice himself, has said that about all the husbands). Baby, and now Egon's face lengthens, and saddens, Baby died in the early Sixties. Drugs.

Lauren: "Oh dear. So in a way Baby was always Baby." She has been unable not to say that.

"Quite." Egon frowns, and then his face brightens as he asks, "You remember Caroline, the mother?"

"Of course, she was wonderful. I always wanted to know her more—"

Caroline, still very much alive at eighty-something is even

more wonderful now, Egon tells Lauren. She still writes letters to papers, to congressmen and senators, and she goes to demonstrations, *still:* for disarmament, against military involvement, anywhere. She has been honored by national peace organizations; he names several. "Most of the time she feels quite well," Egon says. "A little trouble with her back, some other small problems, but she is for the most part all right."

Arne died a long time ago, in the Fifties.

Digesting all this news, which has mostly made her smile with pleasure, Lauren is quiet for a while, stirring and drinking her coffee very slowly, before she asks him, "Tell me, do you happen to know anything about someone named Tommy Russell?"

"No, I don't think so. But the name, something comes. A football star, in high school?"

"Basketball. He was very thin. Blond."

Egon frowns. "No. Now nothing comes."

Surprised at the depth of her disappointment, and afraid that it will show, Lauren tells him, "I, uh, went steady with him for a while that year. And then one night he got really drunk, and I was really scared, and I couldn't tell anyone. And my parents—"

She sees that she has completely lost his interest. A polite glaze has replaced the animation with which Egon described the new-old Caroline and the accomplishments of Julie. And Lauren senses that actually they do not have a great deal more to say to each other. "Such ancient history!" she comments.

"But you must come to see us," Egon next (somewhat surprisingly) says to her. "Julie would be so pleased, I know, and Caroline. Did I say that we are all still there in that same house on the bluff? The house you remember?"

"No, you didn't but that's really great. I will come, what a wonderful idea."

And, sitting there among the fake South Sea Island masks and the real but derelict, neglected tropical plants, Lauren tries to reimagine that house in Madison. How the lake looked at night.

♦ T. Coraghessan Boyle ♦

THE APE LADY IN RETIREMENT

Somehow, she found herself backed up against the artichoke display in the fruit and vegetable department at Waldbaum's, feeling as lost and hopeless as an orphan. She was wearing her dun safari shorts and matching workshirt; the rhino-hide sandals she'd worn at the Makoua Reserve clung to the soles of her pale, splayed, tired old feet. Outside the big plate glass windows, a sullen, grainy snow had begun to fall.

Maybe that was it, the snow. She was fretting over the vegetables, fumbling with her purse, the grocery list, the keys to the rheumatic old Lincoln her sister had left her, when she glanced up and saw it, this wonder, this phenomenon, this dishwater turned to stone, and for the life of her she didn't know what it was. And then it came to her, the word chipped from the recesses of her memory like an old bone dug from the sediment: *snow.* Snow. What had it been—forty years?

She gazed out past the racks of diet cola and facial cream, past the soap powder display and the thousand garish colors of the

products she couldn't use and didn't want, and she was lost in a
reminiscence so sharp and sudden it was like a blow. She saw
her sister's eyes peering out from beneath the hood of her
snowsuit, the drifts piled high over their heads, hot chocolate in
a decorated mug, her father cursing as he bent to wrap the
chains round the rear wheels of the car . . . and then the murmur of the market brought her back, the muted din concentrated now in a single voice, and she was aware that someone
was addressing her. "Excuse me," the voice was saying, "excuse
me."

She turned, and the voice took on form. A young man—a
boy, really—short, massive across the shoulders, his dead-black
hair cut close in a flattop, was standing before her. And what
was that in his hand? A sausage of some sort, pepperoni, yes,
and another word came back to her. "Excuse me," he repeated,
"but aren't you Beatrice Umbo?"

She was. Oh, yes, she was—Beatrice Umbo, the celebrated
ape lady, the world's foremost authority on the behavior of
chimpanzees in the wild, Beatrice Umbo, come home to Connecticut to retire. She gave him a faint, distant smile of recognition. "Yes," she said softly, with a trace of the lisp that had
clung to her since childhood, "and it's just terrible."

"Terrible?" he echoed, and she could see the hesitation in his
eyes. "I'm sorry," he said, grinning unsteadily and thumping the
pepperoni against his thigh, "but we read about you in school,
in college, I mean. I even read your books, the first one, anyway
—*Jungle Dawn?*"

She couldn't respond. It was his grin, the way his upper lip
pulled back from his teeth and folded over his incisors. He was
Agassiz, the very picture of Agassiz, and all of a sudden she was
back in the world of leaves, back in the Makoua Reserve,
crouched in a huddle of chimps. "Are you all right?" he asked.

"Of course I'm all right," she snapped, and at that moment
she caught a glimpse of herself in the mirror behind the halved
canteloupes. The whites of her eyes were stippled with yellow,

her hair was like a fright wig, her face as rutted and seamed as an old saddlebag. Even worse, her skin had the oddest citrus cast to it, a color about midway between the hue of a grapefruit and an orange. She didn't look well, she knew it. But then what could they expect of a woman who'd devoted her life to science and survived dysentery, malaria, schistosomiasis, hepatitis and sleeping sickness in the process, not to mention the little things like the chiggers that burrow beneath your toenails to lay their eggs. "I mean the fruit," she said, trying to bite back the lisp. "The fruit is terrible. No yim-yim," she sighed, gesturing toward the bins of tangerines, kumquats and pale seedless grapes. "No wild custard apple or tiger peach. They haven't even got passionfruit."

The boy glanced down at her cart. There were fifty yams—she'd counted them out herself—six gallons of full-fat milk and a five-pound block of cheese buried in its depths. All the bananas she could find, ranging in color from burnished green to putrescent black, were piled on top in a great towering pyramid that threatened to drop the bottom out of the thing. "They've got Italian chestnuts," he offered, looking up again and showing off his teeth in that big tentative grin. "And in a month or so they'll get those little torpedo-shaped things that come off the cactuses out west—prickly pear, that's what they call them."

She cocked her head to give him an appreciative look. "You're very sweet," she said, the lisp creeping back into her voice. "But you don't understand—I've got a visitor coming. A permanent visitor. And he's very particular about what he eats."

"I'm Howie Kantner," he said suddenly. "My father and me run Kantner Construction?"

She'd been in town less than a week, haunting the chilly cavernous house her mother had left her sister and her sister had left her. She'd never heard of Kantner Construction.

The boy ducked his head as if he were genuflecting, told her how thrilled he was to meet her and turned to go—but then he swung back round impulsively. "Couldn't you . . . I mean, do you think you'll need some help with all those bananas?"

She pursed her lips.

"I just thought . . . the boxboys are the pits here and you're so . . . casually dressed for the weather and all . . ."

"Yes," she said slowly, "yes, that would be very nice," and she smiled. She was pleased, terribly pleased. A moment earlier she'd felt depressed, out of place, an alien in her own home-town, and now she'd made a friend. He waited for her behind the checkout counter, this hulking, earnest college boy, this big post-adolescent male with the clipped brow and squared shoulders, and she beamed at him till her gums ached, wondering what he'd think if she told him he reminded her of a chimp.

*   *   *

Konrad was late. They'd told her three, but it was past five already and there was no sign of him. She huddled by the fire, draped in an afghan she'd found in a trunk in the basement, and listened to the clank and wheeze of the decrepit old oil burner as it switched itself fitfully on and off. It was still snowing, snow-ing like a curse, and she wished she were back in her hut at Makoua with the monsoon hammering at the roof. She looked out the window and thought she was on the moon.

It was close to seven when the knock at the door finally came. She'd been dozing, the notes for her lecture series scattered like refuse at her feet, the afghan drawn up tight round her throat. Clutching the title page as if it were a life jacket tossed to her on a stormy sea, she rose from the chair with a click of her arthritic knees and crossed the room to the door.

Though she'd swept the porch three times, the wind kept defeating her efforts, and when she pulled back the door she found Konrad standing in a drift up to his knees. He was huge —far bigger than she'd expected—and the heavy jacket, scarf and gloves exaggerated the effect. His trainer or keeper or whatever she was stood behind him, grinning weirdly, her arms laden with groceries. Konrad was grinning too, giving her the low closed grin she'd been the first to describe in the wild: it meant he was agitated but not yet stoked to the point of violence. His high-pitched squeals—*eeeee! eeeee! eeeee!*—filled the hallway.

"Miss Umbo?" the girl said, as Konrad, disdaining introductions, flung his knuckles down on the hardwood floor and scampered for the fire. "I'm Jill," the girl said, trying simultaneously to shake hands, pass through the doorframe and juggle the bags of groceries.

Beatrice was still trying to get over the shock of seeing a chimpanzee in human dress—and one so huge: he must have stood better than four and a half feet and weighed close to one-eighty—and it was a moment before she could murmur a greeting and offer to take one of the bags of groceries. The door slammed shut and the girl followed her into the kitchen while Konrad slapped his shoulders and stamped round the fireplace.

"He's so . . . so big," Beatrice said, depositing the bag on the oak table in the kitchen.

"I guess," the girl said, setting her bags down with a shrug.

"And what is all this?" Beatrice gestured at the groceries. She caught a glance of Konrad through the archway that led into the living room: he'd settled into her armchair and was studiously bent over her notes, tearing the pages into thin white strips with the delicate tips of his black leather fingers.

"Oh, this," the girl said, brightening. "This is the stuff he likes to eat," dipping into the near bag and extracting one box after another as if they were exhibits at a trial, "Carnation Instant Breakfast, cheese nachos, Fruit Roll-Ups, Sugar Daffies . . ."

"Are you—?" Beatrice hesitated, wondering how to phrase the question. "What I mean is, you're his trainer, I take it?"

The girl must have been in her mid-twenties, though she looked fourteen. Her hair was limp and blond, her eyes too big for her face. She was wearing faded jeans, a puffy down vest over a flannel shirt and a pair of two-hundred-dollar hiking boots. "Me?" she squealed, and then she blushed. Her voice dropped till it was nearly inaudible: "I'm just the person that cleans up his cage and all and I've always had this like way with animals . . ."

Beatrice was shocked. Shocked and disgusted. It was worse even than she'd suspected. When she agreed to take Konrad, she knew she'd be saving him from the sterility of a cage, from the anomie and humiliation of the zoo. And those were the very terms—anomie and humiliation—she'd used on the phone with his former trainer, with the zookeeper himself. For Konrad was no run-of-the-mill chimp snatched from the jungle and caged for the pleasure of the big bland white apes who lined up to gawk at him and make their little jokes at the expense of his dignity—though that would have been crime enough—no, he was special, extraordinary, a chimp made after the image of man.

Raised as a human, in one of those late-sixties experiments Beatrice deplored, he'd been bathed, dressed and pampered, taught to use cutlery and sit at a table, and he'd mastered 350 of the hand signals that comprised American Sign Language. (This last especially appalled her—at one time he could actually converse, or so they said.) But when he grew into puberty at the age of seven, when he developed the iron musculature and crackling sinews of the adolescent male who could reduce a room of furniture to detritus in minutes or snap the femur of a linebacker as if it were tinder, it was abruptly decided that he could be human no more. They took away his trousers and shoes, his stuffed toys and his color TV, and the overseers of the experiment made a quiet move to shift him to the medical laboratories for another, more sinister, sort of research. But he was famous by then and the public outcry landed him in the zoo instead, where they made a sort of clown of him, isolating him from the other chimps and dressing him up like something in a toy store window. There he'd languished for twenty-five years, neither chimp nor man.

Twenty-five years. And with people like this moon-eyed incompetent to look after him. It *was* a shock. "You mean to tell me you've had no training?" Beatrice demanded, the outrage constricting her throat till she could barely choke out the words. "None at all?"

The girl gave her a meek smile and a shrug of the shoulders.

"You've had nutritional training, certainly—you must have studied the dietary needs of the wild chimpanzee, at the very least . . ." and she gestured disdainfully at the bags of junk food, of salt and fat and empty calories.

The girl murmured something, some sort of excuse or melioration, but Beatrice never heard it. A sudden movement from the front room caught her eye, and all at once she remembered Konrad. She turned away from the girl as if she didn't exist and focused her bright narrow eyes on him, the eyes that had captured every last secret of his wild cousins, the rapt unblinking eyes of the professional voyeur.

The first thing she noticed was that he'd finished with her notes, the remnants of which lay strewn about the room like confetti. She saw too that he was calm now, at home already, sniffing at the afghan as if he'd known it all his life. Oblivious to her, he settled into the armchair, draped the afghan over his knees and began fumbling through the pockets of his overcoat like an absent-minded commuter. And then, while her mouth fell open and her eyes narrowed to pinpricks, he produced a cigar—a fine, green, tightly-rolled panatela—struck a match to light it and lounged back in an aureole of smoke, his feet, bereft now of the plastic galoshes, propped up luxuriously on the coffee table.

*   *   *

It was a night of stinging cold and sub-arctic wind, but though the panes rattled in their frames, the old house retained its heat. Beatrice had set the thermostat in the high eighties and she'd built the fire up beneath a cauldron of water that steamed the walls and windows till they dripped like the myriad leaves of the rain forest. Konrad was naked, as nature and evolution had meant him to be, and Beatrice was in the clean, starched khakis she'd worn in the bush for the past forty years. Potted plants—cane, ficus and Dieffenbachia—crowded the hallway, spilled from the windowsills and softened the corners of each of the downstairs rooms. In the living room, the TV roared at full volume, and Konrad stood before it, excited, signing at the screen and emitting a rising series of pant hoots: *"Hoo-hoo, hoo-ah-hoo-ah-hoo!"*

Watching from the kitchen, Beatrice felt her face pucker with disapproval. This TV business was no good, she thought, languidly stirring vegetables into a pot of chicken broth. Chimps had an innate dignity, an eloquence that had nothing to do with sign language, gabardine, color TV or nacho chips, and she was determined to restore it to him. The junk food was in the trash, where it belonged, along with the obscene little suits of clothes the girl had foisted on him, and she'd tried unplugging the TV set, but Konrad was too smart for her. Within thirty seconds he'd got it squawking again.

"Eee-eee!" he shouted now, slapping his palms rhythmically on the hardwood floor.

"Awright," the TV said in its stentorian voice, "take the dirty little stool pigeon out back and extoimenate him."

It was an unfortunate thing for the TV to say, because it provoked in Konrad a reaction that could only be described as a frenzy. Whereas before he'd been excited, now he was enraged. *"Wraaaaa!"* he screamed in a pitch no mere human could duplicate, and he charged the screen with a stick of firewood, every hair on his body sprung instantly erect. Good, she thought, stirring her soup as he flailed at the oak veneer cabinet and choked the voice out of it, good, good, good, as he backed away and bounced round the room like a huge india-rubber ball, the stick slapping behind him, his face contorted in a full open grin of incendiary excitement. Twice over the sofa, once up the bannister, and then he charged again, the stick beating jerkily at the floor. The crash of the screen came almost as a relief to her—at least there'd be no more of that. What puzzled her though, what arrested her hand in mid-stir, was Konrad's reaction. He stood stock-still a moment, then backed off, pouting and tugging at his lower lip, the screams tapering to a series of dolphin-like squeaks and whimpers of regret.

The moment the noise died, Beatrice became aware of another sound, low-pitched and regular, a signal it took her a moment to identify: someone was knocking at the door. Konrad must have heard it too. He looked up from the shattered cabinet and grunted softly. *"Urk,"* he said, *"urk, urk,"* and lifted his eyes to Beatrice's as she backed away from the stove and wiped her hands on her apron.

Who could it be, she wondered, and what must they have thought of all that racket? She hung the apron on a hook, smoothed back her hair and passed into the living room, neatly sidestepping the wreckage of the tv. Konrad's eyes followed her as she stepped into the foyer, flicked on the porch light and swung back the door.

"Hello? Miss Umbo?"

Two figures stood bathed in yellow light before her, hominids certainly, and wrapped in barbaric bundles of down, fur and machine-stitched nylon.

"Yes?"

"I hope you don't . . . I mean, you probably don't remember me," said the squatter of the two figures, removing his knit cap to reveal the stiff black brush-cut beneath, "but we met a couple weeks ago at Waldbaum's? I'm Howie, Howie Kantner?"

Agassiz, she thought, and she saw his unsteady grin replicated on the face of the figure behind him.

"I hope it isn't an imposition, but this is my father, Howard," and the second figure, taller, less bulky in the shoulders, stepped forward with a slouch and an uneasy shift of his eyes that told her he was no longer the dominant male. "Pleased to meet you," he said in a voice ruined by tobacco.

She was aware of Konrad behind her—he'd pulled himself into the precarious nest he'd made in the coat tree of mattress stuffing and strips of carpeting from the downstairs hallway—and her social graces failed her. She didn't think to ask them in out of the cold till Howie spoke again. "I—I was wondering," he stammered, "my father's a big fan of yours, if you would sign a book for him?"

Smile, she told herself, and the command influenced her facial muscles. Ask them to come in. "Come in," she said, "please," and then she made a banal comment about the weather.

In they came, stamping and shaking and picking at their clothing, massive but obsequious, a barrage of apologies—"so late"; "we're not intruding?"; "do you mind?"—exploding around them. They exchanged a glance and wrinkled up their noses at the potent aroma and high visibility of Konrad. Howard Sr. clutched his book, a dog-eared paper edition of *The Wellsprings of Man*. From his coat tree, which Beatrice had secured to the high ceilings with a network of nylon tow rope, Konrad grunted softly. "No, not at all," she heard herself saying, and then she asked them if they'd like a cup of hot chocolate or tea.

Seated in the living room and divested of their impressive coats and ponderous boots, scarves, gloves and hats, father and son seemed subdued. They tried not to look at the ruined TV or at the coat tree or the ragged section of bare plaster where Konrad had stripped the flowered wallpaper to get at the stale but piquant paste beneath. Howie was having the hot chocolate; Howard Sr., the tea. "So how do you like our little town?" Howard Sr. asked as she settled into the armchair opposite him.

She hadn't uttered a word to a human being since Konrad's companion had left, and she was having difficulty with the amenities expected of her. Set her down amidst a convocation of chimps or even a troop of baboons and she'd never commit a faux pas or gaucherie, but here she felt herself on uncertain ground. "Hate it," she said.

Howard Sr. seemed to mull this over, while unbeknownst to him, Konrad was slipping down from the coat tree and creeping up at his back. "Is it that bad," he said finally, "or is it the difference between Connecticut and the, the—" He was interrupted by the imposition of a long, sinuous, fur-cloaked arm which snaked under his own to deftly snatch a pack of cigarettes from his shirt pocket. Before he could react, the arm was gone. *"Eeeee!"* screamed Konrad, *"eeee-eeee!"* and he retreated to the coat tree with his booty.

Beatrice rose immediately to her feet, ignoring the sharp pain that ground at her kneecaps, and marched across the room. She wouldn't have it, one of *her* chimps indulging a filthy human habit. Give it here, she wanted to say, but then she wouldn't have one of her chimps responding to human language either, as if he were some fawning lapdog or neutered cat. *"Woo-oo-oogh,"* she coughed at him.

"Wraaaaa!" he screamed back, bouncing down from his perch and careering round the room in a threat display, the cigarettes clutched tightly to his chest. She circled him warily, aware that Howie and his father loomed behind her now, their limbs loose, faces set hard. "Miss Umbo," Howie's voice spoke at her back, "do you need any help there?"

It was then that Konrad tore round the room again—up over the couch, the bannister, up the ropes and down—and Howard Sr. made a calculated grab for him. "No!" Beatrice cried, but the warning was superfluous: Konrad effortlessly eluded the old man's clumsy swipe, bounced twice and was back up in the coat tree before he could blink his eyes.

"Heh, heh," Howard Sr. laughed from the top of his throat, "frisky little fella, isn't he?"

Beatrice stood before him, trying to catch her breath. "You

don't," she began, wondering how to put it, "you don't want to, uh, obstruct him when he displays."

Howie, the son, looked bemused.

"You don't, I think, appreciate the strength of this creature. A chimpanzee—a full-grown male, as Konrad is—is at least three times as strong as his human counterpart. Now certainly, I'm sure he wouldn't deliberately hurt anyone—"

"Hurt us?" Howie exclaimed, involuntarily flexing his shoulders, "I mean, he barely comes up to my chest."

A contented grunt escaped Konrad at that moment. He lay sprawled in his nest, the rubbery soles of his prehensile feet blackly dangling. He'd wadded up the entire pack of cigarettes and tucked it beneath his lower lip. Now he extracted the wad of tobacco and paper, sniffed it with an appreciative roll of his eyes and replaced it between cheek and gum. Beatrice sighed. She looked at Howie, but didn't have the strength to respond.

Later, while Konrad snored blissfully from his perch and the boy and his father had accepted first one bowl of chicken soup and then another, and the conversation drew away from the prosaic details of Beatrice's life in Connecticut—and did she know Tiddy Brohmer and Harriet Dillers?—and veered instead toward Makoua and the Umbo Primate Center, Howard Sr. brought up the subject of airplanes. He flew, and so did his son. He'd heard about the bush pilots in Africa and wondered about her experience of them.

Beatrice was so surprised she had to set down her tea for fear of spilling it. "You fly?" she repeated.

Howard Sr. nodded and levelled his keen glistening gaze on her. "Twenty-two hundred and some odd hours' worth, he said. "And Howie. He's a regular fanatic. Got his license when he was sixteen, and since we bought the Cessna there's hardly a minute when he's on the ground."

"I love it," Howie asserted, crouched over his massive thighs on the very edge of the chair. "I mean, it's my whole life. When

I get out of school I want to restore classic aircraft. I know a guy who's got a Stearman."

Beatrice warmed up her smile. All at once she was back in Africa, 2500 feet up, the land spread out like a mosaic at her feet. Champ, her late husband, had taken to planes like a chimp to trees, and though she'd never learned to fly herself, she'd spent whole days at a time in the air with him, spying out chimp habitat in the rich green forests of Cameroon, the Congo and Zaire, or coasting above the golden veldt to some distant, magical village in the hills. She closed her eyes a moment, overcome with the intensity of the recollection. Champ, Makoua, the storms and sunsets and the close, savage, unimpeachable society of the apes—it was all lost to her, lost forever.

"Miss Umbo?" Howie was peering into her eyes with an expression of concern, the same expression he'd worn that afternoon in Waldbaum's when he'd asked if she needed help with the bananas. "Miss Umbo," he repeated, "anytime you want to see Connecticut from the air, just you let me know."

"That's very kind of you," she said.

"Really," and he grinned Agassiz's grin, "it'd be a pleasure."

*   *   *

Things were sprouting from the dead dun earth—crocuses, daffodils, nameless buds and strange pale fingertips of vegetation— by the time the first of her scheduled lectures came round. It was an evening lecture, open to the public, and held in the Buffon Memorial Auditorium of the State University. Her topic was "Tool Modification in the Chimps of the Makoua Reserve," and she'd chosen fifty color slides for illustration. For a while she'd debated wearing one of the crepe de chine dresses her sister had left hanging forlornly in the closet, but in the end she decided to stick with the safari shorts.

As the auditorium began to fill, she stood rigid behind the curtain, deaf to the chatter of the young professor who was to introduce her. She watched the crowd gather—blank-faced housewives and their paunchy husbands, bearded professors, breast-thumping students, the stringy, fur-swathed women of the Anthropology Club—watched them command their space, choose their seats, pick at themselves and wriggle in their clothing. "I'll keep it short," the young professor was saying, "some remarks about your career in general and the impact of your first two books, then maybe two minutes on Makoua and the Umbo Primate Center, is that all right?" Beatrice didn't respond. She was absorbed in the dynamics of the crowd, listening to their chatter, observing their neck craning and leg crossing, watching the furtive plumbing of nostrils and sniffing of armpits, the obsessive fussing with hair and jewelry. Howie and his father were in the second row. By the time she began, it was standing room only.

It went quite well at first—she had that impression, anyway. She was talking of what she knew better than anyone else alive, and she spoke with a fluency and grace she couldn't seem to summon at Waldbaum's or the local Exxon station. She watched them—fidgeting, certainly, but patient and intelligent, all their primal needs—their sexual urges, the necessity of relieving themselves and eating to exhaustion—sublimated beneath the spell of her words. Agassiz, she told them about Agassiz, the first of the wild apes to let her groom him, dead twenty years now. She told them of Spenser and Leakey and Darwin, of Lula, Pout and Chrysalis. She described how Agassiz had fished for termites with the stem of a plant he'd stripped of leaves, how Lula had used a stick to force open the concrete bunkers in which the bananas were stored, and how Clint, the dominant male, had used a wad of leaves as a sponge to dip the brains from the shattered skull of a baby baboon.

The problem arose when she began the slide show. For some reason, perhaps because the medium so magnified the size of the chimps and he felt himself wanting in comparison, Konrad threw a fit. (She hadn't wanted to bring him, but the last time she'd left him home alone he'd switched on all the burners of the stove, overturned and gutted the refrigerator and torn the back door from its hinges—all this prior to committing a rash of crimes, ranging from terrorizing Mrs. Binchy's doberman to crushing and partially eating a still unidentified white angora kitten.) He'd been sitting just behind the podium, slouched in a folding chair around which Doris Beatts, the young professor, had arranged an array of fruit, including yim-yim flown in for the occasion. "Having him onstage is a terrific idea," she'd gushed, pumping Beatrice's hand and flashing a zealot's smile that showed off her pink and exuberant gums, "what could be better? It'll give the audience a real frisson, having a live chimp sitting there."

Yes, it gave them a frisson, all right.

Konrad had been grunting softly to himself and working his way happily through the yim-yim, but no sooner had the lights been dimmed and the first slide projected, than he was up off the chair with a shriek of outrage. Puffed to twice his size, he swayed toward the screen on his hind legs, displaying at the gigantic chimp that had suddenly materialized out of the darkness. *"Wraaaaa!"* he screamed, dashing the chair to pieces and snatching up one of its jagged legs to whirl over his head like a club. There was movement in the front row. A murmur of concern—concern, not yet fear—washed through the crowd. *"Woo-oo-oogh,"* Beatrice crooned, trying to calm him. "It's all right," she heard herself saying through the speakers that boomed her voice out over the auditorium. But it wasn't all right. She snapped to the next slide, a close-up of Clint sucking termites from a bit of straw, and Konrad lost control, throwing himself at the screen with a screech that brought the audience to its feet.

Up went the lights. To an individual, the audience was standing. Beatrice didn't have time to catalogue their facial expressions, but they ran the gamut from amusement to shock, terror and beyond. One woman—heavyset, with arms like Christmas turkeys and black little deep-set eyes—actually cried out as if

King Kong himself had broken loose. And Konrad? He stood bewildered amidst the white tatters of the screen, his fur gone limp again, his knuckles on the floor. For a moment, Beatrice actually thought he looked embarrassed.

Later, at the reception, people crowded round him and he took advantage of the attention to shamelessly cadge cigarettes, plunder the canape trays and guzzle Coca-Cola as if it were spring water. Beatrice wanted to put a stop to it—he was demeaning himself, the clown in the funny suit with his upturned palm thrust through the bars of his cage—but the press around her was terrific. Students and scholars, a man from the local paper, Doris Beatts and her neurasthenic husband, the Kantners, father and son, all bombarding her with questions: Would she go back? Was it for health reasons she'd retired? Did she believe in UFOs? Reincarnation? The New York Yankees? How did it feel having a full-grown chimp in the house? Did she know Vlastos Reizek's monograph on the seed content of baboon feces in the Kalahari? It was almost ten o'clock before Konrad turned away to vomit noisily in the corner and Howie Kantner, beaming sunnily and balancing half a plastic cup of warm white wine on the palm of one hand, asked her when they were going to go flying.

"Soon," she said, watching the crowd part as Konrad, a perplexed look on his face, bent to lap up the sour overflow of his digestive tract.

"How about tomorrow?" Howie said.

"Tomorrow," Beatrice repeated, struck suddenly with the scent of the rain forest, her ears ringing with the call of shrike and locust and tree toad. "Yes," she lisped, "that would be nice."

*   *   *

Konrad was subdued the next day. He spent the early morning half-heartedly tearing up the carpet in the guest room, then

brooded over his nuts and bananas, all the while pinning Beatrice with an accusatory look, a look that had nacho chips and
Fruit Roll-Ups written all over it. Around noon, he dragged
himself across the floor like a hundred-year-old man and
climbed wearily into his nest. Beatrice felt bad, but she wasn't
about to give in. They'd made him schizophrenic—neither
chimp nor man—and if there was pain involved in reacquaint-
ing him with his roots, with his true identity, there was nothing
else she could do about it. Besides, she was feeling schizophrenic herself. Konrad was a big help—the smell of him, the
silken texture of his fur as she groomed him, the way he
scratched around in the basement when he did his business—
but still she felt out of place, still she missed Makoua with an
ache that wouldn't go away, and as the days accumulated like
withered leaves at her feet, she found herself wishing she'd
stayed on there to die.

Howie appeared at ten of three, his rust-eaten Datsun rumbling at the curb, the omnipresent grin on his lips. It was unsea-
sonably warm for mid-April and he wore a red T-shirt that
showed off the extraordinary development of his pectorals, del-
toids and biceps; a blue windbreaker was flung casually over
one shoulder. "Miss Umbo," he boomed as she answered the
door, "it's one perfect day for flying. Visibility's got to be
twenty-five miles or more. You ready?"

She was. She'd been looking forward to it, in fact. "I hope
you don't mind if I bring Konrad along," she said.

Howie's smile faded for just an instant. Konrad stood at her
side, his lower lip unfurled in a pout. *"Hoo-hoo,"* he murmured,
eyes meek and round. Howie regarded him dubiously a moment, and then the grin came back. "Sure," he said, shrugging,
"I don't see why not."

*   *   *

It was a twenty-minute ride to the airport. Beatrice stared out the window at shopping centers, car lots, Burger King and Stereo City, at cemeteries that stretched as far as she could see. Konrad sat in back, absorbed in plucking cigarette butts from the rear ashtray and making a neat little pile of them on the seat beside him. Howie was oblivious. He kept up a steady stream of chatter the whole way, talking about airplanes mostly, but shading into his coursework at school and how flipped out his Anthro prof would be when she heard he was taking Beatrice flying. For her part, Beatrice was content to let the countryside flash by, murmuring an occasional "yes" or "uh huh" when Howie paused for breath.

The airport was tiny, two macadam strips in a grassy field, thirty or forty airplanes lined up in ragged rows, a cement block building the size of her basement. A sign over the door welcomed them to Arkbelt Airport. Howie pushed the plane out onto the runway himself and helped Beatrice negotiate the high step up into the cockpit. Konrad clambered into the back and allowed Beatrice to fasten his seatbelt. For a long while they sat on the ground while Howie, grinning mechanically, revved the engine and checked this gauge or that.

The plane was a Cessna 182, painted a generic orange and white and equipped with dual controls, autopilot, a storm scope and four cramped vinyl seats. It was about what she'd expected —a little shinier and less battered than Champ's Piper, but no less noisy or bone-rattling. Howie gunned the engine and the plane jolted down the runway with an apocalyptic roar, Beatrice clinging to the plastic handgrip till she could taste her breakfast in the back of her throat. But then they lifted off like gods, liberated from the grip of the earth, and Connecticut swelled beneath them, revealing the drift and flow of its topology and the hidden patterns of its dismemberment.

"Beautiful," she screamed over the whine of the engine.

Howie worked the flaps and drew the yoke toward him. They banked right and rose steadily. "See that out there?" he shouted, pointing out her window to where the ocean threw the sky back at them. "Long Island Sound."

From just behind her, Konrad said: *"Wow-wow, er-er-er-er!"* The smell of him, in so small a confine, was staggering.

"You want to sightsee here," Howie shouted, "maybe go over town and look for your house and the university and all, or do you want to go out over the Island a ways and then circle back?"

She was dazzled, high in the empyrean, blue above, blue below. "The Island," she shouted, exhilarated, really exhilarated, for the first time since she'd left Africa.

Howie levelled off the plane and the tan lump of Long Island loomed ahead of them. "Great, huh?" he shouted, gesturing toward the day like an impresario, like the man who'd made it. Beatrice beamed at him. "Woooo!" Howie said, pinching his nostrils and making an antic face, "he's ripe today, Konrad, isn't he?"

"Forty years," Beatrice laughed, proud of Konrad, proud of the stink, proud of every chimp she'd ever known and proud of this boy Howie too—why, he was nothing but a big chimp himself. It was then—while she was laughing, while Howie mugged for her and she began to feel almost whole for the first time since she'd left Makoua—that the trouble began. Like most trouble, it arose out of a misunderstanding. Apparently, Konrad had saved one of the butts from Howie's car, and when he reached out nimbly to depress the cigarette lighter, Howie, poor Howie, thought he was going for the controls and grabbed his wrist.

A mistake.

"No!" Beatrice cried, and immediately the tug of war spilled over into her lap. "Let go of him!"

"Eeeee! Eeeee!" Konrad shrieked, his face distended in the full open grin of high excitement, already stoked to violence. She felt the plane dip out of from under her as Howie, his own face gone red with the rush of blood, struggled to keep it on course

with one hand while fighting back Konrad with the other. It was no contest. Konrad slipped Howie's grasp and then grabbed *his* wrist, as if to say, "How do you like it?"

"Get off me, goddamnit!" Howie bellowed, but Konrad didn't respond. Instead, he jerked Howie's arm back so swiftly and suddenly it might have been the lever of a slot machine; even above the noise of the engine, Beatrice could hear the shoulder give, and then Howie's bright high yelp of pain filled the compartment. In the next instant Konrad was in front, in the cockpit, dancing from Beatrice's lap to Howie's and back again, jerking at the controls, gibbering and hooting and loosing his bowels in a frenzy like nothing she'd ever seen.

"Son of a bitch!" Howie was working up a frenzy of his own, the plane leaping and bucking as he punched in the autopilot and hammered at the chimp with his left hand, the right dangling uselessly, his eyes peeled back in terror. *"Hoo-ah-hoo-ah-hoo!"* Konrad hooted, spewing excrement and springing into Beatrice's lap. For an instant he paused to shoot Howie a mocking glance and then he snatched the yoke to his chest and the plane shot up with a clattering howl while Howie flailed at him with the heavy meat of his fist.

Konrad took the first two blows as if he didn't notice them, then abruptly dropped the yoke, the autopilot kicking in to level them off. Howie hit him again and Beatrice knew she was going to die. *"Er-er,"* Konrad croaked experimentally, and Howie, panic in his face, hit him again. And then, as casually as he might have reached out for a yam or banana, Konrad returned the blow and the plane jerked with the force of it. *"Wraaaaa!"* Konrad screamed, but Howie didn't hear him. Howie was unconscious. Unconscious, and smeared with shit. And now, delivering the coup de grace, Konrad sprang to his chest, snatched up Howie's left hand—the hand that had pummeled him—and bit off the thumb. A snap of the jaws and it was gone. Howie's heart pumped blood to the wound.

In that moment—the moment of Howie's disfigurement—

Beatrice's own heart turned over in her chest. She looked at Konrad, perched atop poor Howie, and at Howie, who even in repose managed to favor Agassiz. They were beyond Long Island now, headed out to sea, high over the Atlantic. Champ had tried to teach her to fly, but she'd had no interest in it. She looked at the instrument panel and saw nothing. For a moment the idea of switching on the radio came into her head, but then she glanced at Konrad and thought better of it.

Konrad was looking into her eyes. The engine hummed, Howie's head fell against the door, the smell of Konrad—his body, his shit—filled her nostrils. They had five hours' flying time, give or take a few minutes, that much she knew. She looked out over the nose of the plane to where the sea swallowed up the rim of the world. Africa was out there, distant and serene, somewhere beyond the night that fell like an axe across the horizon. She could almost taste it.

"*Urk*," Konrad said, and he was still looking at her. His eyes were soft now, his breathing regular. He sat atop Howie in a forlorn slouch, the cigarette forgotten, the controls irrelevant, nothing at all. "*Urk*," he repeated, and she knew what he wanted, knew in a rush of comprehension that took her all the way back to Makoua and that first, long-ago touch of Agassiz's strange spidery fingers.

She held his eyes. The engine droned. The sea beneath them seemed so still you could walk on it, so soft you could wrap yourself up in it. She reached out and touched his hand. "*Urk*," she said.

◆ *Marilyn Sides* ◆

THE ISLAND OF THE MAPMAKER'S WIFE

She trades in antique maps. Her small shop is on Congress Street, three blocks from Boston Harbor. Full of history, tourists drop in from Bunker Hill, Beacon Hill and exclaim in surprise, "You're the owner?" They wonder, often aloud, why does this rather young woman, with only a few glinting silver threads in her hair, why does she spend her time behind the tarnished letters *C.M. Descotes* on the dusty window? What makes her hand linger so on the ancient sea-charts as she smoothes out their creases? An unnatural woman they think, never out loud, to care about latitude and longitude.

The old map-dealers, retired military men and historians in worn tweeds, know better, point out that Descotes is only too predictably a woman. For all her expert abilities—which they admit with grudging respect—to date any map, to attribute it to its designer, to price it for the market, Descotes betrays herself by her specialty. Her passion, the map she knows best and collects for herself, is the frivolous picture map so prized three hundred years ago by fat Dutch wives for their homes.

"Descotes," the dealers reproach her in dismal tones, "merely interior decoration, you know." But it pleases her to think of thin light coming from a window, watery light falling on a white wall spread with a gaily colored map of Europe, Africa—it makes no difference, any annihilation of vast seas and continents to a rectangle will do—bleak light falling further on a table spread with a rich red Turkey carpet, one corner lifted back like a raised skirt. Pure light falling on the woman reading there.

"Ah, Descotes, most unscientific, those maps. Truth? Progress?" But, like her mapmasters, Descotes would sink a newly discovered Alaska for a mermaid billowing her breast on a wave. Descotes would shrink Siberia for a long-whiskered sea monster rolling at the sea-queen's side.

Among the map-dealers, only one indulges her taste without raising an eyebrow. William taught her everything he knew about maps. She learned to love them as much as she loved to pore over his old skin lined and loose until the day, years ago, he decided that he was "Too old for you" and rolled himself up and away from her as she lay still in bed. Between them now there is the cool comfort of shop talk. One afternoon in January, William telephones her from his shop in Salem, a shop with something for people with all sorts of specialities: Indian medicine bags, Chinese chess sets, embroidered chasubles, grass masks with little saucer ears, and maps.

"Two of *your* maps are coming on the market, sweetheart. In Amsterdam, number 4, Prinsengracht. Very fine maps, I hear. Now the dealer's a strange bird, likes to talk out a sale. Won't deal over the telephone. Doesn't care if he loses the business. You're going to have to get up and go there, this time."

"But it's so inconvenient for me to go, right now. I'm expecting offers. You don't have his number, do you? Maybe he'll talk to *me*, I'm good on the phone, you know."

"Sweetheart, not a chance. My friend there says he doesn't even have a number. So, I've said you're on your way and reserved you a seat on the plane for tonight at nine-thirty."

"The maps are good ones, you say, excellent ones? Very good, your friend says? *My* maps, you're sure?"

"Beautiful maps. You won't be disappointed. Good-bye, sweetheart. Good luck."

On a card she writes "Closed 'til Saturday" and tapes it right above her name on the front window. Three days, she tells her answering service. Three days should be enough. No need to loiter once the map is hers. There's nothing else in the world that interests her anymore. For several years, after losing William, before opening her shop, she traveled cheap drugstore map in hand to Italy, Mexico, India, anywhere, for months at a time, every chance she had, wide-eyed, ready to snap a picture, ready to exclaim "how strange, how beautiful" to the man next to her whether it was Stephen, Mark, or Bill, willing to stroke the flesh of Stephen, Bill or Mark lit up by a tropical moon or the northern lights. One morning, however, New Delhi seemed like Paris, like Tokyo, all the same red square on the Michelin maps, the hotels the same black blotches. Bill was as thin, dry, and dark with tiny criss-crossing sentences as Stephen or Mark.

Back in Boston, she "retired," as she likes to put it, and opened her map store. Using her typewriter and her telephone, she manages to find the maps she wants without leaving the city, much less the country. A quiet day spent stroking the downy surface of the thick map paper, then a long walk puffed up and down the shore by fat-cheeked winds, and at last home alone with mad continents of color on the walls—this is a day filled with enough earthly glory for her.

That night the plane cabin seems a prison and a hell. It is drab and smelly, the plastic forks and the passengers make an empty clatter. As the plane rushes past the last lighthouses on the coast and into the blind, shapeless night, she sweats with a fear that, bound to her seat, she can't walk off. She never used to be afraid to fly, what has made her fear to die now? When her mind strays towards the black nothing outside the window—sleep is just as dark, just as much a dense dark fog—she tries to guide it home by sketching out on the airline napkins her favorite maps, so bright, so brimming with ships and flowers and the walls of perfect cities. She makes herself imagine the maps in Amsterdam, very fine maps, William says, very good maps, lovely maps to gaze upon.

*   *   *

In Amsterdam at last, exhausted, she takes a short nap in the hotel room before going to look at the maps. But, she sleeps too long. Waking up in the dark, she angrily reminds herself that there is no time to waste on this trip, and now the shop will be closed. All she can do tonight is walk to the dealer's shop and make sure she knows the way. A good decision, she congratulates herself an hour later, as after several wrong turns in the maze of canals—it has been years since she used a map to find something, the small map is awkward in her hand, the tiny print a strain—she circles towards the shop.

Along Prinsengracht, tall, narrow houses stand stiffly up into the night, the light from their upper rooms blurred by drawn lace curtains in a hundred starry patterns. The maps had better be good, to get her away from home, where she, too, could be behind her curtains in a soft light. Number 4 is a house narrower and darker than all the others. Yet downstairs in the tiny ground floor chamber there glows a heavily shaded lamp. No one comes, however, when she taps, and taps again louder on the cold glass, a sound too loud in the empty street, a neighbor may look out the window and think she is a thief. The door is locked. Pressed against the window, she makes out the quite good things risked in the window—Renaissance globes, Islamic sextants—the maps will be fine ones. Startling her, a face looms up before her eyes, that of a huge cat, dusky yellow with a white tufted bib, who stretches out between an astrolabe and an ancient tome. The cat shakes his head officiously like an old clerk, as if to say, "Closed. Go away."

A cold winter wind turns through the canals. She has to move on. Walking back down the street, she enters into a pub for some dinner. The customers, mostly men, raise their heads to stare at her, but out of habit she looks only at the waiter, nods to him, and follows him to a small table near the central stove that heats up the dark-panelled room. She orders and soon the food comes, promptly and properly hot. As the waiter sets the plate before her, she thinks how long it took to acquire the ability—self-taught—to enjoy eating alone. To make herself served well and courteously, to eat slowly, enjoying her meal, thinking her own thoughts.

A shout of laughter bursts from a group of men standing behind her in one corner. Startled, she looks over at them and a big, tall man, obviously the teller of the joke, catches her eye with his bright, curious glance. Of course, the laugh was raised to make her turn around; it always provokes men, as men, to see a woman alone, making her way without one of them. She must still be quite exhausted to have fallen for that; she knows better. Yet at one time, she suddenly recalls and it's like finding an old dress and thinking instantly of a certain night, at one time, when she used to travel, she would have looked back at this man with a long look and a smile, she would have let him join her for a drink. But now, it's a quiet triumph to have only business on her mind—the maps, her maps, fine maps—once they are in hand she can go home, stay at home. She turns back around, finishes her dinner, pays, and nods good night to the waiter.

*   *   *

In widening circles, squinting at her map over and over, she returns to her hotel and goes to bed. However, having slept too long that afternoon, she sleeps fitfully. Finally falling asleep, she sleeps heavily and wakes up late, again. Rushing through her breakfast, hurrying past canals, she arrives at number 4 by eleven only to find a note saying "Back at eleven-thirty" in Dutch and English. Forced into unwilling tourism, she idles along the canal glancing at the shop windows. But she finds a little pleasure after all. In one window a painting with a map in it, her kind of map, is displayed. A sign she will be successful, she tells herself, and begins to be more cheerful. In the picture only the back of a painter, elegant in a slitted doublet, is visible as he sits before his easel. At the far right corner of the room, placed between a casement window and a heavily carved table, stands a model bedecked with pearls, ostrich plumes, and blue silk brocade. Her face turns slightly away from the artist's gaze. The rival-beauty of the painting is a map of Spain, bordered with panoramic views of the principal cities, which takes up almost all of the back wall. The artist has spent his best efforts on where the light falls from the leaded window—the shirt shining through the doublet on the painter's wide back, the averted cheek of the woman, the gleaming emptiness of sea on the map. These glow in the gloom of the room.

The picture keeps her standing so long enthralled before it that Descotes has attracted the attention of another idler. He has been strolling up and down the street, looking at windows, watching her. She has felt him there, behind her, she realizes. Now he moves closer, in a moment—she remembers how it goes —he will be so close that they will have to say something about the painting, then the weather, then comes an invitation to coffee, to dinner, to bed, if only she keeps standing still for a few more seconds.

But her maps. With a quick glance at her watch she sees it's time for the shop to be open. She turns away as he takes the last step towards her. She used to smile a polite, apologetic smile at moments like these. The practice comes back to her an instant too late now. The man frowns after her.

At number 4, the shop door opens with a grating rumble and shuts with a loud click. The room is as empty as last night, except for the big cat, who rises, stretches, and jumps to her feet. By running at her ankles, he steers her to the desk at the back where the lamp still burns. From the ceiling to the wainscoting are shelves of calf-bound books whose spines glimmer with gold lettering, beneath the shelves wide cabinets of polished drawers, map drawers she knows. A large table blackened with age takes up the rest of the room.

Steps come thumping down some hidden stairs. A big head topped with a shock of red hair, ducks through the low door to the left, the heavy body that follows blocks up the doorway. How this body must fill up this thin, narrow house, how it almost looks at this moment that he is some great hermit crab, carrying his fragile shell house on his back.

*   *   *

Then she sees it is the joketeller from the pub. He recognizes her right away, a grin splits his wide round face. She can see how he could make people laugh, to look at him would make anyone laugh. His brown corduroy suit hangs flabbily around his thick body. His rumpled white shirt sticks out between the waistband of his pants and the thin belt he has hitched up too high and too tight. Part of his shirttail is even caught in his fly, the tuft of it sticks out like a gay white sail before him. She remembers the quick eyes, she sees they are a rich chestnut, curious and direct. His long thin nose along with these eyes gives him the look of a courtly bird. A very funny man, except, it strikes her sharply, for the lips. They are almost too thin, too severe, the lips of an exacting man. Between the upper part of this face and these lips there must run some invisible fault line, along which the two characters, the clown and the master, strain together unevenly.

She hands him her card. "You were told to expect me, I believe."

Throwing up his hands in exaggerated surprise, he exclaims, "Ah, the map-lover. I should have guessed it was you last night. Loitering around the shop, hoping for even one glimpse, a little lovesick already, no? That's a good sign for the dealer, yes? He can charge what he likes. He knows the customer must have the map."

So she's to be paid back for her coolness in the pub.

"I must say that it is rare to encounter a young woman—oh yes, my dear, to a dilapidated, insomniac, old carcass like myself, I'm broken beyond my forty years—yes, yes, you are young, very young—rare to meet a young someone as fervent as you about their trade. Lingering in the cold night simply to be near the maps." He pauses, notes her annoyance with delight, and then turns mock-professional. "Alright, let's be very serious, let's have a look at the maps, the all-important maps."

He bustles over to the locked drawers, at the same time pulling a ring of keys from his pocket. The ring comes out, and along with it an ink pen, a crumpled handkerchief and a leather change purse that falls to the floor spilling coins all around. "You see how clumsy I am—the customer says to herself, 'The dealer is nervous, the advantage is mine.'" He stops and bends over to pick up the coins. As he stoops over with his back to her, his jacket pulls up, his shirt pulls out of his trousers, and he is exposed almost down to the cleavage of his buttocks. Surprised, she thinks "how ridiculous" and at the same time she wants to place her hand there on that skin, it is so fine-grained, smooth, firm almost luminous as if the whiteness were some sheen of silver melted into gold. She'd like to run her fingers down the ridge of the spine to where it ends, she'd like to feel under her palm the muscles playing there so smoothly and powerfully. This must be the center of power for the big body.

*   *   *

Her body starts to tighten up, her thighs, her belly—it has been a long time since she has longed so sharply to touch someone's flesh, to have the feel of it in her fingertips at that moment, knowing it will linger there like a soothing shock for days. Just as she becomes afraid that her hand will go out of its own accord, he straightens up, the clothes covering him in a clumsy bunching of fabric.

In relief she allows herself to smile, she shouldn't let such a silly thing distract her. The maps are all that counts, the maps and going home. Luckily, he has noticed nothing and, unlocking the drawer, has drawn out a roll and pulled the desk lamp over to the big table. He unfurls the map and with a click turns up the power of the lamp to illuminate a beautiful—William was right—beautiful piece of work.

And with one look at the map she is completely back in her mapworld. Here the Netherlands of 1652 have been painted in as a blue heraldic lion rampant on the northern coast of Europe. She almost laughs, for the lion—in spite of his gold crown and elegant tufted tail—looks like a fat blue cat standing on his hind legs to bat at a fly. He could be the royal cousin of the yellow cat gazing at her from the desk. Turning professional, she admires the coloring, a fine wash of blue bice, names the probable date of the map and the mapmaking firm. Impressed, the dealer cries, "Oh, very good, very good, absolutely right. I shall sigh when you're gone. I see only pretentious amateurs and tourists all day long."

She could maybe afford it at what she estimates its price to be. The map of the Battle of Waterloo that she has been holding onto as the price climbed, she could let that go for this. Finishing the thought, she straightens up. He takes the hint, rolls up the map, and then going back to the drawer he produces the second map.

Before her are every fanciful figure of the East, quaint and funny as in a children's book. Ruling the Mongolian plain, the great Khan twirls his mustaches in front of his golden-tasselled tent. Further south Mandarins bow beside their pagodas. A cannibal couple of Borneo, modest in their grass skirts, look shyly at each other over the human elbows they nibble. In the reaches of the sea, fretted calligraphy, like a handwritten letter home, details the terrible marvels of the world.

As she looks the map over, she almost hums; it's good, it's what she had hoped to see. Her explorer's map of the Belgian Congo, she knows a small, rich museum that covets it. To the dealer, again, she names the date and the map-maker. He is delighted, of course, she is right. Now to business, she thinks and prepares her offers in her mind.

However, he has one more map to show her. "A special map. It's not for sale, but if you don't mind, I'd like you to see it. It will give me great pleasure to have you appreciate it, oh, not give it a price, simply see how beautiful it is. I'm rather proud of it and like to show off my good taste." While putting back the second map and bringing back the new map, he tells her that the circumstances of the map's purchase were curious. One day, an old woman had summoned him to come look at a map she had for sale. The map was kept in a locked cabinet in her room. Descotes should imagine a big, tall white-haired woman with the smallest of keys on a blue scrap of ribbon, leading him to her bedroom, shutting the door behind them. The map, she told him, was a gift she had made to herself years ago, with some money left to her by her grandmother, a gift she had kept all to herself all these years, until now when she needed the money to, as she laughed, bury herself. When he saw it, he thought how well she had rewarded herself all those years of her life. "Another mapmistress, she was," he grins at Descotes, "though of only this one map." In fact, he felt very humble in front of her, as if she knew the map better than he, an expert, did. After one look at it, he bought it.

Descotes is immediately wary; declaring the map not for sale, telling the odd story of its former owner—he must be setting her up for the map he really wants to sell her today. She prepares herself to give a cold eye to the map.

But when he lays the map before her, she finds it impossible to do anything but gaze upon it with absolute abandonment to pleasure. This map of South America would have seemed to anyone else a very plain map compared with the first two—but she sees right away it is as lavish, even more so in its own way. She has to admit to herself it is the best of the three maps, truly a superb map beyond comparison. The work could only have been done by the best illuminator of maps in the seventeenth century, Margarethe Blau, the wife of the master printer Theodor Blau. The long spine of the Andes Frau Blau has rendered in the finest golden tincture of myrrh with the western slope reflecting the setting sun in a delicate pink wash of cochineal. Several stands of trees, in a thousand varying shades of green, play the vast rain forest of Brazil. Rivers have been threaded through the continent in indigo banded with magenta. The southern pampas wave their bluish leaves and the golden stalks. Red lead, the color of dried blood, shadows the double cathedral towers of Spanish settlements. Surrounding the land, showing off its gentle brightness, the sea is stippled like shot silk in dark indigo and a wash of lighter blue bice.

*　　　*　　　*

As she examines it, what suddenly strikes Descotes about the map is that its very perfection wants to be saying something, like a child perfectly composed at high tension in order to get the attention of its mother. Taking her magnifying glass from her purse, she works down the western coast, around the Horn, and up the eastern coast to the Caribbean. Everything, every inlet and spit of land, every island, is absolutely correct, and Margarethe Blau has blessed her husband's perfect outlines with her rare colors.

No, here is an island, just off the coast of Venezuela, an island out of place, no, not out of place, for it belongs nowhere else. An imaginary island, drawn in with quick strokes of a pen, not printed. This is what the map's perfection silently strains to tell —the error, the gratuitous island.

The dealer sees Descotes staring at the island and laughs in delight. "So, you've discovered the secret of the map. Frau Blau has sketched in her own paradise: 'Let there be an island and an island appeared on the bosom of the sea.' "

The island *is* a lovely Eden, all for oneself. There are minute patches of greenish gold furze, tiny trees toss in a breeze, tender hillocks—and then Descotes gasps, looks again, narrows her eyes. She can hardly believe it, this exquisitely detailed landscape, its contours, take on the breathtakingly precise outline of a woman embracing a man. That faultless drawing of the upper coast, the taut single line is the woman's exposed neck, her back, the curve of her buttocks, the sweep of her legs superbly clean down to the graceful feet tapering off into the ocean. The arched lower coast is the lover's long back, stretched out afloat on the Caribbean waves. He presses up against her breast and belly and thighs, his thighs and legs flail. His arms are outstretched above his head, grasped by her hands. The good Frau must have found it unbearable to show them—her and her lover, some sailor?—crying out in pleasure, golden hair falls over the woman's face, the lover's face, it flows into the sea, curling and rushing like foam against the rocky shore.

Staring at the island, Descotes feels her own breasts ache, her face must glisten, again a sharp and sudden excitement makes her almost tremble. It isn't fair to be taken so unexpectedly with longing.

"Quite wonderful, no?"

Of course, he knows! He has set up this scene like a voyeur, forcing this upon her, so he could watch her, shock her. Angry, she cannot look at him, she won't give him the satisfaction.

"You don't find the island delightful? Oh, you must, I would be so disappointed!" He seems genuinely puzzled by her silence, his voice innocent of any smile.

Descotes can hardly believe he cannot see, truly see the island. It is so alive, so terrible a picture of possession. He sees only an island, an idiosyncratic island, not a seizure, a conquest, an establishing of rights. It is as if he were an amateur and hadn't recognized the signature or the distinguishing stamp that would make a valuable map in fact priceless. Would she be dishonest if she doesn't point out the true nature of the island to him? But she cannot bear to, it would be like making him aware of her own body pressing, it seems to, against the very walls of the room. Why should she tell him, if he can't see it himself? "Forgive me. I'm sorry, I was lost in it. It's beautiful." Trying to control the tremor in her voice, she adds, "It's so beautiful I'd like to buy it. Would you sell it to me?"

*   *   *

He laughs in triumph. "I knew you would love it. But, as I said, it's not for sale, I simply wanted you to admire it. Now that your immense expertise has confirmed my judgement, I'm very happy. I shall not regret the enormous sum I paid for it."

Descotes, thinking she hears him working up the price, almost smiles and bites her lips. She sings to herself, he's going to sell, he's going to sell.

"We all," he continues, "must allow ourselves an extravagance once in awhile, isn't that right? And this is so beautiful." He looks back down at the map with unfeigned pleasure.

"It's a masterpiece, I agree. Name your price."

Surprised by her insistence, he gives her a long look. Then he laughs, "Oh, forgive me, you must think I'm bargaining with you. No, no, I don't make deals that way. With me, business is always very straightforward. I'm sorry, the map is not for sale. I tell you very honestly, I bought it for myself. It called out for someone who would admire it as much as the old woman."

"But it may be that I admire it more than you and as much as she did. Then, by rights, it should be mine."

He stares at her for several moments. Then, as if testing her, he names a price. It is an immense sum. Almost humiliated to show him what the map means to her—but then he doesn't know what she knows—she swallows and says she can raise the sum, if he will sell the map to her.

His silence is rather cruel, since he must know now that he has her, that she would probably give anything to have the map. When he finally speaks, it is in a serious, friendly tone, a tone that strikes her as only too much like that which William uses with her. "I'm older than you, let me protect you from yourself. Take one of the other maps. They are masterpieces, too, albeit gaudy compared to this one. I'll give you a very good deal on them. For this map, I'll make you beggar yourself."

"That's my affair. I know the business as well as you. I still would like to buy the map. All you have to do, it seems to me, is decide to sell it."

He looks down at the map again, stares at it intently, questioning it, searching it for some answer to her. "It is a fine map, very fine, not another like it, so quiet and calm in its mastery, so happy with its lovely island. Is it really worth so much to you? Why, I must ask myself?"

She manages a crooked smile. "You know women, we have our fancies, our cravings, mine is your map, that's all."

"A woman's weakness? You're that kind of woman, then? Not a map-dealer?" Rolling up the map (oh, my island, gone, she thinks in pain), he puts her off. "Go back to your hotel and think about it. Can you really get the money? I'll see you again at ten o'clock tomorrow. I have to think about it too."

He has to sell to her, he has to give her his word *now*. She wants to argue on, badger him, but she reminds herself, with difficulty, that she has already passed the limit of what is considered civil bargaining among dealers; she consoles herself, with difficulty, that at least she's made him consider selling. Forcing herself to nod, smile, she turns and leaves the shop. Spinning out canal by canal, she hurries back to the hotel and there she places her calls as if she were raising a ransom—quick a matter of life and death. She lies to the manager of her bank and gets a loan. From William, she demands money. She tells him that it is an invaluable map, that she has to have it. When he argues that it is too expensive for her business, she argues back that if he hadn't taught her to prize maps she wouldn't be in the business at all anyway. For the first time in all these years, she makes him feel he owes her something for making her go away, he has to pay her off with the map. He promises her the money and then with a cool good-bye hangs up.

But she doesn't pause an instant to feel ashamed of herself. Adding up the figures, she finds she has the dealer's price. At first she's elated, in the next second frightened at the thought that she is going to throw all this money away for one map. She hastily promises herself she'll work extra hard this spring, she'll move maps round, she'll deal in ways she's refused to before. She's already thinking how she can strip her favorite maps from her own walls, maps she used to treasure as if they were her children; now, she'll sell them down the river—heartless.

At dinner, she starts to worry again. Is the map worth so much? She sketches and resketches the map on a scrap of paper. But her island comes out merely as an island every time. If the island was really that man bound to that woman, he would have seen it. It is only an island, only an island. But, she argues back to her own doubts, the old woman knew it, she kept it secret in her cabinet, an exquisite torment. That was the clue, wasn't it?

She packs, there will not be much time tomorrow to close the deal—he has to sell it!—and make her flight. Trying to sleep, she finds her mind too busy. She is either adding up columns of figures, or sorting out the maps she will have to sell, or attempting to conjure up the island—but it is always only an island. That makes her despair more than she ever has in her life, the very thought of that island being only an island, merely an island.

Only an island—she gets out of bed, gets dressed, she has to go back and look at the island, tonight, she has to know.

*   *   *

Once more, she winds in and in to the shop, by now she has found her footing, she knows every landmark, every bridge, every house along the way. Prinsengracht, #4, cat, lamplight. The door is open, but at the loud click of its closing no one comes. She goes to the back of the shop and in through the small door. Off to one side is a dark kitchen and on the other nothing but a narrow screw of white stairs. Up and up she goes, up into this whelk. At the top is a large room, most of it in the dark except for a light on the table where he sits in a big chair. His jacket is off, the shirtsleeves rolled up over massive forearms, with gilt hairs glinting. He stares at the map, her map. She walks in and over to the table. Looking down at the map, she sees instantly that she was right, yes, the two bodies taut as one still arch in that sea.

"I have the money. I raised it," she has barely any voice.

His eyes are sharp and black, his lips tightened up, as he looks up into her face as if he would read it. "What do you see in my map?"

Her face is made as smooth, as white as thick paper, her eyes almost closed into thin brushstrokes of black lashes. Provoked by her silence, he pushes his chair back, stands up and steps over to her, watching her closely. "Tell me about my map."

She stays perfectly still and says nothing, if she just waits and stays still he'll have to give her the map she says to herself over and over, stay still, just wait, let him find his way to giving her the map, it is inevitable that he will give her the map.

"I won't sell it to you."

Oh, mere defiance easily brushed aside, brushed aside with her hands, reaching out, brushing against that big chest, over across the shoulders, down the arms to take the thick forearms in her hands, to steady herself, to grasp the thick forearms, brushed with gold in the light, to steady him, to keep him on course. She holds fast to them, at the wrists, she wants the feel of them in her hands from the very first, she wants to know the sinews, the bone, the muscle, to feel the grace of flesh—her hands had almost forgotten such grace—she wants to promise herself with this grip, to make a claim with this grip, that she will close her lips over his, she will unbutton his shirt and push him back to the bed she sees over his shoulder, there she will free him from that belt, pants, socks and shoes, she will lay him out on that bed, his fine white legs, the knees knotted intricately like silk cording, the thighs, white and firm as ivory, furzed red-gold, she will smooth him out and then raise up with her hand the long thick spit of land from his bristling thicket of gold, raise it up very long and high, then mount it, as the dawn whirls in and in the canals after her, the light falling on her as she mounts him and holds the wrists down, hard, as she leans over to watch his face in exquisite dread, as she pulls herself up on him, then crashes back down, as he cries out sharp and hard against the white walls of that room, as she washes up gasping in the billowed sheets, the cat lolling in the shallows by their side.

◆ *David Michael Kaplan* ◆

STAND

Some things you just couldn't seem to say good-bye to, Frank thought, as he drove up the dirt road to the summer house. His father had sold it three years earlier, after his mother died, and Frank hadn't been back since helping him close it for the last time. That was also the last time he'd seen his father: each time his father had called, suggesting they get together, Frank had put him off. Now his father was dead, these past six months; he had died suddenly, of a stroke. At age thirty-nine, Frank was alone—mother and father dead, Jena gone, no children. Sometimes he felt this solitude as freedom. He could go anywhere, do anything. As if to prove this to himself, he bought an old Triumph TR3 and began driving on weekends into the New England countryside. These trips had no real destination. They usually ended with his drinking beer in some over-air-conditioned motel lounge and then driving back to Boston with the radio turned up loud on an oldies station. Now, on this Fourth of July weekend, he had come back here to the Berkshires, to the summer house by the lake.

The new owners, whoever they were, were gone—strange, on a holiday weekend. The door was locked, the deck chairs neatly stacked. Frank peered through the porch window, but the sun's slant was wrong and he could see nothing. He walked down to the dock and looked at the rope swing hanging over the water. As a child, he had jumped from it, his skin as pimply as a chicken's in anticipation of the lake's coldness. Frank sat on the edge of the dock and looked up at the house. Everyone he'd thought he loved had been here with him: his parents, Jena, a woman before her, one after. All were gone. He should be too.

He was alone, he told himself, but he was free.

Still—the early evening was fine and musky, and Frank had no desire to return yet to Boston. He'd seen posters at a gas station announcing a fireworks display at the lake. He glanced at his watch—in a few hours the show would start. He could drive back to Boston afterward, or get a motel room along the way. He drove down the road to the Mini-Mart and bought chicken-salad sandwiches, potato chips, and a six-pack. On a display rack he saw a Yankees baseball cap much like one he'd had as a boy. He bought that, too.

The beach was crowded with sunbathers and barbecuers and volleyballers. Frank wanted to be more alone. A quarter mile past the beach the asphalt turned into a narrow dirt road that threaded through thick pines, which hid the shore and prevented parking. Frank was about to back up when he came upon an unexpected clearing, with picnic tables and a dock that jutted into the lake. He heard voices and smelled charcoal. Two pickups, a Ford and a Chevy, were parked off the road. He pulled up beside them: at least this would be quieter than down at the beach. From the dock he'd have a good view of the fireworks.

Four men shared the clearing with him. One was turning hamburgers and hot dogs on a hugely smoking grill while a friend solemnly watched. The other two lazily passed a football, catching with one hand and holding beer with the other. Except for one of the football throwers, who was clean-shaven and long-haired and seemed younger than the rest, they were all bearded and thick-set, their T-shirts hanging loosely over their bellies. Local boys, Frank thought. He took a beer from his six-pack and walked down to the dock to sit apart from them. The grill tender nodded as Frank passed, and his friend belched. The football players ignored him.

Frank sat on the dock and drank his beer. The lowering sun scattered thin rays through the trees on the opposite shore. He shaded his eyes and searched for the summer house but couldn't find it. He raised his beer in a farewell salute and felt strangely guilty, as if he were abandoning the house, leaving it to chance and ruin. It's not mine at all, he reminded himself. It was nothing he had to care for.

*   *   *

A breeze raked the water. Frank crushed his beer can and walked back to the car for the sandwiches. The two men who'd been throwing the football were inspecting the Triumph. The heavyset one had a puffy, bearded face that seemed not to have settled right that day. He nodded at Frank, while his friend, the clean-shaven one, grinned. Up close he wasn't as young as he'd seemed—the long hair had contributed to the illusion—and the corners of his eyes were crinkled, as if he'd been squinting for a long time.

"Nice car." He rubbed his thumb along the fender, so that it squeaked.

"Thanks," Frank said.

"You sure don't see too many of these. Old Porsches, MGs, you see a lot of. Not these."

"I've noticed that," Frank said. He opened the car door and took out the sandwich bag. He had no real desire to talk.

"Ride nice?"

"It's okay."

"I always wanted to have one of these, didn't you, Polk?" His friend grunted. "It's really something." He patted the Triumph's fender. " 'Course I'd never give up my little beauty." He nodded toward the Ford pickup. "You need a truck around here more than a sports car."

"Where you from?" the other man asked Frank. His voice was thick and tarry.

"Boston."

"What brings you up here?"

"The fireworks," Frank said lightly.

"Shit, man—you come all the way here for fireworks? Don't they got fireworks in Boston?"

"I was visiting," Frank said. "My folks used to have a summer house here."

"Did they, now." The clean-shaven man seemed amused. "Well, that almost makes you a home boy, then, don't it?" He pointed to his friend. "That's Polk. I'm Eddie."

"Frank." He offered his hand, but Eddie was already pointing to the men at the grill.

"Over there's Teal and Mace." He shouted, "Teal! Mace! This here's Frank."

The barbecuer waved his hamburger turner, and Frank nodded. "Well," he said to Eddie, "I think I'll go sit—"

"You still got that house, Frank?" Polk asked.

Frank shook his head. "My father sold it a few years ago."

"So who were you visiting?"

"Well, nobody, really."

"So why'd you come back?"

"He told you, Polk," Eddie said. "He came for the fireworks."

"Oh, right."

"Polk's a little slow," Eddie said. "Don't mind him. Have a beer with us, Frank?"

"That's okay. I brought my own."

"Something wrong with our hospitality?"

"No, I just—"

"What you got there anyway, Frank?" Eddie pointed to the paper bag.

"Sandwiches."

"No shit? Let me see." Frank hesitated and then handed him the bag. Eddie pulled out a sandwich. "Chicken." He held it up for Polk to see. "And chicken. Two chicken sandwiches."

"Huh," Polk said.

"Polk, why don't you get our friend here a beer?" Eddie put the sandwiches back, carefully folded the bag, and handed it to Frank, who resigned himself to having a beer with them.

Eddie leaned against the Triumph. "So you say you used to come up here summers?"

"We had a house about a half mile off Lake Road. Up from where that Mini-Mart is now."

"That's not the place burned down?"

"No, no."

Polk returned with the beers, accompanied by one of the men from the grill.

"Mace, what's that place burned down off Lake Road?" Eddie asked the newcomer.

"Brenner place," Mace said.

"Why, I knew them," Frank said. "Mr. Brenner used to go fishing with my dad. They had a daughter who got killed in a car crash."

"That's them."

"Their place burned down?"

"About five years ago."

"Jesus."

"Hard-luck family," Eddie said.

"Brenner got into a little fight with some boys down at the marina about some repair work on his boat," Polk said. "Place burned down over the winter."

"You mean they burned it?" Frank asked.

"No, I don't mean that."

"Things happen sometimes, Frank," Eddie said. "Coincidences. It's spooky. You think there's a connection, but there ain't none. It's just the way things happen."

"Those poor people," Frank said.

"Yeah, they don't come here no more," Polk said.

*   *   *

The four men were silent for a moment.

"Where you from, Frank?" Mace asked.

"Boston."

"Hey—one thing Boston's got that we don't is spooks," Polk said. "You got a lot of them there, don't you?"

"I don't know," Frank said uneasily.

"What—can't see them?" Polk laughed, and Mace did too.

"Come on, Polk," Eddie said. "Don't act ignorant." He winked at Frank. "He don't bother you, does he?"

Frank shook his head.

"Just don't mind him. Some of his best friends are spooks, you know."

"Hell they are," Polk muttered.

Frank took a deep swig of his beer.

"Why're you here anyway, Frank?" Mace asked.

"Damn—" Polk said. "How many times we gotta hear this? He's here for the goddamn fireworks."

"You come all the way up here just to see fireworks?"

"Jesus," Polk groaned.

"I wanted to look around a bit," Frank said. "My folks used to—"

"I hope we don't have to go through all this again just for you, Mace," Eddie said.

"Well, up yours," Mace said.

Frank finished his beer and crumpled the can. "Well—I guess I'll be taking off."

Eddie looked surprised. "I thought you were staying for the fireworks."

"Well, I—"

"Polk didn't offend you, now, did he?"

"Oh, no. No."

"So why're you running off, then?"

"I'm not. I just—"

"You don't mind our company, do you?"

"No, no."

"Well, hell—" Eddie said affably. "Sit awhile. Have another beer."

Frank didn't know what to do.

"Hey, let me see that." Eddie pointed to Frank's cap. "Come on, come on," he urged. Frank handed it to him. Eddie put it on, squared it. "You know," he said to Polk, "I always wanted to have me one of these Yankees caps."

"You're a Yankees fan?" Frank asked.

"Hell, no. I hate that team."

Mace raised his beer. "Red Sox all the way."

"I just always wanted to have one," Eddie said. "It's like wearing your enemy's ears or balls or something. The Hottentots or Genghis Khan or somebody used to do that."

"Niggers," Polk snorted.

"Polk," Eddie said patiently, "Genghis Khan wasn't no nigger." He looked at Frank and shook his head, as if to say, What can you do? He tipped up the Triumph's sideview mirror and stared into it. "Yankees," he murmured. For a moment Eddie seemed absorbed in his reflection. Then he looked up, and his grin was quick and knifelike. "You married, Frank?"

"No—divorced."

"I thought so. I could tell that about you. Any kids?"

"No."

"Footloose and fancy-free, huh?"

"Sure. I guess." Eddie's questions made him uncomfortable. He'd get his cap back; then he'd go.

"Hey, Frank—" Mace had walked to the rear of the Triumph.

"Do you know you got a SAVE THE WHALES bumper sticker back here?"

"Save the whales?" Eddie said.

"Sure enough."

"Screw the whales," Polk said.

"Hey—come on, Polk," Eddie said. "Whales are beautiful." He winked again at Frank. "It's all right. I can relate."

"I seen one at Rockport once," Polk said. "Big, sorry dude. Just threw himself up on that beach there. Just wheezing away. Got himself a real big crowd."

"They say they're pretty smart animals," Mace said.

"Well, what that whale did was real dumb-ass, that's for sure."

"Here's to whales," Eddie said. Except for Frank, who had none, they all raised their beers. "Hey, Frank, you sure you don't want another?"

"No—really, I've got to get going." He waited for Eddie to give him back his cap.

"You know, Frank, I got a sense about you." Eddie tapped the bill of the cap. "Let me guess—I think you're the kind of guy who had a McGovern bumper sticker a few years back, right?"

"That's right," Frank said. "I did."

"And maybe a—who was it?—a McCarthy sticker before that."

"Well, no—"

"Or maybe a GET OUT OF VIETNAM sticker, then. Am I right?"

"No," Frank lied. "I didn't."

"You serve in Vietnam, Frank?" Polk asked.

Frank shook his head.

"How come? You weren't a damn hippie, now, were you?" Polk grinned for the first time, a grin that vanished almost as soon as it came.

"I—had a deferment."

"What for? Got bad feet or something?"

"No." Frank hesitated. "It was an occupational deferment."

"What the hell's that?"

"I had a job the draft board thought was in the national interest."

Polk and Eddie exchanged glances.

"Well, what was this job, Frank?" Eddie asked. "That was so important and all?"

"I was an educator," Frank said.

"A teacher?"

"Well, I—I didn't teach, exactly. I worked for a company that made up tests." Frank saw their puzzled expressions. "You know, standardized tests in reading and math and so on. For young kids. I helped make up test questions."

"They let you out of Vietnam for *that?*" Polk said.

"It wasn't me. It was their decision."

"But you had to ask them for that deferment," Eddie said. "Didn't you?"

Frank was silent.

"Hey, you guys!" Teal shouted from the grill. "Food's on."

"You weren't scared to go, were you, Frank?" Eddie asked.

"Nobody wanted to go to that war."

"That's not what I asked. I asked, were *you* scared?"

"No, I—I—of course not."

"Well, you're a brave man, Frank." Eddie raised his beer in another toast. "I sure was scared."

"You were over there?"

Eddie nodded. "Me and Teal."

"You tell him, Eddie," Polk said. He was smiling again.

Eddie counted on his fingers. "Ben Hu, Qui Duc, the Delta—one lousy place after another."

"Huh," Frank said.

"You know," Eddie said, "a lot of guys over there didn't much care for the guys who got to stay home. I mean, there you were, getting your ass zinged, eating those rotten peaches, and some guy back home was eating a chili dog, screwing your sister—"

"You don't got a sister," Mace said.

"I didn't say this was me, Mace. I'm talking about guys in general. Now, don't worry, Frank. Me—I didn't hate that guy at all. Hell, no—more power to him. He was smarter than me. He got out."

"He got a deferment," Polk said.

"I even *admired* him," Eddie said. "I'd think about the absolute good times he was having, and I just admired him. He was smarter than me. I thought, When I go home, I'm going to shake his hand. And Frank—I'd like to do it." He thrust out his hand. Frank dumbly, automatically, extended his, and Eddie grasped it and shook it once, twice, and let it fall. "There, now."

Polk laughed, and Frank reddened.

Eddie glanced again in the side-view mirror. "Hell, look at me, guys." He fingered a clump of long hair, and laughed. "I'm the one who looks like a hippie now." He tipped Frank's cap back on his head. "You know, I just love this cap."

"Maybe Frank'll give it to you," Polk said.

"Hey—that'd be real nice." Eddie looked at him, and Frank was startled by the challenge in his eyes. They were all looking at him.

"Sure," Frank said. "You can have it."

"Why, that's real nice of you, Frank." Eddie grinned broadly. "Hey, Teal!" he shouted. "Frank here gave me his Yankees cap."

"You guys ever gonna come eat?" Teal shouted back.

"C'mon, Frank," Eddie said. "Let's get us something to eat."

"I should get going," Frank said.

"Oh, come on, now." Eddie clapped him on the shoulder, held him. "You're not scared of our cooking, now, are you?" He guided Frank toward the grill. "You gave me this nice cap, now I've got to give you something. We've got to break bread together, like the old Israelites." Eddie speared a hot dog, put it on a burnt bun, and shoved it into Frank's hand. "We'll eat and have us another beer and then we'll all watch the fireworks, right? Now, you just get yourself some beans and stuff and come sit with us." He turned and walked back to his pickup.

Polk and Mace fixed their hot dogs and hamburgers and went over to sit with him on the tailgate.

*　　*　　*

Frank lingered at the grill. He bit into his hot dog.

Why, why had he given Eddie his cap? He felt stupid. If they hadn't all been standing around, making him nervous—

"Don't let him get to you," Teal said. "Eddie's okay. He just likes to needle folks."

Frank hadn't realized he'd overheard. "I don't think he cares much for me," he said.

Teal flipped over a hamburger. "Eddie don't care much for nobody. That's Eddie."

"Were you in Vietnam together?"

Teal looked puzzled. "What do you mean? Eddie wasn't over there at all. Did he say that?"

"Yes."

Teal grinned. "That crap artist. *I* was over there, but he wasn't. He was in the army, but they'd stopped sending new guys by then."

"But why'd he—"

"He was just kidding you."

Frank looked at the three men eating by the truck. Eddie was saying something to Polk and Mace, and they all laughed. *Just kidding me.* Frank felt foolish but also relieved. Okay, fine. He'd played the fool, he'd lost his cap. So what? Let Eddie have it. He'd just go.

The sun had disappeared behind the trees and the sky was streaked with fire. Frank finished his hot dog. "Well, I better get going," he said.

"Take care," Teal said.

"Hey, Frank," Eddie called as he passed by them. "You're not leaving, are you? The fireworks'll be starting soon."

"No, I've got to go."

"Why? No one's expecting you, are they?"

"I'm a little tired. It's a long drive back."

"Well, it's up to you."

And I'm gone, Frank thought. He'd go down to the beach and watch the fireworks with everyone else.

"Hey, Frank—" Eddie jumped off the tailgate and walked over. "Look, before you go—I was wondering—I got a favor to ask." He seemed hesitant, almost shy. "Could I—you know—take your car for a little spin? Just down the road a ways?"

"I wouldn't let him do that," Mace yelled.

"I can't," Frank said.

Eddie seemed surprised. "Why not?"

"I—" Frank searched for a reason. "My insurance."

"Oh, the hell with that," Eddie said. "Come on—I'll just take a quick spin."

"No, really, I can't."

"You surely don't think something's gonna happen on this little old road, do you?"

"No, I—"

"Well, what are you scared of, then?"

"I'm not scared. I just—"

"You don't have something against *me* driving your car, do you?"

"No, no—"

Eddie spread his hands. "Well?"

Frank didn't know what to say or do. He couldn't argue with Eddie, and he couldn't just get in his car and go. Again they were all looking at him.

"Come on, now," Eddie said, softly, so that only Frank could hear. "I told Polk and Mace you'd probably let me 'cause you're a good guy." He grinned.

"Okay," Frank said. "Just a short ride."

"Hey, Polk," Eddie yelled. "Frank here says we can take his car for a spin."

"Whoee!"

"You're a brave man, mister," Mace called out.

Frank handed him the keys, and Eddie and Polk got in. Eddie revved the engine. Pine needles scattered under the exhaust. He jammed the gearshift forward and the Triumph lurched toward the lake, barely missing Frank's leg.

"Whooee!" Polk yelled.

Ten yards from the bank Eddie braked, glanced back, and ground the car into reverse. Kicking up pine needles and dust, it shot up the slope straight toward a tree stump. He will see it, Frank thought, he will swerve—but Eddie didn't, and the Triumph slammed dully into it.

Frank ran over. Eddie and Polk were already out, inspecting the damage. The rear bumper was dented like a piece of bad fruit.

"Sorry about this." Eddie shook his head. "I don't know where that damn stump came from."

"You saw it!" Frank cried. "Jesus—"

"Sure didn't."

"You rammed it on purpose!"

"Hey, now—" Eddie held up his hand.

"Did you see?" Frank appealed to Mace and Teal, who had just arrived.

"Wasn't watching," Mace said. Teal shook his head.

"It's no big thing," Polk said. "Car'll still run."

"Damn it, why'd you do it?"

"I told you," Eddie said. "It just happened."

"It's just a little bump," Polk said. "You can get a hammer and pound that right out."

"Frank—look here." Eddie pulled two five-dollar bills from his wallet. "Here's ten dollars. That ought to be plenty for getting it pounded out."

"You can't just pound it out! They're going to have to replace the whole damn bumper."

"Here's my ten dollars," Eddie repeated.

"Look at this—" Frank gestured helplessly.

"Real, real sorry."

"Who's your insurance company?"

"Oh, come on, Frank." Eddie looked disgusted. "We don't want to get them involved, now, do we?"

"Somebody's got to pay for this!"

Eddie waved the bills.

"Who's your insurance company?" Frank asked again.

Eddie sighed. "I don't really recall offhand, Frank. It's back there with my papers."

"You can call your agent."

"Don't remember him either." Eddie rocked slightly on the balls of his feet.

"Hey, mister," Polk said. "Are you a lawyer or something?"

"You know who your agent is, don't you?" Frank said.

Eddie's eyes narrowed. "You calling me a liar now too, Frank?"

"Look, I just—"

"Are you?" Eddie's voice rose.

"Look, friend," Mace said reasonably. "Why don't you just take the man's money and go? No trouble. Nothing to get excited about."

"He don't want my ten dollars, Mace," Eddie said. He put the bills in his pocket. "My money's not good enough for him."

"He sure does bitch and moan a lot," Polk said.

"Don't he, though," Eddie said.

"Look—" Frank said. "You smashed my bumper. You—"

"I'm getting real tired of you accusing me of things, Frank," Eddie said angrily. "You know that? Maybe you'd best just get out of here."

Frank looked desperately to Teal. Almost imperceptibly, he shook his head.

"Go on," Eddie said. He came toward Frank. "Get the hell out of here."

Frank stepped back to the car door.

"Get!" Eddie hissed.

Frank opened the door. "I'll call the police," he said, his voice cracking slightly.

"You do that," Eddie said. "Go cry to them."

Frank started to get in. "I need the keys," he said.

Eddie reached into his shirt pocket and threw the keys on the ground between them. His face burning, Frank walked over, stooped down, and picked them up. Someone snickered.

*   *   *

His ears were ringing, and Frank wasn't even aware of driving until he was through the pines, almost to the beach, and then the ringing lessened and he felt only humiliation and the acid taste of shame. He stopped at the end of the road across from the Mini-Mart.

"Bastards!" He hit his palm against the steering wheel. "Goddamn bastards."

He got out and looked at the dented bumper.

"Ten dollars," he muttered. "Ten lousy dollars."

Frank crossed the road to the outdoor phone. He was agitated and couldn't decide whether to call the highway patrol or the local police, and when he decided on the police, he couldn't remember the name of the community he was in. He found a police emergency number in the front of the directory, started to dial, and then hesitated. Even if he could get a cop out here on a Fourth of July evening for a dented bumper, wouldn't Eddie and the others be long gone by the time he arrived? And if they weren't, wouldn't they all stick up for Eddie anyway?

He sure does bitch and moan a lot, Polk had said. He could see them all looking at him with contempt: he'd gone and cried to the police after all.

He hung up. Just go, he thought. Forget it, get out of here.

Frank crossed the road again and got back in the car. He turned on the engine but didn't pull away. Instead, he stared out the windshield.

They humiliated me, he thought. And I let them. His face burned as he remembered. But what else could he have done? He'd been outnumbered. Eddie was crazy; the bumper, after all, wasn't that big a deal. And besides—

You weren't scared, were you? Eddie had asked.

Frank turned off the engine.

I was scared, he thought.

When he'd run from them, he'd been scared. When he'd let Eddie drive the car, when he'd given him the cap, he'd been scared.

And he was scared now.

I got a sense about you, Eddie had said, grinning. And behind him was Polk, and behind Polk, Mace and Teal. And behind them, still others—his father and Jena and the children they'd never had, that he'd never wanted, and he'd been scared of them, too, had run from them just as surely as he was running now.

I've always been scared, Frank thought.

He closed his eyes, and when he opened them, the images were gone except for Eddie, Frank's cap perched mockingly on his head.

Frank started the car and turned back toward the pines.

*   *   *

They were sitting at the picnic table now, passing a joint. Polk raised his arm in a half wave, as if Frank had just gone out for some beer. He parked beside Eddie's truck and walked toward them. They sat in silence, like kings in judgment.

"I want my cap back," he said to Eddie.

Eddie took a deep hit off the joint, held the smoke, and then expelled it harshly. "I thought you gave me this cap, Frank."

"He did, Eddie," Polk said.

"I didn't mean to," Frank said.

"Here, have a hit." Eddie offered him the joint. Frank shook his head. Eddie shrugged and passed it to Mace.

"I'd just like it back," Frank said. His heart was pounding—he was sure they could hear.

Eddie sighed. "That sort of makes you an Indian giver, don't it?"

"He's still hot about the car, Eddie," Polk said.

"I don't care about the car."

Eddie folded his arms. "Why do you want it now, Frank?"

"It—it's mine. I didn't mean to give it away."

Eddie pursed his lips and pulled the cap lower on his head. "How much you want it, Frank?" In the deepening twilight, his face was a mask. Polk laughed sharply.

"You want to fight," Frank said. "That's what you want, isn't it?"

"Hey, now," Mace said.

"Nobody said nothing about fighting," Eddie said. He took off the cap and twirled it on his finger.

"Oh, give him the damn hat, Eddie," Teal said. "Quit kidding around."

Eddie carefully put it back on. Frank flushed. As if they were the words of a stranger, he heard himself saying, "Okay, I'll fight you, if that's what you want. I'll fight you."

"You really want to fight for it, Frank?" Eddie seemed amused. "For this little old hat?" He slowly rose, crossed in front of the table, and stood not more than ten yards away.

"Watch out, now," Polk said.

"Eddie—" Teal said.

"Well, he wants to fight, Teal." Eddie looked at Frank. "Don't you?" Frank felt a lightness in his stomach, as if he were falling. He didn't know what to do. He knew nothing about fighting.

Eddie spread his arms. "Don't you?"

"What—what are the rules?"

Polk groaned. "I told you he was a lawyer, Eddie."

Eddie reached into his jeans and pulled out a knife. "Hey— these are the rules, Frank—" The blade snicked open.

"Eddie—" Teal said, and Mace whistled softly.

Absurdly, Frank said, "That's not fair."

"That's right—it's not. It's just the way things are."

"Eddie, put that damn thing away," Teal ordered. He rose from the table, but made no further move.

"Hey—" Frank said. "Come on."

"Come on where, Frank?" Eddie poked the air between them. "Where do you want to go now?"

"This is crazy!"

"Oh, I am crazy." He began circling Frank. "I'm the craziest thing you've ever dreamed of."

"Eddie," Teal said, "quit dicking around."

Further down the lake a string of firecrackers pop-popped. Frank heard shouts and laughter, impossibly far away. In all the world he was alone.

"You better take off, mister," Mace said.

Eddie circled him but came no closer. And Frank realized that Eddie was going to let him run, that he could if he wanted to—he would be allowed that final humiliation. It was, after all, what was expected of him.

"These are Vietnam jungle rules, Frank," Eddie said, brandishing the knife. "See what you missed?"

"You didn't go to Vietnam!" Frank cried.

Eddie cocked his head. "What's that, Frank?"

"You didn't go to Vietnam either. I know you."

Eddie stared at him, knife at arm's length. He glanced back at the table. "You didn't, Eddie," Teal said.

Eddie grinned. "Well, you sure can't put one over on old Frank, can you?"

"He's a lawyer, Eddie," Polk said.

Something searing, neither rage nor shame but of them both, passed through Frank then, and he yelled, "I'm not a lawyer, goddamn you! You don't know a goddamn thing about me!" He shook his fists at Eddie. "I'll fight you, you son of a bitch! I'll fight you."

"Don't be a fool, mister," Mace said. "Take off."

"No, goddamn it!"

Eddie stood as if frozen, knife extended, the lines of his face tight. "Don't be crazy," he said.

"I don't care," Frank cried. "Come on!"

Eddie squinted, as if trying to see him better in the fading light. The knife blade wavered slightly.

"Come on," Frank said. "You've got the knife."

Eddie didn't move.

"Damn you!" Frank cried. "All your damn talk—" He took a step toward Eddie.

"You're crazy, man." Eddie folded the knife and put it in his pocket. He spread his empty hands and grinned. "I can't fight anybody crazier than me."

He took off the Yankees cap and tossed it at Frank's feet. For a moment Frank couldn't move, couldn't stop watching him. Slowly he unclenched his fists. He picked up the cap and turned it over.

"Happy now?" Eddie said.

Frank put it on.

"Maybe you'd best go now," Teal said.

"I'm not going anywhere," Frank said. His voice seemed to come from far away. "I'm going to watch the fireworks." He walked past them, down the slope to the lake.

*   *   *

Frank sat on the dock's edge: it was dark now, and the lake smelled deep and mossy. His hands shook, lightly at first, then harder, and he hugged himself, as if that might contain the shaking. A first rocket flared and fell, followed by another that opened like a rose. "I won," he said softly.

Frank looked across the lake to the summer house, and, yes, in the rocket's light he could see it. They were all there—his mother and father and Jena, waiting to receive him, to bind his wounds. "I'm not going anywhere," he told them as they opened the door. "I'm staying right here."

The rocket faded; it was gone. He had won, but no one was there to tell, no one to care.

Three more rockets, red and white and yellow, burst over the lake. In their light Frank saw Teal and Polk and Mace and Eddie, faces turned skyward, almost reverent.

"I'm not going anywhere!" he shouted to them, but the men gave no sign of having heard. The rockets faded, they disappeared, and he was alone once more. "I'm not going anywhere," he murmured. "I'm not going anywhere at all."

◆ *Meredith Steinbach* ◆

IN RECENT HISTORY

We had been living in the islands just off the coast for some years when the matter of x. D. suddenly came and went. Though the sun is pleasant enough in spring and summer, our island is hardly tropical. Its rough hide is stony and fraught with gorse. It is a seasonal place. Small lakes dot the area, and along its edges rocky cliffs drop off steeply into a brilliant sea. Autumn does not strip the land completely. There are evergreens, low lying at the center of the island, that tower toward its edges as if the substance of the conifers had been spun out by centrifugal force. Perhaps the most peculiar thing was the presence of the island's predominant small animal. Not squirrels or chipmunks or iguanas, but rabbits had overpopulated the island as if set down by an all encompassing and hocketing wind. These were the rabbits of story books, not your western gray or dusty brown hares. These were the immense fluffy white and black spotted bunnies, brown, white, beige; and the insides of their long thick nappy ears were pink. It was as if everywhere the island had an innocence to it.

One day in June at Egg Lake, Will and I ran across x. d. unexpectedly. Every summer since we'd known him he had been completely occupied with hauling king crab off the coast. We had never seen him enticed by summer events. At the lake some friends had gathered to show off their kayaks. And he was there, too, as an observer, standing off to one side, his yellow-blond hair fallen slightly into one eye, his face ruddy and clear. His shoulders and arms were built up from his job. And his eyes were like new robin's eggs. The irises shone so blue that the whites of his eyes seemed blue, too.

Will and I lived in an A-frame house in the woods. It was a small cabin, and I had fallen for it immediately—with its log walls and its airy interior with the large sleeping loft. We had a wood stove, too, that filled the atmosphere with warmth. And we had our own pond and a brief deck that inclined toward it where I often lay to nap in the late afternoon. But our pond was not Egg Lake, hardly the size for several kayaks to have a running start. We stood next to x. d. that day and watched the enthusiasts on the dock breaking in a new young man. Among them a woman in jeans and bright red flannel shirt delighted us with her brogue and her ready confidence.

"If you're so impertinent as to go taking a dive under," she cajoled the nervous initiate, already in his craft, "don't fight the turn. Whatever you're doing down there, don't turn mollycoddle on us. Remember your moves and don't fight your boat." Then she laughed. "Do one more thing for your old instructor, will you?"

"What's that?" the boy asked.

"Hold your ruddy breath."

With that everybody laughed, the one in the boat least, of course, though he made a good attempt.

"Remember," she said, "it's cold as your old Wisconsin in the underneath, but it's not so dark, and your 'yak will be righting itself if you just swing around like you learned and hold onto your pants."

"How long does it take?" the boy asked. "In case I turn over
—just in case, I mean?"

She smiled warmly at him then. "Not a worry's worth. Ten
counts. You for one can hold your breath that long," she
laughed. She knelt down on the dock and leaned out to pat him
earnestly on the back. "I know that for fact. You're holding it so
tight right now you've practically strangled it. Relax."

Everyone laughed then, including the boy, and he paddled
onto the blue disk of water and set the shimmering reflections
of the trees into motion. It was as if he had stirred them up from
the bottom of the lake.

"Why, x. d.," I said when he turned to us. "I thought you had
abandoned us as of last week. Has anything gone wrong?"

"No no," he said, smiling very broadly. He had a habit of
hanging his thumbs on the front pockets of his jeans, accentuat-
ing the hardy, solid look of his upper torso, the narrowness of
his hips. "I've had a sudden impulse toward retirement—temporarily. I'm roosting on my savings this season, just for once."

He called across the strip of water then to the woman in the
red flannel shirt. Her hair was full and brown. She had a slight
mouth, but her eyes were bright as little green apples; they gave
a real zest to her face. "Tell him again to keep his eyes open if he
turns around," he called to her. "Tell him the water's o.k."

The woman smiled over at x. d. brilliantly, and it was clear
they had met before. Her name was Lindsey, and she'd been in
the States for five or six years, living in many parts. It was hard
to live on the island without being noticed, perhaps impossible.
She had come in May to work at one of the clothing shops for
tourists and had already begun to look for a more permanent
place. It was like that. The same had happened to us. Will and I
had arranged for a two week vacation during a summer break
from college and then we were looking for jobs so that we might
stay on the island for good.

"So maybe we'll be seeing you this summer after all. That's
very good news," Will exclaimed. We enjoyed x. d.'s company

that much. If x. d. and Lindsey had not been together for the
first time recently, it was obvious that they would be soon. Such
happinesses, however brief, pleased us both since we had come
to such deep happiness ourselves after many false starts apiece.

"There you see him—" x. d. said. We looked over in time to
watch wet brown hair like an otter's lifting up with the edge of
the kayak. The boy was upright again. There were his eyes
pinched tight as if drawn by little pursestrings into his face.

*   *   *

One evening not long after the kayak encounter, x. d. and Lindsey came for an evening to our house. How happy they seemed
together, how natural. Neither seemed in competition with the
other; there was none of the telltale mocking humor of a relationship doomed to fail. And there was the steady encounter of
their bodies, one arm brushing the other's, the gentle hand laid
on back or thigh.

We sat together on the deck looking off into the pond, sharing
a pitcher of lemonade under a soft breeze in the pines. Lindsey
had taken off her shoes and rolled up the cuffs of her pants. It
was early June, yet there was already summer heat. She extended her leg and then she waved her foot just at the top of the
water and a circle went out, as if her footprint had been a
dragon fly, something that light.

"So Lindsey," I said, "how do you come to us? Where were
you before you got the island bite and couldn't leave?"

"Ah," she said, "I've left behind an entire career of waitress-
ing. And I miss it—not one bit."

"She came up from Oregon," x. d. volunteered as if he were
responsible for this news. I almost expected from his tone to see
him lean back in his chair. "Yes," x. d. said. "She was raised in
Dublin."

"You can't say 'whiskers' there," she laughed, "without everyone knowing it. According to my relatives I've been married and run off thirty-six times."

Will lifted up his glass. "A toast to Number Thirty-Seven. But tell me, Lindsey, is there any truth in it? Have you ever run off at all?"

She waved her foot and threw back her hair. "Only six or seven times. I've been chased all the way to Galway and back by neanderthals."

"Seriously now."

"Only once, actually," she said, and x. d. leaned forward slightly in his chair. Will later said he thought he saw the hair stand up on x. d.'s ears. "I was shackled up once to the city clerk. He liked most especially to study figures. Any old figure but mine."

"I see, I see," x. d. said mostly to himself, and then to us, "Isn't that hard to believe?" He looked onto her slender form affectionately.

"I guess he must have cared about you after all, at least a little bit," I said. "He chased you down finally in Galway, you say?"

"Tubs to the whale," she exclaimed very cheerfully. "I took refuge in the Church. What could I do? He had himself a gun. I came into a state of sanctuary on the tune that it was not my man at all but my man's friend who was chasing me down with a pistol. 'He's a venomous tufthunter,' I said, 'who is driving my husband and my own self mean. It is lucky,' I said, 'if we don't the pair of us commit a mass suicide.' It was the most secure four hours of my life—hovered over like a fuzzy new chicken by nuns and priests. It wasn't long until the truth came around that it was my own husband trying to get his hairy paws onto me."

"Are you still married to him then?" Will asked gently, almost as if it was of no concern. He scratched thoughtfully along the light brown edge of his beard. I could not help but admire Will. We had been together so long and yet he always seemed handsome and kind and new.

"Oh no," she said gayly. "The Queen has seen fit to sever our hands. I was lucky enough to be married to an infertile man."

Beside her x. d. smiled, and then tenderly he pressed her fingertips. The evening passed lazily and to our delight the two proved themselves to be compatible in conversation as well as in dreams.

*   *   *

The following week I was visiting my friend Lisa in her trailer. She had the piece of land next to ours. Her place was a fifteen minute walk through woods and then there was a clearing of quite high grass and in the center of it sat her trailer. Once I likened her field to a veld and she pointed with her good arm toward the horizon and imagined for both of us a rhinocerous grazing, its tulip ears twirling away flies. The inside of her trailer was hung with tapestries and Peruvian weavings that took away that trailer feeling, nearly completely, of being inside a tin can.

Lisa's right arm had been withered from birth but it had not affected her sunny nature nor her attempts at pleasure in life. She was small with brown hair drawn back into a swinging braid down her back. She had a bad foot, as well; especially the toes were affected. I saw them once when I arrived unannounced. They looked as though they had been bound at birth. I told her that and it gave her great satisfaction to think she might have been made that way—in an earlier life, so she said. That was the way she thought of things.

To support her fascination with the island, Lisa had taken up cleaning house for the wealthy summer residents. On this particular day there had been an alteration in her usual schedule. She was to go to a new customer's house, she said, and continue her preparations for their arrival at the end of the month. She had been there only once, but she was certain I would find it interesting if I wanted to go along.

We set off across the field along the footpath she and her friends had beaten to and from her place. Before me, tilting as she limped, her full black skirt swayed about her calves. The bodice of the dress was also black and she seemed a shadow in the grass when the sun cut through between the trees and caught me in the face. She always wore a dress, she said, when she went off to clean, because it made her feel unlike a true servant in these times. She thought herself more of a character in a book. She always wore one of three or four identical black shirtwaists, and over it a crisp white pinafore. She had also a white triangle with a violet embroidered on it to tie around her braided hair.

The house was set on a point of land jutting into the water. The land did not fall off steeply as it did on most of the island but gradually and by way of a dock that casually stretched out. Soon there would come the summer boats and guests, the people to stand, drinks in hand, and bathe in the dry northern light before retiring to the city for three seasons again. Lisa was considering moving in to keep up the house in the winter, she said.

I looked up at the size of it. Above the gables and unpainted Victorian scallops of the rooms were the many chimneys that would again descend to provide some heat to what I assumed would be large drafty rooms. We had not yet been inside. She had first to show me the small dark huts set about the land where the migrant workers had stayed—how many years ago? —to gather the tart cherries from the summer trees.

I only saw the house that once; but it is the sunroom I remember best: the immense porch with its untuned grand piano, the library adjacent and the worn wooden floor, the tables and their tatted cotton cloths, the brown wicker chairs. It was there I thought I saw them dancing: Lindsey and x. d. floating in the sunlight from off the ocean, both in tight new jeans, their faces glowing with relief.

*   *   *

x. d. had been seeing Lindsey for three weeks when we saw him again. How distraught he was when I opened the door. "Why, what is it, x.?" I asked. "Have you got the summer flu?"

"No no," he said, but his voice was agitated.

"Sit down," I said. "I'll make you some tea or a drink. Will is going to be sorry to have missed you."

x. d. was a tea drinker, a habit he had picked up on some one of his travels he said. We had finished off many pots together, an insignificant fact anywhere else where imported goods were easily got.

In the living room, a roundabout story ensued. I could not make out what the problem was even when x. d. said he'd stated it. He sat in the stuffed chair by the window, his elbows on his knees and his head forward as he stared at his hands. Lindsey, it seemed, wanted to go to the Fourth of July celebration. It was a tradition on the island and everyone would attend. Lindsey, with her enthusiasm, would not have missed such an event.

"I refuse," x. d. exclaimed to me. "I refuse to go to such a ludicrous charade."

"Why not, for heaven's sake?" I tipped up the teapot in front of him, and he watched the brown-black liquid from the orient slip out into the cups. "How do you mean ludicrous?" I asked.

From a pontoon in the middle of Egg Lake at the center of the island, the rockets were shot into the sky. For the event the islanders separated themselves from the tourists by congregating on the mayor's private property around the narrow end of the egg.

x. d. scowled into his cup. "I can't stomach it—to applause! The imitation of bombs. Lindsey thinks I'm berserk."

I laughed, wrongly perhaps, and tapped his arm. "I think you're partly berserk all the time." I smiled very briefly—until I caught the coldness in his eyes. "I'm sorry," I said. "I'd only occasionally thought of it like that."

"It's hideous, it's inhuman," he declared.

I looked at him in such surprise. He had never once seemed

dauntible before. "I guess you're quite upset," I said. I could only think of one possible reason for it; but surely we would have known by then. He stared up from his cup, and I pushed him again. "You don't usually look quite so *hang dog*, x., not even when you're breaking up with your latest love. Tell me what's the matter, please. Maybe it will help. You're not already tired of her?"

He said nothing, just stared at me and then his hands. Quietly he was working his jaw. If he'd been asleep he'd have been grinding his teeth.

"So my sister sent me a book for you," I said, giving him time to come around to telling me, if he wanted it that way. "It's the new book on the psychoanalysis of Freud."

The bookstore on the island was almost completely useless, and the local theatre brought in only children's movies. We were gluttons for imported culture, Will and I, x. D. too. x. D., who was peculiarly fascinated by Freud, barely raised his brow even at this extraordinary news. How many times recently had he mentioned his anxiousness for this book? He said nothing, merely gazed at his own hands, hanging his blond head.

Finally I blurted it out: "After all this time, you're telling me you were in the war, x. D.?" It seemed almost as if he'd already said it anyway. "Is that what you're saying? All this time and all these talks and you've never before mentioned it?"

He looked up because he, of course, had not said any such thing that afternoon. "Yes yes," he said. "I don't like to talk about it."

"I can't believe you never even mentioned it."

He looked at me a long time then, and the blue of his eyes seemed almost heartbreaking in his suddenly worried lean face.

"All right, I was in Cambodia," he said. "The government said we weren't there. I trained mercenaries."

"Mercenaries? I didn't know there were any—"

"Yes," he frowned. "I was an officer, a captain. Yes," he said again, "in the Green Berets." His face had taken on a hardened, white look, as if he were concentrating very hard, or as if he were made of wax beneath the yellow stalks of his hair.

"Oh," I said, startled, for Will and I had been part of the resistance to the war. As x. d. knew, Will had for a time been in jail. "The Green Berets."

He shrugged as I looked on for the first time perhaps, in a quite different way, at his powerful arms. "I got in before anyone knew we had a right not to go. It was early. I'd like to think I wouldn't have gone if it had been later." He told me then one story after another, as though he had no way of stopping himself.

The recollection he seemed most to want me to hear was the one he introduced lightly at first. Adrenaline and the love of a friend, he said, could make a man of one hundred and eighty pounds carry another twenty pounds heavier for miles through brush and fire. It was the episode that upset him the most.

"Yes," he snarled. He leaned over and the glossy male face on the magazine seemed to stare up at him through his empty cup. He had broad shoulders and hands and a construction worker's rather short forearms. His hands and wrists were covered with fine hairs that caught the light as it infiltrated the room. His eyes seemed to tighten with intensity. "You know the incredible heat you feel when another human being is up against you, the satisfaction of it? I felt my own friend cooling against me. He was my warmth and then slowly he was my relief—from the jungle heat, don't you see?" He sighed then and stared at me harshly, almost proudly, as though I would never understand. "I think of that when I make love to anyone for any length of time."

"Is it the celebration itself worrying you? Or have you gotten too close to Lindsey now?" I asked him. "Or is it both?"

His brow furrowed. "You have beautiful hair," he said. "Do you know that? It's like honey—the deep brown golden kind—made from alfalfa or something like that."

The sun was shifting through the trees behind him. Briefly he was a silhouette, his hair golden around his darkened face. I opened the tin of cookies on the table for him. "Tell me, x. d. You're driving us both crazy trying to get started. Jump in, I'm listening."

And so he did begin, suddenly, looking me straight in the eyes. "I was sent to the mountains to train the Montagnards."

"As mercenaries, you said."

"Yes," he said. "A few of our men had been there before me as officers, but they were of lower rank. I was fortunate to have one still there as an adviser when I wanted him, and when I needed it. I hadn't been there long enough to have laid out my gear when the chief of the Montagnards invited me to his tent." As if to veer from the topic his worried eyes went toward the kitchen door. "I won't concern you with the menus of foreign lands."

"Would you like something else, x.?" I asked. "You've had lunch, I hope?"

"Yes, no thank you," he smiled. We leaned together a little over the table between us, just slightly. The light revealed his face again, the crow's feet that never disappeared—happy or sad. He stroked his cup with the thumb of his other hand, cradled it with both, and drank down the remainder of his tea. His lips were drawn tight as if at a touch he might dissolve into tears or rage, it was hard to say which.

"I was still with the rotten translator they'd sent along with me from training camp. The man was like a machine. He thoroughly understood both cultures. But he would never let on when the two were coming to a head. He was a complete asshole. He would just sit back and watch the conflict begin. I think he enjoyed it. In any case, I was at a bad disadvantage with the Chief right away. I bungled along a little with the words I knew.

"Then when we finished eating, a young girl was brought into the tent by several older men. She was nearly sixteen, so the translator told me for the Chief. A lot was made of the fact that her face was very clean and clear. Yes, I agreed, she is very beautiful. She is slender like a willow, I said, smiling and nodding like a fool. The Chief took her hand and held it out to me. A human hand was being offered to me. It seemed absurd. 'No no,' I said. 'I can't.' I waved her away. The Chief let loose a stream of displeasure. 'No, I can't.' The translator did not even offer me an indicative look. But the lieutenant immediately jabbed me with his elbow, his first advice. He excused himself in both languages saying very politely that he had been called by nature. I had the good sense to say the same thing."

Outside, x. d. went on to say, the lieutenant had explained the situation to him. The young woman was the Chief's daughter. He would have to marry her. It was like something out of a fairy tale, x. d. said, you could already sense the upcoming tragic parts.

"So you were to marry a complete stranger right then and there?"

"I had to—for the company's security, to say nothing of the integrity of the girl herself. I was the new, although visiting, chief. That was how they looked at me.

"And so we were married in the middle of a prolonged festival. It seemed then a little like Halloween. And we moved into my tent. At first I resented her. I've always preferred my privacy; and I was not long out of training. Most of the long term men would have given anything to have been in my position."

"She was that beautiful—"

"She was a woman," he said. "Beautiful, yes. The other women in the village were not free to consort with my men."

"You were with her for a long time?"

"Two years. I was very gentle with Pom. I may have killed strangers," he said, "but I was very gentle with her." He looked me straight in the eyes. "I left her behind. I suppose you'll say I've been leaving others behind ever since because of her."

"Why did you leave Pom then—if you loved her so much?"

"I was already married. My wife was waiting for me."

"Oh," I said quietly. Yet another fact about x. d. had come to light. "I see."

"That relationship was already finished, but I didn't find out for certain until I got back. You can't tell that sort of thing from a distance. My wife and I just didn't either one seem to care about the other anymore. And then one day almost a year later a friend wrote that Pom was dead." He rubbed the fingers of his one hand with the other almost as if they were sore. He would not look up.

"I had made a string of gold coins into a necklace for her. We got so much money for each man we brought in dead. The money extended even to us. The necklace was supposed to be her legacy, I said, if I should get myself killed. She wore them constantly. She was superstitious about things. They wouldn't have had to kill her for them. She was very shy. She would never have stood up for herself. Even for me she would have been too much afraid."

He put his hands over both of mine for a moment and I moved closer to him. Then he was holding my hands in his tight fists on his knee. "I'm sorry," I said.

"Yes," he said. "Yes, of course."

We were silent for a long time, suspended over our reflections in the glass table. "And now there is Lindsey," I said. "She would understand, x. d. I'm sure she would. If she didn't, you wouldn't want her anyway."

"No," he said. "It's none of her business. If I thought you would mention it to her—"

"You wouldn't have to tell her the whole story, you wouldn't even have to mention Pom. The war is enough."

"That isn't why I told you."

"Of course not," I said. "I didn't think it was. All the same a friend could help you by talking to her. I could, or Will— It's obvious how much she means to you. You've made that clear to me."

"No." He was adamant. "A friend could not help me."

"You want her to trust you without explanation. Is that it?"

"I don't give a damn about trust," he scowled. "I want her respect."

*   *   *

Dr. Principal was known for a character on the island. He was nearing sixty, tall and wiry, with the same steel-rimmed glasses that he'd had for thirty years, so people said. He always wore short sleeves. It was almost as if he had on wings they stuck out so around his bony arms. He and I had become close friends. I had his confidence enough to hear many of the stories of his work that he would not tell anyone else. In this way I knew that he was very excited about the skull that was found on the island that summer. Roundabout town he had taken on the appearance of the nonchalant.

It was not everyday that he got to see a head without a body, he laughed. It was often enough, he said, that he saw them without brains wandering around town looking for the new sweet shop. He was adamant about sweets. Sweet Edibles, he was certain, was destroying everybody's health and sense.

No, he said, the skull was not the head of the young woman in the rumor I'd heard flying around. That woman had disappeared several years before Will and I had arrived. Dr. Principal himself had helped her to escape her more than tyrannical parents, though he could not publicly say such a thing. He knew her whereabouts still. No, he said to those who became concerned, there was no sense in worrying about that. The head was old, he said, very old, he knew that much.

Fourth of July week, in a flurry of excitement, the expert on bones was sent for and set up in the East Island Inn. A buzz went up among the young unattached women, of course. Even Will and I heard that he was a handsome sort. In any case, he determined that the head was old, quite old, almost Neander- thal, Dr. Principal said. Yes, a real cause for celebration on the

island: a history that went beyond memory, right there under-
foot. Who knew what else had happened on these very
grounds? "Headhunters, that's what happened," Dr. Principal
said to thrill the populace. "I'd bet my car on it." His hard-
driven imported stationwagon was the only emergency vehicle
on the island, short of a plane.

*   *   *

The next time I saw Lindsey was the third of July. She was
brewing up a very large fret about x. d.'s refusal to go with her
to the celebration. Her insistence was almost childish, I thought;
but then I knew the reason behind x. d.'s seeming rejection of
her, and I knew that he had said finally of Lindsey Byrne what
he had not said of anyone else, that in her he had finally found
someone he could both love and trust, the only one since Pom.
The images of his experience had been lingering with me all
week—how he had carried his friend like a child through the
brush, whispering only to himself, "There there, there there,"
afraid to speak aloud to his friend for fear they would be heard
and caught; how the second woman he'd married had been
killed; her throat slit; how he'd said to me—"I kissed that
throat."

Lindsey had decided upon several possible reasons for his
sudden hardness toward her. She had settled too easily on the
idea that it was another woman—either he did not want to be
seen with Lindsey at such a public event or he was going elsewhere with somebody else.

In the back of Sweet Edibles she was telling her side of it to
Molly McAlester when I came popping up the alley, taking the
short cut to the post office. Robust Molly was cleaning up the
malted milk containers and ice cream scoops when Lindsey
caught sight of me. Abruptly they leaned out the back door and
flagged me down.

x. d. had made me promise not to let on even to Will what

he'd said. It was too hard, he said, having other people know about it. They changed their views, he said. They treated you with pity if they knew you'd had pain.

I had tried to tell x. d. obvious things—that everybody had had tragedy. But he said everybody may have had it but everybody didn't tell it.

"Yes yes," I'd said, mimicking him, after an hour and a half of reasoning. "The things you staunch people won't do to save face." With that we had come to a sudden and frosty halt.

Predictably, Lindsey was puzzled by the continued glum view he had taken of the upcoming festive event. "I don't care a rap about the fireworks," she said to me and to Molly. "I want to know why the sudden change in his amorous weather, that's what."

Quickly I slipped out of the sweet shop, making a lame excuse. I have always been bound by my promises. All I said in the sweet shop kitchen—and even that was perhaps too much—was that x. d. never did anything without a good reason and why not leave it at that?

As I turned to leave, I saw in Lindsey's face a new determination. It seemed she and x. d. had talked intimately about many other things. This reversal in his character had frightened her. He had come to mean a great deal to her in such a short time, but she had to look out for herself.

*   *   *

Jamie Hamilton was one of the better liked young men on the island, who had taken his unassuming position as postmaster the year after he graduated from one of the more prominent law schools in the East. Though he had stayed near the head of his class, he soon found that he had no ambition. It was talking to people he preferred, not arguing their stories. His sudden lack of interest in the subjects he had studied was actually held in his favor by the more reclusive native islanders. It was said that the most important thing Jamie had learned in law school was to juggle fruit. Standing in a second floor apartment or office, gazing serenely out one window or another, it was not uncommon to see suddenly three or four, maybe even six, objects whirl up from below. There was no reason to look down. There would be the red hair of the eldest of Mayor Hamilton's remaining redhaired boys, his lean arms a comic blur. Jamie's older brother had not come home from the war. Perhaps this was partially why people approved of Jamie's return even from the profession of his choice.

Now it seemed to everyone as if he had never once been away. "Coming out to Egg Lake for the festivities this year?" Jamie called out when he saw me at the counter. Something about Jamie always reminded me of a young strutting rooster. He was a good looking man with his reddish hair, the long jaw, and very quick way of moving. This year, as in every recent year, Jamie was to be in charge of the fireworks display.

"Of course," I said. "I wouldn't miss your performance for anything."

His head cocked to one side, proudly. "I trained eight years for it. The first thing I learned in Boston was to shoot off my mouth, then I learned how to inflame the average crowd. Finally, I invented the incendiary comment." He didn't often talk about it seriously with people, I guessed. My sister had recently moved east. Perhaps that knowledge and the address on the package had reminded him again. He took out his circular stamp and pressed its red kisses all over the box. "You know," he said, suddenly sincere. "I was never much of a lawyer really; I was never anything but a gossip anyway."

"That's not what I hear," I said, examining the new postage stamp selections.

"Who's talking about me?" he laughed again, pushing forward the sheet of stamps with all the brightly colored birds posturing on the front.

"Why, the whole town is talking, talking about the darling of the harbor, of course."

"Ha," he laughed. If he had been any younger you would still have seen his freckles. As it was you only imagined you saw what had recently gone. "Free legal consultations have earned me a few points."

"It's a miracle you don't go hungry you've got so much give-away business," I said. "So what's new around and about?"

"Have you heard about Dr. Principal's latest patient? The doctor's got a human head in his vault over at the office."

"A human head," I scoffed as if I hadn't heard. "Why, Jamie, now you've gone too far."

"Honest to God," he said, rocking the hand canceling device over the letters he had taken from one of the canvas bags hung up on the wall. "Tourists found it down along Whipple Road. Authorities are trying to put a trace on it."

"But in his vault, Jamie—won't it make a horrible stench?"

"The vault's in the refrigerator where he keeps all his specimens. Took out a few of the racks, I guess. 'Jamie,' he said to me yesterday, 'I never dreamed when I bought the vault I was buying a kind of a hat for a head completely unattached in the world. And now the specimen fridge has turned into a hatbox on me, too. Next thing you know they'll say I'm mad as a hatter myself.'

" 'Dr. P.,' I said, 'The next thing you know is already behind you. Better turn around.' "

*   *   *

Three-quarters of the year, ferries ran only once a day. I loved the isolation of that, particularly in winter. Will and I and some friends had taken up filling in the long winter evenings with writing letters on behalf of imprisoned civil rights activists around the world. We had had some success. In the beginning we had been doubtful that such a small group of us could have an effect, but then there were many groups like us scattered about. But in the summer the nature of the island took on quite another aspect for us. There were thousands of tourists, and the boats came every hour. The cars streamed off like ants. People came wheeling their bicycles down the ramps with their dogs at their heels. Children in groups swarmed after lone beleaguered adults.

Year around, I worked in the small insurance office across the street from Dr. Principal's office. In summer, we often had our sack lunches together, sitting on the big rocks overlooking the small blue port stuck with masts and fishing boats and nets. The little cream-colored restaurant sat below. There the clam chowder was good in late autumn and winter. There no islander would enter during the summer months it was so besieged.

Each year the Fourth of July was particularly rough on Dr. Principal since he was the only doctor on the island. He had made a new partnership with two other doctors but they were not to arrive until the beginning of the year. Each summer the doctor expected numbers of broken limbs and, the way the tourists took the small winding dirt roads of the islands at full speed, perhaps even an automobile accident. An entire family had been lost the year before I came, Dr. Principal said. They'd been so lost that he'd not even seen a body of them until the auto floated up and headed, upside down, into shore at Sheepshead Bay. There it gave a group of holiday bird watchers a terrible start. The Doctor had been napping after work each day now for two weeks, in preparation for the coming weekend's events. Fifteen minutes only, he said, that was all he could give himself, but still he could feel it accumulating under his skin.

There was a joke that Dr. P. was the worst automobile driver around. In all the taverns on the island a jar sat on the bar for the collection of contributions to buy him a siren for his car. It was a small imported station wagon that flew as if it had no speed control at all, no driver at the wheel. Down the winding roads the vague beige vehicle tore in a ghostlike dust. Dr. Principal himself encouraged this modern headless horseman image among both natives and visitors who might drive more responsibly out of fear of meeting him on the road.

Thus it had been rumored, a sort of unintended repercussion of his self-perpetuated story, that Dr. Principal was a mediocre airplane pilot—a truly unjust charge. He was the only doctor not only on our island but on the other three that made up the chain. If a case was really serious, Dr. Principal carried the wounded to the mainland hospital himself in his own Piper Cub. He had never had a scrape.

I was entertaining the thought of taking flying lessons at Dr. Principal's urging. Neither of the nurses in his clinic had wished to be on relentless call as he had, and they as a pair had made it clear that they refused to fly. I would manage the plane, and Dr. P. would be free to watch vital signs and see to the patients while in the air.

As it was, he was confined and nearly helpless with them for a good twenty minutes of crucial time. For years whenever I woke from sleep, I thought of him and considered his plan. I almost believed I could hear the whining of the plane overhead —though that would have been impossible. The tiny cleared field that served as his runway was on the other side of the island—at least fifteen miles away from where we lived on Egg Lake. Dr. Principal frequently reminded me he had liked that idea. We would be good together, he and I. A team.

*   *   *

It was Will's birthday the day before the Fourth and x. D. was at our piano pounding out songs of celebration. *My friend Will,* x. D. sang half in jest, as if from me, since I could not play. The piano had come with the house. I carried in the cake and the three of us celebrated Will's birthday together. At the last moment, in an argument, Lindsey had decided not to come along with him.

That night x. D. again alluded to his love for Lindsey. I remember because Will repeated what he'd said later after he had gone. He and Lindsey were like cougars together, x. d. said, like absolute cougars. He had never experienced anything like it. When I heard it the second time, I thought quietly to myself how much he must have loved the lieutenant, his good friend, whom he had carried desperately through the jungle because the boy had had both of his legs blown off above the knees.

*   *   *

"Do we see you tomorrow at the celebration?" Will asked as we walked him to the door. We always had a small dinner of our own at home, perhaps inviting one or two people to join us before going off to the fireworks which were practically next door at Egg Lake. x. d. glanced at me for a moment but I said nothing.

"You and Lindsey could come over before the fireworks in any case," I said. "No matter what you do later."

"But why wouldn't they go to the fireworks," Will said as if there was no question of it. "You *must* go to the fireworks—since you're going to be around this year. It's the best display any-where. There's something practically Chinese—ancient Chinese —about it. Not the usual popcorn display. Well, you'll see."

x. d. was looking out over the pond, his jacket over his arm. The nightbirds had already begun to fly, and I heard an owl and then a nighthawk and the scamper of creatures in the under-brush. "I guess," x. d. said.

I smiled wanly from the doorway as he drove off. I had come increasingly to resent and pity him for putting me into such a predicament of information.

The next day we had no rain. Rain had been threatened by the mainland weather stations, but the islanders had scoffed. There had never been foul weather on the Fourth in the history of the island as far as anyone could recall. Even in the extended memory of the older and more lucid nursing home patients, no one could report it. I went about gathering things for our supper, enough for four if Lindsey and x. D. should show up. If not, I had no objection to eating leftovers the following day. There were good scallions and tomatoes at the store for our annual potato salad, and I laid in several bottles of wine. Out back there was a layer of rock with mosses and wild strawberries flung over it as if someone had decorated a hat. For dessert we would have strawberries and cake. And we would grill a chicken or two over a maple leaf charcoal fire.

Often we spent this part of the evening alone together, Will and I. Will in the end was the only one surprised when x. D. and Lindsey did not arrive. I was more than a little relieved. Perhaps they had stayed elsewhere on the island to be together quietly, I hoped.

Cars were lined up along the road from Egg Lake as far as we could see as we walked in across the field. On the door of Lisa's silver trailer were strung across the screen perhaps fifty small American flags. The moon was already on the rise, a great red strawberry moon hanging as if by a string in the trees, and beneath it: a pair of deer and a fawn were caught in evening light. Will and I stood looking in turn at them through the binoculars. Lately we had a growing concern for the very young, it seemed. Only within the last few months had we begun to consider aloud the possibility of having a child. I gave Will's beard a little tug and he handed the glasses back to me. How completely large the faun's spots seemed, how lopsided on its quivering young back.

In recent years we had taken up watching the fireworks from the hill. There we were elevated above all the people, yet the display would rise high over us. With the help of the glasses, we could see below in the waning daylight the tourists seated in a vast crowd in the meadow. The much smaller group of islanders gathered near the west end of Egg Lake on the private property of Mayor Hamilton. The only cars in sight now were those of

Dr. Principal, Sheriff Watts, and the Hamiltons. The rest had been left back on the road.

Perhaps ten or twelve of the island's young men were on the pontoon in the middle of Egg Lake which served as a natural barrier to the curiosity of the crowds. There was Jamie Hamilton with his fellows from the Chamber of Commerce making their preparations on the platform. Dr. Principal and his wife were seated on a blue and red plaid blanket with a large picnic basket. "Look, Dr. Principal made it out of the office," I said, and then I sighed a little sadly and handed Will the glasses. "Dr. Principal's having one of Lisa's chocolate pies."

Will looked down across the clearing. It was Dr. Principal's custom to barter his services out to people from the island who couldn't pay. "Don't worry," Will said. "Maybe it's just good will. A friendly gesture. Lisa's been known to do that."

"Yes, that's true," I replied, unconvinced. It was bad enough to be ill without also being broke.

"Lisa looks all right," Will said. "Same as ever. And there's the doctor's usual centerpiece."

Dr. Principal carried his walky talky with him at all times. He received his messages through the sheriff's office, squawking and barely discernible. "Here it comes—" Dr. P. often said to me when the thing went off, "the call of the wild."

We had brought with us two bottles of bug repellent, one in case the other was lost. I was working on Will's back now. First a kiss, then a neck massage and then a cover up of mosquito sauce.

"Don't forget my ears."

"I wouldn't," I said. "What costume's Lisa got on?"

"The usual."

"Hmm," I said. "No embellishments? Not a hat this year? Or a crown?"

"No."

I didn't have to look, though it always amused me to see it. She would be wearing her red, white, and blue ankle-length dress with the one bared shoulder and the immense star over the right breast. Her hair would be let loose from its usual braid to stream wildly about her shoulders; and on her feet were surely the sparklingly red, metallic orthopedic shoes.

"Now I'll do you," Will said, and we exchanged the field glasses for the insect repellent.

I had been surprised to find at our first experience of the island's celebration that there was no music. Nearly fifteen years before, musical instruments had been outlawed indefinitely by the town meeting. A hard rock version of the national anthem, tried out by a few members of the high school band during the grand finale of the display, had been responsible.

The fireflies in the dusk of the meadow below made the field seem vast. And then I saw, in the circles of the binoculars, X. D. and Lindsey on the other side of the egg with the rest of the islanders. There was X. D. sitting close to Lindsey on a blue and red blanket, just like the doctor's, as the sun went down. Lindsey's head was tilted up at X. D. On the pontoon the rockets were lined up along the edges on small posts and there hung all their rope-like fuses. Under our own blanket on the cliff, Will and I would soon be snuggled up together so near and yet so far away from them. "Will—" I said. "There are X. D. and Lindsey."

"Good," he said, but then his head turned up toward me. "What's the matter? Isn't that a good thing?" Will had just finished oiling my ankles and patting the lotion onto my back.

"I promised X. D. I wouldn't tell anyone," I blurted out, "not even you. But I'm afraid, Will. Something might happen tonight. I don't want to be the only one knowing—" Already I felt ashamed for breaking my word.

And so we sat on the cliff and while I told Will all that X. D. had said to me, we watched X. D. stroke the side of Lindsey's face and hair. "No," Will kept saying as I went along, "are you sure?" When I came to the end, we looked down at them together kissing on the blanket in the sunset. Will said, "He told me he was a peace activist during the war."

"He never mentioned it at all to me," I said, incredulous. "I just assumed it, I guess, from all his other talk."

"He even described several marches," Will said. "I remember it clearly. He was arrested, he said. So! he actually felt he had to cover up."

"Why on earth do you think he came." It was not a question. We exchanged the glasses. Far below on the other side of the tip of the egg, their figures seemed mere cutouts, like those of a courtly couple set against a pastel country scene, the kind one sometimes saw in old picture frames. Our friends were staring at one another, talking with very little gesture, completely rapt.

Down below I could see with increasing difficulty the children frolicking at the edge of the woods. Their dogs nosed in zigzag fashions along the ground. Together the people from the nursing home huddled in their lawn chairs, light summer blankets over their laps. Couples everywhere were pressing hands, their thighs close on the grass. And then I could not see any of them. The lake, too, had been obliterated, and with it the pontoon. The sky was all there was.

The initial blast was a loud cracking white starburst and then others whistled out on tendrils, small, carnation-like, in every direction in pink and white and blue. One by one, the missiles catapulted with violent and exhilarating sound into the air, there to explode light and airy as dahlias, like Chinese flowers.

In the dark I felt for Will's hand. It was also the pontoon we were watching, the closest thing to being able to see X. D. who, we knew, would be watching anxiously. First there was the slight glow of the torch and then the arched and leaping brevity of light that was the fuse, and then a high-pitched whistling streak of broader flame as the projectile shot into the air followed by the concussive force above, of air bursting against air. For nearly an hour we looked on at the white and blues, the reds and greens and yellows, the silver and gold. Perhaps the only reason that both Will and I were watching when the rocket misfired was our concern for the way x. d. was seeing things from that blanket on the ground.

There was no whistling of the ascent, only the explosion and a cry of a human or animal in pain, and then the communal gasp of friends and strangers alike across the whole field. Something was burning and screaming on the deck of the boat itself. Almost simultaneously the shouts of young men started up and then a spark on shore as the flashlight of Dr. Principal showed up the lower half of his own face as he grabbed up his medical bag. We saw the shaft of light aim toward the boat. Then there on the shore x. d.'s form was running toward it, too. I saw his body lift up and then his shallow dive. It was maybe fifty yards to the pontoon. Whatever had been burning on deck was no longer on fire. Jack Watts was speaking through his bullhorn in a monotone advising the tourists to stay exactly where they were. We could see almost nothing at all now, as the crowd moved in and we headed down the steep slope along the circuitous long path, moving toward our friends who seemed now so far away in the light of the moon.

On shore Mayor Hamilton had trained the lights of his own car on the boat and was turning on the doctor's, too, when the poignancy of the scene came into view. On the deck in the sudden light lay one of the mayor's red-haired sons. And there Dr. P. stood at the edge of the water waiting as the pontoon started to move its heavy cargo toward the shore. We could not see whether or not x. d. had been pulled aboard. We could hear the heavy churning of water and then the young men were going ashore. Dr. Principal was leaning over someone and then he was running toward the lights of his wagon on the dirt road. To our astonishment the station wagon was then speeding out of its reserved place on the lot; the Hamilton boy had been left exactly where he lay. Mayor Hamilton and the rest of his family bent over him and there, too, was x. d. beside them in the lights from the car. It was as if they were on stage, but we could not see which of the Hamiltons was on the ground until x. d. moved to put his arm around the mayor's wife. "Oh no," I said. But Will had already gripped my arm.

Jamie's features were caught and glowing along with x. d.'s blond hair like two spots of warmth in the dark, among the obscured features of those who were close. As we hurried across the meadow around the tip of Egg Lake, we heard Lindsey calling to Lisa. The sheriff's voice rose again, loud and hollow, devoid of affect, explaining the accident only in general terms at first. The people in the crowd were to drive their cars in single file, he said, along the sides of the meadow and park with their headlights on low beam. When we crossed the opposite corner of the field, we could see in the row of car lights Lisa's wild hair and flowing gown, where she was directing the traffic with her flashlight.

As the rest of the crowd hurried to clear the field, to make the path of light, Will and I reached the boat quite easily. Already the sound of an airplane engine droned increasingly overhead. The field was nearly vacant now, and the long row of lights crept steadily along the borders of the woods. The rectangle was nearly complete. It was as if torchbearers had gathered to hold a silent vigil there. The last pedestrians disappeared then and we stared for a second at the meadow that had been emptied so quickly. We had been too far away, come too late to have been any help at all. The deputy sheriff asked us to stand back, and it was as if we were staring into an empty football field.

Overhead we could hear the doctor coming in. One red and one green speck of light moved steadily against a field of stars. An immense shadow seemed to fill the sky over one end of the clearing, and then the plane dropped down in the dazzling aisle of light. It bounced along the open ground to halt not very far from the lake itself. And then I heard a sound I will never forget, Jamie: high-pitched, desperate, and quavering. Six people were hoisting Jamie in the blanket they had stretched among them; they were running across the field to the plane. Those who had not come in cars were hushed in a body up against the west shore. We heard a quiet purring of automobiles behind the sounds of grief-stricken cries.

We watched the plane lift up out of the broad sparkling runway, a shadow again, and then the lights of the plane grew small like fireflies, and then smaller still as they headed toward the large red moon that hung over the mainland that night. Stricken into silence, we turned homeward, only to pass on our way the young kayak student, who had perhaps seen everything, crouched now, sick and coughing in the reeds. I wanted to stop, but the boy screamed at us more than once to leave him alone. Will pressed me against his side, and we went away.

*   *   *

After x. d. left the island, Dr. P. told me how x. d. had claimed to have been a medic in the war. In that way Dr. Principal had decided to leave Jamie and fetch the plane rather than take him over bumpy roads and fly from the airstrip. He also decided to take x. d. along rather than one of Jamie's relatives, or even some of the islanders trained in first aid. On the pontoon he had handed him his own medical bag.

When they landed, the doctor had been heartbroken to find the bag untouched and x. d. unconscious in a state of shock, both of the young men's torsos soaked in blood. Cheek to cheek they lay, x. d. on top with his face hanging down over Jamie's shoulder, as if he had been whispering in Jamie's ear. Jamie's arms were tightly linked behind x. d.'s back, and x. d.'s blond hair had been newly drenched in sweat. Or was it tears?, the doctor suggested when I told him what I knew. They could not tell at first, which had been the primary victim of the blast. The emergency room attendants had had to pry them apart. The missile fragments lay cradled between the two men in the hollow of Jamie's abdomen.

x. d. had never been a medic at all, Dr. Principal believed. Not even rudimentary attempts to stop any bleeding had been made.

x. D. was treated and released the following day. It was said that
x. D. refused to leave the hospital until Jamie Hamilton's family
had come to carry his body away.

After that night x. D. withdrew from his usual activities. We
saw very little of him before he moved. When he wasn't working on his boat, he stayed at home. He avoided Lindsey and just
as thoroughly avoided us. For some reason it surprised me that
he looked no different when I did see him. How strange and
painful to see his face, as if he had not one secret terrible moment in his heart. How terrifying to watch him turn away down
a street as if he had never lived there at all. Then he simply
disappeared. One day he was there and the next no one could
find him at all.

For a few of us the thought of him seemed slowly to subside,
only to fester again and again along with the thought of Jamie
Hamilton. Each year we sat quietly in reflection while the rest of
the island glittered and rocked. Yet for most of the islanders,
and even for the most fervently affected of us, time, which had
seemed to stop, began again to move. Sadness and remorse gave
way to living, growing things. Finally a catalogue of changes
would seem not to admit that anything had happened at all.

The tourists, as always, come gaily and go. Lisa became the
postmistress and in the summers wears some new costume each
day. This year the mayor's third son went away to the same
eastern law school Jamie once attended. And Lindsey, after worrisome grief and loss of weight, opened a scuba diving shop on
the far end of the island with the man who became her husband, a handsome man, strong and bright. He is the second
cousin of that archaeologist who came to investigate the skull
Dr. Principal kept in his clinic refrigerator—as a talisman, he
said. Here people have come to mark time by that. "That was
the year the Doctor found the skull," people say. They have
forgotten that he only examined it. Dr. P. finally convinced me
to get my pilot's license. He helped me train; and now I work for
him in his office as well as in the air. Soon I will be taking a six

month's break, and a nurse will be coming over from the mainland while I am away. Any day now Will and I, under Dr. P.'s supervision, are expecting to deliver our new little Emily or Christopher.

In a broader sense there have been few incidents. Come autumn last year the usual epidemic of salmonella swept in on the heels of the annual red tide. This time the highest rate of infection occurred among the new technicians at the marine laboratory on the Point. Fortunately no lives were lost. No, it seemed they had never heard of such a thing, Dr. Principal said, though it happened nearly every year and it was their job to study similar things. The famous skull was moved to make way for all the specimens. And—though nearly another year has passed, and it is now once again berry time—the skull still sits on top of the filing cabinet beside the new receptionist's desk where, as Dr. Principal says, people can take a long, hard look at it.

◆ *Claudia Smith Brinson* ◆

EINSTEIN'S DAUGHTER

Like a planarian, I was born with the knowledge of my ancestors and descendants coalescing into one trait, as real as Great-Grandfather Arthur's long nose or Grandmother Reba's red hair. I knew, right from the start, however you want to mark that spot, that you can grow old waiting.

So I drew rocketships, pedalled like mad downhill, ran up escalators. Simple speed was in my bones and blood. And in my head long before I read about it in high school physics, long before I read that tale of twins, one who remains on Earth while the other blasts off at half the speed of light, travels the curve of space-time and returns younger than the twin who stayed on a straight line, who waited.

No wonder women always end up looking older than their men. Starting out even or behind won't save them. Ask Penelope as she sits by her loom; ask Dorothy Parker's character as she sits by her telephone.

My mother did what she could with me. She tried to bring me up right, to train me in the art of waiting. Out of love for her I would practice it even before my time began. The Korean Conflict was over. My father was expected home; I was expected.

"Wait," my mother said, rubbing her hands in small circles, pressing her palms against her tight skin. "Don't come just yet, baby. Wait for your father." I obeyed, lingering for a tenth month in that dark ocean of muted sounds, safe in pending arrival.

My mother (a woman who sits patiently, interminably, ankles crossed, hands clasped, head tilted five degrees to the left) says my hair was unnaturally long at birth, reaching to my shoulders, and tiny red scratches covered my cheeks and chest. That she burst into tears at the sight of my flailing arms and legs, the sound off my angry shrieks. An irritable baby, she says, sucking at her breasts so fiercely the milk would stream down my chin, soaking us both. I would wail, she says, when the precisely timed feedings were over, ten minutes at each breast with four firm pats on my back in between. I would wail long enough, loud enough that often I was left in my crib during the day, the door closed to muffle my impatient yowls, the mobile tightly wound to distract me. So I destroyed it, yanking from their strings the stuffed Little Bo Peep, Little Miss Muffet, and Jack Horner.

When I was with her she strapped me into the infant carrier with its smooth plastic seat and edges, its tight white belt. She strapped me into the yellow and white windup swing with its T-shaped cinch. She stored me in the red, white, and blue playpen with its unscalable mesh walls. So I tipped the infant seat over, splitting it and my lip when we tumbled to the floor. I bounced in the swing until it creaked and rattled and shivered in its resistance to my orbit. The mesh I simply gnawed my way through.

My mother would sit with her decaffeinated coffee, staring out the window. She would lean against the stove, slowly stirring the vegetable soup. She would tuck me tightly in the navy blue carriage and languidly walk the three blocks to a friend's house. And the Longine on her fine-boned wrist would tick its way toward five-thirty and dusk, and, some days, the arrival of my pilot father.

But by the time I could reach that watch and all the other clocks, the metal face between the stove dials, the golden face on the den's mantel, the cat face with the shifting eyes in my room, the luminous face humming by my parent's bed, the neon green face on the car's dashboard, I had left my parents to their own time zones.

As she, and sometimes he, sat through half-hour television shows and thirty-second commercials on a direct path to darkness and sleep, I would crawl to the foot of my canopied bed and watch the past before me: my mother on the brick steps of the tin-roofed farmhouse, Reba and Luke rocking behind her; Susannah holding tightly her stillborn Emily, Arthur in exile in the drawing room's twilight, myself to come in their silences. The probabilities would swirl in the corners of my eyes, and if I turned my head quickly, I could catch the future growing behind. Stasis or travel, symmetry of adventure. Why did I never glimpse myself standing there? I found no lines, no planes, nothing flat or straight, nothing simple, nothing set, only arcs of possibilities to enfold myself in.

Sooner or later the door would crack. As light flooded in, I would travel back to my bed long before the eyes of a proper parent might see. Go fast enough, and to the watcher the clock stops, mass becomes infinite, measurements shrink: disappearance. According to the watcher.

"It's all relative," I told my mother, sullenly I admit. This was my heritage, nothing special, no more than my cowlicked brown hair tinged with red, my green eyes, my slightly crooked nose. So, as the cigarette burned slowly toward her fingers, she told me once she dreamed she could fly. Just once, when she was in love with Danny Blake. She stepped off a balcony, arms out stretched, the air and sun gentle around her, the trees rustling at her passage, her movement finally equal to her soul.

Then, eyes squinting through her trail of smoke, she asked again, "What is it you do?"

I shrugged.

She said, "I saw you once. You were outside, in the back yard by the swing set. Then suddenly, somehow, past the fence and down the block. You were six, but almost gone; still my six year old, but out of my reach."

I looked away, my eyes watering from her smoke.

She gripped my wrist, pulled me across the table toward her. "Answer me," she demanded.

"I'm gaining speed," I said.

"You're my daughter," she said, getting up, turning away from me, searching in her pocket for matches. "You're only nine.

"And you're getting fat," she added, and left the room.

She can't help herself; I know that. She believes what people tell her, believes there are immutable rules and consequences. She's been taught it's all cause and effect. Susannah, Reba, her, me. So she thinks she didn't drink enough milk when she was pregnant or my fall down the stairs when I was two really did give me a concussion or my father has not confessed to some crazy aunt locked away in a closet, and that, right there, that's why I am the way I am. That's what she's been taught to think, that we're just floating down the river together, generations caught in the current.

We're always looking ahead into the past, I want to tell her. When you sit on the porch, Mama, and rock and stare, still, struck by starlight, you're looking back millions of years. But at this point I'm a novice, just beginning to catch speed. So I run out the door, letting the screen slam behind me. I dart back and forth, hands cupped, a pocket of air between to cushion the fireflies. Then, with my hands full of light, I whirl and whirl, fling my arms up, casting the light out, away. The sky spins closer as I spiral into its embrace. And my grandfather, not heard from in thirty years, he laughs and whispers in my ear, "Speed up, speed up. See where it will take you."

The past is there; its images linger on the spent light, and that's where I'm going in my childhood: ahead. I rocket into what's already there. I watch my Grandfather Luke pull the soft, heavy carpetbag from under the iron bed. He shakes its folds out then carefully, precisely stacks in it his three white shirts, their stiff collars, his dark bow tie. From the marble top bureau he takes a photograph of Reba, so prim in her pinned-up hair and high-necked wool dress, two of its jet buttons hidden by a cameo. Her slanted, black-inked inscription, "To my dear Luke No finer husband" is fitted so neatly between the two lines of the Hall New Studio stamp.

Luke is leaving Reba, who teaches school, and my mother and her three sisters to travel eighty-eight miles down the road, into Georgia, where his brother Junius will hire him to sell shoes. He will never work again as a cotton broker. He will move from relative to relative, stranger to stranger, sending letters and money, then just money. For eight more years money will appear in the mail every two months, but he will never reappear.

Reba will not forgive him. Her red hair fades, her thin lips sink deeper into her chin, her large eyes grow pale behind rimless glasses. She takes to striking my mother, the oldest of her daughters. She bangs my mother's head into the pump when my mother cries as her hair is scrubbed under cold water. She knocks my mother to the ground when my mother scorches the lace collar of a dress from Mrs. McKinney's stack of ironing. She slaps my mother hard enough to break my mother's nose when she catches her sixteen-year-old daughter climbing out the window to go riding on a summer's night with Danny Blake, who will marry another, have twin sons, die in a hotel fire in Mississippi, but remain to haunt my mother's heart.

My mother tells me the lump on the bridge of her nose comes from a fall from an apple tree. My mother tells me her father died the year he left the family, and her mother sacrificed, slaved. My mother says her father was selfish, fiddled and fished, played gin rummy in the brokerage office and no wonder the business went under. I ask my mother, "Why did Grandmother Reba pull out hair when you dropped the pitcher of milk? You couldn't help it; that fat yellow cat tripped you." My mother looks at me aslant, not at all surprised at my knowledge. She says flatly, "My mother never hurt me. She only punished me when I was in a hurry and did things wrong. She had to teach me to slow down and pay attention."

Fast as I travel I cannot see it all. I see sparks, cataclysms, thunder, conversations, and sighs you can connect this way or that. She sees strands, chains of the foretold woven together into one tight braid. She would say, there, there is the complete description, this past of linear twists knotted together.

Reba, that red-headed tyrant, whispers in my ear, "I loved your mother best of all. She was my firstborn. I had to teach her to be strong. I had to make her see men will love you, leave you. They want only one thing, girl, then they will fly away from you.

"And you, my hurried granddaughter, your mother must make you sit still and listen. She must keep you safe. Put you in high-laced shoes and doubleknot the ties. Plait heavy ribbons in your hair. Starch your skirts, layer you in petticoats. Make you stay clean and fresh.

"Slow down, child, and listen."

She's too late, though. I've seen through her glasses. I can look into those grey eyes turned mean and see her diverted strength playing into my magic. So I move on, to her mother, to Susannah, who rides horses like a man, who attends one of the first women's colleges in the state, who takes to her bed after her eighth child, the third to die within a month of birth. Who practices statics for seventy more years, directing five children, her husband Arthur, servants, and guests from a red horsehair sofa in a front room and a claw-footed, four poster walnut bed in a back room.

She expects Great-Grandfather Arthur and her children to report their lives and the pace of the world, and they will. The younger girls stitch by her bed; the boys recite texts by the sofa; Arthur reads to her late into the night from ledgers, newspapers, books, eventually grandchildren's letters. And three times a day Reba, the eldest, stands by her mother's swaddled feet and nervously rattles the keys of the household. She timidly recites the contents of the larder or describes the soap or butter slowly forming in the sunlight behind the house. Then Reba listens as her mother details the deficits of last night's dinner or this morning's cut flowers. I watch Susannah, so imperious, so definite in her anchoring, so unmindful of Reba's lost childhood. I wonder, if the amount of energy in the universe is constant, is this where my powers began? Did I accrue what she refused to use?

She shakes a long, thin finger at me. "Don't go looking for trouble, young lady, and it won't find you. Your duty is to love people and to serve people, and you can't do that if you're gallivanting around. You give and you do what you can, and you make sure it's good. That's enough for a woman. Love is enough."

But I am not supposed to be visiting Susannah; I am supposed to be vacuuming the den for my mother. The rattle of a trapped paper clip or safety pin spinning in the machine's throat stops me. I sit to unhook its parts and search for the noisemaker, and the silence draws my mother in. She sees me unemployed, exactly what she expected to see. "Not all here again?" she asks impatiently, arms crossed, eyes surveying the room. She lifts a hassock and finds what she expected, the flat fibers of undisturbed carpeting; she lifts the seat cushion of an armchair and finds what she expected, crumbs. I love my mother, and I love her most intensely when I disappoint her. I am rooted then, grounded by her need for a daughter. She wants more than a replication of bones and blood, more that a womanly echo. I don't meet her ironic gaze. I turn the vacuum cleaner back on, attach the crevice tool, invade the crannies of the chair, my back to her.

If I were to succumb entirely, I would draw a direct line from inertia to now, from daughter to daughter. Instead, I turn my attention to my father, to that part-time presence in our family of three. My father has kept flying, moving from the large, death-delivering planes of the war to the sleek, supersonic planes of commerce. I travel his route and watch him in the neon hues of airport bars, follow him to the motel bed, where he plays a harmonica, his back against two pillows, his shoes tossed by the door.

Sometimes there is a woman in the shower or on the other side of the bed, her flight bag open next to his on the long, polished expanse of the dresser. But among his blue shirts and white underwear is always a present for my mother: French perfume, an Irish linen blouse, a Majorcan pearl necklace, a Scandinavian sweater. He leans on one elbow and murmurs, "God knows I love your mother, but. . . ." He sits up, drapes his arms across his knees, stares deep at his dark reflection in the mirror opposite the bed. "But a house and chitchat about the lawn and the PTA, and nights sitting on the couch with the newspaper and the TV? Don't get me wrong. I love you both. But to be honest, kid, not every day, every night. In doses, you know." It is a simple thing to move fast enough to reach the past, so visible, so well preserved, its light established. There you can spend yourself on your choice of revelations. But I tire of the predictable rhythms, of Susannah's dogged ringing of her silver bell, of Reba's resentful stare into the mailbox, of Arthur eating alone, of Luke staring into a hobo's fire. I grow impatient with my haphazard paths past them. I must set an order to it and chart the consequences.

I retreat to my room, crouch on my pink flowered bedspread, graph paper stretching from foot to headboard so I can record the curves of my constant curiosity. If I can write it down, I can understand it; I can rescue myself. If I can design a family tree, put down names and events my travels have revealed, I will know where I must go and the speed and direction I must use to thwart happenstance and fate. I stare through Saturdays and Sundays at the canyon of Luke's leavetaking, the continuous crests of my father's takeoffs and landings. But I cannot draw the picture whole on the green and white plane.

I focus, instead, on a moment from my own past. I have watched the roller derbies on television and am in love with the hefty, blowsy blondes who crouch low, pumping their arms so sternly as their legs carry them past the linked bodies of their competitors. On weekend mornings I practice secretly, racing up and down the block trying to duplicate that fierce, leg-pumping squat. My rhythm is unnatural, though, interrupted by the bumps of tar welding the long stretches of pavement together. I keep my head low, my eyes marking the black breaks in stride.

"Slow down!" my mother shouts. "Stop! You're going to hurt yourself!" I look up to see her frantically waving from the front porch steps, and in that instant, the wheels of my left foot catch, and I am flying forward, the grit of the pavement peeling my skin as my left hand, my right elbow, my knees hit and skid. What did she think as the pavement rasped against my flesh: I told you so, or I'm sorry; it's my fault, or these things wouldn't happen if you'd behave like a normal girl? Or simply: My poor baby. As she wraps her arms around me, dabs at the blood with her apron, I see her terrible secret. She loves me most when I have failed. It is not that she wishes me evil, but that she wishes me needy.

So I choose another route to pleasing her. I slow down. I satisfy my mother with myself in her path. I cannot please her as much as I would like, cannot bear to spend time on painted toenails or hair wrapped around a curling iron, afternoons in a bubble bath, or evenings in a movie theater, one hand free, the other imprisoned by another. But I can bolt myself to a wrought iron chair next to her on the patio and snap beans to her quiet rhythm. I can take each wet white plate she hands me, hold it briefly under the clear running water, wipe away its wetness, stack it in the cabinet to my left.

And at night, when she would wish my lights on past dark to practice girlish rites: writing in a diary, reading slender romances, or experimenting with eye shadow, I tuck my head to protect my neck. I stare into the thick blackness, curve my shoulders, flex my knees, rock from heel to ball of foot and back until I find my center then auger past the tin barrier of space, spinning past time into time. And in the daytime I drive her, only slightly reckless with my learner's permit, to the nearest mall and follow her from linens to china to fragrances to jewelry to junior dresses. "If you would only slow down, get off that bike of yours," she sighs, "and get to know some boys." She pushes me in front of a mirror, yanks my shoulders back until I stand braced in her clutch as a Marine. "Look at you," she says, her mouth puckering. "Hair hacked off with my scissors so you look like a scruffy orphan. Dirt on your neck." She shakes my hand at the image. "Nails bitten to the quick. The elbows of this sweater black and frayed like you scorched it. Worn out jogging shoes."

"I don't have time to worry about such things," I tell her and wait for her to ask what I mean by that.

But she's wandered three racks away to finger thin linens and pastel cottons. I edge toward the jean jackets. Her mother's eye draws me back beside the long-sleeved lace blouses that stain so easily, the silk dresses intended only for dancing and desire, for slow movement toward traditional resolutions. "Yes ma'am," I reply, pretending to take my reflection seriously as she holds aqua then persimmon against me. She lets the dresses float so slowly to the floor. She pulls me to her, squints wistfully, then lifts my calloused, ragged hands, and kisses the fingertips. "Drive me home, darling," she says, "and stop at the red lights."

We creep along, my mother quiet, her seat belt fastened. I stay behind a grey-haired granny in a green finned Chevy, letting her set our pace. I last for three blocks, five, but I want my mother to see that I, unlike her, am not my mother's daughter. I stare ahead at the road, fighting my foot pressing down, my wrist rigid above the stick shift. I say calmly, evenly, "I'm not going to let gravity wreck me. I'm not going to spend my life at home waiting for some man to show back up. The more you try to tie me to you, the faster I'm going to go."

My mother's tone is ironic; her eyes refuse me and the road ahead, looking instead on her tissue-wrapped purchases. "Do you think any daughter wants to be like her mother? I never met one. I swore I'd best mine, and I did. I kept my husband. And she bettered her mother. She worked hard. She never ran from difficulties. That's all you get, one small change." She looks at me now, her eyes fierce, mother's eyes. "You think you can fly? You're my daughter. I'm bred in you."

I pull the car to the side of the street; I put the parking brake on for her, and I leap. I wish I had the flash of Dorothy's red shoes. I can simply spin, but I show her just how fast I can go, just how fast I can disappear. And this time I go where I can't see; I go into uncertainty, into odds, into probabilities.

I have a bicycle, its frame of titanium, its wheels solid to slice the air and ease me into the slipstream. I have a skateboard, its deck maple, rating ninety-seven on the durometer. I have roller skates, speed skates with leather boots, urethane wheels. I have wheels, for circles let you go, spheres of faith and momentum. But right now I have only myself, and in the bombardment of probabilities I spin and twirl and spiral. I circle my mother in the dark of the living room, her cigarette's red the only heat; my mother in bed, her eyes open and dry and patient. But the light is poor, and I cannot find myself in the house.

Pulling my arms tighter, I hug my ribs and increase the spin, and in the keyholes I catch glimpses of myself, a self blurred— by movement or an insistent nearsightedness I cannot guess. Perhaps she is right: perhaps I can't avoid my blood, and the nature of the geography will coax me into their paths: the easiest path between the wind and loss onto the red sofa, the easiest trail between desire and failure into the shoe store, the easiest route between my mother and father into my room. When I slow down, my hands, so red and raw from my trajectory, are speckled with the dust of the possibilities I could not grasp.

"Mamma," I say, "what do you want?"

"From you?" she asks. "From your father?"

"No," I answer and gulp air. "What do you want from you? For you?"

"I've got what I want, dear," she says, blowing on her coffee. "You, your father, this house, our health. I wish you didn't run off like you do when you get impatient with me."

She sips her coffee, and I taste despair. To her I am a mystery, a mutation, a miracle unasked for; to me she is mass unconverted, gravity's penalty, my immutable mother. "If you could choose to do anything, without consequences, what would you do? Leave Dad? Go back to school? Travel?"

But she is stubborn. "I have what I always wanted. Security. A husband who loves me and won't ever leave me. A healthy child. I've nothing to wish for, nothing to change. That would be greedy." She puts down the cup and shakes her head, mocks herself. "I'd like to get my daughter to wear a dress once in a while. I'd like her to slow down enough to try out mascara. I'd like to wave goodbye to her as she goes out on the arm of some handsome young man. I want to know I'll have grandchildren some day."

I step toward my mother; I reach out and take her in my arms like a dancing partner. I pull her surprised, resisting body to me and whisper past her pearl earrings, "Come with me just once. There's ceaseless motion. So much to see." I could take off with her right then, rocket right out of there, but she pulls back, her weight opposing me, her hands tight on my arms, her face stern.

"Don't you grow up like your grandfather," she hisses. "Leaving people. Don't you turn selfish like some man."

I take her hand, cold and small, and yank her to the center of the floor and twirl; ease my arms around her waist, lock them behind her back and spin; pull my mother into circumrotation, circumgyrations around the fires in the railroad yard, around the yellow cat, around the ironing board, around her lonely self at the breakfast table. The coffee has finished brewing when our feet touch the floor again.

"I'm your mother," she says gently, turning the coffee machine off, taking a cup from the dish drain and filling it. "I've been there before you. What can you teach me that I don't already know?"

I shrug and go upstairs to my room. Hours later I creep back down and out of the house. I sit on the porch steps, lean back on my elbows, tilt my throat to the sky. This is our summer house on the edge of the beach, and on a winter's night like this, when no one else is on the island, there's no electricity to dim the night. The black is silvered with stars, and I am awash in their white light. I walk to the middle of the sandy yard. I am filled with desire and impatience, determined to lose myself in the space of sky and sea.

Yet I don't. To disentangle is to leave my mother where she is, to leave her standing forever in the damp heavy air of the laundry room, her knees pressed into the warm metal of the still humming dryer. To insist she continue to pull from the frayed plastic basket my father's pale blue shirts, my own faded blue denim and chambray. "Come with me," I tell her. "I waited for you once when you asked. I waited for life for love of you. Now you come for love of me."

She pulls one more shirt from the basket, carefully buttons it onto a hanger. She unlocks the back door, walks onto the stoop, and peers at the sky and at me. Her face is sad. She pulls her wedding band back and forth across her knuckle. "I'll walk with you to the dunes," she says. We climb barefoot in the sand toward the sea. Where the sea oats stop, we stop. "Like all children you ask too much," she says.

We clasp hands and lean back, opposing forces, our heels digging into the dune, our backs angled against the sand, our faces to the stars. We start to circle, feeding off each other. I gain speed, reeling on a path past moon-rise, star-rise. Her hands release me, and I rise. Anabatic I rise, heading toward the only possible destination: now, a now of my own making. She has let go of me as we both knew she should. What will she do without me? I dare not stop to ask.

◆ *Felicia Ackerman* ◆

THE FORECASTING GAME: A STORY

Squinting against the sun that was defying her forecast, Charlotte tiptoed into the hospital room just in time to hear the social worker, seated with her back to the door, say to Charlotte's mother, "Hospice care could keep you comfortable and give you personalized attention."

"And all I'd have to do in return is be willing to die just a trifle sooner than necessary," Charlotte's mother said, lifting her chin in a secret greeting as Charlotte's thick fingers made donkey ears behind the social worker's head.

"It's the quality of life," said the social worker. "You wouldn't have to worry about being dependent on machines." Her springy red-gold hair sparkled in the sunlight. Unfair for such vividness to come with such a sappy mind, or was it overwhelmingly fair, a sort of compensation? Charlotte wondered.

Charlotte's mother was emaciated and eighty, twice Charlotte's age and scarcely half her weight. She pushed herself up against the pillows and asked the social worker, "How did you get to the hospital today?"

"What? I drove."

"Do *you* worry about being dependent on machines?" Charlotte's mother said, lifting her chin again. "Charlotte, dear, please tell this lovely young woman I'm not quite so eager to croak as healthy young people think I should be, and if this hospital ever pulls the plug on me, you'll sue the pants off it."

"My mother is not quite so eager to croak as healthy young people think she should be, and if this hospital ever pulls the plug on her, I'll sue the pants off it," Charlotte said pleasantly, stepping over to the bedside.

The social worker said no one had any intention of violating their wishes, she was only trying to find out what they were, and asked if Charlotte was an attorney.

"She's a philosophy professor who likes to think she's a meteorologist, but she knows plenty of lawyers." Charlotte's mother pushed her silver-rimmed glasses up the bridge of her nose. "And now may we be alone, please?"

Getting up to leave, the social worker said how wonderful it was that Charlotte visited her mother every day.

"My mother is one of the two most interesting people I know," Charlotte said, settling her hundred and eighty pounds in the vacated chair, "and the other one doesn't have this much time for me."

"And where would I be without such birdbrains to keep me on my toes?" Charlotte's mother said as soon as the social worker was out of earshot, or possibly a bit before. "And speaking of birdbrains, dear, take a peek at this." She handed Charlotte a magazine opened to an article titled "How Accepting My Mother's Dying Helped Me Grow." The article was part of a series titled "Real-Life Drama." "Charlotte, dear," said her mother, "promise me you will never use my . . . illness as a spiritual stepladder. Or any other kind of stepladder," she added, and Charlotte promised, her eyes filling as if the cold front of her forecast were passing through her head.

A moment later, Charlotte's mother was telling her to stop crying. "I'm going to walk out of here, you know. So why don't you talk about that Republican you seem so enamored of? I still can't figure out how I raised a daughter who could fall in love with a Republican."

Charlotte nodded and, since they were no longer on the subject of her mother's illness, permitted herself a glance at the sky. The sun had slipped behind a cloud, but it was too late. The temperature was already in the 60's. Charlotte's maximum had been 58. She prided herself on exact predictions. She hated forecasts that hedged by saying things like "High around 60, chance of precipitation." "Look," she said, "if I can tell myself he's secretly in love with me, telling myself he's not really a Republican is a piece of cake."

"What kind of cake?"

"Chocolate, of course, with chocolate frosting."

"I do believe I'm going to walk out of here. I merely have anemia; that's why I'm in this delightful place," said Charlotte's mother, who had chronic leukemia that had stopped responding to treatment. "It's called the denial mechanism. I call it the greatest thing since the wheel."

Charlotte swallowed hard and touched her mother's cheek. "Anything anyone does to make his life easier is a psychiatric symptom nowadays," she said thickly, and then in answer to her mother's, "Indulge yourself, dear, and go on about Dale," reminded her that Dale had decided to register as a Republican partly because he'd been asked, "Democrat or Independent?" by someone handing out leaflets on his campus. Dale taught the weather-forecasting course Charlotte drove across the city to twice weekly, since the state college where she taught philosophy had no meteorology department. "He does like talking with me, I'm sure," she said, "well, pretty sure." The older and fatter she got, the harder Charlotte found it to gauge her effect on people. Could being interesting make up for what she looked like? How interesting was she, anyway? Dale talked with her about all sorts of things, laughed at her jokes as well as at many remarks she didn't intend as funny, and was always telling her what exciting and unusual ideas she had. But maybe it was just advanced politeness. He was nice to everyone. Charlotte had gotten into the habit of imagining people in the forecasting course as weather elements, and Dale, she had said to her mother the previous week, was the sun, radiating warmth and light on everyone, when you wanted the warmth and light to be only for you. "Do you want the sun to shine only on you, dear?" Charlotte's mother had asked, and Charlotte had giggled, saying, "At this point, the analogy breaks down," but adding that, of course, possessiveness was part of love. You just had to be ready to give as much exclusive attention and loyalty as you'd demand. Now she leaned forward in her seat and said she felt like screaming when she heard people gush about Dale's niceness, as if being an overprivileged hotshot with an international reputation for your research meant you deserved special credit for being nice, and besides, nice wasn't the same as good. "I mean, I probably don't even cross his mind as a romantic possibility because I'm ten years older and twenty or thirty pounds heavier, and if that's true, it shows he's crummy deep inside, doesn't it?"

"Yes, dear," said Charlotte's mother as obligingly as if they had never had this conversation before, "but so are plenty of people, and you live in a nasty world, just in case you haven't noticed. And I noticed the world gave you a little surprise today," she went on, gesturing toward the window, "and I'm going to give you another one. I have a chance to be in a clinical trial."

"You do?" Charlotte sat up straighter while her mother explained about the new, experimental treatment. "Evidently this place isn't very well coordinated, or that charming social worker wouldn't have come by today to offer me a golden opportunity to bow out gracefully before I can become even more of a burden," her mother ended.

Charlotte's mind barely grazed the surface of her usual thought about a sick person who would rather die than be a burden to his family. Either the family didn't want him to die, so he wouldn't be doing them any favors, or they did, so why should he give a damn about them? "How effective is the experimental treatment?" she asked. She did not ask, How safe? She already knew the answer. Safer than the alternative.

"That, my dear, is what they're trying to find out. Would you believe Dr. Ketchum actually assured me that in any case I would be making a contribution to medical research?"

"I hope you replied that expecting you to think about contributing to humanity at this point is like asking the starving to give to charity."

Her mother smiled. "Remember that documentary about the psychiatrist?"

Charlotte nodded. Two weeks earlier, there had been a television program about a psychiatrist who was training children with terminal cancer to counsel each other. "He made me see I was unhappy because I wasn't helping anyone," a photogenically frail twelve-year-old boy had said earnestly into the camera, and the next day, Charlotte's mother had raged to a sympathetic Charlotte that the poor kid wasn't even allowed to be unhappy simply because he was dying, for heaven's sake. He had to be unhappy because he wasn't *helping* anyone. But Charlotte didn't want to go into that now. "Exactly what did Ketchum say about your chances with this new treatment?" she asked.

"The treatment is very experimental, and no one can predict the future." Charlotte's mother was mimicking a British accent. "I told him to try telling that to my daughter the meteorologist."

"Well, you know what Dale says," said Charlotte. "Everybody has to play the forecasting game."

*   *   *

"Why is it called a game?" Charlotte was asking Dale in the weather laboratory the following week. She gestured at the posted list labeled "Forecasting Game" that placed her third of nineteen people scored on the accuracy of their forecasts. Everyone in the class was on the list; everyone had to turn in two forecasts a week. That was playing the forecasting game. It was, Dale had told her, how most weather-forecasting courses were run. "If a hospital ranked surgeons on how many lives they saved a week and posted the results, would that make it a game?" Charlotte continued. She ran her fingers through her hair and added, "Philosophers spend hours discussing that kind of stuff. It's conceptual analysis. And it never gets resolved. That's the great thing about weather forecasting: you're guaranteed results every day, and you can stick your head out the window and see for yourself how well you did. It doesn't matter what the biggest hotshot in the world says." Dale laughed, the laugh she loved, unusually loud and lively for an adult.

Charlotte glanced out the plate-glass window. Starting out clear, then becoming cloudy later, she had predicted two days before, and the world was cooperating. So far. She turned back to Dale, liking his appearance because it looked as if he cared little about it, which might mean he wasn't crummy, after all, and cared little about other people's appearance, too. He was a trifle dumpy and always wore rumpled pants with a nondescript jacket. Even his longish hair and beard, which on most professors Charlotte would have considered signs of academic trendiness, appealed to her because they weren't what you'd expect of someone who would register as a Republican. They showed his politics weren't just part of his outfit. She could hardly look at him without smiling, and now she could feel her face growing hot and red as the morning's sunrise. Red sky at morning, sailors take warning. Dr. Ketchum had given a warning, Don't expect miracles; but what would she do without the denial mechanism, greatest thing since the wheel? Surely not stand here happily, with no immediate worries beyond whether she could get up the willpower to end this conversation herself, so she could imagine that Dale, who in fact often talked with her for much of the hour until the class, would today feel deprived by the loss.

And even this problem was getting solved, temporarily at least, as Dale opened a package of Life Savers, held it out to Charlotte (who took two), and said he had been invited to speak at a conference in Tel Aviv next winter. Hadn't Charlotte once mentioned she'd visited Israel? What did she have to say about it?

"Well," Charlotte rolled the Life Savers around her tongue, "you're not Jewish, so Israelis will admit you're a foreigner. They didn't with me. I mean, there I was, halfway around the world, and I didn't know anyone, and I didn't know Hebrew, and I couldn't find my way anywhere. And everyone kept saying to me, 'Now that you're in Israel, don't you feel that you've come home?' " Dale burst out laughing again, and she said, "I liked it there, though. A country where three times as many people smoke as jog obviously has plenty going for it." Neither Dale nor Charlotte smoked. But Charlotte liked the idea of smoking, the big taboo.

"Nice to hear there's someplace left nowadays where people know the difference between virtue and a low pulse rate," Dale said. He was barely thirty, but he used the word "nowadays" a lot. Last week, he had shown her a clipping about a California college student who had devised her own interdisciplinary major called "Understanding Myself." It involved courses in psychology, sociology, human biology, American civilization, and women's studies. "See what passes for education in California nowadays," he had said, and Charlotte had replied, "You mean still. That type of thing was much more common fifteen years ago." Now he was saying, "Have you got a dilemma of the week? I can't get through a week without one nowadays." He rocked back on his heels, a motion Charlotte had found she was unable to duplicate without losing her balance.

"This one actually happened," she said, and told him about Lucy, the philosophy department secretary who displayed on her desk a plaque saying, "Success is getting what you want. Happiness is wanting what you get." "And guess what. Her fiancé jilted her last week, and the other secretary said, 'Remember, Lucy, success is getting what you want, and happiness is wanting what you get.' Lucy was furious. So what do you think? Who's the real villain of the story?"

"What do I think? I think you come up with the most amazing situations, Charlotte." Dale rocked back on his heels again and said he wouldn't have used Lucy's slogan against her himself, but he sympathized with the secretary who'd done it, because that slogan was a reproach to people who got things no one could want. "Someone should have told Lucy to hang it in a cancer ward."

Charlotte looked away. She had never told Dale about her mother. Telling him would be too much like using her mother's illness as a stepladder, and anyway, how could it work? What was he supposed to say, Your mother is dying; therefore, I pity you; therefore, I love you? "I couldn't agree more," she said. "Most people I know who are miserable have lives that would make me miserable."

"We're definitely on the same wave length," said Dale.

So why aren't you in love with me, you twit? Charlotte thought. "Well," she said, "I'd better go get started on my forecast."

*   *   *

She walked over to the wall where various kinds of weather maps hung beneath the typed quotation, " 'A forecaster's heart knoweth its own bitterness, but a stranger meddleth not with its joy.'—Sir Napier Shaw, 1854–1945." Charlotte had memorized the quote the first time she saw it, but she kept forgetting to ask who Sir Napier Shaw was. She took down several maps and laid them out on a long laboratory table. "How do you make a forecast?" her mother, a retired milliner, had once asked, and Charlotte had said, "How do you make a hat? There are patterns and standard techniques and rules, and one of the main rules is not to follow the rules too closely. You've got to have a knack." While she and Dale were talking, the room had been filling up with students, innocuous little fillers, like puffy, fair-weather cumulus clouds. All around her now she could hear voices exchanging numbers—58, 64, 62, 65—that could be temperature forecasts or possibly college basketball scores. The students liked sports. They treated forecasting like a sport. Charlotte preferred to think of it as a kind of magic. She even had an old thesaurus that listed "weatherman" and "meteorologist" under "oracle."

Forty minutes later, Charlotte bounded up from her seat—a thunderstorm seemed likely, just the sort of tricky forecasting problem she loved. She started across the room, nearly colliding with Helen Melrose, a flat-faced nineteen-year-old with large, moist, round eyes, who was the only other woman in the forecasting class. Charlotte thought of Helen as a warm front, humid and sticky, casting weak wetness over a large area. It was a special bonus that Helen's curly hair framed her face in little semicircles like the symbols for a warm front on a weather map.

"Hello, Charlotte," Helen was saying. "Are you doing the phone forecast today?"

"Yes, and I'm going against MOS." MOS was the acronym for Model Output Statistics, the computerized forecasts you were supposed to take into account or disregard as conditions required. Charlotte suspected that Helen simply followed these forecasts no matter what. "Just following MOS is like being fed intravenously instead of eating in the usual way," Charlotte said. "The results aren't as good and you miss all the fun." She turned to leave.

"I've been meaning to ask you" (like many warm fronts, Helen took a long time passing through), "how does a philosophy professor come to take up meteorology?"

Charlotte had been asked this so often she sometimes envisioned getting little cards printed up with her answer. "About a year ago, I was driving in a rainstorm," she said, "and it just struck me that it would be exciting, sort of practical and exotic at the same time, to do weather forecasting. For a long time, I figured this had about as much bearing on my life as the idea that it would be exciting to be Emperor of Japan. But when people began telling me I was so obsessed with it that maybe I should see a shrink, I decided it would make more sense to check out the nearest meteorology department instead."

"That's wonderful," said Helen. "You've got your life all together."

"Well, that part of it, anyway," said Charlotte, and noted that the sky was starting to cloud up on schedule. When the world doesn't bear me out, *it's* wrong, she was fond of saying. "I'd better go do the recording," she said. That was a fringe benefit of being in a well-known meteorology program. You could record your forecast over the weather laboratory's telephone line, and people actually called up to hear it.

The recording took hardly a minute, and when she emerged from the booth, Dale was at the radar screen. Charlotte glanced at him hopefully. But, like the sky, she had apparently gotten her share of sunshine. Dale was talking with Helen and two of the male students, and looking as interested and animated as he had with Charlotte. I hate you, Dale, Charlotte thought, recalling how her mother had said, "Even if he wanted you, it wouldn't work out, dear, because people so full of universal niceness aren't capable of single-minded loyalty." And now Dale didn't look her way. His eyes were on the screen. And Helen's eyes, moist and round and sticky as ever, were fixed on Dale like twin suction cups.

*   *   *

"Talk about Dale, dear," Charlotte's mother said, "and don't stint on details. I need a distraction."

Charlotte was sitting beside her mother's bed on what was supposed to be the first day of the clinical trial. But Charlotte was skeptical. The first day had been postponed twice. She glanced out the window (the sky wasn't doing badly, but it could use a few more clouds) and wondered what she could say about Dale that wouldn't sound ludicrously trivial in this setting. But maybe her mother wanted ludicrously trivial. That would be the distraction, Charlotte thought, and began to describe how yesterday she had decided to try a bit of brinkmanship. And so she had told Dale she was going to ask him a personal question and added a lot of build-up about how he obviously didn't have to answer it, but she hoped he would either tell the truth or simply say it was something he didn't want to discuss with her, because this was an area where she wanted very much not to be misled. Charlotte stopped for breath, seeing Dale standing near yesterday's weather maps, as agreeable and unsuspecting as if she were talking about her forecast or the dilemma of the week. "Naturally, he was supposed to wonder what the question was and whether it might even be how he felt about me or if he was involved with anyone else. But he didn't, I'm sure. He didn't because he couldn't see me through my cloak of invisibility. It's called being fat and forty, except that if I make a habit of saying trite things like that, I'll have another cloak of invisibility. Why should I give people an excuse to overlook my mind as well as my body?"

"Anyone who overlooks you is merely betraying his own obtuseness, dear." Charlotte's mother was looking at her watch. "Aren't they ever going to come? They're already two hours late."

"They don't give a damn about patients here, do they?" said Charlotte.

"Oh, they do, dear; we're right up there, ranking fourth after money, prestige, and convenience for the staff. What did you end up asking Dale?"

"I asked him what it was like to be a bigshot," Charlotte said.

"I said fifteen years ago it seemed as if I was going to be one, but it hadn't worked out that way, and I wanted to know if I was missing a lot of thrills." She giggled. "I bet no one ever asked him that before. And he said he could hardly discuss it with just anyone, but of course it was a thrill, especially for someone who'd been such a nerd in college that he couldn't have gotten into a fraternity even if he'd wanted to. But he was afraid he was getting too dependent on it and that it wouldn't last, and it was apt to make people like him for the wrong reasons, although that beat not being liked at all. So at least he has the concept of liking someone for the wrong reasons. So—"

She broke off as a nurse came into the room. Charlotte gripped her mother's hand while the nurse described the procedure: two injections, which might cause sleepiness or nausea. "No real-life drama here," Charlotte's mother murmured. "I don't feel a thing," she said after the injections. But ten minutes after the nurse left, Charlotte's mother abruptly reached for the basin. "If you think—this is disgusting—that's just too bad," she said unsteadily. "I couldn't have put it better myself," Charlotte replied, and held the basin in position until her mother decided she wouldn't be needing it, after all. "Let's assume the nausea means the treatment's strong enough to work," Charlotte said. "Talk some more, dear. Say anything," said Charlotte's mother, and Charlotte said, "You know how self-help books say people don't know what they really want? I think that's a line to keep people from realizing they know exactly what they want and aren't getting it. I know what I want. I want you to get well, and Dale to be in love with me, and all my forecasts to come true, if you'll forgive my mentioning these things in the same breath."

"You didn't," said Charlotte's mother, her eyes closing. "You took a breath before the forecasts. And I don't mind as long as my getting well comes first. It's my *life*, after all."

"It does. I promise," said Charlotte, but her mother was already asleep.

*   *   *

"I promise not to mention your forecast," said Helen eight days later in the university cafeteria. "OK if I sit here?"

"Sure," Charlotte said, not bothering to point out that the promise was automatically broken in the making. Well, maybe the weather betrayed me today, but it looks as if there's going to be a warm front in my life anyhow, she said to herself. She would have liked Helen's lunch to include something, a bowl of clear soup, perhaps, suggesting weak wetness over a large area. But Helen's tray held only a grilled-cheese sandwich. Charlotte was having an all-chocolate lunch, chocolate layer cake and a brownie, to celebrate the fact that her mother's blood count already was marginally better. Besides, Charlotte had made a point of eating fattening food in public ever since reading that most overweight people were too ashamed to—as if they supposed that seeing them eat sparingly might convince an observer it was a diet of lettuce and cottage cheese that was blowing them up like weather balloons. "Well, how are things?" she said.

"Awful," said Helen, instantly jumping up several notches in Charlotte's estimation for not chirping, "Fine, thanks, and you?"

"Do you want to say why?" Charlotte took a forkful of cake, avoiding the frosting, which she felt virtuous for saving till last.

Helen shut her eyes tightly. She opened her mouth, closed it, and opened it again. She's milking this for all it's worth, and why not? Charlotte thought. It beat getting your real-life drama out of magazine articles about other people's tragedies. "I'm sort of in love with someone," Helen said, her eyes still shut. Then she opened them. "You know who it is, don't you?"

Oh, no, Charlotte thought. "Oh, no," she said. "How would I know?"

"It's Dale. I was afraid you might have guessed from the way I acted."

"No, I didn't guess," Charlotte said. "Does he reciprocate? Does he have anyone else?" she added so harshly that Helen gave her a brief, curious glance. But Helen's expression was unsuspecting. I was afraid you might have guessed from the way I acted, Charlotte thought, and scooped up a forkful of frosting ahead of schedule.

"He's always very friendly," Helen was saying. "But he never seeks me out or anything." He seeks *me* out, at least to talk, Charlotte said to herself. "I'm really not sure if he has anyone else," Helen continued, and bit into her sandwich, swallowing so hard Charlotte could hear her. "There's a woman I've seen him with, but it's hard to believe it could be anything romantic. She's a lot older than him. About forty. She's very attractive, kind of exotic-looking, but. . . ."

In class the previous week, Dale had explained how a cumulus cloud could turn into an explosive thunderstorm in barely an hour. Charlotte felt as if this were happening inside her now in barely an instant, and it had to be concealed, compounding the outrage. "So maybe he cares about looks, but not about age," she said evenly. "That would make him only half crummy."

"Just because she looks good doesn't mean he wouldn't like her if she didn't," said Helen.

"He's breaking your heart and you're worried about judging him unfairly?" Charlotte took a vicious bite of the cake. "Anyway, most men care about looks. So do most women, for that matter. Maybe it's original sin or something, but you live in a nasty world, just in case you haven't noticed." She gazed out the window at the nasty world, as calm and bright as if it hadn't even heard her forecast.

"But Dale isn't nasty," said Helen. "He's nice. That's why I'm so crazy about him. He's so nice."

Charlotte put down her fork. "Niceness is a vice masquerading as a virtue," she said.

"What?"

Charlotte giggled, then forced herself to breathe slowly and deeply. Her face felt singed. "What I mean is that if someone's too nice to people he doesn't much care about, he's often apt to make them like and want him a lot more than he likes and wants them. So they end up feeling terrible, and he gets to look and feel like a good guy, and he gets loyalty he hasn't earned."

"But he earns it by being nice," said Helen. "You can't expect people to go around being mean just to make sure no one's going to fall hopelessly in love with them."

Having finished her cake, Charlotte was starting on the brownie. It was fudgy and dense. "They don't have to be mean," she said. "There's a middle ground. There's nice and there's nice. Maybe they ought to be willing to forgo a little personal popularity in order to prevent some broken hearts."

Helen had propped her chin on both fists and was staring at Charlotte. "But—"

"Actually," Charlotte said hastily, "I don't know Dale all that well. I was thinking of the man who supervised my Ph.D. thesis at Cornell." She flicked a mental snicker at her dissertation adviser, a choleric ex-Jesuit about as likely an object of unrequited love as the square root of minus three, and tried to sound as if she were reminiscing. "He made so many people miserable, including me," she said, "because he was so nice and concerned. So, naturally, we all wanted much more from him than we got. I was ashamed of being one of his victims, so on top of everything else, I had to struggle to keep my feelings hidden all the time. It was like being on a maintenance diet—all that effort, and you get nothing to show for it except the bad thing that *doesn't* happen." She decided against mentioning that she knew both sides of that equation. In her thirties, she had lost sixty pounds and kept them off for over a year until, like the dieters she saw written up as object lessons in women's magazines, she had gained the weight back because being slim hadn't made her attractive, let alone changed her life. The magazines made this sound pathological, but Charlotte considered it just common sense. If losing weight didn't bring you happiness, shouldn't you at least have the fun of eating what you liked?

"I still can't believe you really think it's bad to be nice," Helen was saying.

Charlotte wasn't sure how much she thought it, either, but there was a pinch of truth in there somewhere, and besides, she liked the way it sounded. It wasn't what other people would say. Too bad she couldn't try it out on Dale as the dilemma of the week. You come up with the most amazing ideas, Charlotte, he would say. Surely, that other woman was only a friend. If he didn't care about age, wouldn't he know where to turn?

*   *   *

"I'll give you the dilemma this week," Dale said in the weather laboratory two weeks later.

Charlotte was standing in a trapezoid of sunlight at the end of a dustbeam pointing toward her like a wand. She felt enchanted. Anything could happen. Hadn't her mother gained three pounds? Weren't her blood counts progressively improving? No predictions from the doctor, of course, no forecasting game. So Charlotte was playing her own. In her mind, her mother was already convalescing in Charlotte's guest room, with the bay window and the view of the lake. Charlotte beamed at Dale; wasn't he about to say, I'm in love with you, Charlotte; I'm in love with you, and I don't know what to do? I'll tell you what to do, Charlotte thought.

"Do you ever go to the botanical gardens?" Dale said.

Charlotte nodded, wondering what he was leading up to. She had always provided the dilemmas before. "I've been there twice this year, and I haven't run into a dilemma of the week there yet," she said.

Dale laughed and rocked back on his heels. "That's probably because you haven't had someone interrupt a conversation there. My girlfriend and I were sitting by the lily pond and talking about a problem she's had with her work lately, and a man came along and asked how to get to the greenhouse and then to the wild flower garden. I gave him both the directions, but it took a while, and afterward, my girlfriend said I should have pretended I didn't know. 'You put a stranger ahead of me,' she said. Once she put it that way, I realized she was right. It's a matter of priorities. So what do you think?"

What do I think? I think the two of you should freeze to death in a blizzard I deliberately didn't mention in my forecast. Charlotte's mind itself seemed to be freezing over, with all the details horribly in place like separate icicles. So he did have someone, someone like Charlotte, someone Charlotte could have been. Should have been. She had values like Charlotte's, values most people would disapprove of, was as demanding as Charlotte wished she could get away with being, found issues in unlikely places just as Charlotte did. And Dale loved having a girlfriend like this. His face was shining. Charlotte's own face felt ready to burst. "But you seem so universally nice," she said. "You don't seem the type to pretend you don't know directions."

"Being universally nice when loyalty isn't at stake doesn't mean you're going to be that way when it is," said Dale.

So he *was* capable of single-minded loyalty, and he was giving it. To someone else. Someone very attractive and exotic, the woman Helen had seen? Charlotte gripped the edge of a long table. "I think your girlfriend has terrific judgment," she said. "I —this is fascinating. Tell me more about her. Is she a meteorologist, too? How old is she? How long have you been together?"

"She's a violinist and she's forty-two. We've known each other for five months," said Dale, who had known Charlotte for seven, "but—"

But Charlotte had decided that she couldn't stand to hear any more. "Better the devil you know than the devil you don't" wasn't merely a stupid cliché; it was false. Like "Beggars can't be choosers." "Do you believe beggars can't be choosers?" she said. "I think that's a terrible idea. Of course, beggars can be choosers."

"What?" Dale said. "Is this part of the same dilemma?"

"No, we've covered that one. This is the one I have for you." She was talking too fast. Did he notice? "Why do people believe beggars can't be choosers?" she said.

"I suppose the idea is that beggars have no leverage or they wouldn't need to beg," said Dale. "So if they try to be choosy, they're apt to end up with nothing."

"Maybe not." Charlotte felt giddy. "Maybe they can *take* the leverage. Maybe if you show you won't settle for just anything, people will realize you're entitled to a choice. You just have to take a risk." She was always taking risks with her forecasts, going for long shots. Her mother was going for a long shot. "Do you see what I mean?"

"I'm not sure," Dale said. "Do you have any examples?"

"No, I guess I haven't really thought it out." All at once, Charlotte felt calm and confident, her mind closing over the girlfriend like water over a stone thrown into a lake. Suppose Dale had mentioned the girlfriend to tantalize Charlotte and make her jealous. In a few hours, Charlotte would manage to suppose this, not so she would bet on it, but so she could at least fall back on it in her imagination. What harm could this stranger do her? A forecaster's heart knoweth its own bitterness, but a stranger meddleth not with its joy.

*   *   *

Charlotte's joy increased steadily during the next three weeks. Dale didn't talk about the girlfriend again. Perhaps he had invented her, the way Charlotte might have invented a boyfriend in the hope of piquing Dale's interest, if she hadn't been afraid of getting confused and inconsistent about details. Instead, Dale talked about his work. He was afraid of losing his momentum, never making his great contribution, having his spurt of glory dry up almost before it began, like a summer cloudburst. "It can happen," Charlotte said. "It happened to me. You put up with it because you have to, which is what people seem to like to call maturity, but you never stop wanting to make a grand dramatic gesture to show you don't have to settle, after all." "Do you want to make a grand dramatic gesture?" Dale asked. "It varies," said Charlotte, recalling how her mother had said, "Certainly, you shouldn't settle, but grand dramatic gestures look ridiculous and pathetic except to someone who's already interested in you, dear."

And every day, her mother was getting stronger. Every day, she spent more time out of bed. "Her response is encouraging," the doctor told Charlotte, "but remember, her immune system is still depressed. Any little infection could be dangerous." Already Charlotte had washed her guestroom curtains and gotten a new bedspread in her mother's favorite shade of dusky pink. "The results so far are clearly favorable," said the doctor, "but we can't predict the future." Then maybe you should try predicting the past, Charlotte wanted to say. She was first in the forecasting game now, insulated with her mother and Dale in a clear bubble where even the weather—like a snowstorm in a glass paperweight—was under her control. But one day, she came home from a drive along the lake to find a message on her answering machine. "There's an emergency with your mother. Come right away." The message was two hours old, and it was too late.

*   *   *

You could be too desolate to cry, just as it could be too cold to snow. It was three days before Charlotte left her bed except for necessities, three days before it even occurred to her that she had scarcely thought about Dale since the message from the hospital. But now, reading over the newspaper obituary ("Ruth

Corenthal, 80, retired milliner," naming Charlotte as the survivor), she imagined him reading it, too, and wanting to comfort her. Pinpoints of guilt and excitement flared within her like a fireworks display, but she forced them down.

*   *   *

The weather laboratory was unchanged, of course, except that she was no longer first on the forecasting game list. No one was in the room when she returned, and then, a moment later, there was Dale. Again she fought down the excitement.

"Glad you're back," he was saying. "Did you have the flu like everybody else?" His voice was rich and warm, the voice he always had. For everyone.

"Yes," she said. But Dale's eyes were already on the maps. A cold front was headed their way, a front that would give rise to storms and leave things clearer in its wake. Charlotte shivered. Why, that's me, she thought dizzily; I'm a cold front! Starting now. And she shivered again and gripped the edge of a long table and spoke before she could think anything else.

"No," she said. "I didn't have the flu. My mother died last week. Of leukemia."

Dale looked at her, the sun facing the front. "I'm very sorry," he said. "I had no idea." Charlotte said nothing. "How long did she have the leukemia?" Dale asked.

"Not long enough," said Charlotte. "Better dying than dead. That's how she felt, too."

"Hardly anyone admits that nowadays," said Dale. He paused. "I'm really sorry about your mother." There was a longer pause. "Are you doing the phone forecast?" he asked finally.

"Yes," Charlotte said. "Yes, I'm doing the forecast." She laughed—a thick, almost unrecognizable sound. "There's a cold front coming. Right now. Can't you see? I'm the front. No, I'm not cracking up. I've just gotten used to thinking of people in terms of the weather. And you," she continued with a dreadful sense of release, not caring that she was almost screaming, no, glad of it, "you're the sun, shining your warmth and light on everyone, as if 'I'm very sorry' were enough, because you naturally never bothered to think about me long enough to suspect that all along you were making me want—I wanted you to—" She turned, running from the laboratory and into the bathroom, all her stored-up tears streaming down, making her face red and puffier than ever. For a long time she sobbed, then stared at her reflection in the bathroom mirror, knowing what she had done, contemplating the risk, the evilness, and the betrayal, but at least she wasn't settling anymore, and her mother hadn't wanted her to settle, had she? And so half an hour later, eyes swollen but dry, Charlotte returned to the laboratory, no longer fighting the excitement, just holding herself carefully to keep from shivering again.

Dale was alone in the room. He was standing by the window. She walked over to him.

"Dale," she said, "I'm sorry about screaming at you. I. . . ."

Dale turned around but didn't meet her gaze. "Don't worry about it," he said. "When your mother dies, you're not supposed to act like Rebecca of Sunnybrook Farm. I took down the maps if you want to do the forecast," he added, gesturing toward a long table.

A dead sickness flooded through Charlotte. She had betrayed her mother, trying to use her death as a stepladder to Dale, and gotten nothing in return. To sell your soul and gain nothing, maybe that was justice, after all. But in her mind she could hear her mother's voice saying, Justice has nothing to do with it, dear. It's simply that grand dramatic gestures look ridiculous and pathetic except to someone who's already interested in you, and he likes talking with you but he's chosen someone very attractive and exotic, and you live in a nasty world, just in case you haven't noticed.

◆ *Reginald McKnight* ◆

THE KIND OF LIGHT THAT SHINES ON TEXAS

I never liked Marvin Pruitt. Never liked him, never knew him,
even though there were only three of us in the class. Three
black kids. In our school there were fourteen classrooms of
thirty-odd white kids (in '66, they considered Chicanos provi-
sionally white) and three or four black kids. Primary school in
primary colors. Neat division. Alphabetized. They didn't stick
us in the back, or arrange us by degrees of hue, apartheidlike.
This was real integration, a ten-to-one ratio as tidy as upper-
class landscaping. If it all worked, you could have ten white kids
all to yourself. They could talk to you, get the feel of you,
scrutinize you bone deep if they wanted to. They seldom
wanted to, and that was fine with me for two reasons. The first
was that their scrutiny was irritating. How do you comb your
hair—why do you comb your hair—may I please touch your
hair—were the kinds of questions they asked. This is no way to
feel at home. The second reason was Marvin. He embarrassed
me. He smelled bad, was at least two grades behind, was hostile,
dark skinned, homely, close-mouthed. I feared him for his size,

First published in *The Kenyon Review,* vol. XI, no. 3, New Series, Summer
1989. © 1989 by Kenyon College. Reprinted with permission.

pitied him for his dress, watched him all the time. Marveled at him, mystified, astonished, uneasy.

He had the habit of spitting on his right arm, juicing it down till it would glisten. He would start in immediately after taking his seat when we'd finished with the Pledge of Allegiance, "The Yellow Rose of Texas," "The Eyes of Texas Are upon You," and "Mistress Shady." Marvin would rub his spit-flecked arm with his left hand, rub and roll as if polishing an ebony pool cue. Then he would rest his head in the crook of his arm, sniffing, huffing deep like blackjacket boys huff bagsful of acrylics. After ten minutes or so, his eyes would close, heavy. He would sleep till recess. Mrs. Wickham would let him.

There was one other black kid in our class, a girl they called Ah-so. I never learned what she did to earn this name. There was nothing Asian about this big-shouldered girl. She was the tallest, heaviest kid in school. She was quiet, but I don't think any one of us was subtle or sophisticated enough to nickname our classmates according to any but physical attributes. Fat kids were called Porky or Butterball; skinny ones were called Stick or Ichabod. Ah-so was big, thick, and African. She would impassively sit, sullen, silent as Marvin. She wore the same dark blue pleated skirt every day, the same ruffled white blouse every day. Her skin always shone as if worked by Marvin's palms and fingers. I never spoke one word to her, nor she to me.

Of the three of us, Mrs. Wickham called only on Ah-so and me. Ah-so never answered one question, correctly or incorrectly, so far as I can recall. She wasn't stupid. When asked to read aloud she read well, seldom stumbling over long words, reading with humor and expression. But when Wickham asked her about Farmer Brown and how many cows, or the capital of Vermont, or the date of this war or that, Ah-so never spoke. Not one word. But you always felt she could have answered those questions if she'd wanted to. I sensed no tension, embarrassment, or anger in Ah-so's reticence. She simply refused to speak. There was something unshakable about her, some core so impenetrably solid, you got the feeling that if you stood too close to her she could eat your thoughts like a black star eats light. I didn't despise Ah-so as I despised Marvin. There was nothing malevolent about her. She sat like a great icon in the back of the classroom, tranquil, guarded, sealed up, watchful. She was close to sixteen, and it was my guess she'd given up on school. Perhaps she was just obliging the wishes of her family, sticking it out till the law could no longer reach her.

There were at least half a dozen older kids in our class. Besides Marvin and Ah-so there was Oakley, who sat behind me, whispering threats into my ear; Varna Willard with the large breasts; Eddie Limon, who played bass for a high school rock band; and Lawrence Ridderbeck, whom everyone said had a kid and a wife. You couldn't expect me to know anything about Texan educational practices of the 1960s, so I never knew why there were so many older kids in my sixth grade class. After all, I was just a boy and had transferred into the school around midyear. My father, an air force sergeant, had been sent to Viet Nam. The air force sent my mother, my sister Claire, and me to Connolly Air Force Base, which during the war housed "unaccompanied wives." I'd been to so many different schools in my short life that I ceased wondering about their differences. All I knew about the Texas schools is that they weren't afraid to flunk you.

Yet though I was only twelve then, I had a good idea why Wickham never once called on Marvin, why she let him snooze in the crook of his polished arm. I knew why she would press her lips together, and narrow her eyes at me whenever I correctly answered a question, rare as that was. I knew why she badgered Ah-so with questions everyone knew Ah-so would never even consider answering. Wickham didn't like us. She wasn't gross about it, but it was clear she didn't want us around. She would prove her dislike day after day with little stories and jokes. "I just want to share with you all," she would say, "a little riddle my daughter told me at the supper table th'other day. Now, where do you go when you injure your knee?" Then one, two, or all three of her pets would say for the rest of us, "We don't know, Miz Wickham," in that skin-chilling way suckasses speak, "where?" "Why, to Africa," Wickham would say, "where the knee grows."

The thirty-odd white kids would laugh, and I would look across the room at Marvin. He'd be asleep. I would glance back at Ah-so. She'd be sitting still as a projected image, staring down at her desk. I, myself, would smile at Wickham's stupid jokes, sometimes fake a laugh. I tried to show her that at least one of us was alive and alert, even though her jokes hurt. I sucked ass, too, I suppose. But I wanted her to understand more than anything that I was not like her other nigra children, that I was worthy of more than the nonattention and the negative attention she paid Marvin and Ah-so. I hated her, but never showed it. No one could safely contradict that woman. She knew all kinds of tricks to demean, control, and punish you. And she could swing her two-foot paddle as fluidly as a big league slugger swings a bat. You didn't speak in Wickham's class unless she spoke to you first. You didn't chew gum, or wear "hood" hair. You didn't drag your feet, curse, pass notes, hold hands with the opposite sex. Most especially, you didn't say anything bad about the Aggies, Governor Connolly, LBJ, Sam Houston, or Waco. You did the forbidden and she would get you. It was that simple.

She never got me, though. Never gave her reason to. But she could have invented reasons. She did a lot of that. I can't be sure, but I used to think she pitied me because my father was in Viet Nam and my uncle A.J. had recently died there. Whenever she would tell one of her racist jokes, she would always glance at me, preface the joke with, "Now don't you nigra children take offense. This is all in fun, you know. I just want to share with you all something Coach Gilchrest told me th'other day." She would tell her joke, and glance at me again. I'd giggle, feeling a little queasy. "I'm half Irish," she would chuckle, "and you should hear some of those Irish jokes." She never told any, and I never really expected her to. I just did my Tom-thing. I kept my shoes shined, my desk neat, answered her questions as best I could, never brought gum to school, never cursed, never slept in class. I wanted to show her we were not all the same.

I tried to show them all, all thirty-odd, that I was different. It worked to some degree, but not very well. When some article was stolen from someone's locker or desk, Marvin, not I, was the first accused. I'd be second. Neither Marvin, nor Ah-so nor I were ever chosen for certain classroom honors—"Pledge leader," "flag holder," "noise monitor," "paper passer outer," but Mrs. Wickham once let me be "eraser duster." I was proud. I didn't even care about the cracks my fellow students made about my finally having turned the right color. I had done something that Marvin, in the deeps of his never-ending sleep, couldn't even dream of doing. Jack Preston, a kid who sat in front of me, asked me one day at recess whether I was embarrassed about Marvin. "Can you believe that guy?" I said. "He's like a pig or something. Makes me sick."

"Does it make you ashamed to be colored?"

"No," I said, but I meant yes. Yes, if you insist on thinking us all the same. Yes, if his faults are mine, his weaknesses inherent in me.

"I'd be," said Jack.

I made no reply. I was ashamed. Ashamed for not defending Marvin and ashamed that Marvin even existed. But if it had occurred to me, I would have asked Jack whether he was ashamed of being white because of Oakley. Oakley, "Oak Tree," Kelvin "Oak Tree" Oakley. He was sixteen and proud of it. He made it clear to everyone, including Wickham, that his life's ambition was to stay in school one more year, till he'd be old enough to enlist in the army. "Them slopes got my brother," he would say. "I'mna sign up and git me a few slopes. Gonna kill them bastards deader'n shit." Oakley, so far as anyone knew, was and always had been the oldest kid in his family. But no one contradicted him. He would, as anyone would tell you, "snap yer neck jest as soon as look at you." Not a boy in class, excepting Marvin and myself, had been able to avoid Oakley's pink bellies, Texas titty twisters, moon pie punches, or worse. He didn't bother Marvin, I suppose, because Marvin was closer to his size and age, and because Marvin spent five-sixths of the school day asleep. Marvin probably never crossed Oakley's mind. And to say that Oakley hadn't bothered me is not to say he had no intention of ever doing so. In fact, this haphazard sketch of hairy fingers, slash of eyebrow, explosion of acne, elbows, and crooked teeth, swore almost daily that he'd like to kill me.

Naturally, I feared him. Though we were about the same height, he outweighed me by no less than forty pounds. He talked, stood, smoked, and swore like a man. No one, except for Mrs. Wickham, the principal, and the coach, ever laid a finger on him. And even Wickham knew that the hot lines she laid on him merely amused him. He would smile out at the classroom, goofy and bashful, as she laid down the two, five, or maximum ten strokes on him. Often he would wink, or surreptitiously flash us the thumb as Wickham worked on him. When she was finished, Oakley would walk so cool back to his seat you'd think he was on wheels. He'd slide into his chair, sniff the air, and say, "Somethin's burnin. Do y'all smell smoke? I swanee, I smell smoke and fahr back here." If he had made these cracks and never threatened me, I might have grown to admire Oakley, even liked him a little. But he hated me, and took every opportunity during the six-hour school day to make me aware of this. "Some Sambo's gittin his ass broke open one of these days," he'd mumble. "I wanna fight somebody. Need to keep in shape till I git to Nam."

I never said anything to him for the longest time. I pretended not to hear him, pretended not to notice his sour breath on my neck and ear. "Yep," he'd whisper. "Coonies keep ya in good shape for slope killin." Day in, day out, that's the kind of thing

I'd pretend not to hear. But one day when the rain dropped down like lead balls, and the cold air made your skin look plucked, Oakley whispered to me, "My brother tells me it rains like this in Nam. Maybe I oughta go out at recess and break your ass open today. Nice and cool so you don't sweat. Nice and wet to clean up the blood." I said nothing for at least half a minute, then I turned half right and said, "Thought you said your brother was dead." Oakley, silent himself, for a time, poked me in the back with his pencil and hissed, *"Yer* dead." Wickham cut her eyes our way, and it was over.

It was hardest avoiding him in gym class. Especially when we played murderball. Oakley always aimed his throws at me. He threw with unblinking intensity, his teeth gritting, his neck veining, his face flushing, his black hair sweeping over one eye. He could throw hard, but the balls were squishy and harmless. In fact, I found his misses more intimidating than his hits. The balls would whizz by, thunder against the folded bleachers. They rattled as though a locomotive were passing through them. I would duck, dodge, leap as if he were throwing grenades. But he always hit me, sooner or later. And after a while I noticed that the other boys would avoid throwing at me, as if I belonged to Oakley.

One day, however, I was surprised to see that Oakley was throwing at everyone else but me. He was uncommonly accurate, too; kids were falling like tin cans. Since no one was throwing at me, I spent most of the game watching Oakley cut this one and that one down. Finally, he and I were the only ones left on the court. Try as he would, he couldn't hit me, nor I him. Coach Gilchrest blew his whistle and told Oakley and me to bring the red rubber balls to the equipment locker. I was relieved I'd escaped Oakley's stinging throws for once. I was feeling triumphant, full of myself. As Oakley and I approached Gilchrest, I thought about saying something friendly to Oakley: Good game, Oak Tree, I would say. Before I could speak, though, Gilchrest said, "All right boys, there's five minutes left in the period. Y'all are so good, looks like, you're gonna have to play like men. No boundaries, no catch outs, and you gotta hit your opponent three times in order to win. Got me?"

We nodded.

"And you're gonna use these," said Gilchrest, pointing to three volleyballs at his feet. "And you better believe they're pumped full. Oates, you start at that end of the court. Oak Tree, you're at th'other end. Just like usual, I'll set the balls at mid-court, and when I blow my whistle I want y'all to haul your cheeks to the middle and th'ow for all you're worth. Got me?" Gilchrest nodded at our nods, then added, "Remember, no boundaries, right?"

I at my end, Oakley at his, Gilchrest blew his whistle. I was faster than Oakley and scooped up a ball before he'd covered three quarters of his side. I aimed, threw, and popped him right on the knee. "One-zip!" I heard Gilchrest shout. The ball bounced off his knee and shot right back into my hands. I hurried my throw and missed. Oakley bent down, clutched the two remaining balls. I remember being amazed that he could palm each ball, run full out and throw left-handed or right-handed without a shade of awkwardness. I spun, ran, but one of Oakley's throws glanced off the back of my head. "One-one!" hollered Gilchrest. I fell and spun on my ass as the other ball came sailing at me. I caught it. "He's out!" I yelled. Gilchrest's voice boomed, "No catch outs. Three hits. Three hits." I leapt to my feet as Oakley scrambled across the floor for another ball. I chased him down, leapt, and heaved the ball hard as he drew himself erect. The ball hit him dead in the face, and he went down flat. He rolled around, cupping his hands over his nose. Gilchrest sped to his side, helped him to his feet, asked him whether he was OK. Blood flowed from Oakley's nose, dripped in startlingly bright spots on the floor, his shoes, Gilchrest's shirt. The coach removed Oakley's T-shirt and pressed it against the big kid's nose to stanch the bleeding. As they walked past me toward the office I mumbled an apology to

Oakley, but couldn't catch his reply. "You watch your filthy mouth, boy," said Gilchrest to Oakley.

The locker room was unnaturally quiet as I stepped into its steamy atmosphere. Eyes clicked in my direction, looked away. After I was out of my shorts, had my towel wrapped around me, my shower kit in hand, Jack Preston and Brian Nailor approached me. Preston's hair was combed slick and plastic looking. Nailor's stood up like frozen flames. Nailor smiled at me with his big teeth and pale eyes. He poked my arm with a finger. "You fucked up," he said.

"I tried to apologize."

"Won't do you no good," said Preston.

"I swanee," said Nailor.

"It's part of the game," I said. "It was an accident. Wasn't my idea to use volleyballs."

"Don't matter," Preston said. "He's jest lookin for an excuse to fight you."

"I never done nothing to him."

"Don't matter," said Nailor. "He don't like you."

"Brian's right, Clint. He'd jest as soon kill you as look at you."

"I never done nothing to him."

"Look," said Preston, "I know him pretty good. And jest between you and me, it's cause you're a city boy—"

"Whadda you mean? I've never—"

"He don't like your clothes—"

"And he don't like the fancy way you talk in class."

"What fancy—"

"I'm tellin him, if you don't mind, Brian."

"Tell him then."

"He don't like the way you say 'tennis shoes' instead of sneakers. He don't like coloreds. A whole bunch a things, really."

"I never done nothing to him. He's got no reason—"

"*And,*" said Nailor, grinning, "*and,* he says you're a stuck-up rich kid." Nailor's eyes had crow's-feet, bags beneath them. They were a man's eyes.

"My dad's a sergeant," I said.

"You chicken to fight him?" said Nailor.

"Yeah, Clint, don't be chicken. Jest go on and git it over with. He's whupped pert near ever'body else in the class. It ain't so bad."

"Might as well, Oates."

"Yeah, yer pretty skinny, but yer jest about his height. Jest git im in a headlock and don't let go."

"Goddamn," I said, "he's got no reason to—"

Their eyes shot right and I looked over my shoulder. Oakley stood at his locker, turning its tumblers. From where I stood I could see that a piece of cotton was wedged up one of his nostrils, and he already had the makings of a good shiner. His acne burned red like a fresh abrasion. He snapped the locker open and kicked his shoes off without sitting. Then he pulled off his shorts, revealing two paddle stripes on his ass. They were fresh red bars speckled with white, the white speckles being the reverse impression of the paddle's suction holes. He must not have watched his filthy mouth while in Gilchrest's presence. Behind me, I heard Preston and Nailor pad to their lockers.

Oakley spoke without turning around. "Somebody's gonna git his skinny black ass kicked, right today, right after school." He said it softly. He slipped his jock off, turned around. I looked away. Out the corner of my eye I saw him stride off, his hairy nakedness a weapon clearing the younger boys from his path. Just before he rounded the corner of the shower stalls, I threw my toilet kit to the floor and stammered, "I—I never did nothing to you, Oakley." He stopped, turned, stepped closer to me, wrapping his towel around himself. Sweat streamed down my rib cage. It felt like ice water. "You wanna go at it right now, boy?"

"I never did nothing to you." I felt tears in my eyes. I couldn't stop them even though I was blinking like mad. "Never."

He laughed. "You busted my nose, asshole."

"What about before? What'd I ever do to you?"

"See you after school, Coonie." Then he turned away, flashing his acne-spotted back like a semaphore. "Why?" I shouted. "Why you wanna fight me?" Oakley stopped and turned, folded his arms, leaned against a toilet stall. "Why you wanna fight *me,* Oakley?" I stepped over the bench. "What'd I do? Why me?" And then unconsciously, as if scratching, as if breathing, I walked toward Marvin, who stood a few feet from Oakley, combing his hair at the mirror. "Why not him?" I said. "How come you're after *me* and not *him?''* The room froze. Froze for a moment that was both evanescent and eternal, somewhere between an eye blink and a week in hell. No one moved, nothing happened; there was no sound at all. And then it was as if all of us at the same moment looked at Marvin. He just stood there, combing away, the only body in motion, I think. He combed his hair and combed it, as if seeing only his image, hearing only his comb scraping his scalp. I knew he'd heard me. There's no way he could not have heard me. But all he did was slide the comb into his pocket and walk out the door.

"I got no quarrel with Marvin," I heard Oakley say. I turned toward his voice, but he was already in the shower.

I was able to avoid Oakley at the end of the school day. I made my escape by asking Mrs. Wickham if I could go to the restroom.

" 'Restroom,' " Oakley mumbled. "It's a damn toilet, sissy."

"Clinton," said Mrs. Wickham. "Can you *not* wait till the bell rings? It's almost three o'clock."

"No ma'am," I said. "I won't make it."

"Well, I should make you wait just to teach you to be more mindful about . . . hygiene . . . uh things." She sucked in her cheeks, squinted. "But I'm feeling charitable today. You may go." I immediately left the building, and got on the bus. "Ain't you a little early?" said the bus driver, swinging the door shut. "Just left the office," I said. The driver nodded, apparently not giving me a second thought. I had no idea why I'd told her I'd come from the office, or why she found it a satisfactory answer. Two minutes later the bus filled, rolled and shook its way to Connolly Air Base.

When I got home, my mother was sitting in the living room, smoking her Slims, watching her soap opera. She absently asked me how my day had gone and I told her fine. "Hear from Dad?" I said.

"No, but I'm sure he's fine." She always said that when we hadn't heard from him in a while. I suppose she thought I was worried about him, or that I felt vulnerable without him. It was neither. I just wanted to discuss something with my mother that we both cared about. If I spoke with her about things that happened at school, or on my weekends, she'd listen with half an ear, say something like, "Is that so?" or "You don't say?" I couldn't stand that sort of thing. But when I mentioned my father, she treated me a bit more like an adult, or at least someone who was worth listening to. I didn't want to feel like a boy that afternoon. As I turned from my mother and walked down the hall I thought about the day my father left for Viet Nam. Sharp in his uniform, sure behind his aviator specs, he slipped a cigar from his pocket and stuck it in mine. "Not till I get back," he said. "We'll have us one when we go fishing. Just you and me, out on the lake all day, smoking and casting and sitting. Don't let Mamma see it. Put it in y'back pocket." He hugged me, shook my hand, and told me I was the man of the house now. He told me he was depending on me to take good care of my mother and sister. "Don't you let me down, now, hear?" And he tapped his thick finger on my chest. "You almost as big as me. Boy, you something else." I believed him when he told me those things. My heart swelled big enough to swallow my father, my mother, Claire. I loved, feared, and respected myself, my manhood. That day I could have put all of Waco, Texas, in my heart. And it wasn't till about three months later that I

discovered I really wasn't the man of the house, that my mother
and sister, as they always had, were taking care of me.

For a brief moment I considered telling my mother about
what had happened at school that day, but for one thing, she
was deep down in the halls of "General Hospital," and never
paid you much mind till it was over. For another thing, I just
wasn't the kind of person—I'm still not, really—to discuss my
problems with anyone. Like my father I kept things to myself,
talked about my problems only in retrospect. Since my father
wasn't around, I consciously wanted to be like him, doubly like
him, I could say. I wanted to be the man of the house in some
respect, even if it had to be in an inward way. I went to my
room, changed my clothes, and laid out my homework. I
couldn't focus on it. I thought about Marvin, what I'd said
about him or done to him—I couldn't tell which. I'd done something to him, said something about him; said something about
and done something to myself. *How come you're after* me *and not*
him? I kept trying to tell myself I hadn't meant it that way. *That*
way. I thought about approaching Marvin, telling him what I
really meant was that he was more Oakley's age and weight
than I. I would tell him I meant I was no match for Oakley. *See,
Marvin, what I meant was that he wants to fight a colored guy, but is afraid
to fight you cause you could beat him.* But try as I did, I couldn't for a
moment convince myself that Marvin would believe me. I
meant it *that* way and no other. Everybody heard. Everybody
knew. That afternoon I forced myself to confront the notion
that tomorrow I would probably have to fight both Oakley and
Marvin. I'd have to be two men.

I rose from my desk and walked to the window. The light
made my skin look orange, and I started thinking about what
Wickham had told us once about light. She said that oranges
and apples, leaves and flowers, the whole multi-colored world,
was not what it appeared to be. The colors we see, she said, look
like they do only because of the light or ray that shines on
them. "The color of the thing isn't what you see, but the light

that's reflected off it." Then she shut out the lights and shone a white light lamp on a prism. We watched the pale splay of colors on the projector screen; some people ooohed and aaahed. Suddenly, she switched on a black light and the color of everything changed. The prism colors vanished, Wickham's arms were purple, the buttons of her dress were as orange as hot coals, rather than the blue they had been only seconds before. We were all very quiet. "Nothing," she said after a while, "is really what it appears to be." I didn't really understand then. But as I stood at the window, gazing at my orange skin, I wondered what kind of light I could shine on Marvin, Oakley, and me that would reveal us as the same.

I sat down and stared at my arms. They were dark brown again. I worked up a bit of saliva under my tongue and spat on my left arm. I spat again, then rubbed the spittle into it, polishing, working till my arm grew warm. As I spat, and rubbed, I wondered why Marvin did this weird, nasty thing to himself, day after day. Was he trying to rub away the black, or deepen it, doll it up? And if he did this weird nasty thing for a hundred years, would he spit-shine himself invisible, rolling away the eggplant skin, revealing the scarlet muscle, blue vein, pink and yellow tendon, white bone? Then disappear? Seen through, all colors, no colors. Spitting and rubbing. Is this the way you do it? I leaned forward, sniffed the arm. It smelled vaguely of mayonnaise. After an hour or so, I fell asleep.

* * *

I saw Oakley the second I stepped off the bus the next morning. He stood outside the gym in his usual black penny loafers, white socks, high water jeans, T-shirt and black jacket. Nailor stood with him, his big teeth spread across his bottom lip like playing cards. If there was anyone I felt like fighting, that day, it was Nailor. But I wanted to put off fighting for as long as I could. I stepped toward the gymnasium, thinking that I shouldn't run, but if I hurried I could beat Oakley to the door and secure myself near Gilchrest's office. But the moment I stepped into the gym, I felt Oakley's broad palm clap down on my shoulder. "Might as well stay out here, Coonie," he said. "I need me a little target practice." I turned to face him and he slapped me, one-two, with the back, then the palm of his hand, as I'd seen Bogart do to Peter Lorre in "The Maltese Falcon." My heart went wild. I could scarcely breathe. I couldn't swallow.

"Call me a nigger," I said. I have no idea what made me say this. All I know is that it kept me from crying. "Call me a nigger, Oakley."

"Fuck you, ya black ass slope." He slapped me again, scratching my eye. "I don't do what coonies tell me."

"Call me a nigger."

"Outside, Coonie."

"Call me one. Go ahead."

He lifted his hand to slap me again, but before his arm could swing my way, Marvin Pruitt came from behind me and calmly pushed me aside. "Git out my way, boy," he said. And he slugged Oakley on the side of his head. Oakley stumbled back, stiff-legged. His eyes were big. Marvin hit him twice more, once again to the side of the head, once to the nose. Oakley went down and stayed down. Though blood was drawn, whistles blowing, fingers pointing, kids hollering, Marvin just stood there, staring at me with cool eyes. He spat on the ground, licked his lips, and just stared at me, till Coach Gilchrest and Mr. Calderon tackled him and violently carried him away. He never struggled, never took his eyes off me.

Nailor and Mrs. Wickham helped Oakley to his feet. His already fattened nose bled and swelled so that I had to look away. He looked around, bemused, wall-eyed, maybe scared. It was apparent he had no idea how bad he was hurt. He didn't even touch his nose. He didn't look like he knew much of anything. He looked at me, looked me dead in the eye in fact, but didn't seem to recognize me.

That morning, like all other mornings, we said the Pledge of Allegiance, sang "The Yellow Rose of Texas," "The Eyes of Texas Are upon You," and "Mistress Shady." The room stood strangely empty without Oakley, and without Marvin, but at the same time you could feel their presence more intensely somehow. I felt like I did when I'd walk into my mother's room and could smell my father's cigars, or cologne. He was more palpable, in certain respects, than when there in actual flesh. For some reason, I turned to look at Ah-so, and just this once I let my eyes linger on her face. She had a very gentle-looking face, really. That surprised me. She must have felt my eyes on her because she glanced up at me for a second and smiled, white teeth, downcast eyes. Such a pretty smile. That surprised me too. She held it for a few seconds, then let it fade. She looked down at her desk, and sat still as a photograph.

◆ *Bruce Fleming* ◆

THE AUTOBIOGRAPHY OF GERTRUDE STEIN

PART I. 1967

Gertrude Stein was born in 1874 in Allegheny Pennsylvania Alice B. Toklas has told about this in her Autobiography. Gertrude Stein always liked having been born in Allegheny Pennsylvania because she said it gave Frenchmen trouble in spelling it. Allegheny Pennsylvania is in this way not very different from Salawingo Maryland which is where Robert Johnson was born in 1905 and though neither Alice B. Toklas nor Gertrude Stein talks about this there is no reason why they should. For Robert Johnson was after all only one of the many young men who came to visit Gertrude Stein at 27 rue de Fleurus and drank tea while Gertrude Stein sat in her easy chair and talked. Robert Johnson was not one of those who came many times or made a great impression on Gertrude Stein or on Alice B. Toklas who would have mentioned it if he had. He was one of the faceless ones that came to see them and that later was referred to only as one of the many young men who came.

Robert Johnson was born in 1905 in Salawingo Maryland and

Reprinted from *The Gettysburg Review* (Vol. 2, No. 2, Spring 1989), by permission of the editors and author.

grew up there. In 1967 he was sixty-two years old and by then he was nearly bald. He had never had too much hair after the age of thirty-five when it began to thin out and so by the time he was sixty-two he was almost bald. When Gertrude Stein was sixty-two she had just completed what has been described in the Autobiography as her triumphant lecture tour of the United States. Whether or not it was triumphant it is at any rate certain that it pleased her. But as I was saying Robert Johnson in 1967 at the age of sixty-two and bald went to see the grave of Gertrude Stein in Paris in the cemetery of the Père Lachaise the cemetery where are buried Proust and Alfred de Musset and Gertrude Stein along with Alice B. Toklas and which as the Guide Vert or Michelin Guide says is one of the most interesting cemeteries in Paris. Its abundant vegetation it says and the wild terrain accentuate for a simple visitor the funerary impression and there is a map marking the places of the graves of Marcel Proust Sarah Bernhardt Edith Piaf and Gerard de Nerval but the map and the guide book being French there is no mention made of Gertrude Stein no little black x to mark where she is buried with Alice B. Toklas. For the French map and the guidebook she too is only one of the nameless tombs that fill up the spaces between those of the famous people as Robert Johnson too was nameless in her life and in his visits to 27 rue de Fleurus.

Robert Johnson went by taxi to the cemetery and sent it away. He thought it would be wasteful to keep it waiting even though he was not poor having inherited what would be called a small fortune from his grandparents aside from his salary as a book editor. I have always liked this term of the small fortune it implies that after all it is a fortune only small so that we have at once a large thing and a modest word and it somehow does not seem too much. All things being equal it was not a street where he would have wanted to be set down alone by a taxi especially on a dark and cloudy day such as this cool fourth of April. Across the street were stores that could not be seen into because of the darkness of their glass but he could tell they were florist shops selling flowers. Where there are cemeteries there are flower shops. And also there were little cafés with tables that the French and all Europeans love to sit at on long afternoons talking and drinking wine and playing cards and looking out into the street to see what is happening. Nothing is ever happening and they go back to their cards.

Robert Johnson had come to see the grave of Gertrude Stein and also that of Alice B. Toklas though of course he had not expected Alice B. Toklas to be on the map or have her own tiny black x like that of Chopin or Delacroix but he had expected Gertrude Stein to have her own x. But after all Heloise and Abelard are together and they share a single x so perhaps he thought it would be the same with those he had come to see.

There was first the guard house. The guard in the guard house does not have anything to guard but there you are. Robert Johnson stopped at the guard house to see if there was after all not a map which had upon it an x for the grave of Gertrude Stein or perhaps for that of the two together under one alone. There were maps and this was a good beginning. There was also a guard and this showed that the guard house was of some use. Good day said Robert Johnson to the guard who was sitting in a chair looking out the window I have come to find a map and he looked at the pile of maps on the table before him. Yes said the guard and looked also at the pile before him. The conversation thus being at an end the guard looked again out of the window. Thank you said Robert Johnson and taking a map he turned to leave. The guard was abruptly interested he leaned over the table and tapped it. Robert Johnson was surprised. Are the maps sold he asked. The maps are free the guard said it is the service which costs. And this is how Robert Johnson came to spend one franc for a map which did not have an x for the grave of Gertrude Stein.

This is also how he found himself not five minutes later in a room where a woman behind a counter looked in a metal file box and found the name Stein Gertrude and a number for her grave and filled out a card with her name and the date 1946 and there was another little map of the cemetery on which she put an x and pushed it across the counter to Robert Johnson who could not tell from her expression or tone of voice whether or not she recognized the name she had just written down or whether it was the first time she had supplied such a card to a man who was once young and came to see Gertrude Stein as she sat in the armchair and talked at 27 rue de Fleurus.

Even with the maps it was not easy going the wild terrain of which the guidebook speaks is all too truly wild. And the way is curving and winding and it is not always clear what is meant by a path on a map and what is after all not a path but only a shortcut across the grass. But anyhow finally he found the main path that had to be the right one since it was against the wall and one really could not go any further. After all on the other side of the wall there were houses and a crane balancing in the air. The grave of Gertrude Stein was not there instead it was a little further on. Of course the town was misspelled as she always said the French were apt to do she used to say it very solemnly in her booming voice to those officials who were ready with pen poised in air to write down her lieu de naissance her place of birth. And next to it was the grave of Alice B. Toklas that had no stone or name at all and was only outlined in white rocks both of them were dirt without grass or flowers except that on the grave of Gertrude Stein there was the brown skeleton of a geranium plant held up to its neck in the soil and nothing at all on the grave of Alice B. Toklas except for a tuft of crabgrass that the gardener had not pulled off. Dead is dead as Gertrude Stein said in her thousand-page book The Making of Americans.

This was the modern part of the cemetery where the graves were closer to one another and more geometrical and Robert Johnson did not see any more space in Père Lachaise and it may be that there is not any more but in that case nobody famous will be able to die anymore in Paris. Beyond this corner there

are the statues of the nineteenth century that Gertrude Stein
said so often she had escaped and the little dark funeral chapels
in stained glass and stone and rusted metal with their doors
standing ajar to show shadowed insides and dust and bouquets
of flowers dried upon the floors. And as Robert Johnson turned
away from the grave of Gertrude Stein the bells began to ring
over the graves meaning fifteen minutes until the gate was
closed upon them and he looked up at the dark sky and continued along the path where under the trees and among the monu-
ments clustered together there was a grave with a child-sized
statue of a girl with waves of stone for hair and blank eyes with
small gray shoes and crossed feet sitting on a bench as if she
were leaving room for something else to come and sit beside her.

And as he was out of breath on the deserted path Robert
Johnson stopped a minute to look at this which so contrasted
with the clean pure lines of Gertrude Stein's monument like the
clean lines of some of her prose such as Ida of which a critic has
said it has the purity of a Bach fugue and as he looked at this
fascinated by its difference from the grave of Gertrude Stein he
suddenly saw something move at the stone girl's feet and he felt
afraid it was after all near dusk and cold and the bells to leave
were still echoing in the air. It was a mother cat with her yellow
eyes wide with fear surrounded by her kittens that had taken
shelter under this seat of marble and that he had at first thought
a part of the sculpture a part of the stone of the sightless girl
and the half-empty bench and that had suddenly moved. And
he felt strange and he hurried on down the deserted path in the
cemetery the gravel crunching under his feet. And that was the
grave of Gertrude Stein.

But when a few days later in his hotel room Robert Johnson
read another copy of the Autobiography of Alice B. Toklas that
he had found in the stall of a bookseller by the Seine wrapped
in plastic he could not finish it not because there was in it the
sounds of things remembered or things that made him regret
but rather because the book seemed finally to him unspeakable.

It seemed to him incredible that a person sixty years of age should demand so openly and in so public a way what she had demanded privately all her life in her writings and in her person the justification of her self and of her existence by the forms of art. An incredible thing that someone who was denied this justification in the eyes of others for so long should still demand it and what was worse still believe in it.

For he saw as he read in this book the strange failure of Gertrude Stein and that of any individual against the world the failure of sentences saturated with self-assertion and the anecdotes that were amusing only because the people about whom they were told had in fact been willing to submit themselves as Gertrude Stein had not to the confines of forms and become famous doing so. And nowhere in this book was there relief from the attempt to convince the world by mere force of assertion that the author was among the group of the chosen ones who were different from ordinary ones and that this justified writing down everything that could be remembered. It seemed to Robert Johnson that Gertrude Stein all her life had confused the personal with the artistic thinking her life the same as art merely because it was her life and she wanted recognition and saw that artists got it.

Robert Johnson let the book slide from his fingers onto the spread in the room and saw the blank blue wall and burst into tears feeling the hot liquid on his fingers. And when it was evening he sat down with a pile of paper and a pen and began to write.

PART II. 1905–1925

But as I said Robert Johnson was born and raised in Salawingo Maryland he was born there in 1905 and had done what growing up he was going to do there by the time when he was sixteen and left and went to Johns Hopkins where he grew up some more. There was a small but excellent school for young ladies in Salawingo that had been founded in 1891 by Miss Nettie P. Turkington who had come to visit a friend and had been as she later said shocked that there was not an academy for the young ladies and as Miss Nettie P. Turkington was well to do as they said in those days and came from Philadelphia she decided to stay and set up the Turkington Academy which soon changed its name to Marshall College after a benefactor. It became one of the most select schools for young ladies both from the surrounding area and the city of Baltimore and one of the most refined.

The parents of Robert Johnson had come to Salawingo in 1894 when it was still a tiny seaport town still dark and dingy from the neglect it had suffered after the period of its greatest wealth in the 1860s with little streets lined with wooden houses inclining down to the water and the bay enclosed by the sand spits that opened around it and made it calm. The bay lapped slow and quiet against the side of the dark wood of the dock smelling of creosote where Robert Johnson sometimes sat watching the water in the afternoons when his parents did not know where he was. There were some large brick houses from the 1708s in Salawingo on these streets radiating down to the water from the courthouse that sat in the center on the top of the hill but some of these were empty behind their brick walls facing the street with their gardens gone to waste or filled with the lone old survivors of the age of the town's glory when the seaport was busy and people walked on the streets. Now it was mostly silent.

Marshall College had only just before the arrival of Miss Nettie P. Turkington been a private estate gone to ruin. It had white columns in the front and a greenhouse and formal gardens where clogged fountains trickled and stone figures of Pan sat on pedestals overgrown by the vines. Miss Nettie P. Turkington is said to have taken a look put a monocle to her eye and said it is sufficient simply it is sufficient and nothing more and then the gardens were cleaned the house was opened restored and supplied. The first year Miss Nettie P. Turkington had ten young professors and a student body of nearly fifty. Robert Johnson's father came three years later with a degree in mathematics fresh from Johns Hopkins to this little town run down and abandoned and the nearly silent port and the hills stretching around them where tobacco was grown and horses were raised.

Robert Johnson's mother was named Marie by her parents in Baltimore after Marie Albani who was an opera singer then touring the east whose name was really Roberta Smith but she had changed it. She had given a program at the end of which she had sung Home Sweet Home accompanying herself on the piano and Ralph Shapey the grandfather of Robert Johnson had cried though he had not cared for the songs preceding it. His grandmother a frail thing who liked her roses and a little needlepoint soon gave birth to a daughter and named her after the singer who had brought tears to her husband's eyes. Ralph Shapey was well to do as they said in those days and was in business. And every time Robert Johnson was taken to Baltimore still called home by both his parents he was taken to a big house with a little old lady who spoiled him and fed him sugar cookies so lacy and thin they dissolved on the tongue and let him play with the bell pull on the wall that brought the maid.

But anyhow their daughter Marie was brought up in comfortable surroundings and as her parents were influenced by modern ideas they sent her to Paris from which she returned three years later full of modern ideas herself. She met Robert Johnson's father at Johns Hopkins at a talk where he was at that time a student and the next year in one of the biggest events of the season married him wearing a dress that reached half way up the aisle. The next month they left for Marshall College which was soon to have such a reputation. Marie Johnson was a big woman with her own ideas and a belief in the new woman and so she was delighted to be married to Matthew Johnson a teacher at Marshall College for Women and she put all of her energy into her husband's job and his world. Perhaps this is strange.

Many years later Robert Johnson was to remember going to receptions with his mother and father in the big high-ceilinged living room of the college main hall with the dark wood walls and the Persian rugs and the portraits over the fireplace and the alcoves with sofas and chairs and the young women standing about balancing tea cups on saucers that Robert Johnson always hoped would fall off just to see what would happen and the little cookies and the clusters of lights in threes on the wall. It was his mother who was good at organizing who organized May Day every year on the lawn when the Queen of the May was crowned and the families were invited to come and there was a maypole with the girls in white skirts against the green trees.

Thus Robert Johnson grew up in a house on one of the quiet side streets of this town that he had known since he was young he must leave in a house behind the county courthouse with the benches along the walkway up to its door where the old men sat under the oak trees in the afternoons. Robert Johnson was an only child he was as I said born in 1905 there had been a baby after him a girl that had died early on and after that there could be no more. And Robert Johnson grew up confused though he did not know it he could not reconcile the knowledge that he would leave this town to the fact that it was after all his life. Was life then someplace else. He spent many hours reading novels and poetry and other things that were not true and of this of course his parents approved his father was a professor.

And so Robert Johnson grew up alone his father occupied with his position his mother with organizing. There were to be sure other children of faculty men and these he knew fairly well in fact he went to Johns Hopkins with one a pale blond boy named Marcus after the Roman emperor Marcus Aurelius but there were only a few and they were not very interesting. And though sometimes Robert Johnson thought about how pretty a girl was that he saw in passing in the corridors or on the lawn this was when he was alone up close they seemed large and sure of themselves and so when he was sixteen and went to Johns Hopkins with the other boys it was something of a relief. And when he left Salawingo it seemed as if finally he must be about to enter the dream world of Baltimore that he knew only from visits and yet that his parents referred to as home these plain brick buildings on the Homewood campus that he had visited with his parents so often and not far from the large dark house of his grandparents in the rich dark Baltimore of after the War.

At first each thing at Johns Hopkins seemed a part of the dream fresh and new the buildings the other young men the pathways overhung with elm trees the voices of the professors. But of course as is true with all dream worlds it simply with the passage of time became real it simply and slowly as the days passed that first winter disintegrated into the sensation of the edge of his desk against the palm of his hand the sound of the tree branches on his window the chill of the water against his face in the morning. And he felt it leaving and it was then that Robert Johnson understood for the first time the difference between what is imagined and what is lived it was the first time he felt this strange flattening of life that he was to know once more in his life felt the world lose its golden glow and turn dull.

And for the first time in his life he was afraid. He had always been solitary but it had never bothered him now he felt as if others threatened him by their very being. That spring he read political history he did not know why it seemed as if he must understand to control this world of other people and he was afraid. And yet time passed one year and then two and Robert Johnson led a solitary life meeting some people who were amusing some that were interesting but no one he really cared for and around the end of the third year after many courses in politics and having settled on the idea of reading law the fear that had laid under the surface all this time simply disappeared. He was not aware of its going but one day he was aware that it was gone and he became peaceful.

And in his last year he began to read books in literature again and one day in late winter while watching the rain against the windows from his room he had the thought that he might become a writer. And he sat down right then and wrote a poem about the rain on the window and he was pleased with himself. And for the rest of the year he read and wrote poems. In the spring there was a poem of his published in the literary magazine the Calumet and he said to himself now I am a real writer.

PART III. 1926–1927

After graduation that June he went to Paris with letters of introduction to a family with whom his mother had been friends and with the intention of finding the artistic life he had heard just a little about at Johns Hopkins. And it was late in the fall of this year that Robert Johnson with a renewed interest in literature where it seemed that the person was no longer threatened by others came to visit 27 rue de Fleurus and to meet Gertrude Stein.

He had heard at Johns Hopkins about Gertrude Stein and the artistic life and he set out to find them. The people with whom he was staying knew someone who knew a friend of Gertrude Stein and so it was that he knocked on the door at 27 rue de Fleurus and heard the deep contralto voice of Gertrude Stein ask after a pause de la part de qui venez-vous on whose part do you come and he stuttered at first he was unsure as to what to say and while he was still tongue-tied the door swung open and there was a large woman in a shapeless dress and sandals saying well come in anyway perhaps it will be all right after all.

And after he had introduced himself as Robert Johnson from Johns Hopkins the woman had said well come in Robert Johnson and turning abruptly had padded towards a room where there were lights and already several people. The woman settled herself in her chair again motioning Robert Johnson to a place by two other young men who got up quickly to shake hands with him neither of them seemed to speak English and then they all sat down quickly and turned again to Gertrude Stein who motioned towards a thin woman with a hooked nose in the corner with another woman who had not ceased talking quietly. Miss Toklas she said and the other woman was not introduced then she cleared her throat and as I was saying she went on and she leaned back in her chair half-closing her eyes for a moment.

And so Robert Johnson met Gertrude Stein when he was twenty-one. He came back several times to 27 rue de Fleurus always listening always awed by this new world opening up to him after the easy well-to-do stuffiness of Baltimore and Johns Hopkins the world of the paintings on the walls of the people he saw and sat with this large woman who commanded the most self-assured of all and who ruled this room if not possibly also the world. It seemed as he walked along the Seine at night looking at the glittering lights of the boats reflected on the water that here was the only solid world this world of people becoming history by their own activities producing works that lived independently of them and would live beyond them this was the possible dream the justification of art. Robert Johnson did not talk much when he went to the rue de Fleurus but he talked and so he was invited back three times. Gertrude Stein had at first evidently taken an interest in this quiet and interested young man from Baltimore later she may have lost it or decided that he was too quiet or not interested enough. But he did go three times.

Robert Johnson had found a room not far from the Pantheon and he had friends now men and women writers models actors he had met in bars other writers and painters who had parties in tiny rooms filled with smoke. He saw Ernest Hemingway in bars and Picasso at the picture exhibitions everyone saw everyone at the picture exhibitions. Robert Johnson sold two poems at this time they were nice poems and one day on the street he met Gertrude Stein again with Alice B. Toklas they were perched high up in the car that was stopped for a traffic light he bowed and Gertrude Stein inclined her head and Robert Johnson was convinced that she must have read his two poems otherwise she would not have bowed and he was heartened. He wrote to his parents telling them he wanted to be a writer he was happy his parents did not say no.

Robert Johnson felt the power of art to turn people into objects beyond mere life felt it because it was in the air and in the beliefs and talk of all these people the painters he saw on the street and the writers he sat up late with over wine in the cafés their belief in their greatness present or to be. This was the year when he read Tender Buttons and saw the Bonheur de Vivre and thought them daring and strange and altogether wonderful and saw the people who had made them Matisse with his gold spectacles like a German professor and Gertrude Stein. Here he thought lay the answer to the difference between dream and reality that had so bothered him human beings could turn themselves into art.

PART IV. 1927–1967

And yet this period of Robert Johnson's life ended not long after. His parents had given him the money for about a year saying we will see when the year is up when it ran out they said they could not they had recently had large expenses they had repaired the roof and he would have to find some other source and with their letter Robert Johnson was at first bitter then philosophical then bitter again for now Robert Johnson knew he was on his own.

At first he thought of writing to his grandparents in Baltimore then he was ashamed then he thought of getting a job like some of the others in the cafés but suddenly he realized that he did not want this sort of work on the edges of life serving others he wanted to control the world not be in it. So this period of his life ended when faced with the sudden reality of these things he would have to endure and the realization that he would be cut off from the life he wanted either by accepting its charity or living in a way to which he was not accustomed that he realized that this year had only been a dream the power of art a dream. He realized this in his room with the sun of early summer coming in the window and falling on the sheet of his unmade bed and with the realization of the weakness of art and the strength of the real world what had seemed the legitimization of the self in the eyes of others through art seemed only a charade.

And so for the second time in Robert Johnson's life the glow left the world only this time it seemed a blinding glow that was gone rather than a gentle one like a sun that had made everything unclear so that when it went away there was only the neutral world of everyday things no more and no less and himself a person among others who could act within the world. The next week he wrote to a book publisher he had some contacts with in New York and asked for a job as an editor since after all there seemed no point in letting this year of the literary life go to waste the production of books was like the production of everything else. So in 1927 Robert Johnson moved from Paris to New York and his youth came to an end. He took his job as a book editor and he felt in himself a calmness and acceptance he had never felt before and an interest in other people in the motions of the world its actions and the feelings of others and he was not unhappy.

At first it was difficult to form personal relationships with other people especially women. In Paris there had been women of easy virtue and fellow artists almost like brothers but now it was different. One woman he knew in New York told him that she was not a mother or a whore and so was not for him and this time was the coming to adulthood of Robert Johnson.

Yet finally in the fall of 1930 Robert Johnson was married to a woman that he continued to love off and on until she died in 1962 at the age of fifty-five and this was the longest period in

his life. She was named Geneviève she was a Frenchwoman
visiting in New York who never went back to France she had
beautiful hands and smooth thighs she played the piano and
belonged to the flower club and though Robert Johnson never
understood her he felt bound to her by forces that he could not
comprehend and did not want to. They had no children and for
his part Robert Johnson was just as glad and so life passed on
and during the time that this happened a world war had come
and gone and a whole new generation of people coming of age
and beginning to grow old.

Then his wife died and suddenly she was gone and this period of his life so much longer than any other was over and in
the months after her death he began to think that he was like
Rip van Winkle and the world had changed. He felt afraid that
in a strange way he had missed knowing something he should
know as if there were questions that had been merely postponed in his life not answered. Was this love of one person not
an escape from those questions was it all there is.

He found it difficult to work at his job at night the apartment
seemed too large and empty perhaps for the reason that his life
with another person was gone but his life alone still existed
somewhere. He began to think about the youth that had ended
in 1927 before he had become a part of the world and fallen in
love. And finally he took a vacation from his job and went
traveling going back to Paris for the first time in nearly forty
years longer after all than the time that Gertrude Stein was gone
from the United States the country of her youth.

PART V. 1967

He walked along the narrow streets of the Latin Quarter in the
Paris he had not seen since he left seeking things he recognized.
Of course he found little he recognized except the streets them-
selves forty years is a long time. It was all so hidden by the

students in blue jeans and the Communist slogans painted on the walls the stores of white and plastic and the girls and boys with frizzy hair walking in the fountain on the Boulevard St. Michel. Almost a week later having seen the grave of Gertrude Stein he sat in his hotel room with the window open over the lights of the city and Sacré Coeur white against the sky to let in the cool and freshness of the coming spring with the traces of tears on his fingers and a pile of paper before him.

What was the seductive promise of art. It was the dream of becoming something that was not merely one person among many the attempt to legitimize a single person by creating a world in which he was king and it is literary forms that effect this illusion. What are literary forms. They are the parts and aspects of a work stripped of any association to a single person. In place of these forms of the overall work Gertrude Stein substituted a succession of much smaller units within the work so that there were no larger forms left to distinguish any work from any other certainly not on generic grounds the plays like the poems like the novels and all these playing at being kinds of literature totally emptied a false detective story a false drama a false lyric poem.

It is these tiny forms which as a result and in the absence of larger ones are the most visible aspect of her works what some call her radically personal forms which is to say radically absent forms given that forms are impersonal and the effect produced on the reader of these tiny units within the works is that of repetition. Later on Gertrude Stein said that the repetition had been the point that which she was attempting to achieve yet the works of Gertrude Stein cannot be understood if they are understood as the result of a desire to produce a certain kind of work they are instead the result of a certain perception of self. For Gertrude Stein believed that anything that happened to her or that she made was important not because it was constructed to be so but rather because it happened to her or she made it. It is this that she called the continuous present. In fact by making the artistic forms so small and so close together Gertrude Stein turned these into the most substantial content of her works more interesting than the references possibly to her dog a picnic she had or her pile of writing such as the long sentence followed by the short the question with a period. However the references which may be to her dog her day her pile of writing are not sufficiently interesting to hold up the minute shiftings of her repetition since everyone has the same minutiae of life we do not need that of Gertrude Stein.

Later on as well she tried to justify these tiny bits of content on the basis of the need for repetition but this is it seems a rationalization after the fact. It would of course have been the tiny content that was most important to Gertrude Stein not the repetition which is thus not cause but effect. Some people have said that in her writing Gertrude Stein was finally achieving the goal of Flaubert to write about nothing but this is not so for her it was very much something because for her she was very much someone and it was the content of her life. Gertrude Stein in fact confused her perception of her life with others' perception of her life and so believed that others would be willing to read what she was willing to write. The proof of this is that she never understood why others did not perceive her works as she perceived them that is as perfectly unexceptionable and very interesting. It is very interesting she said this often in her thousand page book The Making of Americans.

But writing is more interesting than reading and others are not like one's self. Other people conclude we are someone because of what we write Gertrude Stein thought she was someone therefore she must write. Gertrude Stein demanded that her life not be deformed more than just a little bit to art or not at all. Yet she wanted in return the acclaim that she had learned from the Romantics is given to people who are willing to squash their lives into the forms of art since it is only these that create the illusion of the impersonal. Gertrude Stein it may be said put the cart before the horse yet as far as that went did she not finally after all deform her life with forms reducing it to personality and selling it so that her strangeness was interesting because people did not believe that someone like her could exist so self-assertive and yet so dependent on their acceptance. Was it not her failure in literature that made her a success as a personality and thus finally did turn her life to art not as a success but as a failure yes it was.

The interest it seems of Gertrude Stein is that she tried to make literature a minor art for only in this way could it mirror and so legitimize her own life which was in essence like many other daily lives. That this was productive of something new and perhaps instructive is certain that this was productive of something major because minor is less certain. It was finally legitimization of her life by the grounds of art that Gertrude Stein had asked for and all of those who had ever wanted this deep down but had realized that it could not be asked for directly and so who had submitted their lives to the shapings and disfigurations of forms and suffered from it stood speechless with envy for the impossible thing she had demanded and that it seemed almost gotten. The nature of what Gertrude Stein had demanded took Robert Johnson's breath away that night in his hotel room causing him to look around to see if those who took reprisals on this sort of temerity had overheard half in awe of the enormity of what it was that she had dared to ask for.

Yet Robert Johnson had learned from his life in Salawingo Maryland and from Johns Hopkins and from Geneviève his wife that all of us are born a part of the world among others and stay that way. This is the world in which we love or are loved or suffer or not suffer and in which we finally die. And Robert Johnson was tired he ran his hands across his bald head and felt his scalp and the cool air on it and raised his head to see that it was getting light and he felt tired. If there is a love that dare not speak its name it is the love that Robert felt at that moment for Gertrude Stein precisely because she had been so wrong. He drew his hand again across his forehead but like Gertrude Stein he was not fond of seeing the sun come up so he stretched out and closed the shutters and went to bed.

Gertrude Stein has said I am I if my little dog knows me by which she means that there is no justification of being save in life itself yet Gertrude Stein did not believe this thing. Sometimes it is easy to believe this thing and sometimes it is not easy and sometimes it is easy to be puzzled about what to believe and sometimes it is not after all necessary to choose for sometimes the form and the individual come together into the work of art and we can believe for just the few minutes of writing or reading that it is after all this which solves the problem.

fin

◆ *Devon Jersild* ◆

IN WHICH JOHN IMAGINES HIS MIND AS A POND

When John woke in the morning he was thinking of Ann: the earnest look on her face when she asked him how he was getting along, her silence at the dinner table, her attention to the children. She grinned when jokes were made, looked pensive when the talk was serious.

She was married to Graham. He wrote articles on international economics, and when John's wife said she had a friend who was also an economist, Graham said, "Oh yes, I've met him. He wishes he were me."

Ann didn't seem embarrassed. John thought she treated Graham as if he were her guest, someone she respected but didn't know well.

He hadn't seen her beauty at first. Her shoulders tipped forward, and you could see how she would look when she was old: crooked, bony, in need of a cane. She wore her hair frizzed and electric from a perm, or limp and clinging to her face, or sometimes, short and spikey on the top with a long braid down her back. John's wife thought Ann couldn't make up her mind about how to present herself.

First published in *The Kenyon Review,* vol. XI, no. 3, New Series, Summer 1989. © 1989 by Kenyon College. Reprinted with permission.

"Mmm," she said, pulling the sheet up to her chin and stretching appealingly, "Couldn't you get me a cup of coffee?" The sheet formed itself to her body: the two stiff legs, the cloud of hair between them, the concave belly. Kristina always slept naked, even though John said it wasn't great for the kids to come into their room and know she was unclad beneath the sheets. "*I'm* undressed," she had answered, "but you're wearing at least two pairs of pajamas, so they know there's no chance of funny business." Kristina thought John was sexually repressed, probably because his father hated homosexuals, so that John had to deny his same-sex impulses as an adolescent, thus setting the pattern of repression. "Bullshit," said John. "I just get cold at night."

He pulled her next to him. For ten years they had spent their nights tucked into each other, and mornings before he opened his eyes he would smell the sleep in her hair, on her neck, her breath. Her scent was faint; when she skipped her morning bath, her body smell got richer. "Coffee for you?" he said. "Why should I get you coffee?"

"Mmm, I need coffee. Go, before the kids get up. I want a peaceful morning."

John touched his finger to his tongue and ran it from her Adam's apple down along her breastbone toward her navel, where her skin got fuzzy and warmer. Many of his friends said they didn't know how strongly they could love until they had children. John loved his kids, but that wasn't his experience. For him, it was Kristina who had shocked him out of his youthful narcissism, tramping into his life in shorts and hiking boots, offering him a joint. She was strong but fine featured, feathery blond hair on her arms and legs. He had been reading. For a moment, he thought he had imagined her.

"Don't get started," she said. "Coffee, coffee."

"You can't deny me," he said. "You'll only add to my problems. I'll be having a mid-life crisis soon."

"You're so simplistic," she said. "Anyway, you're usually the one who turns me away."

John rolled the covers off his legs and searched for his sneakers. Time to turn the heat up. By now he should have weatherproofed the house. Old as it was, no one had ever bothered to outfit it against the elements. Rain poured off the roof where there should have been a gutter, then leached into the basement. Cold air breathed through the cracks in the molding and in through the kitchen fan. What precious heat the radiators could produce went straight through the attic into heaven. In Vermont, houses needed to be stuffed, wired, and wrapped in space suits, to take them through the winter.

He wondered, was Ann awake across town? Was she thinking about him?

*   *   *

He first saw her several years ago, when she wasn't aware that anyone was looking. In the parking lot of the nursery school, with her three-year-old daughter and her infant son in their car seats behind her, she reached her hand into her blouse to adjust her bra strap. Then she smoothed her hands over her breasts as if they were hurting her, as if the milk in her ducts were uncomfortably stored. When she stepped out of the car and caught his eye, her face reddened for a moment: you could tell she was thinking, did he just see me? Ann showed everything on her face. The nervous eyes, the rapid and subtle changes of expression, the hint of a smile—clearly, nothing passed her by.

"Hi," John had said, holding out his hand. "Our daughters must be the same age. This is Karen."

"Out of the car," Ann said to the girl in the back seat, who made no sign of moving. John suppressed a smile. Other mothers would have said, "Shall we get out of the car now, sweetheart?" or, in the more current, firm mode, "I need you to get out of the car." Parents within a two-block radius of the nursery school were always incredibly polite.

John poked his head into the car. "What's her name?" he asked, not looking behind him.

"Polly," she said.

"Polly," said John, "you won't believe what I saw inside the Kangaroo School this morning. I saw a cookie as big as the moon, a huge ball of a cookie, and all the children were munching on it. And you know that little boy who wears clogs? Well, he was sitting on *top* of the cookie and eating his way down through the middle of it."

Polly took her long face out of her lap. Her breath smelled of Cheerios. "What kind of cookie?"

"I didn't get close enough to see. Maybe we'd better go before the other kids eat it up." She let him unbuckle her and pull her out of the car, crumbs falling from her lap.

As they went in, Ann said, "So what are you going to tell her when she gets there and there's no cookie?"

"I'll think of something," said John.

"God," said Ann. "It takes too much energy to be an imaginative parent. I like the old way better."

"Anything that works," said John. He looked at Ann and took in the edge of shyness, the distracted, blunt manner. All this, he thought, is superficial. He saw in the flare of her nostrils a kind of fierceness, and he felt something solid and purposeful underneath her skittishness. He was thinking, "I like you." Even then—before their children started playing together, before the town meetings, before the dinner parties—he liked her, he felt as if he knew her. Back then she was wearing her hair straight, and it was just the shade of his own hair, dark and rich, the color of wet bark. A loose strand hung over her forehead.

*   *   *

All day long he had dinner to look forward to. They were having their Christmas party tonight, and Ann and Graham were coming. He imagined what would happen if he could get Ann alone for a while: if they could talk. Maybe they would agree that the house was too hot—so many people—and would step outside together, where the wind would take away their breath. Moisture from her eyes would bead and freeze on her lashes. She would step close to him, fragile and delicate, and his heart would expand with tenderness for her.

Saturdays, Kristina worked at the gourmet shop she'd opened a couple of years ago; she didn't dare neglect the store in spite of the party that night—Sundays were her only day off. John indulged in fantasies as he cleaned the kitchen after breakfast, took the children for their Saturday walk, flipped through his briefcase. Weeks ago, the plays unfolding in his mind had been almost innocent—simple exchanges of affection between John and Ann. John would be driving in his car, for instance, and Ann would be beside him. They would have a long distance to cover—maybe through the country, with the moon hanging in the sky, the smell of corn and cow manure whooshing through the vents. They would talk happily, and then, when they reached her house and she put her hand on the door, he would turn to her and say, "You're dear to me." She would meet his gaze. "You're dear to me," she'd whisper back.

Because he had been married to Kristina for ten years and saw the world so much through her eyes, John occasionally was confronted by the image of himself lying on a psychiatrist's couch, repeating these fantasies. The one about driving in a car was embarrassing enough—so corny, so *kitsch!*—but even worse was the intricate drama he sometimes replayed, involving the deaths of Kristina and Graham, their funerals on a rainy day, the subsequent sorrow, courtship, and marriage of John and Ann. Only a coward would have a fantasy like that. Unbelievable what he went through to dream himself into bed with her.

Lately, though, John's daydreams began and ended on a different note. He called Ann on the phone; she came to his house when no one was there. They both knew what they wanted. They held each other. Then they were in bed, silky foot to silky foot, and he was rising on his elbows above her. What he wanted most was to see her face just as he came inside her. He wanted to see her expression break into pain and pleasure. And he wanted her to see his face, too. He wanted her to see him.

Once in a while, again because of Kristina's presence in John's mind, this daydream was impeded by a double pair of pajamas. If, in an act of defiance, he ripped the clothing from this figment of himself, revenge came as distraction: just when Ann's face began to turn, a draft from the window crept along his legs.

John had been raised in the puritan tradition, and his first impulse was to scold himself for his fantasies. He thought he should restrain himself, though he knew this was an ancient way to chaos. For centuries his forebears had denied their bodies' urgings, ignored them as if they did not exist, only to find themselves in astonished adulterous embraces. These were the people who took their sins so seriously that they felt obliged to follow up: to divorce their husbands and wives, abandon their children, and spread the general misery into the next generations.

At the same time, John knew that the more he played out these desires in his mind, the stronger they became. In fact, he was worried. Painful as it was to imagine himself alone in his fantasies, and much as he longed for a sign from Ann, he knew it could be worse if she became his co-conspirator. Think how he missed her already; think how she kept him from his work, his time in the here and now. What if she wanted him in the same way: wouldn't that be even worse? If they acknowledged the attraction between them, how could he live away from her?

Lately, he'd been reading about meditation, and for half an hour each morning he sat cross-legged against the wall, eyes closed, thinking of nothing but his breathing: in and out, in and out. The air tickled his passageways coming in, felt warmer going out. He forgot about time; his breathing grew shallow. When the telephone rang or an ambulance went by, he concentrated harder, trying to discern something about his breath that he hadn't noticed before. He was getting better at it. Afterward, his mind was clearer, empty of static. He could go to his office and concentrate.

The Buddha said to think of the mind as a clear, deep pond. Sometimes rain stirs up the bottom and muddies it. Sometimes clouds pass over and obscure the surface. If a twig or branch drops from a tree, ripples circle out from its center. All these disturbances come and go, but the pond remains. Desire, anger, confusion: these pass through the mind like weather. One should not try to restrain them (how can you stop a natural force like rain?), nor should one identify with the force, and think, for instance, that the mind *is* angry when anger passes through. Rather, the Buddha encourages one to acknowledge the weather dispassionately, to observe it, and watch it pass by.

This is good, John thought. The technique involved neither restraint nor indulgence. He thought he could make it work—as when a month ago, he ran into Ann at the bookstore. She reached up high to take a book from an upper shelf, and as she did, he was overwhelmed with desire. He took a deep breath. He focused on his breathing: coming in, going out. His heart had doubled, tripled, in his chest. He felt sad and anxious. His breath came in and out.

"Have you read this?" Ann asked, holding up a novel. "My brother said it's wonderful. I'm giving it to myself for Christmas." She pulled down on her skirt in the back. A child leaned out of his stroller and spun the calendar rack.

John took the book from her and read the back cover. How wonderful to feel calm in her presence. His breath came in and out. He could enjoy his attraction to her. It did not agitate him.

"Actually," Ann said, "I should know better than to act on my brother's advice. The last book he sent me proved that all wars have been caused by people eating animal flesh. He is so flaky."

"Where is this child's mother?" said a clerk. "That rack is going to fall on top of him."

"Let's hope he has better taste in fiction," said John, giving the book back to Ann. Their hands touched for a moment.

They smiled at each other, and John saw in the crease of her forehead how her daughter looked like her. He'd met Ann's father once, too. He was like Ann in a thoughtful mood: long, delicate features, a serene or troubled expression—hard to say which.

"Don't tell me what you're buying," she said. "Poetry?"

"Why," said John, "would a lawyer buy poetry?"

"You're a poet-lawyer, I'm sure of it."

"I'm not buying anything today." He raised his empty palms.

"Okay," she smiled.

John left the store and turned once more to wave. As she waved back, she lifted her chin and her nostrils flared, and he felt they had experienced an intimacy. Walking down the street, exhilarated by her image in his mind, he thought they could be close without fear of a dangerous involvement. What they shared would mean more without the drama of sex.

But this sort of thing was getting harder to keep up. Last week he had seen her twice. The first time was at a meeting about the lack of housing for low-income families—the need most recently close to Ann's heart. Would he have gone if not for the chance of seeing her? When they spoke afterward, Ann seemed nervous, and he wondered, afraid, if perhaps she recognized his feelings and wanted to push him away. Then on Sunday, Kristina took Karen over to play with Polly, and later Ann brought Karen home. He had gone to answer the door, to let his daughter in, and Ann stepped inside with her arms full of Karen's playthings. She handed him the glitter-markers and the books, the tops and the bag of jacks, and then she held up Karen's plastic iguana to look it over. It was a funny-looking creature, its tail arched, its lizard tongue cherry red, its ludicrous, happy expression. John smiled. Ann leaned forward, and as if with a burst of feeling, she kissed the iguana on its lips.

*   *   *

Vermonters, John thought, feel a special pressure in the holiday season. They know that people across the country have an image of Christmas that has little to do with the cornfields or the deserts or the palm trees where they live. Since Currier and Ives, America's vision of Christmas has been set in the white towns of Vermont. That's where the sleigh bells jingle; that's where the carolers go from door to door. Snow drifts into mounds; the air shimmers; human-scale mountains peak on the horizon. And for the most part, people (and the weather) try to live up to those expectations. If you picked any quaint, tree-lined street and walked along the sidewalk at night, you'd see in the windows of the houses: the Christmas trees, the strings of cranberries and popcorn, the bobbing heads, the electric candles on the sills. You imagine that in every living room women in red blouses stand with eggnog in their hands, while men in red or green ties drink whiskey and water; red tricycles wait beneath the tree (and plastic machine guns in the homes of the unenlightened and defiant). Every husband goes out on Christmas Eve to buy a piece of jewelry for his wife; every wife, seeing the amount written in the check register, pretends not to notice.

These visions do not include the Christmas suicides, the Christmas divorces, or the Christmases in the barely heated homes of people, who, if they are lucky, open donated cans of yams and little green peas.

Every year John delivered this sermon to Kristina, and every year, about December, he got nostalgic for the music of Phil Ochs. As presents began arriving in the mail, as he and Kristina wrapped packages for each other and the children, always there was Phil Ochs in the background, singing, "They don't have

Christmas in Kentucky, / There's no holly on a West Virginia door, / For the trees don't twinkle when you're hungry, / And jingle bells don't jingle when you're poor." This was the sort of irony that John savored. If he couldn't get out of the holiday round, the buying and the rush, at least he could be fully aware throughout. He preferred to acknowledge his complicity in the Christmastime perversion of generosity.

Kristina's gesture of nonconformity was their annual party on the twenty-eighth, an extravaganza of Swedish food and drink. She brought her Scandinavian inheritance from the china cabinet: the wooden, orange horses with painted saddles, ranging from two inches high to one crude, two-foot version; the blue and white porcelain featuring maids and geese; a Swedish sampler. For weeks in advance she pulled the bones out of herring with tweezers and set it aside to pickle. She soaked veal in salt water and then weighted it with bricks, to make into rollepolz. She served potatoes in cream sauce, boiled lutfisk and fruit soup. One year the lutfisk—an imported fish soaked in lye, the consistency of a jellyfish—was so gelatinous that as John tried to strain it, it slipped through his fingers and into the garbage disposal. That year they ate canned ham in disgrace.

Kristina served glög, too. She poured whiskey and wine into a pot on the stove and simmered it with raisins, almonds, sugar, cloves, cinnamon, and cardamom. John thought that people got drunk on it too fast, and that it was too sweet. This year he had talked her into letting him indulge his taste for expensive wine. On a day last week he had driven two hours to his favorite wine store in Burlington. He studied the labels, talked to the manager, and finally chose a case of Haut Médoc, 1979, $13.99 a bottle. He loved it—one sip and your head was full of its spirit. John played it cool with the manager, pressing down his excitement. It was a dream of his: a gracious house, its bounty known by fine wine breathing in every corner. It made him think of Jonson's poem "To Penshurst," praising the manor "whose liberal boord doth flow, / With all, that hospitalitie doth know!"

John thought it was a good thing that Kristina didn't know about the poem, and how he identified with it. She would have teased him mercilessly. She would have framed it and hung it in the entryway, next to the cross-country skis, an ironic commentary.

John loaded his trunk with the wine. Driving home, he felt only a little bit guilty. Phil Ochs would not approve, but then, Ben Jonson would not approve of Phil Ochs.

*　　*　　*

When Ann and Graham arrived at the door the night of the twenty-eighth, John didn't trust himself to greet them. His palms were sweaty; his skin was cold. He had been wrong to think so much of seeing her. Now talking to her would be impossible. From the corner of his eye he watched Graham give Kristina a kiss.

"Vermont is changing fast," Mr. Kelly was saying to him. "The thing is, it's going to happen whether you like it or not, so you might as well keep some of the profit from the wrong people."

"You've made some good investments, I'm sure," John said. Across the room, Ann made her way to the herring and rollepolz, where she stood alone. Graham had gone off in another direction—she didn't have a glass of wine. Was she afraid to talk to him? Had he just imagined their mutual attraction? Nearby, Kristina gestured to a small crowd of listeners. He could see that she was telling the story about their car being towed from a legal parking spot on their trip to New York. They had gone from official to official with no luck anywhere, until Kristina bribed one of them with tickets to a baseball game.

"You know that row of brick houses where they just put in the A&P?" Mr. Kelly was saying. "Mine."

"You're kidding," said John. Kristina's audience was laughing now. It was an exhilarating story: Kristina using all her wit and daring to free them from an inhuman system. Enterprising, she was. She would have made a better lawyer than he.

"Well, I'm small potatoes compared to some of them. I'm a big fish in a little pond, if you know what I mean."

"I know what you mean," said John.

"Aw, go on," said Mr. Kelly.

"Excuse me," said John. "Looks as if I better attend to the wine." He took a bottle off the mantel and refilled Mr. Kelly's glass.

"Here, Nancy," he said. "Let me give you some more wine."

"No, no," she said. "I'm still working on this. Come back later."

"Ellis, how about you?"

"Sure, fill 'er up." The Médoc flowed.

"Michael, wine?"

"I've got whiskey, John. Kristina showed me."

"Over here, John, I need some," said Susan Henley, their next-door neighbor. "This is heavenly. Where'd you get it?"

He tipped the bottle over her glass. "Thanks," he said. "I got it in Burlington—the cheese outlet sells wine."

"Any white?" she asked. "Chad's allergic to red."

"Ask Kristina," said John. He emptied the bottle into a spare glass on the coffee table and picked up another from under the lamp. If he went around the room like this he could make his way naturally to Ann.

"No more, John," said Norman Ikely. "One can only drink so much."

"Drink!" said John. "There's plenty."

"So I see," said Norman. "Maybe I better eat something first."

"Try some herring," said John. "And with every bite you take, think of Kristina's tweezers, which saved you from choking on a bone."

Someone tugged at the elbow of his jacket. He turned. It was Kristina, holding their four-year-old.

"Can you take him?" she said. "I've got to see to the food."

"I thought he was in bed."

"He was." Kristina peeled the boy's hands from her neck. "Go to Daddy, Nicky. Mommy's busy now."

John put down the wine and took the boy into his arms.

"I don't want to go to bed," Nick started to cry. *"Mommy. I want Mommy."*

"Now, don't be a baby, Nick. Let's go upstairs and see if the reindeer is waiting on the roof for you." John headed for the stairway.

Nick rubbed his nose into John's shoulder. "But I don't want to go to bed," he cried. "No, no, *no.* I want to stay up with the people."

"But Nicky," said John, "we're all going sledding tomorrow. If you stay up late you'll be too tired to go sledding. You'll be a grouch and then *no* one will be happy."

"Hey, Nicky."

John stopped, and then his face flushed. It was Ann. She had extracted herself from Mr. Kelly to come over to them. "Hey," she said, "did you know it's snowing outside? And do you know what I saw on my way to your house?"

Nick stopped crying and looked up at her.

"Come here," she said. "I'll show you."

Nick let Ann take him. She started up the stairs with him. On the landing she turned, and John pointed to the end of the hall, where Nick's room was. She went up, her skirt swaying at her ankles.

John went halfway up the stairs, too, and sat down on the landing. A wall separated him from the living room. Kristina was laughing in the kitchen; someone was telling a noisy joke; the Christmas record scratched to its end. From upstairs, he could hear nothing. He saw through the window that it *was* snowing. Snow fell through the branches of the trees and onto the cars parked along the street. The scene set off an echo in his mind, he wasn't sure what—a poem, a sequence in a story. He was moved. He took a deep pull of air, and then let it out. He looked at the snow and thought of his breathing.

When Ann came down, shadows from the railing cast bars of light across her skirt.

"I thought you said you weren't any good with kids," said John.

"Did I say that?" She sat down next to him. "Oh well, children are better for people they don't know. He's a sweetie, Nick is."

"You got him to sleep?"

"Mmm. Almost." She leaned her head against the railing and looked out the window ahead of them. John thought, she could have rested it against my shoulder. She looked beautiful to him —because of her hair against her sweater, because of her sweet bared ankles and the curve of her hip beneath her skirt—but also because of something else, something he couldn't say. He loved the familiarity of her features—the flare of her nostrils, her daughter in her forehead. He knew her face by heart. And something else, too. He felt that whatever he said to her, whatever he risked, she would be equal to it.

"Nice snow," she said. "Snow like this, and a party downstairs—it reminds me of something, of a story I read once."

After a pause, John said, "I think I want to tell you something."

She looked away from the snow, looked at him.

"I miss you," he said. "I miss you when you're not with me."

For a moment her eyes got bigger. He didn't know what she was thinking. And now he had said it. She took one of his hands and held it between hers. "I think of you, too," she said.

"Ann—"

"Shhh." She pressed her finger against his lips. Light wavered on her face. Standing, she said, "Come and be host." He watched her ankles going, quickly, down the steps ahead of him.

*   *   *

After the guests had swept the snow from their cars, and after all of them had driven away, half a dozen bottles of Haut Médoc, 1979, stood uncorked and still breathing.

"That was some miscalculation," said Kristina.

"Can you believe it?" said John. "All of my beautiful, beautiful wine."

"I think the glög goes over better." She picked up a few empty glasses.

"Thanks," said John. *"Shit.* I can't tell you how horrible this makes me feel."

"Don't worry. We'll cork it now and drink it every night this week. If it goes bad I'll use it in a stew."

"Thanks," said John. *"Shit."*

"Hey," said Kristina, "I'm not insulting *you."*

"You should know better," said John, "than to insult a man's taste in music or wine."

Kristina laughed, putting down the empty glasses. "Come here," she said. She pulled him down on the couch with her. "Let me comfort you."

"See if you can," he said.

*   *   *

The next morning, he woke up early, while the house was still. The snow had kept falling—he knew this without looking, because of the blue light from the windows. He had dreamed of Ann. His dream had brought him face to face with her, but now he was awake, while she still drifted back in the mist of sleep. He felt at one with the little room he slept in; he felt it glowing with loneliness. He rolled the covers off his legs, tucked them around Kristina's shoulders, and bent to find his sneakers. The humidifier had steamed up the windows, so he couldn't see out.

Kristina kept sleeping. Who knows, he thought, what she might be dreaming.

He closed the door behind him and stepped down to the window on the landing, where he had sat with Ann the night before. From here, the world looked like a Japanese screen, two dimensional. The snow shagged the evergreens and the thinnest twigs. The field beyond their house was sunk in a wintry drowse. When you looked out the window on a day like this, you could see that the earth had given itself to winter. Everything else was gone. Everything else was forgotten.

The blankness, the whiteness, made him think of his meditation, and he wondered, could he let go of his desire? Could he give it up? Could he give it to the snow and look outside without feeling the pangs of what he wanted?

Upstairs—it surprised him—his daughter was getting up. He heard her filling the tub, he heard the water rumbling. Then she turned it off. For a moment, the water lapped, and then the house was quiet again. She was a perfectionist, his daughter, and she liked her rituals. John knew what she would do next. She would go to the bathroom closet and take out her frog. She would stand over the tub and drop the frog into the water. She would listen to it plop and watch as it sank to the bottom and then, slowly, it would rise back up to the surface. The entire time she took her bath, it would bob there in the corner, riding on the little currents.

◆ *Janice Eidus* ◆

VITO LOVES GERALDINE

Vito Venecio was after me. He'd wanted to get into my pants ever since tenth grade. But even though we hung around with the same crowd back at Evander Childs High School, I never gave him the time of day. I, Geraldine Rizzoli, was the most popular girl in the crowd, I had my pick of the guys, you can ask anyone, Carmela or Pamela or Victoria, and they'll agree. And Vito was just a skinny little kid with a big greasy pompadour and a cowlick and acne and a big space between his front teeth. True, he could sing, and he and Vinny Feruge and Bobby Colucci and Richie DeSoto formed a doo-wop group and called themselves Vito and the Olinvilles, but lots of the boys formed doo-wop groups and stood around on street corners doo-wop-ping their hearts out. Besides, I wasn't letting any of them into my pants either.

Carmela and Pamela and Victoria and all the other girls in the crowd would say, "Geraldine Rizzoli, teach me how to tease my hair as high as yours and how to put my eyeliner on so straight and thick," but I never gave away my secrets. I just set my black hair on beer cans every night and in the morning I teased it and teased it with my comb until sometimes I imagined that if I kept going I could get it high enough to reach the stars, and then I would spray it with hairspray that smelled like red roses and then I'd stroke on my black eyeliner until it went way past my eyes.

The kids in my crowd were the type who cut classes, smoked in the bathroom, and cursed. Yeah, even the girls cursed, and we weren't the type who went to church on Sundays, which drove our mothers crazy. Vito was one of the worst of us all. He just about never read a book or went to class, and I think his mother got him to set foot in the church maybe once the whole time he was growing up. I swear, it was some sort of a holy miracle that he actually got his diploma.

Anyway, like I said, lots of the boys wanted me and I liked to make out with them and sometimes I agreed to go steady for a week or two with one of the really handsome ones, like Sally-Boy Reticliano, but I never let any get into my pants. Because in my own way I was a good Catholic girl. And all this time Vito was wild about me and I wouldn't even make out with him. But when Vito and the Olinvilles got themselves an agent and cut a record, "Teenage Heartbreak," which Vito wrote, I started to see that Vito was different than I'd thought, different than the other boys. Because Vito had an artistic soul. Then, on graduation night, just a week after Vito and the Olinvilles recorded "Teenage Heartbreak," I realized that, all these years, I'd been in love with him, too, and was just too proud to admit it because he was a couple of inches shorter than me, and he had that acne and the space between his teeth. There I was, ready for the prom, all dressed up in my bright red prom dress and my hair teased higher than ever, waiting for my date, but my date wasn't Vito, it was Sally-Boy Reticliano, and I wanted to jump out of my skin. About halfway through the prom, I couldn't take it anymore and I said, "Sally-Boy, I'm sorry, but I've just got to go over and talk to Vito." Sally-Boy, who was even worse at school than Vito, grunted, and I could tell that it was a sad grunt. But there was nothing I could do. I loved Vito and that was that. I spotted him standing alone in a corner. He was wearing a tux and his hair was greased up into a pompadour that was almost as high as my hair. He watched me as I walked across the auditorium to him, and even in my spiked heels, I felt as though I was floating on air. He said, "Aay, Geraldine, how goes it?" and then he took me by the arm and we left the auditorium. It was like he knew all along that one day I would come to him. It was a gorgeous spring night, I could even see a few stars, and Vito put his arm around me, and he had to tiptoe a little bit to reach. We walked over to the Gun Hill Projects, and we found a deserted bench in the project's laundry room, and Vito said, "Aay, Geraldine Rizzoli, I've been crazy about you since tenth grade. I even wrote 'Teenage Heartbreak' for you."

And I said, "Vito, I know, I guessed it, and I'm sorry I've been so dumb since tenth grade, but your heart doesn't have to break anymore. Tonight I'm yours."

And Vito and I made out on the bench for a while, but it didn't feel like just making out. I realized that Vito and I weren't kids anymore. It was like we had grown up all at once. So I said, "Vito, take me," and he said, "Aay, Geraldine Rizzoli, all right!" He had the keys to his older brother Danny's best friend Freddy's car, which was a beat-up old wreck, but that night it looked like a Cadillac to me. It was parked back near the school, and we raced back along Gun Hill Road, hoping that Sally Boy and the others wouldn't see us. Even though Vito didn't have a license, he drove the car a few blocks away into the parking lot of the Immaculate Conception School. We climbed into the backseat and I lifted the skirt of my red prom dress and we made love for hours. We made sure I wouldn't get pregnant, because we wanted to do things just right. Like I said, I was a good Catholic girl, in my own way. Afterward he walked me back to Olinville Ave. And he took out the car keys and carved VITO LOVES GERALDINE in a heart over the door of the elevator in my building, but he was careful to do it on another floor, not the floor I lived on, because we didn't want my parents to see. And then he said, "Aay, Geraldine Rizzoli, will you marry me?" and I said, "Yeah, Vito, I will." So then we went into the staircase of the building and he brushed off one of the steps for me and we sat down together and started talking seriously about our future and he said, "Aay, you know, Vinny and Bobby and Richie and me, it's a gas being Vito and the Olinvilles and singing those doo-wop numbers, but I'm no fool, I know we'll never be rich or famous. So I'll keep singing for a couple more years, and then I'll get into some other line of work and then we'll have kids, okay?" And I said sure, it was okay with me if he wanted to sing for a few years until we started our family. Then I told him that Mr. Pampino at the Evander Sweet Store had offered me a job behind the counter, which meant that I could start saving money right away. "Aay, Geraldine, you're no fool," he said. He gave me the thumbs-up sign and we kissed. Then he said, "Aay, Geraldine, let's do it again, right here in the staircase," and he started pulling off his tux, but I said I wasn't that kind of girl, so he just walked me to my door and we said goodnight. We agreed that we wouldn't announce our engagement until we each had a little savings account of our own. That way our parents couldn't say we were too young and irresponsible and try to stop the wedding, which my father, who was very hot-tempered, was likely to do.

The very next morning, Vito's agent called him and woke him up and said that "Teenage Heartbreak" was actually going to get played on the radio, on WMCA by the Good Guys, at eight o'clock that night. That afternoon, we were all hanging out with the crowd and Vito and Vinny and Bobby and Richie were going crazy and they were shouting, "Aay, everyone, WMCA, all right!" and stamping their feet and threatening to punch each other out and give each other noogies on the tops of their heads. Soon everyone on Olinville Ave. knew, and at eight o'clock it was like another holy miracle, everyone on the block had their

windows open and we all blasted our radios so that even the
angels in Heaven had to have heard Vito and the Olinvilles
singing "Teenage Heartbreak" that night, which, like I said, was
written especially for me, Geraldine Rizzoli. Vito invited me to
listen with him and his mother and father and his older brother
Danny in their apartment. We hadn't told them we were engaged, though. Vito just said, "Aay, Ma, Geraldine Rizzoli here
wants to listen to 'Teenage Heartbreak' on WMCA with us,
okay?" His mother looked at me and nodded, and I had a feeling
that she guessed that Vito and I were in love and that in her
own way she was saying, "Welcome, my future daughter-in-
law, welcome." So we sat around the kitchen table with the
radio set up like a centerpiece and his mother and I cried when it
came on and his father and Danny kept swearing in Italian and
Vito just kept combing his pompadour with this frozen grin on
his face. When it was over, everyone on the block came pounding on the door, shouting, "Aay, Vito, open up, you're a star!"
and we opened the door and we had a big party and everyone
danced the lindy and the cha-cha all over the Venecios' apartment.

Three days later "Teenage Heartbreak" made it to number
one on the charts, which was just unbelievable, like twenty
thousand holy miracles combined, especially considering how
the guidance counselor at Evander Childs used to predict that
Vito would end up in prison. The disc jockeys kept saying
things like "These four boys from the streets of the Bronx are a
phenomenon, ladies and gentleman, a genuine phenomenon!"
Vito's mother saw my mother at Mass and told her that she'd
been visited by an angel in white when she was pregnant with
Vito and the angel told her, "Mrs. Venecio, you will have a son
and this son shall be a great man!"

A week later Vito and the Olinvilles got flown out to L.A. to
appear in those beach party movies, and Vito didn't even call
me to say goodbye. So I sat in my room and cried a lot, but after
a couple of weeks, I decided to chin up and accept my fate,

because, like Vito said, I was no fool. Yeah, it was true that I was a ruined woman, labeled forever as a tramp—me, Geraldine Rizzoli, who'd made out with so many of the boys at Evander Childs High School but who'd always been so careful never to let any of them into my pants, here I'd gone and done it with Vito Venecio, who'd turned out to be a two-faced liar, only interested in money and fame. Dumb, dumb, dumb, Geraldine, I thought. And I couldn't tell my parents because my father would have taken his life savings, I swear, and flown out to L.A. and killed Vito. And I couldn't even tell Pamela and Carmela and Victoria because we'd pricked our fingers with sewing needles and made a pact sealed in blood that although we would make out with lots of boys, we would stay virgins until we got married. So whenever I got together with them and they talked about how unbelievable it was that skinny little Vito with the acne and the greasy pompadour had become so rich and famous, I would agree and try to act just like them, like I was just so proud that Vito and Vinny and Bobby and Richie were now millionaires. And after a month or so I started feeling pretty strong and I thought, Okay, Vito, you bastard, you want to dump Geraldine Rizzoli, tough noogies to you, buddy. I was working at the Evander Sweet Store during the day and I'd begun making out with some of the guys in the crowd in the evenings again, even though my heart wasn't in it. But I figured that one day someone else's kisses might make me feel the way that Vito's kisses had made me feel, and I'd never know who it would be unless I tried it.

And then one night I was helping my mother with the supper dishes, which I did every single night since, like I said, in my own way, I was a good Catholic girl, when the phone rang and my mother said, "Geraldine, it's for you. It's Vito Venecio calling from Los Angeles," and she looked at me like she was suspicious about why Vito, who'd been trying to get into my pants all those years when he wasn't famous and I wouldn't give him the time of day, would still be calling me at home, now that he was famous and could have his pick of girls. When she'd gone back into the kitchen, I picked up the phone, but my hands were so wet and soapy that I could hardly hold onto the receiver. Vito said, "Aay, Geraldine Rizzoli," and his voice sounded like he was around the corner, but I knew he was really three thousand miles away, surrounded by those silly-looking bimbos from the beach party movies. "Aay, forgive me, Geraldine," he said, "I've been a creep, I know, I got carried away by all this money and fame crap, but it's you I want, you and the old gang and my old life on Olinville Ave."

I didn't say anything, I was so angry and confused. And my hands were still so wet and soapy.

"Aay, Geraldine, will you wait for me?" Vito said, and he sounded like a little lost boy. "Please, Geraldine, I'll be back, this ain't gonna last long, promise me, you'll wait for me as long as it takes."

"I don't know, Vito," I said, desperately trying to hold onto the phone, and now my hands were even wetter because I was crying and my tears were landing on them, "you could have called sooner."

"Aay, I know," he said, "this fame stuff, it's like a drug. But I'm coming home to you, Geraldine. Promise me you'll wait for me."

And he sounded so sad, and I took a deep breath, and I said, "I promise, Vito. I promise." And then the phone slipped from my grasp and hit the floor, and my mother yelled from the kitchen, "Geraldine, if you don't know how to talk on the phone without making a mess all over the floor, then don't talk on the phone!" I shouted, "I'm sorry, Ma!" but when I picked it up again, Vito was gone.

So the next day behind the counter at the Evander Sweet Store, I started making plans. I needed my independence. I knew I'd have to get an apartment, so that when Vito came back, I'd be ready for him. But that night when I told my parents I was going to get my own apartment they raised holy hell. My mother was so furious she didn't even ask whether it had something to do with Vito's call. In fact, she never spoke to me about Vito after that, which makes me think that deep down she knew. The thing was, whether she knew or didn't know, seventeen-year-old Italian girls from the Bronx did not leave home until a wedding ring was around their finger, period. Even girls who cut classes and smoked and cursed. My parents sent me to talk to a priest at the Immaculate Conception Church, which was right next door to the Immaculate Conception School, the parking lot of which was where I gave myself to Vito in the backseat of his older brother Danny's best friend Freddy's car, and the priest said, "Geraldine Rizzoli, my child, your parents tell me that you wish to leave their home before you marry. Child, why do you wish to do such a thing, which reeks of the desire to commit sin?"

I shrugged and looked away, trying hard not to pop my chewing gum. I didn't want to seem too disrespectful, but that priest got nowhere with me. I was going to wait for Vito, and I needed to have my own apartment ready for him, so the instant he got back we could start making love again and get married and start a family. And besides, even though the priest kept calling me a child, I'd been a woman ever since I let Vito into my pants. I ran my fingers through my hair, trying to make the teased parts stand up even higher, while the priest went on and on about Mary Magdalene. But I had my own spiritual mission, which had nothing to do with the Church, and finally I couldn't help it, a big gum bubble went *pop* real loudly in my mouth and the priest called me a hellion and said I was beyond his help. So I got up and left, pulling the pieces of gum off my lips.

The priest told my father that the only solution was to chain me up in my bedroom. But my mother and father, bless their hearts, may have been Catholic and Italian and hot-tempered, but they were good people, so instead they got my father's best friend, Pop Giordano, who'd been like an uncle to me ever since I was in diapers, to rent me an apartment in the building he owned. And the building just happened to be on Olinville Ave., right next door to my parents' building. So they were happy enough. I insisted on a two-bedroom right from the start, so that Vito wouldn't feel cramped when he came back, not that I told them why I needed that much room. "A two-bedroom," my mother kept repeating. "Suddenly my daughter is such a grown-up she wants a two-bedroom!"

So Pop gave me the biggest two-bedroom in the building and I moved in, and Pop promised my father to let him know if I kept late hours, and my father said he'd kill me if I did, but I wasn't worried about that. My days of making out with the boys of Olinville Ave. were over. I would wait for Vito, and I would live like a nun until he returned to me.

My mother even ended up helping me decorate the apartment, and to make her happy I hung a velour painting of Jesus above the sofa in the living room. I didn't think Vito would mind too much, since his mother had one in her living room too. I didn't intend to call Vito or write him to give him my new address. He'd be back soon enough and he'd figure out where I was.

And I began to wait. But a couple of weeks after I moved into the apartment I couldn't take not telling anyone. I felt like I'd scream or do something crazy if I didn't confide in someone. So I told Pop. Pop wore shiny black suits and black shirts with white ties and a big diamond ring on his pinky finger and he didn't have a steady job like my father, who delivered hot dogs by truck to restaurants all over the Bronx, or like Vito's father, who was a construction worker. I figured that if anyone knew the way the world worked, it was Pop. He promised he'd never tell, and he twirled his black mustache and said, "Geraldine Rizzoli, you're like my own daughter, like my flesh and blood, and I'm sorry you lost your cherry before you got married, but if you want to wait for Vito, wait."

So I settled in to my new life and I waited. That was the period that Vito kept turning out hit songs and making beach

party movies and I'd hear him interviewed on the radio and he
never sounded like the Vito I knew. It sounded like someone
else had written his words for him. He'd get all corny and sentimental about the Bronx, and about how his heart was still there,
and he'd say all these sappy things about the fish market on the
corner of Olinville Ave., but that was such crap, because Vito
never shopped for food. His mother did all the shopping, Vito
wouldn't be caught dead in the Olinville fish market, except
maybe to mooch a cigarette off of Carmine Casella, who worked
behind the counter. Vito didn't even like fish. And I felt sad and
worried for him. He'd become a kind of doo-wop robot, he and
the Olinvilles, mouthing other people's words. I noticed that
he'd even stopped writing songs after "Teenage Heartbreak."
Sometimes I could hardly stand waiting for him. But on
Olinville Ave., a promise was a promise. People had been found
floating facedown in the Bronx River for breaking smaller
promises than that. Besides, I still loved Vito.

Pamela married Johnny Ciccarone, Carmela married Ricky
Giampino, and Victoria married Sidney Goldberg, from the Special Progress Accelerated class, which was a big surprise, and
they all got apartments in the neighborhood. But after a year or
two they all moved away, either to neighborhoods where the
Puerto Ricans and blacks weren't starting to move in, or to Yonkers or Mount Vernon, and they started to have babies and I'd
visit them once or twice with gifts, but it was like we didn't
have much in common anymore, and soon we all lost touch.

And Vito and the Olinvilles kept turning out hits, even
though, like I said, Vito never wrote another song after "Teenage Heartbreak." In addition to the doo-wop numbers, Vito had
begun letting loose on some slow, sexy ballads. I bought their
forty-fives and I bought their albums and every night after
work I would call up the radio stations and request their songs,
not that I needed to, since everyone else was requesting their
songs, anyway, but it made me feel closer to Vito, I guess. And
sometimes I'd look at Vito's photograph on the album covers or

in the fan magazines and I'd see how his teeth and hair and skin were perfect, there was no gap between his front teeth like there used to be, no more acne, no more cowlick. And I kind of missed those things, because that night when I gave myself to Vito in the backseat of his older brother Danny's best friend Freddy's car, I'd loved feeling Vito's rough, sandpapery skin against mine and I'd loved letting my fingers play with his cowlick and letting my tongue rest for a minute in the gap between his front teeth.

So, for the next three, four years, I kind of lost count, Vito and the Olinvilles ruled the airwaves. And every day I worked at the Evander Sweet Store and every night I had dinner with my parents and my mother would ask whether I was ever going to get married and have babies and I'd say, "Come on, Ma, leave me alone, I'm a good Catholic girl, of course I'm gonna have babies one day," and my father would say, "Geraldine, if Pop ever tells me you're keeping late hours with any guys, I'll kill you," and I'd say, "Come on, Pa, I told you, I'm a good Catholic girl," and then I'd help my mother with the dishes and then I'd kiss them goodnight and I'd go visit Pop for a few minutes in his apartment on the ground floor of the building and there would always be those strange men coming and going from his apartment and then I'd go upstairs to my own apartment and I'd sit in front of my mirror and I'd tease my hair up high and I'd put on my makeup and I'd put on my red prom dress and I'd listen to Vito's songs and I'd dance the lindy and the cha-cha. And then before I went to sleep, I'd read through all the fan mags and I'd cut out every article about him and I'd paste them into my scrapbook.

Then one day, I don't remember exactly when, a couple of more years, maybe three, maybe even four, all I remember is that Carmela and Pamela and Victoria had all sent me announcements that they were on their second kids, the fan mags started printing fewer and fewer articles about Vito. I'd sit on my bed, thumbing through, and where before, I'd find at least one in every single mag, now I'd have to go through five, six, seven magazines and then I'd just find some real small mention of him. And the radio stations were playing Vito and the Olinvilles less and less often and I had to call in and request them more often because nobody else was doing it, and their songs weren't going higher than number fifteen or twenty on the charts. But Vito's voice was as strong and beautiful as ever, and the Olinvilles could still do those doo-wops in the background, so at first I felt really dumb, dumb, dumb because I couldn't figure out what was going on.

But I, Geraldine Rizzoli, am no fool, and it hit me soon enough. It was really simple. The girls my age were all mothers raising kids, and they didn't have time to buy records and dance the lindy and the cha-cha in front of their mirrors. And the boys, they were out all day working and at night they sat and drank beer and watched football on TV. So a new generation of teenagers was buying records. And they were buying records by those British groups, the Beatles and the rest of them, and for those kids, I guess, an Italian boy from the Bronx with a pompadour wasn't very interesting. And even though I didn't look a day older than I had that night in the backseat of Vito's older brother Danny's best friend Freddy's car, and even though I could still fit perfectly into my red prom dress, I had to face facts too. I wasn't a teenager anymore.

So more time went by, again I lost count, but Pop's hair was beginning to turn gray and my father was beginning to have a hard time lifting those crates of hot dogs and my mother seemed to be getting shorter day by day, and Vito and the Olinvilles never got played on the radio at all, period. And I felt bad for Vito, but mostly I was relieved, since I was sure then that he would come home. I bought new furniture, Pop put in new windows. I found a hairspray that made my hair stay higher even longer.

But I was wrong. Vito didn't come home. Instead, according to the few fan mags that ran the story, his manager tried to

make him into a clean-cut type, the type who appeals to the
older Las Vegas set. And Vito left the Olinvilles, which, the fan
mags said, was like Vito had put a knife through their hearts.
One mag said that Vinny had even punched Vito out. Anyway,
it was a mistake on Vito's part not to have just come home right
then. He made two albums and he sang all these silly love songs
from the twenties and thirties, and he sounded really off-key
and miserable. After that, whenever I called the disc jockeys,
they just laughed at me and wouldn't even play his records. I'd
have to go through ten or fifteen fan mags to find even a small
mention of Vito at all. So I felt even worse for him, but I definitely figured he had to come home then. Where else could he
go? So I bought a new rug and Pop painted the wall. And I sat in
front of my mirror at night and I teased my hair and I applied
my makeup and I put on my red prom dress and I danced the
lindy and the cha-cha and I played Vito's albums and I'd still
cut out the small article here and there and place it in my scrapbook. And I hadn't aged a day. No lines, no wrinkles, no flab, no
gray hair. Vito was going to be pleased when he came home.

But I was wrong again. Vito didn't come home. He went and
got married to someone else, a skinny flat-chested blond model
from somewhere like Iowa or Idaho. A couple of the fan mags
ran little pieces, and they said she was the best thing that had
ever happened to Vito. Because of his love for her he wasn't
depressed anymore about not having any more number one hits.
"Aay," he was quoted, "love is worth more than all of the gold
records in the world." At first I cried. I kicked the walls. I tore
some of the articles from my scrapbook and ripped them to
shreds. I smashed some of his albums to pieces. I was really
really angry, because I knew that it was me, Geraldine Rizzoli,
who was the best thing that had ever happened to him! That
blond model had probably been a real goody-goody when she
was growing up, the type who didn't cut classes or smoke or
tease her hair or make out with lots of guys. No passion in her
skinny bones, I figured. And then I calmed down. Because Vito

would still be back. This model, whose name was Muffin Potts, was no threat at all. Vito would be back, a little ashamed of himself, but he'd be back.

Soon after that, Vito's mother and father died. A couple of fan mags carried the story. They died in a plane crash on their way to visit Vito and Muffin Potts in Iowa or Idaho or wherever she was from. I didn't get invited to the funeral, which was in Palm Beach. Vito's parents had moved there only six months after "Teenage Heartbreak" became number one. Five big moving vans had parked on Olinville Ave., and Vito's mother stood there in a fur coat telling everybody about the angel who'd visited her when she was pregnant with Vito. And I'd gone up to her and kissed her and said, "Goodbye, Mrs. Venecio, I'm going to miss you," and she said, "Goodbye, Carmela," like she was trying to pretend that she didn't remember that I was Geraldine Rizzoli, her future daughter-in-law. The fan mags had a picture of Vito at the funeral in a three-piece suit, and the articles said he cried on the shoulder of his older brother Danny, who was now a distributor of automobile parts. There were also a couple of photos of Muffin Potts looking very bored.

Then I started to read little rumors, small items, in a few of the magazines. First, that Vito's marriage was on the rocks. No surprise to me there. I was surprised that it lasted an hour. Second, that Vito was heavy into dugs and that his addiction was breaking Muffin's heart. Really hard dugs, the mags said. The very worst stuff. One of the mags said it was because of his mother's death and they called him a "mama's boy." One said he was heartbroken because of his breakup with the Olinvilles and because Vinny had punched him out. And one said he'd been doing drugs ever since Evander Childs High School, and they had the nerve to call the school a "zoo," which I resented. But I knew a few things. One, Vito was no mama's boy. Two, Vito and the Olinvilles still all loved each other. And, three, Vito had never touched drugs in school. And if it was true that he was drowning his sorrows in drugs and breaking Muffin

Potts's heart, it was because he missed me and regretted like hell not coming home earlier!

Soon after that I read that Muffin had left him for good and had taken their child with her. Child? I stared at the print. Ashley, the article said. Their child's name was Ashley. There was no photo, and since Ashley was a name with zero personality, I wasn't sure whether Ashley was a girl or boy. I decided it was a girl, and I figured she looked just like her mother, with pale skin and a snub nose and milky-colored hair, and I wasn't even slightly jealous of that child or her mother because they were just mistakes. True, Vito kept acting dumb, dumb, dumb, and making some big fat mistakes, but I didn't love him any less. A promise was a promise. And I, Geraldine Rizzoli, knew enough to forgive him. Because the truth was that even I had once made a mistake. The way it happened was this. One day out of the blue, who should come into the Evander Sweet Store to buy some cigarettes but Petey Cioffi, who'd been one of the guys in our crowd in the old days. A couple of years after graduation he married some girl from the Grand Concourse and we all lost touch. But here he was in the old neighborhood, visiting some cousins, and he needed some cigarettes. Anyway, when he walked in, he stopped dead in his tracks. I could tell he was a little drunk, and he said, "Aay, Geraldine Rizzoli, I can't believe my eyes, you're still here, and you're gorgeous, I'm growing old and fat, look at this belly, but not you, you're like a princess or something." And it was so good to be spoken to like that, and I let him come home with me. We made out in my elevator, and I felt like a kid again. I couldn't pretend he was Vito, but I could pretend it was the old days, when Vito was still chasing me and trying to get into my pants. In the morning, Petey said goodbye, looked at me one last time, shook his head and said, "Geraldine Rizzoli, what a blast from the past!" and he slipped out of the building before Pop woke up. He probably caught holy hell from his wife and I swear I got my first and only gray hair the next morning. But my night with Petey Cioffi made it easier to forgive Vito, since I'd made my mistake too. And I kept waiting. The neighborhood changed around me. The Italians left, and more and more Puerto Ricans and blacks moved in, but I didn't mind. Because everyone has to live somewhere, I figured, and I had more important things on my mind than being prejudiced.

Then I pretty much stopped hearing about Vito altogether. And that was around when my father, bless his heart, had the heart attack on the hot dog truck and by the time they found him it was too late to save him, and my mother, bless her heart, followed soon after. I missed them so much, and every night I came home from work and I teased my hair at the mirror, I put on my makeup, I put on my red prom dress, I played Vito's songs, I danced the lindy and the cha-cha, and I read through the fan mags, looking for some mention of him, but there wasn't any. It was like he had vanished from the face of the earth. And then one day I came across a small item in the newspaper. It was about how Vito had just gotten arrested on Sunset Strip for possession of hard drugs, and how he was bailed out by Vinny of the Olinvilles, who was now a real estate salesman in Santa Monica. "I did it for old times' sake," Vinny said, "for the crowd on Olinville Ave."

The next morning, Pop called me to his apartment. He had the beginnings of cataracts by then and he hardly ever looked at the newspaper anymore, but of course, he'd spotted the article about Vito. His face was red. He was furious. He shouted, "Geraldine Rizzoli, you're like my own daughter, my own flesh and blood, and I never wanted to have to say this to you, but"—he waved the newspaper ferociously, which was impressive, since his hands shook, and he weighed all of ninety pounds at this point, although he still dressed in his shiny black suits and those strange men still came and went from his apartment— "the time has come for you to forget Vito. If he was here I'd beat the living hell out of him." He flung the paper across the room and sat in his chair, breathing heavily.

I waited a minute before I spoke, just to make sure he was

going to be okay. When his color returned to normal, I said, "Never, Pop. I promised Vito I'd wait."

"You should marry Ralphie."

"Ralphie?" I asked. Ralphie Pampino, who was part of the old crowd, too, had inherited the Evander Sweet Store from his father when Ralphie Sr. died the year before. It turns out that Ralphie Jr., who'd never married, was in love with me, and had been for years. Poor Ralphie. He'd been the kind of guy who never got to make out a whole lot. I'd always thought he looked at me so funny because he was constipated or had sinuses or something. But Pop told me that years ago Ralphie had poured out his heart to him. Although Pop had promised Ralphie that he'd never betray his confidence, the time had come. It seemed that Ralphie had his own spiritual mission: he was waiting for me. I was touched. Ralphie was such a sweet guy. I promised myself to start being nicer to him. I asked Pop to tell him about me and Vito, and I kissed Pop on the nose and I went back upstairs to my apartment and I sat in front of my mirror and I teased my hair and I put on my makeup and I put on my red prom dress and I listened to Vito's songs and I danced the lindy and the cha-cha.

The next day, Ralphie came over to me and said, "Geraldine Rizzoli, I had no idea that you and Vito . . ." and he got all choked up and couldn't finish. Finally, he swallowed and said, "Aay, Geraldine, I'm on your side. I really am. Vito's coming back!" and he gave me the thumbs-up sign and he and I did the lindy together right there in the Evander Sweet Store and we sang "Teenage Heartbreak" at the top of our lungs and we didn't care if any customers came in and saw us.

But after that there wasn't any more news about Vito, period. Most everyone on the block who'd known Vito and the Olinvilles was gone, and I just kept waiting. Just around that time an oldies radio station, WAAY, started up and it was pretty weird at first to think that Vito and the Olinvilles and all the other groups I had spent my life listening to were considered "oldies" and I'd look at myself in the mirror and I'd think, Geraldine Rizzoli, you're nobody's oldie, you've got the same skin and figure you had the night that you gave yourself to Vito. But after a while I got used to the idea of the oldies and I listened to WAAY as often as I could. I played it every morning first thing when I woke up and then Ralphie and I listened to it together at the Evander Sweet Store, even though most of the kids who came in were carrying those big radio boxes turned to salsa or rap songs or punk and didn't seem to have any idea that there was already music on. Sometimes when nobody was in the store, Ralphie and I would just sing Vito's songs together. There was one deejay on the station, Goldie George, who was on from nine in the morning until noon and he was a real fan of Vito and the Olinvilles. The other deejays had their favorites too. Doo-Wop Dick liked the Five Satins, Surfer Sammy liked the Beach Boys, but Goldie George said he'd grown up in the Bronx just two subway stops away from Olinville Ave. and that he and his friends had all felt as close to Vito as if they'd lived on Olinville Ave. themselves, even though they'd never met Vito or Vinny or Bobby or Richie. I liked Goldie George, and I wished he'd been brave enough to have taken the subway the two stops over so that he could have hung around with us. He might have been fun to make out with. One day Goldie George played thirty minutes straight of Vito and the Olinvilles, with no commercial interruptions, and then some listener called in and said "Aay, whatever happened to Vito anyway, Goldie George, he was some sort of junkie, right?"

"Yeah," Goldie George said, "but I'm Vito's biggest fan, like you all know, because I grew up only two subway stops away from Olinville Ave. and I used to feel like I was a close buddy of Vito's even though I never met him, and I happen to know that he's quit doing drugs and that he's found peace and happiness through the Chinese practice of T'ai Chi and he helps run a mission in Bakersfield, California."

"Aay," the caller said, "Goldie George, you tell Vito for me that Bobby MacNamara from Woodside says, 'Aay, Vito, keep it up, man!' "

"I will," Goldie George said, "I will. I'll tell him about you, Bobby, because, being so close to Vito in my soul when I was growing up, I happen to know that Vito still cares about his loyal fans. In fact, I know that one of the things that helped Vito to get through the hard times was knowing how much his loyal fans cared. And, aay, Bobby, what's your favorite radio station?"

"WAAY!" Bobby shouted.

And then Goldie George played another uninterrupted thirty minutes of Vito and the Olinvilles. But I could hardly hear the music this time. I was sick to my stomach. What the hell was Vito doing in Bakersfield, California, running a mission? I was glad he wasn't into drugs anymore, but Bakersfield, California? A mission? And what the hell was T'ai Chi? I was so pissed off. For the first time I wondered whether he'd forgotten my promise. I was ready to fly down to Bakersfield and tell him a thing or two, but I didn't. I went home, played my albums, danced, teased my hair, frowned at the one gray hair I'd gotten the night I was with Petey Cioffi, and I closed my eyes and leaned my head on my arms. Vito was coming back. He just wasn't ready yet.

About two weeks later I was behind the counter at the Evander Sweet Store and Ralphie was arranging some Chunkies into a pyramid when Goldie George said, "Guess what, everyone, all of us here at the station, but mostly Vito's biggest fan, me, Goldie George, have arranged for Vito to come back to his hometown! This is Big Big Big Big News! I called him the other day and I said, 'Vito, I grew up two subway stops from you, and like, you know, I'm your biggest fan, and you owe it to me and your other loyal fans from the Bronx and all the other boroughs to come back and visit and sing "Teenage Heartbreak" for us one more time,' and I swear Vito got choked up over the phone and he agreed to do it, even though he said that he usually doesn't sing any more because it interferes with his T'ai Chi, but I said, 'Vito, we love you here at WAAY, man, and wait'll you hear this, we're going to book Carnegie Hall for you, Vito, not your grandmother's attic, but Carnegie Hall!' How about that, everyone. And just so you all know, the Olinvilles are all doing their own things now, so it'll just be Vito alone, but hey, that's okay, that's great, Vito will sing the oldies and tickets go on sale next week!"

And I stood there frozen and Ralphie and I stared at each other across the counter, and I could see a look in his eyes that told me that he knew he'd finally lost me for good this time.

Because Vito was coming back. He may have told Goldie George that he was coming home to sing to his fans, but Ralphie and I both knew that it was really me, Geraldine Rizzoli, that he was finally ready to come back to. Vito worked in mysterious ways, and I figured that he finally felt free of the bad things, the drugs and that boring Muffin Potts and his own arrogance and excessive pride, and now he was pure enough to return to me. I wasn't wild about this T'ai Chi stuff, whatever it was, but I could get used to it if it had helped Vito to get better so he could come home to me.

Ralphie sort of shook himself like he was coming out of some long sleep or trance. Then he came around the counter and put his arm around me in this brotherly way. "Geraldine Rizzoli," he said really softly, "my treat. A first row seat at Carnegie Hall."

But I wouldn't accept, even though it was such a beautiful thing for Ralphie to offer to do, considering how he'd felt about me all those years. I got teary-eyed. But I didn't need a ticket, not me, not Geraldine Rizzolli. Vito would find out where I lived and he'd come and pick me up and take me himself to Carnegie Hall. He'd probably come in a limo paid for by the station, I figured. Because the only way I was going to the concert was with Vito. I went home after work and I plucked the one gray hair from my scalp and then I teased my hair and I put on my makeup and I put on my red prom dress and I danced and sang.

All week Goldie George kept saying, "It's unbelievable, tickets were sold out within an hour! The calls don't stop coming, you all remember Vito, you all love him!"

On the night of the concert Pop came by. He had to use a walker to get around by then and he was nearly blind and lots of things were wrong. His liver, gall bladder, stomach, you name it. He weighed around seventy-five pounds. But he still wore his shiny black suits and the men kept coming in and out of his apartment. And he sat across from me on my sofa, beneath the velour painting of Jesus, and he said in a raspy voice, "Geraldine Rizzolli, I didn't ever want to have to say this, but you're like my own daughter, my own flesh and blood, and as long as Vito wasn't around, I figured, Okay, you can dance to his albums and tease your hair and wear the same clothes all the time and you're none the worse for it, but now that he's coming home I've got to tell you he won't be coming for you, Geraldine, if he cared a twit about you he would have flown you out to L.A. way back when and I'm sorry you let him into your pants and lost your cherry to him, but you're a middle-aged lady now and you're gonna get hurt real bad and I'm glad your mother and father, bless their souls, aren't around to see you suffer the way you're gonna suffer tonight, Geraldine, and I don't wanna see it either, what I want is for you to drive down to Maryland tonight real fast, right now, and marry Ralphie, before Vito breaks your heart so bad nothing will ever put it together again!"

I'd never seen Pop so riled up. I kissed him on the nose and I told him he was sweet, but that Vito was coming. And Pop left, shaking his head and walking slowly, moving the walker ahead of him, step by step, and after he left, I played my albums and I teased my hair and I applied my lipstick and I danced the lindy and the cha-cha and I waited. I figured that everyone from the old crowd would be at the concert. They'd come in from the suburbs with their husbands and their wives and their children, and even, I had to face facts, in some cases, their grandchildren. And just then there was a knock on my door and I opened it and there he was. He'd put on some weight, but not much, and although he'd lost some hair he still had a pompadour and he was holding some flowers for me, and I noticed that they were red roses, which I knew he'd chosen to match my prom dress. And he said, "Aay, Geraldine Rizzoli, thanks for waiting." Then he looked at his watch. "All *right,* let's get a move on! Concert starts at nine." And I looked in the mirror one last time, sprayed on a little more hairspray, and that was it. Vito took my arm just the way he took it the night I gave myself to him in the backseat of his older brother Danny's best friend Freddy's car, and we went downtown by limo to Carnegie Hall, which was a real treat because I didn't get to go into Manhattan very often. And Carnegie Hall was packed, standing room only, and the crowd was yelling, "Aay, Vito! Aay, Vito! Aay, Vito!" and Pamela and Carmela and Victoria were there, and all the Olinvilles came and they hugged Vito and said there were no hard feelings, and Vinny and Vito even gave each other noogies on the tops of their heads, and everyone said, "Geraldine Rizzoli, you haven't aged a day." Then Goldie George introduced Vito, and Vito just got right up there on the stage and he belted out those songs, and at the end of the concert, for his finale, he sang "Teenage Heartbreak" and he called me up onstage with him and he held my hand and looked into my eyes while he sang. I even sang along on a few of the verses and I danced the lindy and the cha-cha right there on stage in front of all those people. The crowd went wild, stamping their feet and shouting for more, and Goldie George was crying, and after the concert Vito and I went back by limo to Olinville Ave. and Vito gave the limo driver a big tip and the driver said, "Aay, Vito, welcome home," and then he drove away.

And ever since then Vito has been here with me in the two-bedroom apartment. He still does T'ai Chi, but it's really no big thing, an hour or two in the morning at most. Pop died last year and Vito and I were with him at the end and his last words were "You two kids, you're like my own son and daughter." Vito works in the Evander Sweet Store now instead of me because I've got to stay home to take care of Vito Jr. and Little Pop, who have a terrific godfather in Ralphie and a great uncle in Vito's older brother Danny. And, if I'm allowed to do a little bragging, which seems only fair after all this time, Vito Jr. and Little Pop are very good kids. They go to church on Sundays and they're doing real well in school because they never cut classes or smoke in the bathroom or curse, and Vito and I are as proud as we can be.

Biographies and Some Comments by the Authors

Felicia Ackerman is a professor of philosophy at Brown University. This is her first appearance in the *Prize Stories: The O. Henry Awards.*

"Like Charlotte in 'The Forecasting Game: A Story,' I am a philosophy professor who got the idea that it would be exciting to forecast the weather. I now teach at Brown University and study meteorology and do weather forecasting at the University of Lowell. I began writing fiction in my thirties, and my stories have appeared in *Commentary, Playgirl, The Providence Sunday Journal Magazine, Ascent,* and other publications."

Alice Adams is the author of six novels and four collections of stories, most recently *After You've Gone.* She has been frequently included in *Prize Stories: The O. Henry Awards* and in 1982 she received the Special Award for Continuing Achievement.

"Like Lauren Whitfield from Enid, Oklahoma, I did spend the winter of 1940–41 in Madison, Wisconsin—and to me, coming up from North Carolina, Madison seemed a most beautiful, glamorous, sexy, and sophisticated place. Through an accidental circumstance having to do with Southern schools, I was two years younger than my classmates— fourteen to their sixteen—a big difference at that age. And like Lauren, at fourteen I was much more concerned with the next dance or the next fall of snow than with what might happen in Europe. However, in retrospect I see that we all to some degree felt that cloud, that heavy horrible menace, Hitler's Germany. I have always wanted to write

about that year, and when I actually came to do so, I was both surprised and interested to find that the very politically active, passionate
writer of letters to newspapers, the mother of a friend (I did not know
the mother well at all) presented herself as a central figure, in fact the
person through whom I would tell much of that story."

James P. Blaylock, having lived in Southern California most of his life,
now lives with his wife and two sons in Orange, the city where "Unidentified Objects" is set. His most recent novel is entitled *The Last Coin.*
His short stories have been published in *TriQuarterly, OMNI, Isaac
Asimov's Science Fiction Magazine,* and in various anthologies. In 1986 his
story "Paper Dragons" won the World Fantasy Award.

"I've always been compelled, for reasons I don't entirely understand,
to wonder at trifles. Certain oddball little objects gleaned from random
years of my life seem to generate their own small magic. That's why
this story is full of camellia blossoms and tin toys and Popsicles and
starfish—scattered trinkets and baubles from my childhood. Unlike
Proust's madeleine cakes and lime-flower tea, such odds and ends do
not often recall for me vast tracts of forgotten time. My memory hasn't
held up that well; sometimes I'm lucky to recall my own phone number.

"What happened here was that somewhere in the course of my writing 'Unidentified Objects,' these trinkets seemed to insist that they
were more than mere things; heaped together, they wanted to take on
metaphoric weight—something like the several objects arranged just so
in a Cornell box. Out of the arrangement came a structure to the narrative, implying secret patterns, until I fancied that I could follow those
patterns as if they were colored lines on a road map and so arrive at a
sort of vista point from which I might see a landscape laid out below
me—one that I hadn't before been able to see, because I had been too
close to it.

"In other words, I was trying to work a sort of literary sympathetic
magic—a magic, by the way, that I believe in utterly. Common sense
would suggest that I resist the temptation to think in these terms. A tin
toy is just a tin toy, it would say, giving me a grave and knowing look.
All of these colorful trinkets are frivolous things, a box full of rhine-
stone jewelry, but hardly the sort of treasure that can be put out at

interest. . . . Then it would become distracted by the world, and would undertake to sell me a life insurance policy, a condominium, and a prepaid cemetery plot."

T. Coraghessan Boyle has previously appeared in *Prize Stories: The O. Henry Awards.*

" 'The Ape Lady in Retirement' is a sequel of sorts to a story I wrote as a student at the Iowa Writers' Workshop, a story that became the title piece of my first collection, *Descent of Man.* The link between the two stories is Konrad. In the early piece, he was a highly accomplished three-year-old living at a Yerkes-like establishment, not merely communicating linguistically, but composing symphonies, translating Darwin into Yerkish, and vying for the romantic attentions of the narrator's girlfriend, Jane. The current story is perhaps less absurd (it is loosely based on an actual incident), but like its predecessor it is concerned with interspecies communication, if not interspecies sex.

"I began as a short story writer and am committed to the form. I've published three collections—*Descent of Man, Greasy Lake,* and *If the River Was Whiskey*—as well as three novels, and I do not see the stories as three-finger exercises or ditties to fill the gaps between writing novels. There are full-length ideas, such as *World's End* or *Water Music,* and there are smaller ideas, like 'Greasy Lake' or 'Ike and Nina.' They are equally deserving of expression.

"And why are my stories so bizarre? A question I am often asked. Let me say this: I live in Los Angeles."

Claudia Smith Brinson has published stories in *Iowa Woman, Crescent Review,* and *Kalliope.* She lives in Columbia, South Carolina, where she is a senior writer for *The State* newspaper. She has also taught writing at the University of South Carolina. This is her first appearance in *Prize Stories: The O. Henry Awards.*

"Four years ago I decided facts were not enough to tell a story true. So I began, on the nights and weekends my children were gone, to try my hand at fiction, and there I discovered the place I wanted to spend the rest of my life. 'Einstein's Daughter' takes advantage of my obsession with time and interest in physics. Explanations about time–space fascinate me, especially the tale of the twins, and I began jotting down other tidbits in preparation for this story: time is not linear, but our perception of time is; because light needs time to travel, we're always looking into the past; the faster a particle moves, the longer it lives; clocks slow when in motion; people, if the temperature is raised, underestimate the time between events. Coincidentally, I stumbled upon one of those depressing lists on how many years we spend in one life bathing, dressing, and so on; included was 'three years waiting for something to happen or someone to arrive.'

"I thought I was writing a story about time and the quandaries of waiting. But the voice telling the story quickly pushed its own agenda, insisting, in addition, on telling a story about mothers and daughters, the paths family histories etch for us, and the obligations and dangers imposed by past generations. Eventually, the narrator and I shared a question: Can any of us escape the fate genetics and parental love insist upon?"

Janice Eidus has published a novel, *Faithful Rebecca* (1987), and a collection of stories, *Vito Loves Geraldine* (1990), of which the title story appears in this volume.

She has lived in the Virgin Islands, California, Maryland, Iowa, and upstate New York. She is currently back home in New York City, where she was born and raised.

" 'Vito Loves Geraldine' is not autobiographical. It is, however, a story in which many of the various threads of my life—and of my literary vision—are merged.

"I spent my childhood in the Bronx, and so, first and foremost, 'Vito Loves Geraldine' is my fictional homage to the kids in my old neighborhood. I was a generation younger than Vito and Geraldine would have been, and I idolized the kids like them: the boys with their slick pompadours and the girls with their teased dyed hair. 'Vito Loves Geraldine' is also an homage to the rock 'n' roll music of the fifties, and I like to think that it's a kind of rock 'n' roll song in its own right.

"I've heard it said that a writer must 'love' all of her characters, but I don't think that's true. At least, that hasn't been true for me. Some of the characters about whom I write engage me in other ways: they disturb me, or anger me, or provoke or amaze me perhaps. But I can say honestly that I do love Vito and Geraldine.

" 'Vito Loves Geraldine' is a humorous story, and I've always had an irrepressible urge to be funny—in life, and in fiction. Also, when I write, I like to blend elements that are real with elements that are fantastic, and to create a kind of magical territory somewhere between. In 'Vito Loves Geraldine,' for instance, the world of the 1950s northeast Bronx is very real. On the other hand, the fact that Geraldine never gains a pound and never looks a day older than she did at her senior prom—well, that's absolutely *fantastic* (and I mean it in both senses of the word)."

Bruce Fleming appears in *Prize Stories: The O. Henry Awards* for the first time.

"Like Robert Johnson, I grew up in a small town in Maryland, and I too have been fascinated by Gertrude Stein since I first read her works. I have also visited her grave in Père Lachaise—though as a younger man than Robert Johnson was when he did so.

"I teach modernist and world literature to midshipmen at the United States Naval Academy in Annapolis, Maryland's lovely but rapidly "developing" eighteenth-century capital (which looks suspiciously like Robert's hometown). When I came to Annapolis in 1987, I had been out of the country for five years. After receiving a Ph.D. in comparative literature from Vanderbilt in 1982, I spent a year first in Siena, then on a Fulbright Fellowship in Berlin, then taught for two years at the University in Freiburg im Breisgau. Subsequent to this, I spent two years as the Fulbright Professor at the National University of Rwanda. While I was there, I visited the game parks, and began a novel set in Africa called *Tonight in Kigali*.

"I had graduated from Haverford College in 1974 with a degree in philosophy and no clear idea of what to do with my life. 'Perhaps,' I thought, 'I might be a writer, but how will I earn a living?' I worked as a motel night clerk, a census taker, a substitute teacher, and for a year as a surveillant at the French Lycée in Washington, D.C. Nine months at the University of Chicago produced an M.A. in comparative literature. Thereupon followed a year and a half in Munich, and finally the offer of a graduate fellowship at Vanderbilt.

"I had been rereading *The Autobiography of Alice B. Toklas* in preparation for a course and it struck me differently than it had ever done before.

Stein's phrases began buzzing around in my head, and I wrote the story in one great rush. A number of revisions later—some of the most useful of which were suggested by my editor at *The Gettysburg Review,* Peter Stitt—and the piece seemed finished. When I sat down to write it, I had thought it would be a short novel, but the fine line I was trying to walk between originality and appropriation petered out at the length of a short story. Of course, it is better so. Surely this particular kind of tightrope walk would be tiresome in a longer work."

Jane Brown Gillette: "I was born in Indiana in 1943 and attended Vassar College. My first short story was published in 1963, and I've had lots of dry spells since—both in writing and publishing. I've written three unpublished novels and around thirty unpublished stories. I've sold stories to a number of magazines that have gone under, plus *Mademoiselle, Shenandoah, The Virginia Quarterly,* and *The Yale Review.*

"Literature has always been the focus of my life. Right after college, I got a Ph.D. in English from Yale, and about the time I wrote this story, after some twenty years of teaching part time, I gave up on academe, realizing at last that I would never get a regular appointment. One day I got a call from an old Vassar friend, who'd married an accountant, had three children, and gone to live in Maine. She was getting a divorce. Her life was falling apart. She wished that I would write a story about the death of her boyfriend; her therapist didn't understand the ambiance of the times.

"I did just that. It seemed a little boring. I changed things—in some cases by simply reversing what really happened. Finished, the story hardly seemed a suitable document for a therapist—or a friend. But I felt loyal to it. After it was published, I fearfully sent it to my friend. She loved it. Aside from a few details, she found it accurate. I can no longer remember exactly what I made up.

"People have asked me if I hate the girls—so cold, so unfeeling! This year I am going back to my twenty-fifth reunion at Vassar: Eleanors and Dianas will be all over the place. I am looking forward to seeing them. Trying to do the brave thing and failing, changing one's mind, suffering intelligently, do not seem contemptible to me. People demand a good deal more love than is good for them."

Joanne Greenberg was born in Brooklyn, New York, and graduated from American University, Washington, D.C. She has studied at the University of London and the University of Colorado. She is the author of ten novels and three collections of stories. She lives near Lookout Mountain, Colorado, with her husband and their striped cat named Ripoff. This is her first appearance in *Prize Stories: The O. Henry Awards.*

"There are stories that seem to come out of nowhere, to relate to nothing in a writer's experience, present difficulties, or insights. 'Elizabeth Baird' is such a story. I have been to Japan and know the area of Ebisu Station in Tokyo quite well. I was a girl during World War II and remember much of the ambience of those times. Long ago I had been told about life in a prison camp in the Pacific. These were all unconnected and I never had a conscious plan to gather this combination of experience and hearsay or to form something from its unpromising scraps. It was when I began to think about my character—an odd, elfin little girl who had a slight brain lesion—that I found them there, waiting.

"I reread the story six months after I had written and revised it, to be able to see it as an objective piece of work, parted from my wishes for it. It was then I realized that it carried not only the marks of my manner of approach but was very much in the line of my interest, the claim I seem to have staked out for myself and had been working for years. This has to do with inquiry into the meaning of isolation and belonging —how each comes, how each is dealt with, how it changes. Can isolates in one society belong comfortably in another? When? Where? How? Did Lefcadio Hearn fit in his adopted country? Would Elizabeth Baird have fit in? Where? How?

"World War II presented us with all kinds of changes and paradoxes along this line. Shy, traditional girls learned state-of-the-art technology in factories. College professors became mechanics and people found in themselves capacities they never knew they had—some easy to live with, some not.

"This was true of the Japanese also. I once knew a veteran of Santo Tomas, a Japanese camp in the Pacific, and he had spoken to me of the deadening effects of starvation and overwork, the heat and fetid humidity, the reduction of adult prisoners to childlike dependence.

"Finally, I had the choice of returning Elizabeth to Ionia, to a town unchanged, but if World War II did nothing else, it remade life in thousands of out-of-the-way villages, particularly in the American South, so I let my young woman come back to what some of the New South would be like. And once there, I was confronted, as she was, by a world in which, though it was hers, she did not belong."

Devon Jersild lives in Middlebury, Vermont, where she is an editor at *New England Review and Bread Loaf Quarterly.*

"I was born outside of Chicago in 1958 and raised in Rock Island, Illinois. While a senior at Dartmouth College, I took a term off to write a novel. That was a way of testing the waters, to see how it felt to sit down and write every day. I found the process exhilarating and, compared to writing poetry (which I'd done a lot of), something like a steady job. Since then I've arranged my life to spend a few hours writing every day. The other hours I've spent variously—mostly teaching and raising two small sons. I also write book reviews for publications such as *USA TODAY* and the *New York Times Book Review.* I'm just finishing a novel set in southern Utah during the Depression, and I have two practice novels in a drawer, but the story here is my first published piece of fiction.

"I often experience the frustration of conceiving of a story beyond my technical ability; the words on the page seem only to hint at the small universe of what I can imagine. Writing 'In Which John Imagines His Mind as a Pond' was entirely different. I felt my energies gathering; I felt all the prose I'd written before supporting each new paragraph. With every section of the story I asked myself, 'Can I do this?' And then it just seemed to happen."

David Michael Kaplan: "I grew up in western Pennsylvania and have lived in New England, North Carolina, California, and the Midwest. I suppose that's why my stories are set in so many different places: rootlessness, for better or for worse, seems to be a fact of life in late-twentieth-century America. I've variously been a social worker, educational consultant, documentary film editor and director. Currently, I live in Chicago, where I teach fiction writing at Loyola University.

"My first short story collection, *Comfort,* was published by Viking Penguin in 1987. "The idea 'Stand' evolved over a number of years. I'd long been intrigued by the idea of someone innocently encountering a group of strangers in an isolated setting and being psychologically bullied by at least one of them. And then achieving some sort of victory over that bully. It all seemed pretty flat, however, until I realized that the important thing was not Frank's 'victory' but rather its hollowness, the emptiness of a victory achieved too late. If you win, and have no one to share it with, have you really won? Or put it another way: If you win only for yourself, have you really won much at all? Isn't taking a stand for others—indeed, *having* others to take a stand for—the most important thing, after all? What Frank has really won is the realization that he's lost."

Leo E. Litwak: "I grew up in Detroit, left for war, lived in New York, moved to St. Louis, and after a decade settled in San Francisco, where I still teach at San Francisco State University. The Detroit I knew is long gone but remains a focus of my writing. A Detroit novel, *Waiting for the News,* published twenty years ago, will be republished by Wayne State University Press this year. My stories have appeared in *TriQuarterly, The North American Review, The Partisan Review, Esquire,* and other places. I've written a book of nonfiction, *College Days in Earthquake Country,* in collaboration with Herbert Wilner. Articles have appeared in the *New York Times Magazine, Look,* and elsewhere.

"The origin of 'The Eleventh Edition' is complex and not easily unraveled, but I recall one source clearly. We had just moved to San Francisco. An old man lived in the flat below us. He was alone and fading fast. His recollection of San Francisco before the earthquake was detailed and vivid. About his present circumstances he was very dim. We knew him briefly and then one day he disappeared. A month went by and the landlady finally emptied his apartment and dumped his goods in the rear entryway and there, alongside the garbage cans, I found a carton containing the Eleventh Edition of the *Encyclopedia Britannica,* in mint condition, the pages uncut. It is a great *Encyclopedia,* published in 1911, composed by an assemblage of scholars who spoke in a voice of imperial confidence. Six volumes were missing. I looked into the old man's storeroom and immediately spotted the missing books on a barrel, almost in reach. What separated us was a legion of rats. The old man had been in the seed business and had left behind two bulging sacks of grain. Large rats swarmed over the grain and carpeted the floor. I am uncomfortable with rats and the room pulsed with them, but it's a great *Encyclopedia* and I took a giant step. The rats parted for me and I had the books.

"The rats aren't in this story, but the treasure they guarded is. I summoned up Detroit, removed San Francisco, made adjustments in time, and so the story began."

Peter Matthiessen was born in New York City in 1927, and graduated from Yale University in 1950. His first short story was published in *The Atlantic Monthly* in 1951. Since then he has written, published, and traveled widely. His works include *Far Tortuga* (fiction) and *The Snow Leopard* (nonfiction; National Book Award). This is his first appearance in *Prize Stories: The O. Henry Awards*. He lives in Sagaponack, Long Island.

" 'Lumumba Lives' has two broad sources. In the winter of 1961, I was hitchhiking through remote southern Sudan, near its border with Zaire and Uganda, when Patrice Lumumba was assassinated across the border with the apparent connivance if not at the instigation of the CIA. In the firestorm that swept all across Africa, a number of whites died, and although we had never heard of Lumumba, the three of us who were caught there at the border, at the mercy of the border guards and a wildly excited populace, might very well, we felt, have been among them. Since then I have had a keen interest in Lumumba, a far more dedicated leader than the Army puppet imposed on the Zairean people by United States and western European interests.

"The setting of the story is the Hudson River Valley, where I lived as a small boy—indeed, the house in the story is roughly based on our old house, which overlooked the river at Irvington. In recent years, as a resident in Zen training at a seminary in Riverdale, I had the habit of taking long solitary walks via the railroad tracks along the river, which renewed my old associations with this scene. But of course the Hudson, though still majestic, is sadly degraded since my childhood, and the omnipresence of pollution—the industrial poisoning of the Hudson, and the dumping of toxic wastes in Africa—brought together the broad sources of the story."

Reginald McKnight appears in *Prize Stories: The O. Henry Awards* for the first time.

"I was born in Fürstenfeldbruck, Germany, in the mid-fifties. My father was an Air Force sergeant, and Mother has worked in the child-care business for most of her life. Just like the character in my story, I grew up in places all over the country: New York, California, Colorado, Texas, Louisiana, to name but a few. I graduated from high school in Colorado Springs, then joined the United States Marine Corps. I'm a Vietnam-era veteran, but never served in combat. After my discharge, I went to Pikes Peak Community College in Colorado Springs, and took an A.A. degree, then went on to get my B.A. in African literature at the Colorado State College in the same town in 1981. Then, on a Watson Foundation Fellowship, I went to Senegal in west Africa, where I taught English, wrote eight to sixteen hours per day, and got sick all the time. My first book, *Mustapha's Eclipse,* winner of the Drue Heinz Literature Prize, was published in 1988. I'm now teaching fiction writing at the University of Pittsburgh, and I enjoy it very much. It certainly beats the socks off the other jobs I've had."

Joyce Carol Oates has twice received the Special Award for Continuing Achievement in this series. Her most recent book is the novel *Because It Is Bitter, and Because It is My Heart.* She is Distinguished Professor in the Humanities at Princeton University.

"My first story to appear in *Prize Stories: The O. Henry Awards* was in 1963, but I must confess that each story I write seems to me a new departure, and certainly a new and often frustrating challenge. For the past two years, I have been experimenting with 'tone clusters' in prose, especially in short fiction: the tone of 'Heat' is that of the piano used as a nonvibrating instrument, without the use of the pedal, in which chords struck and lifted, do not resonate or echo but exhibit an eerie disconnection with one another. This tone seemed to me perfect to express a narrative viewed through the prismatic lens of Time, by way of which all events seem equidistant: thus the 'floating' paragraphs, seemingly disconnected and without transition in many instances.

"In 'Heat' too, of course, I was exploring the mysterious relationship between twins, about which I've written elsewhere in short fiction and in pseudonymous novels. It is a subject that exercises an uncanny fasci-nation for me—yet the more I contemplate it, and write about it, the more powerfully I seem to be drawn into it; the act of writing is not an exorcism."

Carolyn Osborn was born in Nashville, Tennessee, moved to Texas in 1946 when she was twelve, received a B.J. in 1955 and an M.A. in 1959 from the University of Texas. She wrote for newspapers and radio, and returned to the university to be a part-time English teacher from 1968 to 1978. She's married to an Austin lawyer; they have two children.

By 1962 she'd begun to have stories published in little magazines. Her work has appeared in *The Antioch Review, The Paris Review, The Georgia Review,* and most recently in *New Letters* and *Shenandoah.* Her third short story collection, *Warriors and Maidens,* scheduled for publication in 1991, will include "The Grands."

"I first wrote a story called 'The Greats,' which celebrated kin so distant they were only vivid fragments in the narrator's mind. Moving closer to 'The Grands' was a natural progression. It was often called 'a reminiscence' by uninterested editors. Of course it's partially reminiscence. A good many stories are. But why do such stories persist, and how does one use a family's collective memory? Obviously a fiction writer invents; the imagined family invents also, so there's overlapping. The need to tell the stories, the variety of kinship, the necessity of mythology, the mystery of reality are all entwined here. I didn't think about any of that when I was writing it. I thought mainly about the people riding on mules, dancing on porches, meeting on trains."

Julie Schumacher was born in Wilmington, Delaware, in 1958 and graduated from Oberlin College in Ohio. She received an M.F.A. from Cornell University in 1986, and her short stories have appeared in *The Atlantic Monthly, The Best American Short Stories: 1983, The Quarterly, New Letters,* and other magazines. She now lives in St. Paul, Minnesota, and is working on a novel.

"In early versions of 'The Private Life of Robert Schumann' Mr. Zinn taught science instead of music. But when I decided to set the ending of the story in a church (one that, to my mother's dismay, actually exists), I knew he had to direct the choir. Knowing almost nothing about music, I began leafing through encyclopedias, looking for information about composers. When I stumbled on the romance between Robert

Schumann and Clara Wieck, I knew I *had* Mr. Zinn: I felt I had pinned him; he wasn't going to get away."

Lore Segal left her native Vienna at the age of ten and moved to England, where she lived with a number of foster families. After receiving her B.A. from the University of London in 1948, she went to live in the Dominican Republic until her American quota allowed her to come to New York in May, 1951. Her first novel, *Other People's Houses*, was based on those refugee experiences and early travels. Mrs. Segal was married to the late David Segal and has two children.

Lore Segal has taught writing at Columbia University's School of the Arts, at Princeton, Bennington College, Sarah Lawrence, and at the Bread Loaf Writers' Conference. Since 1978 she has been professor of English at the University of Illinois at Chicago. This is her first appearance in *Prize Stories: The O. Henry Awards*.

" 'The Reverse Bug' situates itself neither in the person of the screamer nor the person of torturer but in that part of your and my head where we bury the knowledge that pain is inflicted and suffered even as I write this, as you read it. I wanted to imagine what would happen if pain were exposed so that we could *not* not imagine it. What does the story recommend that we do about it? Why, bury it! Bury it again, so that we can live. It won't stop the howling."

Marilyn Sides makes her first appearance in *Prize Stories: The O. Henry Awards*.

"I currently live in Somerville, Massachusetts, and teach at Wellesley College. 'The Island of the Mapmaker's Wife' was my first published story. Before I started writing stories, I filled up my time by traveling as much as I could, reading, teaching, writing love letters, and walking. The story began with a footnote by Jonathan Swift, in his *A Tale of a Tub*: 'This [O. Brazile] is an imaginary Island, of Kin to that which is call'd the *Painters Wives Island*, placed in some unknown part of the Ocean, meerly at the Fancy of the Map-maker.' I was delighted with the notion and read up on maps. There were imaginary islands, and there were wives of mapmakers who worked as expert colorists in the family firm. The best seventeenth-century maps came from Amsterdam, a city I once had occasion to walk in for several days. It was a pleasure to work on the story, to give myself and the reader something to look at."

Meredith Steinbach was raised in Storm Lake, Iowa. She is the author of two novels, *Zara* and *Here Lies the Water,* which was published in the winter of 1989. Her first collection of stories, *Reliable Light,* is appearing in the spring of 1990. Ms. Steinbach is a graduate of the Iowa Writers' Workshop and has been awarded fellowships, including those from the National Endowment for the Arts and the Bunting Institute of Radcliffe College, Harvard University. On the faculty of Brown University, Ms. Steinbach previously has taught at Antioch College, Northwestern University, and the University of Washington. Recently she has completed her third novel, *The Birth of the World As We Know It; Or, Teiresias,* and is at work on her fourth.

Magazines Consulted

The Agni Review, P.O. Box 229, Cambridge, Mass. 02238

Alaska Quarterly Review, Department of English, 3221 Providence Drive, Anchorage, Alaska 99508

Amelia, 329 "E" Street, Bakersfield, Calif. 93304

Antaeus, Ecco Press, 26 West 17th Street, New York, N.Y. 10011

The Antioch Review, P.O. Box 148, Yellow Springs, Ohio 45387

The Apalachee Quarterly, P.O. Box 20106, Tallahassee, Fla. 32304

Arizona Quarterly, University of Arizona, Tucson, Ariz. 85721

Arts Alive: A Literary Review, 17530 South 65th Avenue, Tinely Park, Ill. 60477

Ascent, Department of English, University of Illinois, Urbana, Ill. 61801

Asimov's Science Fiction Magazine, Davis Publications, 380 Lexington Avenue, New York, N.Y. 10017

The Atlantic Monthly, 8 Arlington Street, Boston, Mass. 02116

Balcones, P.O. Box 50247, Austin, Tex. 78763

The Black Warrior Review, P.O. Box 2936, University, Ala. 34586

Borderline, c/o Doug Hitchcock, 26–15 9th Street, Astoria, N.Y. 11102

Boulevard, 4 Washington Square Village, 9R, New York, N.Y. 10012

California Quarterly, 100 Sproul Hall, University of California, Davis, Calif. 95616

Canadian Fiction Magazine, P.O. Box 46422, Station G, Vancouver, B.C., Canada V6R 4G7

Capital Region Magazine, 4 Central Avenue, Albany, N.Y. 12210

Carolina Quarterly, Greenlaw Hall 066-A, University of North Carolina, Chapel Hill, N.C. 27514

The Chariton Review, The Division of Language and Literature, Northeast Missouri State University, Kirksville, Mo. 63501

The Chattahoochee Review, DeKalb Community College, North Campus, 2101 Womack Road, Dunwoody, Ga. 30338–4497

Chelsea, P.O. Box 5880, Grand Central Station, New York, N.Y. 10163

Chicago, WFMT, Inc. 3 Illinois Center, 303 East Wacker Drive, Chicago, Ill. 60601

Chicago Review, 970 East 58th Street, Box C, University of Chicago, Chicago, Ill. 60637

Chicago Tribune, Nelson Algren Award, 435 North Michigan Avenue, Chicago, Ill. 60611–4041

Cimarron Review, 205 Morrill Hall, Oklahoma State University, Stillwater, Okla. 74078–0135

Clockwatch Review, 737 Penbrook Way, Hartland, Wisc. 53021

Colorado Review, Department of English, Colorado State University, Fort Collins, Colo. 80523

Columbia, the Magazine of Columbia University, 3 Claremont Avenue, New York, N.Y. 10027

Columbia, the Magazine of Poetry and Prose, 404 Dodge Hall, Columbia University, New York, N.Y. 10027

Commentary, 165 East 56th Street, New York, N.Y. 10022

Concho River Review, c/o English Department, Angelo State University, San Angelo, Tex. 76909

Confrontation, Department of English, C. W. Post of Long Island University, Greenvale, N.Y. 11548

Cosmopolitan, 224 West 57th Street, New York, N.Y. 10019

Crazyhorse, Department of English, University of Arkansas at Little Rock, Little Rock, Ark. 72204

Crosscurrents, 2200 Glastonbury Rd., Westlake Village, Calif. 91361

Cutbank, c/o Department of English, University of Montana, Missoula, Mont. 59812

Denver Quarterly, Department of English, University of Denver, Denver, Colo. 80210

Descant, Department of English, Texas Christian University, Fort Worth, Tex. 76129

Epoch, 254 Goldwyn Smith Hall, Cornell University, Ithaca, N.Y. 14853

Esquire, 2 Park Avenue, New York, N.Y. 10016

Farmer's Market, P.O. Box 1272, Galesburg, Ill. 61402

Fiction, Department of English, The City College of New York, N.Y. 10031

Fiction International, Department of English, St. Lawrence University, Canton, N.Y. 13617

Fiction Network, P.O. Box 5651, San Francisco, Calif. 94101

The Fiction Review, P.O. Box 1508, Tempe, Ariz. 85281

The Fiddlehead, The Observatory, University of New Brunswick, P.O. Box 4400, Fredericton, New Brunswick, Canada E3B 5A3

The Florida Review, Department of English, University of Central Florida, Orlando, Fla. 32816

Four Quarters, La Salle College, Philadelphia, Pa. 19141

Gallery, 401 Park Avenue South, New York, N.Y. 10016

Gargoyle, P.O. Box 30906, Bethesda, Md. 20814

Gentleman's Quarterly, 350 Madison Avenue, New York, N.Y. 10017

The Georgia Review, University of Georgia, Athens, Ga. 30602

The Gettysburg Review, Gettysburg College, Gettysburg, Penn. 17325–1491

Grain, Box 1154, Regina, Saskatchewan, Canada S4P 3B4

Grand Street, 50 Riverside Drive, New York, N.Y. 10024

Granta, 13 White Street, New York, N.Y. 10013

The Greensboro Review, University of North Carolina, Greensboro, N.C. 27412

Hard Copies, Department of English and Foreign Languages, California State Polytechnic University, Pomona, Calif. 91768

Harper's Magazine, 2 Park Avenue, New York, N.Y. 10016

Hawaii Review, Hemenway Hall, University of Hawaii, Honolulu, Hawaii 96822

High Plains Literary Review, 180 Adams Street, Suite 250, Denver, Colorado 80206

The Hudson Review, 684 Park Avenue, New York, N.Y. 10021

Indiana Review, 316 North Jordan Avenue, Bloomington, Ind. 47405

Interim, Department of English, University of Nevada, Las Vegas, Nev. 89154

Iowa Review, EPB 453, University of Iowa, Iowa City, Iowa 52240

Kalliope, a Journal of Women's Art, Kalliope Writer's Collective, Florida Community College at Jacksonville, 3939 Roosevelt Boulevard, Jacksonville, Fla. 32205

Kansas Quarterly, Department of English, Kansas State University, Manhattan, Kansas 66506

Karamu, English Department, Eastern Illinois University, Charleston, Ill. 61920

The Kenyon Review, Kenyon College, Gambier, Ohio 43022

Ladies' Home Journal, 641 Lexington Avenue, New York, N.Y. 10022

The Literary Review, Fairleigh Dickinson University, Teaneck, N.J. 07666

Mademoiselle, 350 Madison Avenue, New York, N.Y. 10017

The Magazine of Fantasy and Science Fiction, Box 56, Cornwall, Conn. 06753

Malahat Review, University of Victoria, Victoria, British Columbia, Canada V8W 2Y2

The Massachusetts Review, Memorial Hall, University of Massachusetts, Amherst, Mass. 01002

McCall's, 230 Park Avenue, New York, N.Y. 10017

Memphis, 460 Tennessee Street, P.O. Box 256, Memphis, Tenn. 38101

Michigan Quarterly Review, 3032 Rackham Building, University of Michigan, Ann Arbor, Mich. 48109

Mid-American Review, 106 Hanna Hall, Bowling Green State University, Bowling Green, Ohio 43403

Midstream, 515 Park Avenue, New York, N.Y. 10022

Minnesota Monthly, 15 South 9th Street, Suite 320, Minneapolis, Minn. 55402

The Missouri Review, Department of English, 231 Arts and Sciences, University of Missouri, Columbia, Mo. 65211

Mother Jones, 1663 Mission Street, San Francisco, Calif. 94103

MSS, Box 530, Department of English, SUNY-Binghamton, Binghamton, N.Y. 13901

The Nebraska Review, The Creative Writing Program, University of Nebraska-Omaha, Omaha, Neb. 68182–0324

New Directions, 80 Eighth Avenue, New York, N.Y. 10011

New England Review and Breadloaf Quarterly, Middlebury College, Middlebury, Vt. 05753

New Letters, University of Missouri-Kansas City, Kansas City, Mo. 64110

New Mexico Humanities Review, The Editors, Box A, New Mexico Tech., Socorro, N.M. 57801

The New Renaissance, 9 Heath Road, Arlington, Mass. 02174

New Virginia Review, 1306 East Cary Street, 2-A, Richmond, Va. 23219

The New Yorker, 25 West 43rd Street, New York, N.Y. 10036

The North American Review, University of Northern Iowa, 1222 West 27th Street, Cedar Falls, Iowa 50613

North Dakota Quarterly, University of North Dakota, Box 8237, Grand Forks, N.D. 58202

Northwest Review, 129 French Hall, University of Oregon, Eugene, Ore. 97403

Oak Square, P.O. Box 1238, Allston, Mass. 02134

The Ohio Review, Ellis Hall, Ohio University, Athens, Ohio 45701

OMNI, 1965 Broadway, New York, N.Y. 10067

The Ontario Review, 9 Honey Brook Drive, Princeton, N.J. 08540

Other Voices, 820 Ridge Road, Highland Park, Ill. 60035

The Paris Review, 541 East 72nd Street, New York, N.Y. 10021

The Partisan Review, 128 Bay State Road, Boston, Mass. 02215/552 Fifth Avenue, New York, N.Y. 10036

The Pennsylvania Review, University of Pittsburgh, Department of English, 526 C.L., Pittsburgh, Penn. 15260

Phylon, 223 Chestnut Street, S.W., Atlanta, Ga. 30314

Playboy, 919 North Michigan Avenue, Chicago, Ill. 60611

Playgirl, 801 Second Avenue, New York, N.Y. 60611

Ploughshares, Box 529, Cambridge, Mass. 02139

Prairie Schooner, Andrews Hall, University of Nebraska, Lincoln, Neb. 68588

Puerto Del Sol, English Department, New Mexico State University, Box 3E, Las Cruces, N.M. 88003

The Quarterly, 201 East 50th Street, New York, N.Y. 10022

Raritan, 165 College Avenue, New Brunswick, N.J. 08903

Redbook, 230 Park Avenue, New York, N.Y. 10017

Sailing, 125 E. Main Street, P.O. Box 248, Port Washington, Wisc. 53074

Salamagundi, Skidmore College, Saratoga Springs, N.Y. 12866

The San Francisco Bay Guardian, Fiction Contests, 2700 19th Street, San Francisco, Calif. 94110–2189

Santa Monica Review, Center for the Humanities at Santa Monica College, 1900 Pico Boulevard, Santa Monica, Calif. 90405

Self, 350 Madison Avenue, New York, N.Y. 10017

Sequoia, Storke Student Publications Building, Stanford, Calif. 94305

Seventeen, 850 Third Avenue, New York, N.Y. 10022

The Sewanee Review, University of the South, Sewanee, Tenn. 37375

Shenandoah: The Washington and Lee University Review, Box 722, Lexington, Va. 24450

The Short Story Review, P.O. Box 882108, San Francisco, Calif. 94188

Sidewinder, Division of Arts and Humanities, College of the Mainland, 8001 Palmer Highway, Texas City, Tex. 77591

Sonora Review, Department of English, University of Arizona, Tucson, Ariz. 85721

The South Carolina Review, Department of English, Clemson University, Clemson, S.C. 29631

South Dakota Review, Box 111, University Exchange, Vermillion, S.D. 57069

Southern Humanities Review, Auburn University, Auburn, Ala. 36830

The Southern Review, Drawer D, University Station, Baton Rouge, La. 70803

Southwest Review, Southern Methodist University Press, Dallas, Tex. 75275

Special Report, c/o Whittle Communications L.P., 505 Market Street, Knoxville, Tenn. 37902

Stories, 14 Beacon Street, Boston, Mass. 02108

StoryQuarterly, P.O. Box 1416, Northbrook, Ill. 60062

St. Andrews Review, St. Andrews Presbyterian College, Laurinburg, N.C. 28352

St. Anthony Messenger, 1615 Republic Street, Cincinnati, Ohio 45210–1298

The Sun, 412 West Rosemary Street, Chapel Hill, N.C. 27514

This World, San Francisco Chronicle, 901 Mission Street, San Francisco, Calif. 94103

The Threepenny Review, P.O. Box 9131, Berkeley, Calif. 94709

Tikkun, Institute of Labor and Mental Health, 5100 Leona Street, Oakland, Calif. 94619

TriQuarterly, 2020 Ridge Avenue, Evanston, Ill. 60208

Twin Cities, 7834 East Bush Lake Road, Minneapolis, Minn. 55435

University of Windsor Review, Department of English, University of Windsor, Windsor, Ontario, Canada N9B 3P4

U.S. Catholic, 221 West Madison Street, Chicago, Ill. 60606

Venus Rising, P.O. Box 21405, Santa Barbara, Calif. 93121

The Village Voice Literary Supplement, 842 Broadway, New York, N.Y. 10003

The Virginia Quarterly Review, University of Virginia, 1 West Range, Charlottesville, Va. 22903

Vogue, 350 Madison Avenue, New York, N.Y. 10017

Washington Review, Box 50132, Washington, D.C. 20004

Webster Review, Webster College, Webster Groves, Mo. 63119

Welter, English Department, University of Baltimore, 1420 North Charles Street, Baltimore, Md. 21201–5779

West Coast Review, Simon Fraser University, Burnaby, British Columbia, Canada V5A 1S6

Western Humanities Review, Building 41, University of Utah, Salt Lake City, Utah 84112

West/Word, The Writers' Program, U.C.L.A. Extension, 10995 Le Conte Avenue, Los Angeles, Calif. 90024

Wigwag, 73 Spring Street, New York, NY 10012

Wind, RFD Route 1, Box 809, Pikeville, Ky. 41501

Witness, 31000 Northwestern Highway, Suite 200, P.O. Box 9079, Farmington Hills, Mich. 48333–9079

Woman's Day, 1515 Broadway, New York, N.Y. 10036

Yale Review, 250 Church Street, 1902ʌ Yale Station, New Haven, Conn. 06520

Yankee, Dublin, N.H. 03444

Yellow Silk, P.O. Box 6374, Albany, Calif. 94706

Zyzzyva, 41 Sutter Street, Suite 1400, San Francisco, Calif. 94104

BOOK MARK

The text of this book was set in the typeface Palatino
by Berryville Graphics, Berryville, Virginia.

It was printed and bound by R.R. Donnelley, Crawfordsville, Indiana.

Designed by Patrice Fodero